A COLLAR OF JEWELS

With her young son William in her arms, Ellie Berman waits on the dockside in Southampton whilst her husband Max finalises their immigration papers. She is filled with relief, for Max's involvement in a railway strike had led to Ellie and William receiving death threats and her mother's offer of money to get them to England had come just in time. After hours on the dockside, Ellie is eventually informed that her husband was last seen boarding a boat returning to New York. Abandoned by her husband, with a young child to support, Ellie will face much hardship in her desperate fight for survival.

A COLLAR OF JEWELS

A COLLAR OF JEWELS

by
Pamela Pope

Magna Large Print Books
Long Preston, North Yorkshire,
England.

British Library Cataloguing in Publication Data.

Pope, Pamela
    A collar of jewels.

A catalogue record for this book is
available from the British Library

ISBN 0-7505-1449-3

First published in Great Britain by Century, 1994

Cover illustration © Roberts by arrangement with Allied Artists

Published in Large Print 2000 by arrangement with Pamela Pope

Magna Large Print is an imprin
Library Magna Books Ltd.
Printed and bound in Great Britain by
T.J. International Ltd., Cornwall, PL28 8RW.

For Alan,
Whose help, support and encouragement
make all the difference.

'Therefore pride is their collar of jewels and violence the robe that wraps them round.'

Psalms LXIII. 6
(NEB)

ACKNOWLEDGEMENTS

I extend very grateful thanks to Beth Buker of Baton Rouge, Louisiana, for her invaluable help with American research.

I also thank the Historic Pullman Foundation of Chicago for assistance, especially for recommending the book *Pullman: An Experiment in Industrial Order and Community Planning 1880–1930* by Stanley Buder.

My thanks too, to the staff of the Reference Library at Southampton, to Dr David Tuddenham, and to the many other kind people who helped in so many different ways.

PROLOGUE

It was half an hour since Ellie Berman had watched her husband leave the disembarkation shed, his long green coat flapping about his legs as he went out into the drizzling rain. She'd heard the warm ring of his voice as he shared a last joke with friends they had made on the seven-day journey across the Atlantic to Southampton on the steamship USMSS *New York,* and then he'd been lost from view among the seething mass of passengers and port officials.

'I have to go to the immigration office,' Max had told her. 'There's a few formalities to get through before they'll let us stay.'

She looked up at the iron girders criss-crossing the roof, from which hung notices about baggage clearance and signs pointing to the London-Waterloo train. It had all been so exciting when they'd first docked, but now she was too edgy to take an interest in these new sights and sounds. Half an hour without Max was too much, and she was worried that something had gone wrong with his papers.

She paced up and down with the baby pressed against her shoulder, willing her husband to reappear. Her face was pale and she was holding William too tight, so that he gave little unhappy cries of protest. Surely it wasn't Max's Jewish identity that was proving difficult? She'd not heard of any problems in Britain. Or what if someone had telegraphed ahead to say that Max Berman was a troublemaker, and shouldn't be allowed into the country? It was not true, of course, but after all that had happened over the past months anything was possible. Questions tumbled through her mind.

Porters with trolleys were transporting luggage to the London train and the crowd had begun to thin out.

'I hope your husband won't be too long,' said the woman from Boston who had been so good helping Ellie with the baby. 'We're due to leave in fifteen minutes, I understand.'

'I didn't expect him to be gone so long,' Ellie admitted.

'Would you like my husband to ask the porter to be taking your luggage?'

'Thank you, Mrs Faber, but I'd rather wait for Max.'

'Well, don't leave it too late, my dear.'

In ten more minutes Max still hadn't returned. When the last people had left, Ellie was alone in the vast hall where now every sound echoed. Panels on runners were being wheeled into place to form a wall along the open side of the building, shutting her in, and the noise of the iron wheels screeched through her head.

A porter came up to her. 'Are you going to London? If you want this lot shifting, ma'am, you ain't got much time.'

'Yes, we're going to London,' said Ellie. 'But I don't know where my husband is.' Her voice trembled but she kept her head up and tried to look confident.

'Reckon he's deserted you,' the man laughed. She'd heard about the English sense of humour. 'Can't hold up the train, ducks. There's the mail to be got in on time.'

She was getting desperate. *'Please* can you see if he's still at the immigration office?' she begged.

'I'll send a boy, ma'am.' The man's hand was cupped to receive a gratuity.

'I've no money on me. My husband has it.'

The wretched creature's manner changed. 'Afraid it'll take a while to find someone who ain't busy.'

So this was England! Ellie had been full of joy a short time ago as the steamship edged towards the quay in Southampton's Empress Dock on that September morning of 1894. It had felt wonderful to arrive in this new land, even in such dismal weather. She'd painted rosy pictures of England in her mind which had refused to be dampened by her first glimpse of the drizzle-shrouded shore, but now her joy turned sour as she shivered in the draught.

A forbidden picture came into her mind of what she had sacrificed in order to marry Max, and her eyes blurred. In his anger, her father had declared there was no longer a place for her in the family if she married a penniless Jew; she had made her choice and hadn't regretted it for a single instant. Whenever she looked at Max's handsome Jewish profile her heart gave a jerk. She loved him with a passion which

11

sometimes frightened her, and as long as they were together nothing could dim her happiness. Such high hopes she had for their future in this new land... He was strong and ambitious, afraid of nothing, and they were so fortunate to be putting the troubled times behind them.

William, who was four months old, began to cry in earnest now, beads of moisture settling on his forehead as he grew hot with anger at having to wait for nourishment. Ellie found his milk bottle and sat on the portmanteau to feed him from it.

There was plenty of activity on the quay still. Dockers shouted and joked in raucous voices, their accent strange to her American ears. The rain was heavier now. Through the murky greyness she saw a ship edging away from its berth further up the dock, the tide taking it so that the bows swung gently to point down Southampton Water towards the Solent and the open sea. Ellie's heart was beating unevenly, and just briefly she wondered if they ought to have stayed on the other side of the Atlantic.

Another fifteen minutes passed and she was becoming frantic. She couldn't leave the luggage to go and look for Max and everyone seemed too busy to help her. Finally the same porter returned.

'Ain't no one in the immigration office, lady,' he said. He looked at her with more compassion, seeing how young and ill-equipped she was to be left in this predicament. 'Do you want me to get a cab for you?'

'No. I can't go anywhere until my husband gets back.'

'Scarpered, has he? Perhaps it's a copper you need.'

The slang was like another language to her. 'I don't understand.'

'Police,' the man said.

'Oh, no.' Beads of perspiration gathered round her neck and made her thick dark hair damp. William had never felt so heavy. 'There must be some simple explanation. He'll be here any minute, I know he will.'

'Well, if he ain't here sharpish give us a shout and someone'll come and lend you a hand,' the man said, with bluff kindness. 'What's his name?'

'Berman. Max Berman,' Ellie told him. 'He's very tall and dark and he's wearing a green overcoat that comes down to his ankles.'

He touched his cap respectfully. 'Don't you worry, ma'am. I'll ask around.'

When he had gone she sat down again on the portmanteau in the middle of the empty hall. Her hands wouldn't stop trembling and her legs felt too weak to hold her. Every sound was amplified as the rain began to beat on the roof and she hadn't felt so frightened since the start of the trouble in Chicago.

'Oh William, where *is* your papa?' she cried to the baby who now closed his eyes contentedly, untroubled by this fearful turn of events.

Presently she heard someone running and jumped to her feet with a great surge of relief. Max would be desperate at having left her for so long and she started out to meet him. But the man who appeared through the curtain of rain was not Max. It was once again the porter, and she could tell by his expression that something was terribly wrong.

'What is it? Where is he?' She could hardly get the words out for the lump in her throat.

Rain was dripping from the man's hair into his eyes and when he shook his head it splashed her. 'I don't know how to tell you this, love.' He took her arm and led her to the window, pointing at the sister ship to the *New York* which she had recently seen leaving its berth. It was now well underway. 'A man by the name of Berman boarded the *Paris* at the last minute. Very tall, he was, and wearing a green coat like you said. Reckon he's on his way back to America on it.'

'Max? On his way back to America!' Her eyes were so wide she felt a cold wind rush into them. 'I don't believe you. He wouldn't leave me here.'

'I'm really sorry, ma'am. He had a return ticket to the States in his pocket.'

'But what am I to do? I've no money—nothing.'

Ellie swayed, and held William in a vice-like grip. If the iron girders above her head had fallen in on her she couldn't have felt more devastated. She didn't know which was greater, the terrible discovery that she had been deserted, or the paralysing fear as to what she should do next.

PART ONE

MAX

ONE

As usual it had been a wonderful vacation on Martha's Vineyard. Every summer the Harveys spent several weeks at their New England seaside house on the island, away from the smoke of Chicago, passing the time idyllically, swimming, fishing, or just walking across the top of the high cliffs. This year they were leaving a little earlier.

'Just because Drew's having a fight with Papa,' complained Ellie. 'It isn't fair. I don't want to go home yet.'

'Your father is very worried about him,' said Mama, supervising while servants Prudence and Maisie packed the trunks. 'Drew has to be stopped from throwing away his education.'

'He only wants to earn a living.'

'He doesn't *have* to earn a living—well, not on the footplate of an engine, anyway! Your father already has a place for him on the Board. Drew has brains and he'll be even more successful than Frederick in time, provided he gives his mind to it.'

Ellie was prepared to argue all day for her favourite brother. 'He's always wanted to be an engineer, you know he has.'

'All boys wants to be engineers,' scoffed Mama, 'but they usually grow out of it before they're sixteen. Drew is now twenty-one and

17

mature enough to know that driving a train is no occupation for the son of the President of the Union Atlantic Railroad.' She snatched a silk shawl from the tray about to be deposited in the trunk before the lid was closed. 'Not that, Maisie. I shall want it on the boat.'

Ellie knew it would be no use pleading with her father. Conrad Harvey had been in one of his darkest moods ever since the telephone call from Drew saying that he had taken a job as a fireman for the Chicago, Burlington & Quincy Railroad Company.

'The fool's taken leave of his senses,' Papa had stormed. 'What the hell does he think he's doing?' And the next day he had commanded Mama to arrange the packing, curtly informing Lionel, Jefferson and Ellie that they were returning home.

Elena Harvey was fifteen, that summer of 1890. Going home meant growing up. Away from the freedom of Martha's Vineyard she was obliged to walk instead of run, to dress with decorum in gowns which emphasised the new fullness of her figure, and to speak graciously like Mama. No more romping with her brothers. No more wearing bloomers or climbing trees. Next summer she would be leaving to spend nearly two years at a finishing school in France, and it felt as if the vacation was over forever.

Early that morning they crossed the channel at the south-west tip of Cape Cod where strong tides rocking the boat were too much for Mama's delicate stomach. On the mainland, at Woods Hole, they boarded the train for New

York. Papa was to travel on to Chicago with the boys, but Mama had insisted that her planned visit to their oldest son Frederick must still go ahead, as his wife had recently given birth to a second child.

'Elena and I will continue the journey in a Pullman car after you leave the train at Boston,' she said.

Conrad Harvey had his own private railcar for travelling, made in the workshops of his friend George Pullman, the man whose first sleeping car had been used to carry the body of Abraham Lincoln and the mourners from Chicago to Springfield in 1865. The Harvey car was the ultimate in luxury for the President of the United Atlantic; it was equipped with the finest upholstery, carpets and carved wood, as well as the Pintch system of gas-lighting with ornate glass shades, and there was ample room to move about inside it. In the course of business, Conrad Harvey arranged for railroads to carry his private car upwards of a hundred days a year.

This day was 19 August 1890, and the express train was making good time. Elena hated having to sit still for so long. She amused herself by drawing caricatures of the family—a talent which made everyone laugh but sometimes caused ruffled feelings since she was able to pick out faults as well as redeeming features. She sketched Papa with his newspaper, a frown on his high forehead indicating his disapproval of any reading matter other than the *Chicago Tribune* His lips were disguised by a large moustache, and his thick hair, the colour of a hazelnut, showed no sign of receding. He was a tall, proud, handsome man, and Ellie loved him dearly. Her four brothers declared him to be a martinet, but as the youngest of his children and the only girl she could usually get her own way.

Mama was doing her embroidery, a simple design chosen for the journey which could be worked without wearing the spectacles that vanity kept her from using. She was beautiful. Ellie took pleasure in watching her, admiring the set of her narrow shoulders and the tilt of her head which revealed the slenderness of her neck. Elegance flowed from her long, posed fingers, the index and third fingers usually raised higher than the second, the smallest one extended outwards. In every drawing Ellie did of her mother the hands were a feature, sometimes mockingly so, though the young artist didn't intend it. Mama's hair was as dark as midnight and the colour of her eyes had been likened to rich chocolate. Although the eldest of her five children was already twenty-five and had now made her a grandmother twice over, her figure was still youthful and she chose clothes to grace it with the expertise of one used to spending a great deal of money. Dear Mama ... so beautiful, yet so cool. Sometimes Ellie yearned for some gesture of affection, but those were reserved for Sibylla Harvey's sons.

Lionel was studying. He thumbed self-importantly through a textbook, making notes on a pad under the heading *Financial Advantages of Providing Good Working Conditions for the Unskilled.* Lionel was eighteen and made in his father's mould, the same as Frederick. When he went back to University in the fall he would be boringly conversant with Euclid, and as ignorant as ever of life's lighter pleasures. Ellie's pencil deftly caught his studious attitude, magnifying the lower lip which protruded further the more he concentrated.

Jefferson, who was only a year older than herself, was easy to draw. He smiled readily with an appealing lopsidedness which made women want to mother him, and his brown hair always flicked forward in spite of Mama's attempts to control it with pomade. For Jeff, this journey was a series of new delights and he rarely left the window. When he exclaimed at seeing a herd of buffalo, Ellie quickly looked out, but the train had entered a tunnel and she saw only a reflection of herself.

She was becoming so like Mama it was embarrassing.

'Why, child, you're going to outshine your mother, I do declare,' had been the latest comment. At this Mama hadn't looked too happy.

Ellie moved her head to try to see her profile, her eye muscles aching as she tried to observe her straight little nose, curved brows, neat chin and full, sensual lips. Yes, she resembled her mother quite strikingly, though her eyes were of a different colour. George Pullman, her godfather, had once described them in a rare poetic moment as being 'like violet petals'. She hurriedly included an exaggerated sketch of herself in the Harvey family group, then linked them all within the outline of their mansion home in Prairie Avenue, Chicago. Only Drew was missing.

'Papa, may Lionel take me to the dining car?' Ellie was too restless to sit a moment longer.

'A meal will be served here presently,' Papa said. 'Can't you wait?'

'I could, but it would be so grown-up just to be escorted by Lionel. Good for my education. You will take me, won't you, Lionel?'

He closed his book. 'If Father agrees.'

Papa deliberated, then consented. 'Elena will be your responsibility, Lionel. See that she behaves like a dignified adult. I want no word of complaint to reach my ears.' He touched his youngest son's shoulder. 'Do you wish to accompany them, Jefferson?'

'Aw, no,' said Jeff. 'Why go to the mountain when the mountain will come to Mohammed?'

Mama made Ellie stand still while she smoothed the crumpled skirt of her travelling gown. 'It's time you learnt more decorum, Elena. Be a credit to Lionel now he's so kindly agreed to chaperone you.'

'Oh I will, Mama.'

Flushed with success, Ellie followed her brother through the elastic diaphragm which firmly joined the vestibule cars together with spiral springs. The rocking almost unbalanced her, but she planted her feet firmly and passed along the next Pullman car without mishap, aware that admiring glances followed her. In

22

the dining car the pair were shown to a table covered with snowy white linen and set with silver cutlery, and were offered a choice of menu which included elk, beefsteak, grouse or antelope.

'I can recommend the grouse, madam,' the waiter said.

Ellie looked up. The young man was foreign and he was one of the few white waiters. His hair swept back from a peak on his forehead and had a natural gloss which made it appear blue-black. Black eyebrows almost met the sideburns growing thickly above strong cheek and jawbones, and his cleanshaven chin jutted powerfully. His eyes were a warm brown. There was something about him which made her think he might be Jewish.

'The grouse then, please,' murmured Ellie, her voice hardly more than a whisper. She couldn't find breath to speak any louder, having been robbed of it at the sight of this fascinating man in white uniform jacket and black trousers. Her mouth was dry. She took a sip of water from the glass he had placed before her, but an extra jerk of the train made her spill some on the cloth. Instantly he soaked it up with the white serviette he'd been carrying over his arm, and gave her a reassuring smile before taking Lionel's order.

'Try not to be so careless,' Lionel admonished, when the waiter had gone. 'You heard what the parents said.'

'Don't be so pompous, Lionel,' said Ellie. She languished in her seat, a glow stealing over her.

Perhaps being grown-up was not such a bad thing, after all. She touched her hair which Prudence had coaxed into six long ringlets, four of which were pinned up on the top of her head. With trembling fingers she found some stray pins, lifted the other two ringlets from her back and included them in the coil, saying: 'Isn't it hot in here?'

All through dinner Lionel criticised their second eldest brother.

'I don't mind going back early, but it's hard on Mama. How selfish of Drew. It's the first year we haven't all been together on vacation and I was surprised Father agreed to him staying in Chicago in the first place. No doubt he'll be home when we get there. He'll never stand the hard work and conditions.'

Ellie answered in monosyllables, her support for Drew having temporarily evaporated. She watched for the waiter to appear at the end of the car and walk sure-footed along its length, his head almost touching the lamps, and she ordered extra vegetables so that he would have to return one more time to the table. He seemed pleased to do so. When he served the dishes she studied his hands, admiring the deft movements and marvelling at the dark silken hair covering the backs of them. She wanted to touch.

'Will madam take coffee?' he asked, when the meal was finished. Was she imagining it, or was there a softer tone in his voice now? His slightly foreign accent gave the impression of cultured speech, and she warmed to the deep ring of it.

'I'd love some coffee,' she said, though normally she only drank fruit juice. She deliberately flirted when their eyes met a few seconds later. 'Thank you.'

Then, without warning, something happened that was destined to change the whole course of Ellie's life...

One minute she was watching the coffee being poured from a silver pot, and the next the train suddenly started to shake and buck in a terrible fashion. Hot liquid cascaded into her lap, scalding her legs. She screamed, jumping up. From all sides the sound was repeated as the shuddering grew more violent and passengers panicked.

'Get away from the window!' yelled the waiter. And to Lionel: 'You too, sir. It's a derailment.'

Sure enough, the dining car lurched and careered into the back of the carriage in front, only stopped from being telescoped by the strength of the vestibule springs, but as it left the rails it tipped forward and broke almost in two. The noise was deafening, the dust choking.

Ellie was terrified. She put out her hands to save herself but everything seemed to be sliding towards her. Shattered glass tore at her skin and clothing. The waiter caught hold of her, protecting her from the worst of the impact, and as they fell he pushed her clear of a shaft of splintered wood which came cracking down from the roof into the débris. The last thing she remembered was his agonised cry as he was trapped by his legs under the wood and tables, which could have killed her, had he not been so quick-witted and brave.

There followed a terrible silence. The engine was a tangle of smoking metal. The train settled, the front cars tilting drunkenly and fire starting from an overturned stove.

A few moments before the disaster happened Jefferson Harvey, keen-eyed, saw a crew of repair men come into view round a bend in the track on the Old Colony Road near Quincy, Massachusetts. He saw them desperately trying to stop the express, but though the brakes were applied immediately it was impossible to halt the huge engine before it struck an upright ratchet jack which had become jammed in the rails.

It seemed like forever before rescue came. Ellie had only lost consciousness for a few minutes, and when she revived she was unable to move clear of the débris hemming her in. Blood was drying on her face from superficial cuts and she felt sure she was covered in bruises, but apart from that she seemed to be unhurt. She tested her legs and found them in good working order. Her arms likewise, though one wrist ached from taking the brunt of her fall.

She was very fortunate indeed to be alive. Only a few inches from her head lay the heavy wooden shaft which would have killed her if the waiter hadn't risked his own life to push her aside. Through dust-filled eyes she saw him lying only a foot away, the wood across his legs.

'Help me, someone!' she cried, desperately

afraid. Fear made her struggle to get free from the mess, but it was as if she were in a cage. 'Lionel, where are you?'

'Lie still,' came a voice from her side. 'Do you want the whole lot to fall in on us?' Miraculously the waiter opened his eyes and with his free hand, he reached out to restrain her, though the movement made him wince with pain.

'Where's my brother? Is he dead? Oh, Holy Mother, please don't let him be dead.'

'He's gone to get help. Be patient.'

Ellie heard new sounds. Men were clawing at the wreckage to free the injured, and it was likely to be a while before they reached the dining car. Ahead of it the need for help was greater. She wanted to ease the pain for the young man at her side, but didn't know what to do. His eyes closed again.

'You won't die, will you,' she pleaded.

His lips twisted into a painful smile. 'No. It'll take more than this to kill Max Berman.'

'Is that your name?' She snatched on the information to take her mind off what was happening.

'Yes. What is yours?'

'Elena Harvey. Everyone calls me Ellie, except Mama and Papa.' With difficulty in the confined space she managed to remove the jacket of her lavender-coloured travelling dress, folded it and lifted his head to put it underneath. 'Is that any better? What else can I do for you? You saved my life.'

'Just keep talking. I must stay awake.'

'What shall I talk about?'

'You.'

So Ellie told him about the vacation on Martha's Vineyard, described her brothers and told him how beautiful her Mama was, and how strict Papa could be. Then she cried a little. 'Do you think they're all right? Our car was near the end of the train.'

'I'm sure they are. You're very brave, Ellie.' Max stared at her for several seconds admiringly, then shut his eyes once more.

'Don't go to sleep,' she urged, leaning over him with fresh anxiety. Beads of perspiration had collected on his forehead and she wiped them away with her fingers, conscious that he was a stranger and she was being very familiar. Yet it seemed natural to touch him. The feel of his skin beneath her fingertips caused new and disturbing sensations to excite her. She willed him to open his eyes again, longing to look into them. Dear Holy Mother, she'd never felt like this before. 'Tell me about *you*. I want to know all about you.'

'I am very uninteresting,' he said.

'No one is uninteresting. I like people. Where do you come from?'

'Russia.' He sounded exhausted but forced himself to go on speaking. 'My family live in Chicago now.'

'Oh, how wonderful. I live there too.'

He stroked her face, and she shivered. 'In a very different part of the city, I'm sure. My father is a tailor. He wanted me to learn the trade but already my older brother Laban is helping him and there wouldn't be enough for us all to do.'

'So you took a job on the railroad.'

'I have to earn money, but I want to create things. I'm very clever with my hands.' He flexed his fingers experimentally. 'If I lost the use of them I don't know what I'd do. I want to make beautiful furniture.' There was a chair balanced above him which was covered in velvet and quilted with buttons. The silk fringe danced in the dust. 'So much I should like to do that,' he murmured. Then the effort to talk was too great and his head lolled sideways against her.

To her enormous relief voices soon came closer, shouting reassurance. Men arrived to free victims trapped in the dining car, and dust flew in renewed clouds as they started to heave aside the obstructions. Ellie called as loudly as she could to direct the rescuers to herself and Max.

'Please get this man out,' she shouted. 'I think his legs are broken.'

She refused to be moved first and stayed beside Max to cushion him against extra pain as they lifted him clear. When he was safely lying on a rug at the grassy side of the track with experienced people to help him she let willing hands ensure her own safety, and she shook uncontrollably with delayed shock as soon as she was free.

Papa appeared, panting, dishevelled and grey with worry. Lionel and Jefferson were with him, both unscathed.

'Elena, my darling, it's all right,' her father cried, gathering her into his arms. 'Papa's here.

29

You're safe now.' She had never seen him so agitated.

'Where's Mama?'

'Your Mama is all right, too. Very shaken, like you.'

'It's all so awful,' Ellie wailed.

'I know, I know.'

She let herself be comforted for several minutes while her brothers joined the rescue operations, and she heard the beat of her father's heart as she rested against his chest. Then she pulled away.

'I owe my life to that man over there,' she told Papa, indicating the group a few feet away. 'He pushed me clear and was trapped himself by his legs. He's badly hurt. You must do something for him.'

'He'll be rewarded,' Papa promised. 'I'll make enquiries.'

'I know his name and all about him. His name's Max Berman. He's a waiter...'

'Hush now, sweetheart. I'm only interested in getting you somewhere safe.'

Her father picked her up and carried her away from the devastation, away from the man she had known only the briefest time, but whom she would never forget. She looked back but couldn't see him, and she began to weep.

Later, the family was recovering in an hotel in Quincy. In the aftermath of a disaster which had claimed the lives of fifteen people and left forty-six seriously injured, time was needed for the track to be repaired and the wreckage cleared before another train could take the

Harveys home to Chicago. The delay was another worry on top of the previous day's trauma, but it gave Ellie time to work on her father's sympathies before the problem of Drew became all-important again.

'You promised to help Max Berman, Papa,' she reminded him.

'I've already arranged for the man to have every care and attention in hospital at my expense.'

She took a breath and suggested something which had come to her overnight. 'I want you to speak to my godfather and get Max a job in the Pullman Works where he can learn to make furniture.'

'My dear girl, what gave you such an extraordinary idea?' Papa was very surprised.

'You've got to help him to get the kind of job he wants, when he's well.'

'Aren't you asking too much?'

'He saved my life,' Ellie said, refusing to give up. She twined her arms about his neck and kissed him. 'How much am I worth to you?'

'Everything, of course, my darling.'

'Then please, for my sake, speak to Mr Pullman.'

Papa could never resist her wheedling. Elena was his shining light, his treasure, his adored only daughter. He had never denied her anything within reason that she truly wanted.

'Very well,' he promised. 'I'll ask George as a favour to give the man a trial, but if your protégée proves useless, George must have the right to stand him off without question. I can't see a waiter becoming a skilled worker in a hurry.'

Ellie squeezed him with gratitude. 'Thank you, Papa.'

She could relax. There was no doubt at all in her mind that Max would make the most of the opportunity she had won for him.

So it was that Max Berman, a fiercely proud and independent young man, became entangled with the Harveys. The first thread was in position which would draw him slowly into a world of materialism, a world in which wealth and influence were all-powerful. The thread appeared to be golden.

As soon as his leg was mended, Max was invited to present himself to the foreman of the upholstery shop, part of the vast Pullman Palace Car Company in the model town of the same name situated on the outskirts of Chicago. He was to be trained as a craftsman.

'You sure must have powerful friends,' said the foreman. 'Mr Pullman himself sent word you're to get special training.' The man barely disguised his opinion of favouritism. 'In disgrace, are you? Kicked out of your rich home without a dime? Well, I'm telling you, sonny, this is no soft option. You'll have to work your guts out here.'

'I was a Pullman Car waiter,' Max answered, struggling to remain polite, 'but I'm working my way up. I've never met Mr Pullman—he just heard of me.'

'Smart guy, eh?'

'I'm capable of better things than being a

waiter, but I wouldn't go crawling. It just so happened I was owed a favour, and I'm to be given the chance to learn about upholstery from a good craftsman, sir—if you'll accept me. I don't aim to make a habit of being helped up the ladder. I shall do it my own way, but right now I'll be real grateful for your help.'

The foreman's attitude remained sceptical, but he admired initiative. He was to discover that Max Berman had a lot of talent and plenty of ambition, which soon made him one of the most skilled men in the workshop. He also got on well with everyone—but he would not be put upon.

Within two years of arriving at Pullman, Max was working on intricate chairs which adjusted to give rest to every part of the anatomy while travelling. These chairs had foot-rests and reclining backs which could be locked into whatever position afforded the best comfort, and were scientifically designed to support the shoulders, pelvis, back and lumbar regions; if complaints were received, it was diplomatically pointed out that the passenger must be at fault. He used rich fabrics and hand-carved wood of the finest quality to construct seating which could have graced the most luxurious parlour. And considerable interest was shown in the drawings he submitted of new ideas he wanted to implement. In a very short time, Max Berman had graduated with honours from waiter to craftsman.

His improved wages enabled him to rent a tenement apartment in the town of Pullman. For his three-roomed flat on the third floor of one of the blockhouses on Fulton Street, he paid eight dollars a week, and this included a gas cooking stove and lighting, a sink and water tap, and a pantry. The place was too large just for one so his sister Katrina came to keep house for him. Within a few months she had found herself a husband who was only too happy to move in as well.

Max's physical needs were taken care of by a girl called Mariette Schuman, but he didn't feel inclined to make her his wife. She lived in a predominantly Jewish area of Chicago close to his parents, and as she too was Jewish no doubt he would have received their blessing if he'd had a mind to marry her. Katrina had hurt them greatly by marrying outside the faith. However, although he was fond of her, Max didn't feel that Mariette would fit in with the other Pullman wives.

After a while Max almost forgot that he owed his current prosperity to a pretty dark-haired girl whose life he had saved—but whose face he couldn't remember.

TWO

There was a lantern hanging from every tree in the garden on Elena Harvey's eighteenth birthday—a big, round, rosy-red lantern with a lighted candle inside to illuminate the delicate

34

cherry blossom. And between the lanterns fluttered huge paper butterflies, colouring the warm May evening with their brilliance. Saké was being served in a tea-house erected by the maple trees, and liberal consumption of the seemingly innocuous drink of fermented rice caused laughter to gust out at intervals. It vied with the sound of the samisens playing tinkling music in a minor key, which was far too sad for the frivolous occasion.

This was the most lavish party seen in Chicago in a long time, and everyone of any social standing had been invited. Seven hundred guests filled the garden, no expense had been spared and there was no indication that a recession was biting in that spring of 1893. The party theme was Japanese, and as costumes were obligatory, it was difficult to pick out the rich and influential from those with less prestige.

Elena flitted around her guests like an exotic bird, graciously receiving gifts.

'Why, Mrs Canter, how kind of you. Mr Dean, how thoughtful. Mrs Fairman, I can't wait to see what's inside this gorgeous wrapping.' And the presents were piled high, to be opened later.

'Elena, there are still people arriving,' her father said, catching up with her as she moved among friends whom she had not seen since her return a week ago from the Paris finishing school. 'You should be greeting them on the terrace. Take my arm—I'm afraid you'll fall in that ridiculous footwear.'

Ellie happily slotted her hand through the proffered arm. It was so good to be home!

The two years in France had been a wonderful experience and she had enjoyed it, but the call of this gracious house and the love of her family had tugged at her all the while she was away. Jefferson had gusted in from college like a whirlwind to be at her party, and Lionel had brought two friends from University whose suitability in the marriage stakes even impressed Papa. Frederick was here from New York with his wife and brood of three solemn children, another having been added, and this evening only her brother Drew was missing. Papa's stubborn refusal to forgive him, and Drew's obstinate resolution to please himself, caused her such heartache.

She hurriedly put aside the one shadow hanging over her birthday and asked a very important question. 'Papa, have the Pullmans arrived yet? Is Florence here?' She hoped to impress the eldest Pullman daughter, who never let anyone forget she had an hotel and a boulevard named after her in her father's town on the west shore of Lake Calumet. There was something else too, something she was dying to find out. 'I *must* see my godfather.'

'Hoping for a special present?' Papa teased. 'Yes, they're here, except for Mrs Pullman who is unwell.'

Ellie excused herself from a group of adoring young men and went with her father to the terrace where music more to the American taste was supplied by a quartet of musicians playing a selection from the latest operetta. She was one of the most eligible girls in the city and there was much competition to gain favour. Her beauty was unmatched this evening and she was aware of it as she moved among the guests, dressed as a geisha in a kimono of heavily embroidered vermilion silk. Traditional shoes on platforms made walking a precarious business, but this didn't mar her poise, and her black hair was styled in elegant Japanese fashion, with a ricepaper butterfly on top fluttering in the breeze.

George Pullman's face lit up when he saw her. 'Elena, my dear, happy birthday. I made sure I would be home for it.' He was an elegant man, though conservative in his choice of clothes, and his only concession to the request for Japanese apparel was a green robe hand-painted with dragons, worn over his suit. A self-made man from Portland, he had moved up from being a clerk in a general store to the exalted position of 'sleeping-car king', for George Pullman had made rail travel a far more comfortable experience. Along with his vast industrial empire, he had also built the town to house his workers on drained prairie land beyond Chicago, and though he was a hard man in business he had the respect of his employees.

'Dear Mr Pullman, I'm so glad,' Ellie said, accepting a kiss on the cheek. 'I'm really sorry your wife isn't well.'

'My wife's health is a worry,' the great man admitted. He had a broad face with a deeply indented upper lip, and from beneath his lower lip flowed a narrow white beard as soft and silken as his shirt. 'These are difficult times one way and another.'

Ellie nodded knowingly. 'Papa tells me the recession is beginning to cause industrial unrest.'

'Sadly, I've had to lay off some men and cut down on hours. It grieves me, but I have no alternative.' He turned to Papa. 'Your daughter has matured, Conrad. She's a credit to you—*and* to all the school fees you've been paying out.'

'You'll soon have to watch out, George,' laughed Papa. 'She's developing quite a head for business.' Pride made him stand a little taller. 'I'll leave you two together.'

Ellie and Mr Pullman strolled along the terrace. The two families had been friends and neighbours for as long as she could remember, and Ellie happily answered all his questions about her French education. She waited a suitable time before putting a question of her own.

'Mr Pullman, nearly three years ago, after we were in that bad train accident, Papa asked you to give a job to the man who saved my life. His name was Max Berman.'

'Berman. Ah yes, I believe he is doing rather well.'

An inner leap of excitement made her draw in her breath. Memories of Max had stayed with her though they'd been an ocean apart, and her keenness to have news of him was not even overshadowed by this gala entertainment.

'He's still with your company, then?'

'A talented young man, so I hear.'

38

'I'm glad you were generous enough to give him a chance.'

'For you, Elena, I will do much. You make it so easy for me to fulfil my duties as a godparent.'

Ellie longed to ask more about Max Berman but it would have been unseemly to show too much interest, and the main thing was that she knew where he could be found.

'I'm very lucky,' she said. Her attention was then diverted as more guests were announced and she clapped with delight. 'Oh, the Markhams have come at last! Will you excuse me, Mr Pullman?'

'Of course. Enjoy yourself, Elena. Youth is only fleeting.'

Ellie shrieked with laughter at seeing her best friend's fair hair covered with a black wig. 'Clarissa, you look so different!'

'Well, we can't all be perfect for the part,' Clarissa said. 'Happy birthday, Ellie.' She looked round, her eyes shining. 'Isn't this wonderful! I'm so glad you didn't have a Columbian evening like everyone else this year.'

'I wanted to be different. Have you been to the Exposition yet? I went with Mama and Papa to the opening on the first of May and we were right beside President Cleveland when he flicked the gold switch. It was just wonderful. Flags went up everywhere at once.'

'No, I haven't been yet, but I heard the ships' guns on the lake,' Clarissa said. 'Just fancy—nineteen countries exhibiting in great white pavilions.'

'I've seen them.' Ellie's enthusiasm grew. 'All those hundreds of acres of parkland and the Midway turned into a fair! It's unbelievable.'

'I do so hope I can see it soon.'

The World's Columbian Exposition, held to celebrate the four-hundredth anniversary of Christopher Columbus discovering America had been a main topic of conversation ever since the first building had been erected in Jackson Park last October. Papa had given financial backing, of course, and Mama, who was very influential, had become a member of Mrs Potter Palmer's Board of Lady Managers.

'I'm to be allowed to go again with Lionel and his friends next week,' said Ellie. 'I'll ask if you may come with us.'

'Oh Ellie, thank you.' Clarissa was the only child of doting but elderly parents who were out of touch with the youthful element of society. Her tone became wistful. 'How nice if Drew could have been with us, too.'

'Don't let my Papa hear you say that.'

'Nothing's changed, then?'

'Nothing. Lionel says Drew's now got involved with someone called Eugene Debs who heads labour unions.'

A sigh escaped Clarissa. 'Why does he have to be so different?'

'Why, indeed.'

A gong beat reverberated through the garden and supper was announced. At once there was movement towards the tables laden with food just inside the house, and Ellie found herself strangely irritable with the young men who pushed and strutted and swanked on their way up from the garden. She was given priority and she laughed as her plate was piled high with delicacies, but something had happened to the evening.

Mentioning Max's name had unsettled her. She stood aside for a moment, and above the cacophony of voices she heard another long-remembered one in her head. 'You are very brave, Ellie,' Max had said, and his eyes had done more than admire her. The timbre of his voice remained with her even now and touched a chord somewhere deep inside. Her stomach contracted with a peculiar spasm, leaving her devoid of appetite. Throughout her time in France she had held memories of him so close it had seemed as if he'd always been in her life, and she had built up a dream. How foolish. She knew next to nothing about the man, and yet she continued to weave an imaginary future in which Max loved her and was forever at her side. Thoughts of meeting him again were sheer fantasy, yet they coloured her reverie and refused to fade.

After supper there were flattering birthday speeches to which she replied with confidence touched with humility. Ellie included everyone in her words of thanks, from Papa and Mama who had provided this wonderful party, to the waiters who served. But beneath her exuberance remained a layer of discontent and she felt strangely close to tears.

It was then that a waiter addressed her quietly. 'Excuse me, Miss Elena, there is a gentleman

41

wishing to speak to you privately in the drawing room.'

She didn't ask who it was. The waiter was from a catering company and wouldn't have known. Mystified and with renewed excitement, she slipped indoors.

The drawing room was lovely. Ornate stucco-work decorated the ceiling and pale walls; a huge organ with pipes painted in red, blue and gilt patterns dominated the space between two doors, and a potted palm filled one corner. A leopardskin rug was splayed out on the parquet floor like a penitent at prayer, and a painting of Sibylla Harvey was displayed on an easel.

At first she thought no one was there. Then she was aware of a young man sitting in one of the armchairs, his face hidden by the wing. He heard her and looked round, a beaming smile on his face. Heavens! Oh, such joy! It was Drew.

She gasped with delight. 'Drew! Oh, I'm *so* pleased to see you.' Tears now filled her eyes and she hugged him fiercely.

'Happy birthday, little one. My, how beautiful you look. Even Father couldn't keep me away from your party.'

'You haven't seen him yet?'

'No, but I'm still a son of this house even though he calls me a bum with no ambition.'

'Then you should be outside, acting like one of the family instead of skulking in here.'

He had changed. In almost three years of separation he had become a man, the fat from good living honed away leaving him muscular and handsome. His dark hair was well-groomed, but his cleanshaven face bore lines to confirm the rough life he had been leading and his hands were ingrained with grease and coal dust from hard, honest work. He no longer had the fashionable style of his brothers, yet he was far more compelling in the serviceable clothes which he wore well. Ellie ached with love for him.

There was so much to say and so little time, but in brief sentences they tried to catch up.

'It was wonderful in France, but I missed everyone...'

'I've been with the CB & Q all this time—as an engineer. It's exciting on the footplate, everything I knew it would be.'

'I haven't seen you since I was nearly killed in the derailment.'

'I was in one myself. A bridge was swept away in a storm...'

Yes, so much to say.

She would be missed. She had to go back to the party and she wanted Drew to come with her, but he was not ready.

'Ellie, will you do something for me?' His tone changed and he clasped his sister by the shoulders. 'I want to come back home.'

Her face lit up; her heart sang. Drew wanted to return at last, and just hearing him say it brought her more happiness than all her birthday gifts put together. 'That's the most wonderful news,' she cried, almost strangling him in her excitement. 'Let's go and tell Mama and Papa.'

'No, that's just it. I don't want to see them tonight. I don't want to have to grovel to Father.

43

Will you speak to him for me, pave the way? It would be so much easier.'

'Why can't you speak to him yourself? You'll make Papa the happiest man in the world.' Surely he would be treated like the Prodigal Son!

'He wants my capitulation. No half measures —he wants me to admit I was wrong and to repent of my sins, like he was God, but I can't do that. Please, Ellie, sweeten him up. He'll do anything for you.'

'Why do you want to come home, then?' Ellie didn't understand him. 'Have you had enough of the rough life?'

'I know that I can do more for the working classes if I go into management. Father always said there would be a place for me at the Union Atlantic. I want to take it.'

'And undermine his authority? That's not right, Drew.'

'No, you goose.' Drew ran an affectionate finger down her cheek. 'But I want to have a say in the way workers are treated. I understand their needs now I've been one of them. There's a lot of things I want to put right but no one will listen to an engineer.'

He put up a persuasive argument, and while he was talking Ellie's excitement increased. If Drew was so desperate for her help she could bribe him into giving help in return. He was the answer to her own dilemma.

'All right, I'll speak to Papa,' she promised, 'but only if you do something for me in exchange. I want to meet someone who works

44

in Pullman.' She told Drew all she knew about Max Berman, ending with the latest news, that he was doing well as an upholsterer. 'Max saved my life and I want to see for myself that everything's fine for him.'

Drew grinned, not fooled for a minute. 'He must be special for you to be this concerned. Okay, how do I arrange this meeting?'

'Bring him to the Exposition next Wednesday evening. I'm going with Lionel and his friend and Clarissa, and I'll make sure we're at the Ferris wheel by eight-thirty. Only don't tell Max that.'

'I'll see what I can do.'

'You'll do it, I know, and I'll plead your case with Papa so well it'll bring tears to his eyes.' It was not only her father Ellie could twist round her little finger.

When Ellie returned to the party she didn't know how to contain her exhilaration. She was bursting with secrets which mustn't be told, not even to Clarissa, and when Jefferson drew her into a circle of his college friends she was in a scintillating mood.

'Are you still good at dancing, Ellie?' Jefferson asked. 'Dance for us now.' He jumped on the platform where the Japanese musicians were playing. 'My sister's going to dance for us.'

'I can't,' she protested.

'What have they done to you at that froggy school? You wouldn't have been so bashful before you went away.'

'She was a child then,' said Lionel, coming upon the scene.

'She's still our Ellie,' insisted Jefferson. 'Come on, Sis, dance on your birthday.'

And because she was so deliriously happy she at last kicked off the crippling shoes and started to dance alone inside the circle cleared for her on the lawn. Lessons in Classical Greek movement had done wonders for her deportment and had given her added confidence. She became carried away by the rhythm, and the vermilion kimono slipped to the ground where it lay on a carpet of fallen petals. In a clinging gown of ivory crêpe she danced barefooted to music played on the samisens. Slowly and gracefully she moved, stretching up until the ivory crêpe rippled over her body and the ricepaper butterfly on top of her head seemed alive, its wings lifting and falling with the music. Pins fell from her hair and the elegant coiffure became a dark curtain round her shoulders. She felt gloriously alive.

Conrad Harvey also came down to the lawn at that very moment. When he saw Ellie's performance his face took on a purple hue and he pushed aside the nearest of the audience to make a path through, his brow dark and his eyes glittering with anger.

'Elena! Stop this outrageous display this minute,' he commanded. 'You've been drinking too much saké.'

Ellie hovered like a hummingbird, poised on her toes in mid-movement, and slowly she lowered her arms. 'I haven't had anything to drink except lemonade, Papa. I'm just so happy.'

'Go indoors and don't come out again until

you are fully clothed and every hair of your head is back as it was. I shall speak to you tomorrow.'

'Yes, Papa,' said Ellie.

Jefferson interceded. 'Don't be hard on her, Father. It was my fault.'

'Then you should be ashamed.'

Papa's anger could have blighted the evening, but Ellie's happiness was undiminished as she picked up the kimono and went indoors. *Drew was coming home.* But even more intoxicating was the thought of meeting Max again...

Max Berman first spoke to Drew Harvey at the Turner Hall in Kensington. It was at a packed meeting which had been called by Eugene Debs, whose support for railroad workers was fast turning him into something of a folk hero. With depression sweeping across the country, it was necessary to have someone supporting the countless workers who were daily losing their jobs, and Debs was the one to do it.

'The strike is the weapon of the oppressed,' Debs said. This lean man of six foot two, with a balding head and long, pointed chin, had shovelled coal into the cavernous firepits of locomotives in his early days. Now his influence as a spokesman for the men's rights had made him an awesome figure. 'Labour unions have striking power, and if such power is surrendered we become slaves.'

There were shouts of, 'Never!'

Eugene Debs had learnt through long experience how to hold an audience, and his speech

47

was full of sense. It was also inflammatory. The division between rich and poor was becoming more deeply felt since the start of the recession and he urged all working men to join together in support of fair deals.

'Brotherhoods and labour unions must be better organised if we're to strike,' he cried. 'We've tasted violent strikes across the east in the past, but they didn't have the strength of unity and they would have bred revolution. We don't want that. Nor do we want our men blacklisted and forced to leave their home towns for breaking the law. What we want is one powerful union.' He raised both arms high and clenched his fists. 'Let's unite, brothers, for the common good.'

Men were standing shoulder to shoulder. Max's neighbour spoke to him. 'Looks like this is only the beginning.'

'Heard tell Debs'll soon be launching a national labour newspaper in New York,' said Max. 'But we need more than a newspaper. Strike action's the only answer.'

'A strike means halted production, frustration and loss of money. There must be another way.'

'Whose side are you on?' The meeting was over and they started moving with the throng towards the entrance.

'Negotiation, that's what's needed.'

'And fair bosses. We will not get any improvement while they continue to line their pockets at our expense.'

'Or until someone on the inside has the

interest of the workers at heart.'

'And that will be when pigs fly ... to use a strange American expression.'

'You're a foreigner, then?'

'Max Berman, son of Russian Jewish immigrants.'

'My name's Drew.'

The two men spent the rest of the evening together at one of the forty or so bars in Kensington. This fellow Drew seemed keen to have his company and Max had nothing better to do so he went along with it. He liked him, even though he disagreed with some of his opinions. The bar served food but there was little light to see to eat it in the wood-panelled booth, and a candle flickering between them burnt down to a stub of reeking tallow.

'What work do you do?' Max asked his companion.

'I'm an engineer with the CB & Q.'

'The engineers are least likely to want an amalgamation. They refused before and they're always at odds with either the firemen or the switchmen.'

'I'm no grand chief, but I'll fight for their rights.' The light accentuated Drew's high forehead and gave his eyes a glow of idealism. An engineer's job was fraught with danger. Frequent accidents on the line were caused by bad track-laying, collisions with cattle, and numerous other hazards. The pay was far too low for the risks, and if there was no train to take out, a man could be waiting in some distant town for hours or even days. 'We need better tracks and more safety devices on locomotives, for a start—and better conditions. I aim to make the industry listen.'

Max was sympathetic but sceptical. 'And how do you propose to do that? Would you be in agreement with one union for all railroad men?'

'Would you?' countered Drew.

'I work for the Pullman Company. Wages are being cut, production reduced. Yes, I would support it wholeheartedly. There's a lot of unrest.'

'I hope George Pullman doesn't know you've been at a labour meeting. He wouldn't approve of a subversive element in his paradise.'

The candle gave a final splutter and died, leaving them with only the light from the bar across the room. The adjoining booth was unoccupied. Max reached over the partition and took the candle from that table, causing a spiral of smoke to follow in its wake as he set it down between them.

'What I do outside Pullman is none of his business.'

Max was puzzled by his companion. He was not quite what he seemed—a spy perhaps, planted by management? Max had the distinct impression that he had been deliberately sought out, but surely an upholsterer was not a likely source of inside information? He needed to be wary. Events in his past had taught him to trust no one, and fear of treachery made him naturally suspicious.

His family had come to America in 1882 when the May Laws in Russia forbade Jews to

50

settle in villages. Max had been fifteen then. The journey from Russia remained vividly in his memory, as did the persecution which had preceded it, and though he tried not to let it colour the present, he could never rid himself of the horror. Pictures of his mother's suffering were always there to remind him of man's inhumanity to man. His father had quickly obtained employment in the new country, but neither he nor Momma had relinquished a single Jewish custom and they refused to become Americanised. Their only concession had been to shorten their name for the sake of ease in business, Bermanovitch being difficult to spell.

'What work do you do in Pullman?' he was asked.

'I make the luxury furniture for Pullman cars.'

'Sounds a secure job. Why were you at the meeting?'

'No job is secure. Last week my wages were cut again.' Max pulled the lining out of one of his pockets to demonstrate his financial state. 'Some men are being stood off.'

'It's happening everywhere.'

'Things are not as straightforward in the Pullman Company. We are at the mercy of the corporation for everything. George Pullman is fine but he is never there. Foremen show favouritism and because we are mostly on piecework they see their friends get the best pickings. Oh, there is much that is underhand, believe me.'

He didn't elaborate further. He'd already said too much, but if anything *did* lie behind the friendliness, he still couldn't help liking this Mr Drew. There was something vaguely familiar about him and he felt as if he'd known him for some time, though he couldn't think why. It was the eyes mainly which attracted his attention, so light in colour compared with the darkness of his hair, and somewhere at the back of Max's memory was a recollection of eyes a similar shade. The set of the head, too, he seemed to have seen before. As they talked he puzzled over it, and finally he had to ask.

'Forgive me, but I feel we might have met before. Is this possible?'

'I think not,' said Drew. 'But I'd be happy for us to meet again.'

'A pleasant thought.' Max was noncommittal.

'On Wednesday I've got time off to meet my sister and one of my brothers at the Exposition. Would you care to come along as well? You'll like my sister.'

He'd been on the point of making a polite refusal, but something prompted him not to be too hasty. Perhaps it was the elusive familiarity. Or it could have been the prospect of being introduced to a girl who promised to be fine-looking if she resembled her brother.

'All right,' Max said. 'Thank you, I shall be pleased to join you.'

The two men rose, stretched their bodies to ease the cramp from sitting so long and prepared to go their separate ways—but not to lose sight of each other completely. In fact, from that evening on their lives were destined to be linked ever more closely.

THREE

While at school in France, Ellie had missed all the excitement of Chicago over the past months. She hadn't seen the buildings being erected in Jackson Park, or heard the arguments about the millions of dollars being spent on the World's Columbian Exposition, though Papa had told her it was more than thirty-three million in all, of which ten and a half was to be found by the city itself. On top of this there were bills for cleaning up Chicago to impress the world's visitors. It was all a remarkable achievement, an artistic triumph for the man called Olmstead who had planned it, and Ellie's first sight of that vast, unimagined feat had taken her breath away. She couldn't believe that this was the same park through which she had occasionally driven with Papa and Mama in an open carriage.

There was so much to see that one visit merely whetted the appetite for more, and Ellie was looking forward immensely to the evening there with Lionel and Clarissa. By the time Wednesday came, the hope that Drew wouldn't fail her added extra spice to her anticipation, and the possibility of seeing Max Berman again made her feel quite lightheaded. She kept having to breathe deeply to steady her nerves.

Sensibly, Ellie was prepared for disappointment when she saw him. The memories she had kept so green over the past three years were based on hero-worship, and she reminded herself that the first love of her life at fifteen might not appeal to her at all now that she had matured. All the same, as she walked at last beside the lagoons and turreted buildings in Jackson Park that evening she was full of anxiety. Supposing Drew had failed! Max was probably a married man by now. What would she say to him if he did come? Questions and suppositions tumbled through her mind like a waterfall, waiting to be answered at half-past eight.

Replicas of foreign places gave the feel of travelling abroad on a magic carpet. There was a Moorish palace, an Irish village, an Egyptian temple, and many more such wonders all within walking distance. They came upon the camel in an area of the Midway which could have been a bazaar in some Middle Eastern country. The huge animal plodded through the crowds, led by a coloured boy wearing a tunic and round felt hat, while up on its back rolled two ladies seated side-saddle. The ladies simpered and giggled, clinging to the blanket covering the beast's neck.

'Come for a ride on it with me,' urged Randolph Sale, Lionel's friend.

She declined politely. 'I'd rather not.' She would hate to look so silly.

'I'll hold you. You won't fall.'

'I don't want to go on the camel, thank you.'

Ellie didn't care for him and wished he wasn't there. It was irritating having to put up with him when she was nervous and preoccupied. Randolph was a gangling law student with a pedigree going back to the Pilgrim Fathers, and with Lionel's encouragement he was determined to impress her.

'Come with me to the Dancing Theatre then.' His persistence was as vexing as the gnats she had to keep flicking away.

'I think not,' she said, and raised her parasol, tipping it so that he could no longer get too near.

'Ellie, give the man a chance,' said Lionel. 'What's the matter with you? I thought we were going to have some fun.'

'*I'll* decide what I want to see and do, and with whom,' she answered, her tone copied from Mama. The secret she hugged to herself made her impatient. Tension caused irritability.

Crowds had gathered across the road from the theatre to see a dark-eyed beauty known as Little Egypt perform the hootchy-kootchy in a mock Cairo street. Ellie left the men to drool over the girl's gyrating hips and hurried to catch up with Clarissa.

'There's something bothering you, isn't there?' Clarissa remarked. 'Do tell. Don't you like Randolph?'

'I dislike him more every minute.'

'He's done nothing improper, I hope.'

'No, nothing.'

'Then why are you all on edge?'

Ellie longed to confide in Clarissa but it

would be too risky, knowing her friend's lifelong devotion to Drew. When they met him it must appear quite unexpected. She evaded the question, glanced at the diamond-watch brooch pinned to her bodice, and saw that at last it was approaching eight-thirty.

'I'm just dying to go on the wheel, aren't you?' she said, new life in her voice. 'They say you can see Indiana and Wisconsin and the whole of Illinois from the top!'

The most imposing thing in the whole Exposition was the Ferris wheel, so large that it was visible from every direction. Thirty-six cars were hanging on the rim like great baskets, and Ellie's eyes were drawn to it with dreadful fascination. Somehow she managed to manoeuvre everyone so that they were at the entrance to the wheel with just a few minutes to spare. The 264-foot revolving contraption with great spokes looked like an enormous bicycle wheel, and there were queues to ride on it.

'We're not going on that,' declared Lionel, looking up at the swinging gondolas as big as tramcars.

'But it's the most exciting thing at the fair,' cried Ellie. 'You're only saying that because you're scared.'

'I am not scared.'

Ellie daren't look round for Drew. She was so nervous she could hardly stand still. The moment had come. Oh, if only she could remember exactly what Max Berman looked like. Her legs felt so wobbly she wished there was something she could hold onto, and she leaned so hard on her parasol that the flimsy thing bent with the weight.

Drew turned up while they were still debating. He approached Lionel first, for all the world as if the meeting were pure coincidence.

'Lionel, if this isn't a surprise!' he exclaimed. 'And Ellie! A proper family reunion.'

'Well,' Lionel snapped, plainly disconcerted, 'so my errant brother turns up at last. Do engineers actually have time off? No, don't shake hands, I don't want coal dust on my cuffs.'

'Coal dust provided the means to pay for your expensive clothes, brother,' said Drew. 'Perhaps you shouldn't forget it.' And he kissed Ellie and greeted Clarissa, who gazed at him in delight.

Ellie was in a turmoil. She had thought for a moment that Drew was alone, but he had been temporarily separated from his companion by the crowds, and a moment later she saw Max coming towards them. She recognised him instantly. He wore a white shirt, a soft bow tie of sapphire blue, a multi-coloured waistcoat under his brown jacket, and a boater tilted at a jaunty angle over his dark hair. She had always pictured him in a waiter's uniform so it came as a surprise to see how well he dressed. Oh yes, he was everything she remembered—and more.

The sight of him started up a throbbing in her body which was so intense she clasped her hands tightly against her stomach to try to quell it, and in so doing, she dropped her parasol. They stooped together to retrieve it, and while her back was still curved their glances met. Then he picked up the parasol and as he handed it to her she saw recognition dawn in his keen dark eyes.

'We've met before,' he said. The timbre of his voice was also exactly as she remembered.

'Just outside Quincy,' she answered, trembling. 'The rail disaster. I was afraid you were going to die.'

'Max, this is my sister Ellie Harvey,' said Drew.

Max looked from one to the other, summing them up. He had acquired an air of confidence since she had seen him last, and it suited him. When he addressed her brother, one eyebrow was raised. 'You said your name was Drew.'

'My Christian name.'

'So you are also a Harvey?'

'I am, though I've been tempted to call myself something else.' Drew turned to the others. 'Now, shall we spend the rest of the evening together as one happy family?'

'Stay out of our way,' advised Lionel pompously. 'Father wouldn't want us to associate.'

'You grow more like him. I pity you.'

A bitter exchange followed and it looked as if there was going to be a scene right there amidst the crowd. Ellie backed away, hearing her brothers quarrel as if she were a spectator at a play. Her senses responded only to Max Berman.

'I hate all this,' she murmured to him. 'Will you think me very forward if I ask you to take

58

me on the wheel, Mr Berman?'

She was afraid he would refuse, but she was taking the initiative for fear this meeting might lead to nothing after all her careful planning. It was a dreadful thing to do, of course, quite unseemly and contrary to everything she had been taught in France, but she was unashamed.

He hesitated. 'You must ask your brothers' permission first.'

'How can I when they're at loggerheads? Anyway, Lionel's been spoiling my evening by trying to pair me off with his awful friend. I'll be much obliged if you'll rescue me. And Drew won't mind.'

Max smiled slowly, his eyes on her. 'I am wondering if this was planned,' he said. 'If so, who am I to refuse the advances of a very beautiful young lady? Come.'

Ellie's face burned with embarrassment as he took her hand and guided her away, but her heart was singing. Lionel was too busy being his father's son to notice her going, and quite likely Drew's reason for antagonising him more was to win time for her. She had to make the most of it.

Max boldly infiltrated the head of the queue for the wheel and they were quickly counted among the next sixty people filling a gondola at ground level. Once inside with the door closed Ellie was panic-stricken. She was imprisoned with a virtual stranger in a cage which rose a few feet from the ground and then stopped for the next gondola to be filled, and already the ground looked a long way down.

'Oh dear, I think I want to get off,' she quavered, feeling foolish.

Max cupped her chin. 'Look at me,' he said. 'Don't look down.'

'It doesn't feel safe.'

'*I'm* with you. I'll look after you.'

She concentrated on his strength and gradually her fears subsided as they swung there. He was by far the most handsome man in the car. The wheel, which carried over 2000 people, climbed slowly until each gondola was filled, and all around them couples were linking arms and drawing closer, seeking support from each other for the coming ride.

'Can you see Drew and the others?' she asked.

'No. We don't want them with us anyway, do we, Miss Harvey?'

Oh, how he devastated her. She swallowed hard, partly because her ears were affected by the height, but more because the question was provocative. This was the kind of adventure she'd invented in school in France to enthral her friends, only better. Papa would never forgive her for allowing herself to be separated from Lionel but she didn't care.

The moment he set eyes on Elena Harvey that evening Max was captivated. She was the loveliest girl imaginable and he couldn't stop looking at her. His heart drummed, his loins suddenly ached, his throat went dry, and he drank in the vision before him like a man with an unquenchable thirst. She was poised

60

and aristocratic in a green silk dress with a triple layer of frills at the back, but he could tell the hauteur was only recently acquired by the way she dropped her parasol at seeing him. The suppleness of her body when she bent at the same time as himself to retrieve it excited him dangerously. It was not until he met her eyes that he knew who she was.

Then Drew made the introduction and Max knew he had been right to suspect intrigue. There was not enough surprise in Ellie's greeting. She had known she was going to meet him, was too quick with her reply when he said they had met before. But what pleasant intrigue. While the Harvey men indulged in argument his gaze stayed on Ellie and when she asked him to take her on the wheel the reason behind this meeting was unimportant.

Max was well aware of the power of his dark, brooding good looks and Ellie was as vulnerable as a newly hatched chick in this grown-up world, but the tremor through her body when he took her hand revealed a sensuality ready to be fully awakened. She was out of his class, of course. It seemed wrong to want her in the same way he might want a girl who lived in the same tenement block as himself, yet that was how she had affected him straight away.

They reached the pinnacle of the Ferris wheel, swayed on the final stanchion in preparation for descent, and Max slipped an arm round her. She held herself rigid and tried not to show her nervousness, both of him and the dizzy height. The wheel began to turn, gathering

61

speed, and as it plunged earthwards she gave a cry. Forgetting all protocol she buried her face against his jacket which smelt of cigar smoke, and when her hat tipped back he touched her hair. The ride had only just begun and they soared again towards the sky. After the second rotation she dared to look out, and all at once the magic of the experience took hold.

'I feel as if I'm flying,' she exclaimed, laughter now transforming her face. Her eyes shone and she clapped her hands.

Max kissed her. 'I knew you would like it.'

He dropped the inconsequential kiss onto her mouth as if it was the natural thing to do. It was only the lightest, briefest touch, but so unexpected Ellie recoiled with shock. Perhaps he had misinterpreted the signals.

'Impertinent man!' she cried. She was quivering from head to toe, but he would have bet his last dime the blush on her cheeks was not caused by anger. 'We're hardly acquainted. Don't think you can take liberties with me.' He smiled at her imperious tone and watched her brush her lips with the tips of her fingers as if to sustain the sweet sensation.

'We know each other very well, I think,' said Max. 'We were once so close I could see myself in your eyes.'

How could he have forgotten her? She'd been playing at being grown-up that day of the disaster, he recalled, but she had been lovely even then. And now the promise of great beauty had been fulfilled.

He didn't look for Drew Harvey or his brother

when the ride was over and Ellie walked with him alongside a lagoon chatting freely about her French education, her birthday party, and the extravagant living she accepted as normal. They rubbed shoulders with girls in gingham dresses and young men with coat-tails swinging. Ellie stood out among them like an orchid in a daisy field, and when she asked him about *his* family he found himself wanting to shock her.

'I saw my mother dragged from our house in Russia,' he said. 'She was beaten because she was expecting another child and she lost it. I saw her almost bleed to death and she could never have any more. They said there were too many Jews in Russia. My father was whipped for sowing new seed and my brother and sister and I were made to watch with our wrists and ankles bound.'

Ellie was horrified. Max saw tears gather in her eyes and was slightly ashamed. In her protected world she knew nothing of such inhumanity or what hatred could do. Not that he elaborated. It was not the time or place for morbid recounting, but it set the scene to his background just as Ellie's description of her party had proclaimed hers.

'You make me feel it's wicked to have so much money spent on me,' she said. 'Yet I'd die if we were poor.'

'Money can't buy everything,' said Max.

He took her to see a map made out of pickles with vinegar lakes and rivers; a Bolivian who was over nine feet tall, and midgets in a village of their own. He bought her sweetmeats, and an Irish lace handkerchief. They saw tapestries which Queen Victoria had loaned from her castle in England, Zulus showing how diamonds were mined, and they had drinks served by Dutch girls in national costumes.

And then there was the Transportation Building where Pullman cars were on view. One was the 'Santa Maria', a car of such luxury that even Ellie Harvey seemed impressed. Along both sides were armchairs thickly quilted in rich velvet and with silk tassels to cover the legs; chairs so beautifully designed they would have graced a palace.

'This is the work I do,' said Max, indicating the magnificent upholstery. 'I'm beginning to design furniture of my own.'

'I'm very pleased.' Her smile was gentle, as if she knew it was what he would be doing. He'd always been grateful to Conrad Harvey for finding him work in Pullman's upholstery shop, but he had often wondered what had prompted him to do it. 'Recompense' was the word used—a reward for putting his life in danger to save the young Elena, but it was a mystery how the Union Atlantic President had known exactly what job would suit him. It hadn't occurred to Max that he might have told Ellie of his ambitions while he was lying dazed with pain. Now he understood, and he felt vaguely uneasy.

'Come, and I'll show you where I live,' he said.

By the main entrance was a large plaster of Paris model of Pullman, the company town

George Pullman had established so that his workers might live in a well-ordered community free from all bad influences. It was laid out to scale, showing the factories, the tenements, the Arcade Building and library, the artificial lake and the parkland landscaped to give the place a rural appearance. Max pointed to one of the tenements.

'I share this with my sister Katrina and her husband. She's married to an Irishman.'

Ellie was surprised. 'Is he Jewish, then?'

'Lord, no! Oliver's as Catholic as they come.'

'But I thought...'

'That Jews only married Jews? My father and mother were very upset, but Katrina's happy and they've forgiven her. They try to understand that in America it's necessary to become American. My brother Laban has a good Jewish wife, and they give thanks for that.'

'We're Catholic, too,' Ellie said.

He liked Ellie. She was intelligent and charming, and though obviously indulged by her family she was not affected. So his present success was due to her. It amused him the way she had conspired with her brother, and he was flattered. He was also self-complacent. If he continued to please her, who could tell what fresh opportunities might come his way. In spite of somewhat radical views Max had a lot of personal ambition, and he knew it would be prudent to keep in with the Harveys.

Lionel appeared along the path a few minutes later with his friend. His young face was contorted with rage, and the element of surprise enabled him to grab Max by the lapels of his coat.

'What's the idea?' Lionel demanded. 'Is this how you repay my father's generosity, by kidnapping my sister? Oh yes, I remember you—the waiter who got lucky. Well, you won't get away with this!'

'Lionel!' Ellie cried. 'Have you gone mad?'

'Take your hands off me.' Max's tone was cool and dignified. He was a head taller than his assailant and he flicked him aside as easily as swatting a fly. 'Money obviously doesn't breed manners.'

'Shall we teach him a lesson?' asked Randolph, who was a baseball hero at University.

'Where did you meet Drew and how did you bribe him to bring you here tonight? What more do you expect to get from my family?'

Ellie was furious. 'Stop all this nonsense. What have you got against Mr Berman?'

'He's a Jew.' Lionel spat the word out as if it were unclean. 'We all know the lengths *they'll* go to, to get rich.'

Max's eyes narrowed and a muscle moved in his jaw. 'I trace my roots back to Abraham,' he said. 'If you could do the same I would respect you as an equal, but I doubt if your family even knew the Columbus this fair commemorates. Don't tangle with me, Harvey.'

'Leave this man and come with us, Ellie,' Lionel commanded.

'I won't,' said Ellie. 'Where's Drew?'

'Drew has taken off with Clarissa.'

'And you are jealous ... well, don't take it out

on me. I'm an adult now, Lionel, and you can't tell me what to do.'

She was wrenched from Max's side. 'You'll behave properly, miss. I'm responsible for you and I say you'll stay with me, not gallivant with any riffraff that takes your fancy. Especially a Jew.'

Max struck him. He knew immediately his fist made contact that it was the most foolhardy thing he could have done. The blow landed just beneath the cheekbone and Lionel reeled from it. Randolph was the one who retaliated first, bringing Max to the ground in a tackle which would have won applause in a sports stadium. Ellie screamed. A whistle blew.

Crowds gathered as the three men struggled, and the police had a job to get through. Lionel immediately addressed the law, his good looks marred by a red swelling of the cheek which he nursed with a cupped hand.

'I'm Lionel Harvey,' he said officiously, and pointed at Max. 'Arrest that man! He attacked me.'

Two policemen took over and hauled Max aside. 'C'mon. A night behind bars ought to cool you off, mister.'

Max was held prisoner but no one could rob him of his dignity. 'You'll regret this,' he said to Lionel. 'I warn you, one day you'll have to come to terms with all I stand for.'

As he was led away Ellie bent to retrieve his boater which had bowled to her feet and she refused to give it up to anyone.

No charges were laid against Max Berman, and he was allowed to walk free from the police cell later that night with no more than a warning not to let it happen again. He suspected that Ellie was responsible for his quick release, but he was as yet only partly aware of the power of her persuasion.

'Thank you, Papa, dearest,' Ellie said, when Conrad replaced the telephone after speaking to the most senior officer on duty and explaining it had all been a family misunderstanding. She dried her eyes on a delicate lace handkerchief. 'I knew you would be as upset as I was at the way Lionel provoked poor Mr Berman. It was unforgivable. Mr Berman of all people, to whom we are so indebted.'

The state of her father's feelings was dubious, but Ellie had played upon them until the desired result was achieved. She had marched indoors ahead of Lionel, Randolph and Clarissa, determined to present her side of the story before anyone else had a chance. Her defence of Max had been breathtaking, and it had left Lionel in a position where anything he said made the case against him sound worse. Conrad Harvey had succumbed.

'And now, Papa, we're again in Mr Berman's debt. He's brought Drew back to us—isn't it wonderful?'

'A coincidence that they met,' said her father. 'Nothing more.'

'It was *meant* to be,' beamed Ellie. 'Now I will tell you the most wonderful news of all. I spoke to Drew and I've persuaded him to come home, if you'll not be hard on him. I know he regrets the mistake he made but I said you've forgiven him and want to make a fresh start. You'll do that, Papa, won't you? You'll take him into the company and not be angry any more?'

'I'll hear him say first that he was wrong to defy me.'

'No, Papa. You'll never get him back if you do that.' The lace handkerchief fluttered again as Ellie's voice trembled. 'I know you miss him more than anybody. And *I* want him back more than anything in the world.'

A week later Drew Harvey took his place on the Board of the Union Atlantic Railroad Company.

FOUR

Her experiences at the Exposition had plunged Ellie into a dilemma. The meeting with Max Berman had confirmed that her emotional obsession over the last three years had not been wasted. Seeing him again had brought fresh life to her fantasies, only now they had become reality. She had nearly fainted with desire when his lips had touched hers in that brief, exquisite kiss, and she wouldn't rest until the contact was repeated, though she was at a loss to know how that could be managed.

Now that Drew was back in the family fold it was unlikely he would have any further contact with Max, and so there was no hope of another chance meeting even if she took Drew into her confidence. Ellie racked her brains for a solution but came up with nothing, since it was out of the question for her to approach Max in person at his place of work. She thought of asking her godfather to help, but he was away on one of his visits, and even if he had been available she wouldn't have known what to say without arousing suspicion. There remained only the option of writing a letter.

Ellie stayed in her room the whole of one morning composing a missive which would let Max know she wanted to see him again, yet without seeming to be a cheap invitation. When she finally sealed the envelope and gave the letter to Prudence to post, she felt reasonably confident that her words wouldn't be misinterpreted, but her nerves were raw nevertheless.

'Dear Mr Berman,' she had written. The paper was decorated with pink rosebuds all down one edge. 'I feel sure my brother Lionel will not apologise to you for the terrible things he said, so I am taking it upon myself to let you know that his sentiments are not shared by anyone else in the family. Please can you find it in your heart to forgive his behaviour? I couldn't bear it if you were to think I hold the same opinions, for it doesn't slip my mind for a minute that were it not for you I might not be here today, and I am eternally grateful.

'How extraordinary that you know my dear brother Drew. It is surely Fate.

'It would put my mind at rest if you could let

70

me know that you do not bear a grudge. Yours in anticipation, Elena Harvey.'

She didn't know whether he would even reply. He'd been very angry that evening at the Exposition, quite rightly so, and he might not want anything more to do with the Harveys. At night she clutched the corner of her frilled pillow for comfort the way she had done when things had worried her as a child, and willed him to understand that she very much wanted to see him again.

Three days later Ellie was coming down the curved staircase which was such a grand feature of the house in Prairie Avenue, and she almost tripped when Prudence called up to her from the hallway.

'Telephone, Miss Elena,' Prudence said, holding out the earpiece. 'Gentleman by the name of Mr Berman.'

Ellie took a deep breath, then swept down the remaining stairs with a nonchalant air which hid an inner quaking.

'Good evening, Mr Berman,' she said. 'This is Elena Harvey speaking.'

'I received your letter, Miss Harvey,' said Max. There was humour in his voice. Surely he hadn't thought it funny! 'Please don't let your mind be uneasy any longer. I bear no grudge.'

'Oh, thank goodness.'

'I hope our association at the Exposition didn't cause you any trouble.'

'Oh no,' said Ellie, now a little breathless. 'None at all.'

71

'I was afraid your father might be angry that you became separated from your brothers.'

'Well ... just a little. But I reminded him that I was perfectly safe with you.'

'You hardly know me.'

'No, but you once saved my life. In whose hands could I be safer?'

'I don't wish to hear that little matter ever mentioned again,' Max said, sounding vexed. Then he laughed. 'And I'm sure I have to thank you for my prompt release from custody, so please consider the debt cleared. Now, I won't keep you—I know you must be busy.'

'No...'

'I'll bid you goodnight, then.'

'Goodnight,' murmured Ellie, as the line went dead.

Oh, the disappointment. He hadn't even expressed a wish that they might meet again some time in the future. Nothing. When the gong sounded for dinner, Ellie entered the dining room knowing it would be impossible for food to pass the lump in her throat, and she had to excuse herself on the pretext of being unwell.

The following evening Drew waylaid her in the conservatory where she had languished uncharacteristically for most of the day.

'Little one, I know the symptoms,' Drew said, drawing a chair close to hers. 'Would a fellow by the name of Berman be the reason for this attack of the doldrums?'

Ellie flushed crimson. 'How did you guess?'

'As I said, I've suffered myself.' He picked up

72

her hand and traced the heart line deeply etched across the top of her palm. 'Tomorrow evening I've asked Clarissa's parents if I may take her to a concert given by the Chicago Symphony. I'm afraid I took the liberty of saying that you would come with us as chaperone. You will come, won't you, Ellie? It'll take your mind off things.'

'You'd no right—' she began. Then she saw how disappointed her brother would be if she refused, and fought against her disinclination to do anything. 'You never used to like Clarissa.'

'She was gawky and freckled. How was I to know she would grow into a red-headed beauty while I was away?'

'She adores you, Drew.'

'Of course! Doesn't everyone?' He teetered backwards on the chair when she pushed him for teasing, but when he righted himself he was serious. 'I'm glad to be back home, Ellie, for many reasons, but one of the main ones could be Clarissa.'

'I'm glad. And of course I'll come tomorrow.'

Ellie dressed with care for the concert in a gown of apricot silk. She longed to wear dark velvet like Mama, which would have made her look older and more sophisticated, but Mama had said that at eighteen pastel shades were more becoming and had refused to let her even try a fabric of midnight blue against her pale skin, yet Ellie knew instinctively that with her colouring it would be striking.

Drew was allowed to use the new vis-à-vis carriage with curtain quarter which had been made specially for Papa by Brewsters of New York, and they arrived early at the concert hall where the great Theadore Thomas was to conduct the orchestra. Clarissa, in turquoise satin, clung to Drew's arm with excitement while Ellie walked on the other side of him, feeling that she was decidedly in the way.

The foyer was already overflowing with elegant concert-goers. Drew bought programmes and sweetmeats and as he had predicted, the atmosphere lifted Ellie out of her misery. She loved coming here and looked around with pleasure at the well-known society figures with whom she was sharing the evening. A Theadore Thomas concert was not to be missed, and it was almost a social obligation to be seen at one. It was amazing, therefore, to spot Max Berman shouldering his way through the crush, his head proud, his eyes seeking someone. Ellie was suddenly so hot she thought she was going to faint. It was the last place she would have expected him to be.

He came up to them while she was still fearful of seeing him approach some female other than herself. That he was to join them was too good to be true.

'Max,' said Drew, attracting his attention. 'Glad you're here. I didn't tell the ladies you were coming just in case you couldn't make it.'

'It was kind of you to invite me,' Max answered. He bowed over Clarissa's hand with continental good manners, and lingered a fraction longer over Ellie's. 'My experience of the theatre has only been melodramas and variety shows at the Arcade in Pullman.'

'Do you like classical music, Mr Berman?' asked Clarissa.

'Greatly, though I hear little of it.' They began to move towards the auditorium, Drew with Clarissa, Max falling in beside Ellie. 'I didn't know you were coming, Miss Harvey.'

'I didn't know you were either, Mr Berman. I'm very glad to see you.'

It was the greatest understatement. She was ecstatic. All through the first half of the concert she was conscious of him and kept glancing surreptitiously at his strong hands resting on his knees. Her own were clasped to stop them trembling. And once she caught him looking in her direction rather than at the stage. Their eyes met briefly and they smiled at each other in the dimness, and though they didn't have a chance to speak alone she knew that Max was pleased to have her company.

Arriving home later, Ellie was hardly inside the door before she flung her arms around Drew.

'You're the dearest, kindest brother in all the world,' she told him, close to his ear so that no one else should hear. 'It was wonderful what you did for me ... inviting Max, I mean.'

'I didn't invite him for you,' said Drew, disentangling himself. 'I needed to pass on a message. I guess it's I who should be thanking you for bringing Max and me together. We can do business.'

'I don't understand—what business?'

'The less said the better. And I'd rather you didn't say anything to Father.'

'Oh, Drew.'

Ellie was uneasy, but not for long. Max Berman had asked to see her again and that was much more important.

Several times over the next few weeks Ellie met Max in town, but always through an arrangement made by Drew and without Mama or Papa knowing that she was seeing him. She would carry a letter to deliver, but once it had changed hands Max seemed pleased enough to spend an hour or two with her walking through one of the parks or along the waterfront.

Once he took her to the wharf where the Goodrich boats left daily for Milwaukee and Grand Rapids and they watched passengers leave the SS *Columbus* glowing from the bracing lake air.

'It's a pity we can't go cruising on it one Sunday,' Max said. 'I'm afraid your family wouldn't approve.'

'I can't think of anything I'd rather do,' cried Ellie, knowing as well as he that such a trip was out of the question, but the fact that he had suggested it set her heart racing.

She lived for the times they were together. Not that Max ever let their meetings develop into a personal relationship. He was very correct. They talked of formal things, and it seemed as if he had forgotten the time they had kissed on the Ferris wheel. But he began to call her Ellie. When she used his given name for the first time it felt as sweet as honey on her tongue.

'I like being with you, Max,' she said, as they were parting one evening. 'Would you still want to see me if Drew didn't have any more messages to pass on?'

He leaned into the carriage, his keen eyes holding hers, his lips curving fractionally upwards. 'We get on well, Ellie. I enjoy your company.' He wouldn't say more and she tried to be content, but when her body felt as if it was on fire if his hand so much as brushed against hers, it was difficult to find much hope in the comment.

Ellie was forced to trust Melksham, the family coachman, who drove her to some unlikely destinations to meet Max without any show of surprise. She was supposedly visiting various aunts scattered about the city. Then one dreadful day the deceit was discovered. One of the aunts made unexpected contact with Papa and he said how pleased he was that Ellie had become so caring. The fact that she had not been visiting at all was soon discovered, and poor Melksham almost lost his job. Part of the truth came out under Papa's angry questioning. Ellie had never been at the receiving end of his cold, hard anger before and it was frightening, reducing her to tears which this time failed to move him.

'Max Berman!' Papa spat the name out. 'Not only have you lied, Elena, you have betrayed my trust and behaved like a cheap factory girl. You have kept company with a man not fit to clean your shoes—an immigrant, a Pullman employee, an adventurer!'

'Don't speak about Max like that,' Ellie cried.

Papa's nostrils flared. 'He sees you as an easy means of getting his hands on money.'

'He doesn't. He isn't like that, Papa.'

'He knows you see him as some sort of hero and he's playing on it. It's all part of his scheme, girl, but you're too young and innocent to see it. Oh, I understand the attraction but I thought you would have had more sense than to be taken in by a fortune-hunter.'

Drew was not mentioned and Ellie held her tongue.

Her punishment included confinement to the house unless Mama was free to accompany her, no letters which were not first seen by one of her parents, and she was utterly forbidden any contact with Max Berman.

Max was acquainted with the situation via another letter smuggled out. He didn't try to communicate with her except for once sending fresh flowers which Mama consigned to the rubbish bin. And once he telephoned but was refused a hearing.

Ellie suffered frustration and misery and heartbreak. She realised it was an unsuitable friendship and she tried to be an obedient daughter, but being cut off from Max was like being starved of oxygen and life seemed meaningless. She sat forlornly in the garden beneath the cherry trees pining for him.

'I'm sorry, Sis,' Drew had said. 'Sorry for you, and sorry my line of communication's broken.'

'I love him,' Ellie quavered. 'I'll never love

anyone else in my whole life.'

'You'll get over it.'

'No, I won't. I'd give up everything to be with him, just like you did to be an engineer.'

'Ellie, you wouldn't last a week without new gowns and a maid to help dress you.' He pinched her cheek affectionately. 'You're very young. Write it off as experience.'

She was furious. 'You're a hick, Drew—you've got no feelings. And I hate being a woman so I can't just go out and get what I want. Why do I have to stay here? Why can't I go right over and tell Max how I feel?'

'Because you're too well-bred. And because Max has too much pride to appreciate being chased.'

She took a deep breath. 'All the same, I might write him another note.'

'You'll be taking a risk.'

'I know. But anything's better than sitting here letting life pass me by. It's not my way.'

'No, it isn't.' He gave a wry smile. 'So I suppose if you're silly enough to write him a note I'll have to be the fool who sees he gets it.'

'Will you? Oh Drew, please.'

'Just for you,' he promised.

Max was surprised how much he missed Ellie. Meeting up with her had been an amusing pastime and he had quite looked forward to their time together, but in a way it had been a relief when the association had come to an end. He'd become increasingly aware that Ellie was taking everything too seriously, and while he was flattered by the adoration she couldn't hide, it also embarrassed him.

Part of the problem was that he found her so sexually attractive. If she had been of his class he would have taken her to bed and enjoyed finding out if the signals she gave were genuine, but it was too risky to play around with the daughter of the President of the Union Atlantic Railroad Company. If any harm came to her there would be hell to pay. His new career would be in ruins and all hope of ever setting up in business on his own would be gone. So he pushed her to the back of his mind.

Then he received yet another letter in her neat copperplate writing.

'Dear Max,' Ellie had written. *'You were so kind to send me flowers. I'm so sorry I wasn't allowed to speak to you on the telephone. Please can you try again on Thursday next between eight and ten o'clock in the morning. I miss our outings. Yours sincerely, Ellie.'*

The text was no more than friendly but Max knew enough about her now to deduce that much thought had gone into the wording. Ellie was a very determined young lady and she was not used to being thwarted. Something out of reach was bound to be exciting, and the fact that their backgrounds were so different probably led her to glamorise the situation. If he wanted to discourage her before he himself was drawn into deep water then something positive had to be done.

For two weeks he hadn't heard her voice.

When she answered the telephone on Thursday the sound of it caressed his ear and he felt as if he were being seduced.

'I'm so very pleased to hear you,' Ellie cooed. 'I felt I had to give you the chance to get in touch. I was afraid you might think I felt the same way as my parents about our friendship.'

'Your father disapproves.'

'I've been threatened with being sent to live in New York with Frederick and Henrietta if I disobey him.'

'And yet you wish to see me.'

'Oh yes,' she breathed.

'I should like you to see where I live,' Max said. 'My sister Katrina has a new baby and it would be nice for you to meet.'

'That would be wonderful—but I can't go anywhere without Mama. How can I possibly manage it?'

'I shall be at the corner of State and Madison streets at two o'clock on Sunday and I'll wait one hour. If you are as keen as you say you'll find a way to be there.'

Max replaced the receiver without giving her the chance to answer. He didn't doubt that she would be there on time, and he would take her to Pullman. The apartment in Fulton Street was at present cluttered with all the paraphernalia necessary for a newborn baby, and the comparison with her own luxurious home would be so apparent it was to be hoped she would see how pointless it was for them to become involved with each other.

All the same, he stood for a few minutes

in the telephone booth at the upholstery shop after replacing the receiver, his mind troubled. He couldn't be absolutely sure that dissuasion was the real reason why he had invited her to his home.

The corner of Madison and State was said to be the busiest in the world, but Ellie had no qualms about planning to go there alone on Sunday. It would be easy to mingle with the crowds and no one would recognise her, but first she had to find a way of getting there.

Thursday night was hot and Ellie couldn't sleep after speaking to Max. Her body ached. When she closed her eyes pictures of him were so clear she stretched out her arms and almost expected to feel him bending over her. Her fingers combed through her black hair as she imagined it was his, her lips parted in futile anticipation. She gasped at the fantasies he inspired and grew hotter in her pink and white frilled bed.

When she could lie there no longer she went to the window and pulled back the heavy rose brocade drapes. Her bedroom overlooked the terrace and shadows were like figures in the moonlight. For one silly moment she thought Max was leaning against the stone balustrade and she opened the casement, his name on her lips, a Juliet convinced that her lover had risked everything to wait beneath her balcony. There was no one there.

How had it happened, this business of falling in love? She ought to have been carefree and looking forward to a season of balls and parties in the company of Chicago's most elegant young men. Instead she was obsessed with a Jewish immigrant far removed from her own social circle who made other men pale by comparison. Max had only to look at her and the world went spinning out of orbit.

Love wasn't just in his touch, though the mere brushing of his arms against hers produced enough electricity to light a department store. It wasn't only in the magnetism of his eyes, or the timbre of his voice. It wasn't in the words he spoke, the way he looked, or the life he led, but a combination of all these things. Ellie had no idea what drew her to him with such force, both mentally and physically. She felt as if she was drowning in emotions she didn't understand and a practical streak in her wanted to rebel against this subjective state, but just hearing Max at the other end of the telephone had made her resistance collapse like a house of cards. Love, whatever it was, controlled her every waking thought.

There was no question of not meeting him on Sunday. If it meant further punishment she would have to bear it.

On the Saturday, Ellie went shopping with her mother to Marshall Field's store to choose new drapes for the morning room. They spent two hours comparing designs and fabrics, and returned to their carriage after finally placing an order, only to find that the street was blocked by men demonstrating against working conditions. It was an ugly scene.

'Ban the monopolies!' was the chant. 'Halt the lay-offs. A fair wage for a fair day's work!'

There were banners waving and traffic was stopped while a procession of several hundred workers jammed the thoroughfare. Sibylla and Ellie Harvey got into their open carriage to wait for the marchers to pass, sitting high in the seat and shading their heads from the sun with parasols. Unfortunately their exalted position made them a target.

'How'd you like to go hungry, duchess?' came a derisory cry, and raised faces leered at the two fashionable ladies in their vehicle. Melksham tried to turn them away but he was a lone voice against angry men.

Eggs were thrown and one landed on one of the enormous bell-sleeves of Mama's blue walking dress, unbalancing her momentarily, but she recovered her poise straight away and brushed the slime clear with a gloved hand.

'Trash, the lot of them,' she said, with icy aplomb. 'Mark them well, Elena, and perhaps you will understand why your Papa has been so strict. Such men are ill-bred and loud. I'm not saying they're not decent-living in their own communities, but that's where they belong and there's a great divide between our society and theirs. That's how it should be.'

'Have you no feelings, Mama?' Ellie had been viewing the incident through eyes which saw into the poverty and hardship provoking it, thanks to earnest discussions with Drew and Max. 'You've no idea of the desperation that drives men like these to demonstrate.'

'Perhaps I have more idea than you,' said Sibylla, removing her eggstained gloves. 'My father wasn't always rich.'

Rarely did Mama speak of her early life. Ellie knew only that she was from the British aristocracy and that Papa had wooed and won her in the summer of 1864 when he had been on an extended visit to England supervising the shipment of railway locomotives to Chicago. Sir Robert Cromer, Mama's father, had given them his blessing and a vast dowry which had enabled Papa to fulfil ambitions which his own well-connected but financially impoverished family had been unable to do. No mention was ever made of Mama's British side of the family. So the statement came as a surprise.

'Tell me about my English grandfather,' Ellie urged, while they waited for the road to be clear.

'He was a railway contractor. He started with nothing and as a child I wore clogs, or went barefoot. It was dreadful.' The last of the demonstrators turned into another street and were lost from view. 'My father took risks,' Sybilla went on, 'and he was lucky. Once he put out a tender to build a magnificent station when he was penniless and he won the contract. Don't ask me how he managed, but he did. We didn't see him for months and my mother had to accept charity from the parish.'

'Oh Mama, is that why you never talk of him?'

'I've better things to do.' Sibylla dropped a coin to a smelly urchin selling flypapers while

Melksham gathered up the horses' reins and edged the carriage away from the sidewalk. 'I wouldn't have mentioned him now if you hadn't assumed that I'm ignorant of the effects of poverty.'

'Then why do you have no sympathy?'

'I have a position to keep and I prefer to forget. You will not mention my disclosure to anyone.'

'No, Mama.'

Ellie was very quiet on the journey home. Life held so many surprises, and none greater than the revelation that her mother, that essence of grace and refinement, had once worn clogs.

FIVE

On Sunday, Ellie went to morning Mass with the family but declined to have lunch, saying that she felt sick and couldn't possibly eat a thing. It was quite true. Nervousness made her pale and queasy, and she had hardly known how to sit still in church. She was about to defy her father. If he found out she trembled to think of the consequences, but nothing was going to prevent her from meeting Max.

Prudence came and drew the drapes in Ellie's room, clucking with sympathy when she saw the wan girl reclining on her bed. She had brought a tray of light food which she left on a side-table.

'I hope you soon feel better, Miss Elena,' she said.

'Prudence, will you tell my mother and everybody that I don't want to be disturbed, please?'

'Yes, Miss Elena.' There was concern in the soft brown eyes. Prudence was more than a servant. Often she had given comfort when mother-love had been absent and neither nursemaid nor governess had been a suitable substitute. 'You're not thinking of doing anything silly, are you?'

A little colour stole into Ellie's pale cheeks. 'Now, would I?'

'Sometimes I know things, miss, and I know it's a young man causing all these vapours.'

'You want me to be happy, don't you, Prudence?'

'You know I do.'

'Then if I should want some air presently you won't tell anyone I've gone out, will you?'

'Trust me, Miss Elena.'

As soon as she was alone Ellie changed into her least conspicuous dress and hat, made sure there was money in her purse, and left the house unobserved by the west gate. The impression of calmness she gave was due to years of deportment lessons in which she had been taught that hurrying was undignified. The urge to run had never been greater but she managed to control it. For the first time in her life she took a trolley into the city, and arrived at State and Madison ten minutes before the appointed time. Max was not yet in sight, but already her heart was galloping like a stampede of horses.

Even on a Sunday there was industrial smoke in the air which caught at her throat, and the smell of the lake and prairie beyond was something Ellie always associated with Chicago and had remembered while she was abroad. A woman was riding a horse straddlewise; rich men strolled past, lethargic after midday dining at hotels like the Richelieu. Heads turned and admiring glances flickered over the dark-haired young woman waiting uncertainly on the corner. Ellie knew she ought not to be standing there alone. It was dangerous, even in daylight.

She saw Max when he was still in the distance and the eccentric beat of her pulse drummed in her ears. He was striding along, head held high and arms swinging so that other pedestrians stood aside for him. She savoured the joy of watching him before he was aware of her. Then she was flying towards him.

'Steady.' He'd no option but to catch her in his arms. It might have been wishful thinking, but surely he kept hold of her longer than was necessary to make sure she didn't fall.

'I'm so pleased to see you,' she cried.

'So it seems,' laughed Max. 'We're taking the train to Pullman. I've told Katrina you're coming.'

'I haven't been there since I was a little girl.'

'Yet it's a favourite weekend occupation for people from Chicago to look at our excellent living conditions in Pullman.'

'Papa says no man can build a Utopia.'

'Just so,' Max assented. 'But he can try.'

Trains went to Pullman every half hour. Max bought two fifty-cent round-trip tickets for the forty-minute journey and Ellie found herself pressed against him in the crowded railcar.

'You'll like my sister,' Max said. 'She's gentle and beautiful like Momma. Usually she keeps the apartment so clean and pretty. Always she puts fresh flowers in the window. But now there's the baby—it's a girl. Her name's Galina.'

His accent became more foreign when he talked about his family, as if they closed round him in spirit. Ellie listened, absorbing every detail, but at the same time was conscious of his thigh tight against hers. It was hot in the train and she hoped her dress wouldn't stain with perspiration, for she was melting away.

The route edged the shore of Lake Michigan and Grant Park for a while. Prairie Avenue was over to the west and Ellie pictured her parents resting in the drawing room unaware, she hoped, of their daughter's deception. A stretch of open country followed, and after a fourteen-mile journey the workshops of Pullman appeared. Ellie exclaimed at a gigantic engine behind a plate-glass window near the entrance to the car works main building.

'I remember that—it's the Corliss engine! We came when Mr Pullman brought friends in his private car to see Florence push the button to start it.'

'It powered the machinery in all the car shops.'

'And water from it filled Lake Vista.' The Corliss engine had been built to supply power for the Philadelphia Centennial in 1876, and afterwards George Pullman had bought it for 130,000 dollars to keep for posterity. Ellie drew up her shoulders with delight at every new sight. 'Oh, isn't it a wonderful day!'

Max smiled at her indulgently, and when he squeezed her hand she seized the opportunity to capture his, holding onto him for the rest of the journey.

The conductor called out 'Pullman!' and Max helped Ellie to alight. Leaving the station she was surprised to see flowerbeds everywhere, lawns stretching down to border the artificial Lake Vista, and wide streets leading into town. The Arcade Building extended for a whole block, where shops catered for everything Pullman citizens needed, though it was closed for the sabbath.

Max pointed out a long, low building belonging to the maintenance department, and a stable nearby. 'That's known as the Casino,' he said. 'Goodness knows why, because horses are kept in it. If you've got money and own a horse you have to stable it there, and if you haven't you can rent one with a carriage for three dollars a day to take the family out. Oliver says he's going to take Katrina and the baby for a drive as soon as she's strong enough.'

At that moment the doors of the Casino were flung open and the water wagon belonging to the volunteer fire company was driven out at great speed, the horses snorting and foaming as they were whipped into action. Passersby stood back in alarm. A man who had obviously called out the firemen came running from the door in pursuit, still gasping for breath as he started to follow. Then he spotted Max.

'Max! God, man, something terrible's happened. There's been a gas explosion in one of the Fulton Street block-house apartments.'

Ellie had grasped his arm and she felt the muscles grow taut. She remembered him saying once that he lived in Fulton Street, and she saw the colour drain from his face. Her own heart seemed to stop momentarily and start up again at twice the pace.

In his haste to get to the scene Max dragged Ellie along, stumbling, tripping. A thin column of smoke was now visible about two blocks away and they headed towards it, others collecting up on the way. Fear nearly choked her. There was no knowing what sight she would see and she was afraid of failing Max. And she was not used to such haste. Her skirt hampered her so she bunched it up and exposed her ankles without thought, anxious not to delay them. An acrid smell stung her nose.

When they turned the corner into Fulton Street the scene was dreadful. A tall house about halfway down had flames coming from the top-floor window. Neighbours were screaming, children crying, and it seemed as if everyone in Pullman was congregating to either stare or shout advice.

'Oh my God,' Max breathed. 'It's *my* apartment.'

For a moment he froze with horror, then he pushed Ellie from him and ran to soak his handkerchief in a puddle by the roadside. He tied it over his nose and mouth and flung his jacket to Ellie. 'Stay here—I'm going inside.'

'No! Don't go,' Ellie screamed. Her stomach surged with fear and she tried to stop him, but he shrugged her off almost angrily and disappeared. She clutched his coat to her breast and prayed. 'Oh Holy Mother of God, dear Virgin Mary, keep him safe. I love him.'

The fire company men were erecting ladders. An old woman was being helped out of the ground-floor apartment as the whole building was evacuated.

'Heard this terrible bang,' someone said.

'There was a big flash,' said another. 'Windows broke.'

'Someone get Katrina Devlin out!' screamed a young girl. 'She's in there with that new baby.'

Katrina! Now she knew why Max had been so desperate. Ellie began praying again—there was nothing else she could do. She hopped from one foot to the other in anguish, a stranger in the midst of these people, anxious to help but only too aware of her own inadequacy. The possibility that she might never again see Max alive was just too awful, too frightening. Pain shot through her.

'There's wooden stairs in that building,' said the woman next to her.

'You mean people at the top are trapped?' Ellie was horrified further.

'Only a few weeks ago a man from the Labour Commission said there ought to be another way out.'

Tears were streaming down Ellie's cheeks as she gazed at the window where firemen were at last dousing the flames. If Max had managed to reach his sister she prayed he would be able to get back. He was not alone. Others were there evacuating families from the ground and middle-floor apartments, and their first thought would have been to rescue Katrina. Burnt drapes ripped against broken glass and the charred window-frame crumbled, bits of scorched wood falling into the crowd as the blaze died down.

'How could it have happened?' Ellie's voice shook and she felt quite faint from the smell.

'Gas is funny stuff. I never did trust these new-fangled stoves.'

Ellie pushed her way up the steps to the main door and tried to see inside, but her way was barred, the hallway clogged with people.

'Keep back.' Men had arrived with a stretcher. She stood on tip-toe and saw Max coming down the stairs carrying a young woman in his arms, fair head lolling against his chest, eyes closed. Ellie's tears flowed anew, this time with relief that he was safe, but his grim expression sent more tearful shivers through her. Beads of sweat studded his brow, his shirt was torn. His eyes were red from the smoke, and the bleakness in them brought silence to the crowd. Ellie held back, afraid to intrude.

There was a new commotion. A man with red hair was thrusting his way through.

'My wife!' he was crying. 'I've got to get to my wife.' A path was cleared for him and sympathetic hands pressed his shoulders as he headed for Max and Katrina. This, then, must be Oliver Devlin. 'Thank God. I feared the worst. Tell me she's all right.'

Max shook his head as he gently laid his sister on the stretcher. 'She's dead, Oliver. Dead. The fumes killed her.' His voice was thick. He embraced his brother-in-law as they shared a grief too great for words.

Ellie watched, too shocked to move, and all her nerves felt exposed. In her pampered life she'd had no experience of raw pain. At the derailment she had been sheltered from the dying and hadn't known any lives were lost until she was safely away from the scene. Now she couldn't take her eyes off the girl on the stretcher. Apart from burns to her hands and clothes she looked as if she was sleeping, and Ellie ached intolerably.

The tragedy affected the crowd. All around there was the strongest feeling of love and sympathy, as if the shocked community fused into a compassionate shield. The people of Fulton Street knew about suffering in a way that would have been foreign to Prairie Avenue.

Ellie moved towards Max, longing to express her sorrow, yet knowing instinctively that now was not the time to remind him of her presence. Instead she looked down at the serene face of Katrina Devlin and cried for the life that was lost. She was beautiful. Her mouth and nose resembled Max's, but she had much lighter hair. Her hands were small and capable, and Ellie pictured them handing round cakes as they should have been doing at this moment. Quite likely she could have made a friend of Katrina, and she deeply regretted that they had not spoken to each other. It was all too awful for words and she desperately wished there was something she could do, not only for Max's sake.

'Where's the baby?' someone was crying.

'The cradle was just cinders,' said the man who had come downstairs behind Max.

Fresh weeping broke out among the women. Ellie could no longer stand her own inactivity and for no explicable reason she felt driven to investigate inside the house of tragedy. It was more than morbid curiosity. She felt sucked into the doorway, now cleared of people, and she entered the building without anyone trying to stop her.

There was no smoke on the stairs, only the acrid smell which made her cough, and she climbed towards the sound of voices, not caring that her skirt trailed through rivulets of water. Up and up the narrow wooden stairs she climbed, past doors left open on the first floor when the family living there had been hastily evacuated. Up here was the room where she could have been sitting herself when the explosion occurred.

Suddenly above the din of voices and banging and splashing water Ellie heard the most unexpected sound. The cry of a newborn child was like a thin reed-pipe tune penetrating the atmosphere. She rushed up the final set of stairs, following the sound, and found herself in a small, smoke-filled bedroom with a brass bedstead by the window. Choking and coughing, she dashed across to the bed and flung back the sheet. There was the baby, wrapped in shawls and kicking feebly as it tried to draw enough breath to survive. It was a wonder it hadn't already suffocated.

Ellie wasted no time. She picked up the bundle and rushed back to the landing.

A fireman tried to stop her. 'What do you think you're doing here? Get to hell out of it.'

'I found the baby alive,' she gasped. 'I've got to get it to safety before the fumes damage its lungs.'

'Holy Jesus, it's a miracle.'

Other men echoed the exclamation, stopping momentarily to see for themselves as Ellie started back down the stairs with the bundle of smoke-grimed shawls protecting the infant in her arms. On the lower landing she paused, feeling dizzy, and for one moment she gazed at the tiny face of Galina Devlin. There was a look of Max about the baby. Ellie trembled as with extraordinary insight she saw her future life tied up with this child, these people.

'Get on down, woman!' the fireman yelled down over the banister. She had never been spoken to in such a way, but felt no indignation.

Someone pounded up the remaining stairs towards her. It was the man with red hair. He snatched the precious bundle from Ellie and buried his face against it.

'Holy Mother of God be blessed,' he sobbed, over and over again.

A sheet was found to cover Katrina's body. Max kissed the lifeless hands of his sister before crossing them over her breast. His heart was breaking and he could hardly bear it when the sheet was drawn up over her beloved face.

They had been through so much together. With arms supporting each other they had been forced to witness their parents' agony in an ordeal so terrifying it remained scorched into the soul. They had experienced poverty and statelessness, and a bitter journey across land and sea to a new country where their language was not understood. Hunger and cold had aged them prematurely, but they had survived. He had rejoiced at last when Katrina had found a husband, and he had seen her happiness complete when the baby was born. No one had deserved it more. Now her life had been snuffed out like the pinching of a candle-flame.

Max got to his feet. There was no sign of Oliver, nor of Ellie Harvey, whom he'd almost forgotten.

He turned to face the tenement, his eyes lifted the upper storey where his home smouldered. It could be rebuilt. George Pullman would send in workmen to clean the bricks, replace the windows, and strengthen the floors. Everything would be put back in prime condition, with another gas-stove installed, and life would go on for those left.

He frowned. What was Ellie Harvey doing

coming out of the building? Where had she been? He tried to move towards her, but his feet felt leaden and he had no spirit to cope with the capriciousness of the society beauty he had hoped to discourage with a domestic scene outside her experience.

She was dishevelled, her cheek streaked with soot as if she had rubbed against something, and he remembered how she had looked when they were trapped together in the débris of the train at Quincy, when she had talked to keep him awake. She was always babbling about him having saved her life, but in all fairness she had done much to save his own. She had courage.

Suddenly he was ashamed. Ellie had not wept or fainted when confronted with disaster. She kept her head and tried to see what she could do.

Now she came to him. 'The baby's alive, Max. Your brother-in-law's bringing her down.' She placed the palm of her hand gently against his cheek. 'I'm here for you. What can I do?'

Oliver appeared with the baby held close to his chest and there were gasps of joy from the crowd still thronging round. Eager, motherly hands reached out to relieve him of the burden but he wouldn't relinquish it. The stretcher was lifted and he walked beside it as his wife's body was borne away to rest in the church, a broken man with his bright head bent over the shawls containing his child.

Max didn't go with them.

'Come away,' said Ellie gently.

'No. I've got to go back and see what can

be salvaged. And you must go home. There will only be more trouble if your parents know you have been with me.'

'I can't go home. I love you,' she said. 'I must be with you.'

He was in no mood to argue, and when he went back into the building he was glad of her company. Each stair he climbed increased the pain of his loss. Ellie came up behind him in silence.

The firemen were leaving with a loud clatter of buckets, and they pressed his shoulder as they passed him on the first landing, no words being adequate. From the apartment came a nauseous smell of gas and wet charred timber, and water trickled round his feet. Max trod on the burnt floorboards of the kitchen and rocked with anguish as he surveyed the devastation. It was practically gutted. Glass was everywhere, a black, skeletal chair was all that was left of the furniture, and there was not a stick worth saving.

Saddest of all was a flowerpot set amidst the débris, with one of Katrina's bright red geraniums still bravely flourishing in it, as if she had left behind a single sign of hope. Max picked it up. His shoulders shook and his tears fell on the brilliant petals.

Ellie led him away from the kitchen and into the bedroom where the baby had been found alive. Soot hung in the air, but the room was intact. She took the flowerpot and stood it on the washstand, then put her arms round him, her sympathy flowing without any emotional declaration. Her presence was very soothing and strangely he didn't mind her seeing his weakness at this moment.

'I'm so sorry, Ellie. You ought not to be involved in all this.'

'How can you say that? It was meant for us to share things.' She slipped a hand through his arm and drew closer to his side. 'I believe in Fate, you know, and the way our lives are linked in times of trouble can only mean that we're here to help each other.'

He stopped and turned to her, and saw the beauty of her nature beneath the elegant façade. He had maligned her. It had amused him to play along with what he had thought to be a game when she had sought him out so obviously, but it had not been a light-hearted diversion after all. She had spoken of loving. And oh, how lovely she was.

He bent his head towards her upturned face and with his thumb he wiped away the sooty marks. She was breathing erratically.

'You're a very surprising person, Ellie.'

'Am I?'

His lips touched hers, brushing against their fullness and meeting with such sensitivity his loins immediately throbbed. An inner voice challenged him, demanding to know how he could be doing this when Katrina had just died in this place, but the feel of Ellie's mouth drove him on to explore with his tongue, and when she melted against him he was lost. Kissing her released him temporarily from suffering. For several minutes they were locked in a hungry embrace, his hand sliding down to press her even closer, but when he felt her respond to the intimacy he came to his senses.

'I'm sorry,' he said, forcing her away. 'I'm using you. Forgive me.'

'There's nothing to forgive.' She regained her composure, taking a deep breath. 'I'll do anything for you, Max, anything at all which will ease the pain. Don't send me away.'

Her face was still dangerously close and compassion made her yielding. He could feel her warmth and suppleness like a force drawing him irresistibly nearer, and his hands hovered against her shoulders as he fought to shake off temptation. But the sweetness of her femininity, the chance to forget everything, were too much for his willpower, and he gave in.

They were alone now. He drew her against him again, breathing in the fragrance of her skin as he kissed her, and together they sank onto the damp, soot-stained bed. Her arms enfolded him, comforted and strengthened him. Her fingers miraculously kneaded the tension points in his neck, and her lips fluttered over his temple where the pain was bad. She aroused him until restraint was impossible.

Much later he was to feel terrible shame that he had taken her virginity with such selfishness, but at the time there was only blessed relief from the agony of this day's events in Ellie Harvey's willing body.

Max had to put Ellie out of his mind over the next few days. He and his brother Laban made all the arrangements for Katrina's funeral as Oliver Devlin had little knowledge of Jewish customs and was too distraught to make any effort to help. Nor did Oliver have the ability or the will to cope with his child, much to everyone's surprise. It was thought that Galina would bring him comfort, but after the first thrill of finding her alive, he seemed unable to even look at her and his lack of interest was incomprehensible. The baby was left with Momma, who cried over her incessantly, and at the end of that terrible week of grieving all their lives had changed.

Soon after their dear Katrina had been laid to rest, Oliver came to the Berman house and said he was going to Philadelphia.

'I can't stay here without my wife,' he said. 'I've got friends in Philadelphia and I've a hankering to visit them, just until I can pull myself together. You'll look after Galina for me, won't you, Momma Berman? She's too young to go travelling yet.'

Max was angry. 'You can't do this. Momma shouldn't be burdened with a baby at her age.'

'Then who shall I be leaving the child with? Would you rather she went into an orphanage?'

'Don't fret, either of you!' Momma said, cradling her grandchild. 'I'll bring the little one up as if she were my Katrina all over again. I'll love doing it.'

'I knew you would,' said Oliver. 'I knew you'd understand, Momma.'

He left the next day. Perhaps it was for the best. Momma, who had been inconsolable since her daughter's death, began to take an interest in things again, and after a few more days could be heard crooning softly to the baby in her care.

'A child costs money,' grumbled Poppa. 'He didn't leave us anything to provide for the child.'

'What does it matter,' she said. 'We shall manage.'

'We can hardly manage to feed ourselves. Business is bad, Hedda. The recession means no one is buying new suits.'

'We've lost Katrina, but God spared her child to take her place. Would you have grudged our daughter the slightest thing?'

'Of course not.'

'Then we will think of Galina as another precious daughter.'

Jacob Berman took the baby from his wife's arms and rocked her as he had done their own. 'You're right, Hedda. And you're a wonderful woman.'

Max was living with his parents until the tenement in Pullman was habitable again. At night the baby cried and Momma paced up and down with it in the next room, and in the mornings she was so tired her face looked as grey as her hair. It broke his heart to see her so overburdened, and he did what he could to relieve the strain, but he couldn't help financially. On top of everything else there were problems at work which made him so bitter he felt like starting a revolt, though that would have cost him his job altogether and he was not that foolish.

It was all to do with the assistant foreman called Warren, a 'straw boss' whom no one liked. The man had no scruples. Max had devised a new and easier method for piping the patterned plush which was to cover the chairs in a new parlour car, but the credit he had expected went to Warren, who claimed the idea was his own.

'You're no more than a common thief,' Max accused him. 'The idea was mine, and I want recognition for it.'

'I thought of it before you set foot in this shop,' blustered Warren.

'Then why haven't we used it before? You're a liar.'

'You cause trouble, Berman, and I won't pass your work.'

Like most of the men, Max was on piecework, and when the foreman kept him idle for many unpaid hours there was no higher authority to which he could complain. Warren could also see to it that the price for the job the crew was working on was unfairly divided, and at the end of the week there was precious little money in Max's pocket.

As a result of this he attended a convention called by Eugene Debs, and he became one of the first members of the newly formed American Railway Union, trusting the promise that the ARU would bring about higher wages and better working conditions.

Sometimes he called on Mariette Schuman, hoping for respite, but he found none. Since possessing Ellie Harvey he felt restless and unhappy, angry with himself for having given way to temptation. And yet the fault had not been entirely his. Ellie had done a lot of encouraging, and that worried him. Making love to her had been an exciting experience in spite of the circumstances, or perhaps because of them, but he couldn't get over the feeling that she was a danger to his freedom. She was a young lady with a great sense of purpose, and no doubt she'd got what she wanted all her life, so remembering her declaration of love made him uneasy.

Each night he tossed on his bed, sweltering in the Chicago summer heat which seemed worse in the cramped space behind the tailor's shop than it did in the third-floor tenement in Fulton Street, and thoughts of Ellie Harvey oppressed him.

SIX

It was thanks to Drew and Prudence that Ellie's traumatic visit to Pullman went undiscovered by her father. A call from Max on the telephone had brought Drew to collect her in the gig and Ellie had been smuggled up to her bedroom by the back stairs, feeling frightened but elated, and so much in love she could do nothing except lie on her bed and dream. Her mother had come to see her later and had wanted to send for the doctor, but Ellie had persuaded

105

her to wait until the next morning, by which time she had managed to collect her feelings, and to conceal the inner turmoil which made food seem completely indigestible.

Next day, the story of the fire in a Pullman tenement was in all the Chicago newspapers, and much was made of the tragic death of Katrina Devlin. Max Berman's name was mentioned, the apartment being rented by him, but if Mama and Papa noticed it they made no comment.

Ellie worried incessantly about Max. She wanted to be with him, but she couldn't intrude without invitation. All the week she wore her darkest clothes and waited, making excuses for him when no word came. The middle of the following week, Drew brought her a letter, and with fast-beating heart she fled to her room to read it.

'*My dear Ellie,*' Max had written. The endearment thrilled her. '*I cannot tell you how sad this past week has been. Remembering your compassion has helped me through. I am writing to thank you, and to say again that I am sorry to have involved you so deeply in my affairs.*

'*Please don't think me ungrateful when I say that it would be foolish for us to meet again.*' Her joy evaporated, and now she was stricken. With fear she read on. '*I am sure you will agree that there are too many difficulties preventing us from becoming closer friends. Your father would forbid it, and mine would frown upon it. Believe me, I think very highly of you and things might have been different in different circumstances. As it is, I can see that further meetings would only cause*

106

trouble for you, and I have no wish to do that. So this is a letter of goodbye. I hope your future will be happy and I wish you well.

'Goodbye, Elena. I shall remember you with affection and gratitude. Max.'

Ellie let out a cry of despair. All her hopes were snuffed out, all her love spurned. She was desolate, and she couldn't accept that his feelings for her were any less than hers for him, not after the intimacy they had shared.

She had just read the letter through for the third time when Drew knocked and came in.

'He doesn't want to see me again, Drew,' she gasped. Her face was white and she was trembling. 'It's too awful.'

'It's for the best,' said Drew. 'Max is a decent sort. He's got the grace to be honest with you, and that counts for a lot.'

'But I love him so much. What am I going to do?'

'You'll survive.'

'I'll never love anyone else.' Ellie flung herself on her brother and clung to him, weeping. 'I love you, too. You've got to help me.'

'Not any more, Ellie. For your own good you've got to put Max Berman out of your mind.'

'Not ever,' she vowed.

Nevertheless she was sensible enough to know that Drew's advice was sound. Papa *would* be terribly angry if he ever found out that she had disobeyed him, and without doubt she would be immediately despatched to New York. The thought of having to live with Frederick and

107

Henrietta depressed her more than ever, and so she tried to be strong.

Over the next two weeks she went visiting with Mama, met Clarissa for girlish gossip, and hid her heartache beneath a veneer of smiles. She wove a fantasy in which Max was suffering equally, and in her mind he became a martyr who had sacrificed everything for her sake. That way she was able to cope.

It was well into the fourth week after the fire that she had to admit the plan was not working. She felt continually unwell. Each morning she woke up so dejected it became a physical malady and she had to rush to the closet to be sick.

Nothing escaped Prudence's notice. After the third attack of sickness the coloured woman came to Ellie's room with fresh towels and sponged her down in the hipbath. She was silent until the job was done, then she looked at the girl speculatively.

'Miss Elena, I'm going to ask a question and I want a truthful answer,' she said. 'Have you been doing anything you'd no business doing?'

'Prudence! No, of course I haven't,' Ellie protested. Then: 'What sort of thing?' Her heart was beating very fast.

'I'd say, missy, that you're going to have a baby, and I'm never wrong.'

'You're lying, Prudence. How dare you!' she cried in anger. Yet her protests were a defence against the terrible truth she had suspected.

'I hope I am, Miss Elena,' Prudence said quietly.

Oh, at school in France she had giggled with

her friends about the peculiarities of marriage, and there had been plenty of guessing about what a husband did to a wife to produce babies. But what had happened between herself and Max had been so wonderful and natural and it had made her feel so deliriously, so ecstatically happy, she could hardly credit it was the dreaded act she'd heard a woman had to put up with in order to be a good wife. It was, of course, but there had only been the single time. Surely nothing so momentous could have occurred in that brief moment of loving Max with every part of her.

She touched her stomach. It felt tender, but that was because she had just been sick. She looked at herself in the long cheval mirror and saw that the reason why her bodice had felt tight this last week was because her breasts were fuller. Mercy. She knew nothing about the intricacies of pregnancy, but as her fingers explored her body she had to accept that this was what was the matter with her.

The truth was appalling, yet her first experience of intimacy with Max had affected her profoundly and the thought of having his child overwhelmed her.

She took a deep, shuddering breath. 'So what am I going to do, Prudence?'

How cold it was. Her skin felt raw and she was shivering.

'I should say, miss, that you should get yourself a husband just as soon as you can, then no one need know it isn't an early baby. There's plenty of young men wanting to marry you.'

'I'll never marry anyone except Max.'

'Then see him right away. You can't go wasting no time.'

Ellie wrapped the towel round her, drawing it tight as if the warm folds would take this thing away. 'I'm frightened, Prudence. I'm terrified. What if Papa and Mama find out?'

'They won't hear anything from me, I swear. But there'll be no hiding what you've got inside you in a few more weeks. Take my advice and go see the young man today.'

'Papa will never let me marry him.'

'Your Papa loves you, Miss Elena. He's never denied you anything you really want, now has he?'

Ellie took the train to Pullman. She sat in the carriage looking out on scenery she had viewed with Max on that eventful day which had totally changed her life, and she could hardly believe that everything looked just the same.

Prudence had lent her a plain dress which wouldn't attract attention, and she wore a hat with a veil. She was glad of the veil. It enabled her to observe one of the women opposite without appearing to do so. She looked to be not much older than herself but she had a child of about a year old wriggling on the seat beside her because room on her lap was limited by the swelling beneath her drab frock. It was the first time Ellie had studied a woman who was obviously pregnant. The mound looked uncomfortable, and the girl kept moving as if the hard seat made her back ache, but she looked happy. There was a glow about her.

This is how I shall look, Ellie thought. She had spent all of the precious day reconciling herself to a fact which couldn't be changed, and now she felt stronger. She was going to give Max the most precious gift it was possible to give—the gift of creation. He couldn't fail to be moved by it. For the first time since the discovery of her condition Ellie began to feel excitement. She wanted to be with Max for the rest of her life, and Fate had conspired to make that possible.

Pullman looked different on a working day. Shops were open in the Arcade and there was bustling activity around the school and the Florence Hotel. No one took any notice of her and when she asked the way to the upholstery shop it was assumed she was going there for a job.

At the office she asked for Max Berman, but had to wait until lunch-time before she could see him. His surprise was almost comic and if the situation had not been so serious she would have laughed.

'Ellie!' he exclaimed, as she lifted the veil. 'What on earth are you doing here?'

'I have to talk to you,' she said. 'It's very important.'

'I've no time. And I meant what I said in my letter about us not meeting again.'

'I'm expecting a baby, Max.' If he had no time then it was vital to shock him into listening. 'I want to know if you'll marry me.'

He opened his mouth, but no sound came. For a moment he stared at her as if she had confronted him with some vicious lie, then he bowed his head and appeared to be doing battle with his emotions.

'Are you certain?' he asked.

'Quite certain. But nobody knows except Prudence.'

He walked with her along the path bordering Lake Vista and they talked of the dilemma haltingly, in staccato sentences, questions and answers solving nothing.

'I don't love you, Ellie,' he said.

'But I love you enough for us both.'

'People would say I'd married you for your dowry.'

'Does it matter?'

'Your father would never agree.'

She faced him, her heart beating so erratically it made her voice quiver. 'If you don't marry me, Max, I'll have to accept Randolph Sale. Before he went back to University with Lionel he swore his undying love and I know he would jump at the chance. Then you'd never see our baby.'

'You're trying to blackmail me.'

'No, I'm being practical.'

'You're carrying my child. I care about you.'

'Then say you'll ask my father for my hand. I'll get Drew to speak for you, too. He knows how much I love you.'

Max let out his breath on a long sigh. 'Oh Ellie, what a mess.'

'No, it isn't,' she said. She tucked her hand into his and their fingers automatically twined. 'I'll make you a good wife.'

'I must have my own father's blessing.'

He was weakening. She began to feel easier. 'Of course. You must arrange for me to meet your parents. I've always wanted to.'

They had reached 111th Street, the wide boulevard which formed a boundary between the factories and the community. Over to the right, beyond the Florence Hotel, lay the network of streets where the tenements were. Max turned her to face him and he grasped her shoulders.

'Would you live here with me, Ellie?' he asked. 'Would you sacrifice your fine life in Prairie Avenue and all the luxuries that come with it to be with me here in Pullman?'

'Yes, Max—but it won't come to that. Papa will set us up with a nice home and you might be able to work alongside Drew in the Company.'

'Supposing I don't want that? I'm proud. I won't be humiliated, not for your sake.'

'Please, Max. For the sake of our child.'

He looked fierce, his eyes boring into her. His silence while he made up his mind was frightening. Then: 'All right, Ellie Harvey, I'll ask your father, but I'll not go grovelling.'

He bent to claim her mouth in an angry kiss which forced her lips against her teeth and bruised them. But after the initial onslaught he became more gentle. Passers-by turned to stare; Ellie didn't care. She pressed herself close to him, by her response showing agreement with anything he suggested.

Sibylla Harvey considered the arranged meeting

to be one of her best diplomatic victories. She had persuaded her husband to allow Max Berman into the house to speak with him. It had pacified Ellie, satisfied the overbearing young man, and it would bring a swift end to all the unpleasantness of the past weeks, because Conrad would forbid the association once and for all.

The appointed time was seven-thirty that early August evening. There was no food on offer, and the small anteroom in which she interviewed prospective employees was chosen for the meeting. Sibylla had instructed Ellie and Max to be punctual, but kept a different schedule for herself and Conrad. It was better that the miscreant was kept waiting to stew a little.

At just after eight, their English butler showed Sibylla and Conrad into the ante-room where the young couple appeared to be quite unconcerned by the delay. They actually looked as if they had welcomed the extra time together, moving apart guiltily as the door opened. There was no time to lose. Sibylla was dressed in a sumptuous gown of emerald silk and she wore impressive jewellery which would highlight the difference in status between the Bermans and the Harveys. She had worked hard at setting the scene. Now it was all up to Conrad.

She had never met Max Berman. She expected him to be an uncouth man of the labouring class with a veneer of charm which had temporarily turned her daughter's head. It was a surprise then, to see someone who could pass for one of their own social circle. Max was impeccably dressed in a frockcoat of finest quality serge, his shoes were polished until the toecaps gleamed, and he wore a high collar with a soft, expertly-tied maroon bowtie. There was nothing flashy about him, nothing she could immediately criticise, and she was annoyed with herself for experiencing a hint of excitement at the sight of someone so handsome.

Sibylla arranged her skirt and sat on a high-backed chair, leaving Conrad to open the proceedings. But the initiative was taken from him.

'Sir, I'm very pleased to meet you again,' said the forward young man, extending his hand.

'I regret to say the pleasure is not mutual,' said Conrad, ignoring the gesture. 'In fact, we are seeing you very reluctantly.'

'Papa!' cried Ellie at his rudeness.

'I understand from my daughter Elena that you have the audacity to wish for her hand in marriage. I presume you have taken no account of the effect it would have on her, in the unlikely event of permission being given.'

'I have, Mr Harvey. It's what we both want.'

'He's right, Papa,' Ellie said, as eager as a puppy. 'I've never wanted anything more than to be married to Max.'

'My father has built up a good tailoring business in Chicago,' Max went on. Ah, thought Sibylla, that explains the cut of his clothes. 'At present, thanks to you, I am working for Mr Pullman making luxury furnishings. I am good

115

at it, the best in the company. One day I intend to have a furnishing company of my own.'

'Which you hope to set up with my money, no doubt.'

Max Berman raised his eyebrows. 'Sir, I am a proud man. I will achieve my ambitions by my own merit.'

Sibylla saw the flicker of admiration in Conrad's eyes, which was quickly hidden. It was obvious the fellow was not coming over the way he had expected either, but there would be no weakening. Poor Conrad. Was he remembering what he owed to *her* father? Of course, there the similarity ended. In marrying Conrad Sibylla had bettered herself socially. She had been welcomed into his old colonial family with open arms and introduced proudly as Sir Robert Cromer's daughter. Fortunately, no one had ever found out that the rich Sir Robert had no breeding and was ostracised in his own country.

Max Berman had nothing to recommend him except looks and style.

The two men discussed Max's prospects for several minutes out of courtesy, and Sibylla's eyes rested on her daughter who was hanging on every word. For the first time she had a certain amount of sympathy for her. Ellie was clearly in love and it was easy to see why. Max had a direct, penetrating gaze, an intelligent forehead, and a handsomeness guaranteed to melt the heart of any woman. He was tall, his body perfectly proportioned, and his mouth would be firm and irresistible for kissing. Sibylla had always secretly appreciated such things. Without any feeling of guilt she slightly envied Ellie, and even pitied her that the liaison must end.

'Mr Berman,' said Conrad, 'would you be prepared to embrace the Catholic faith and renounce Judaism?' This was the crux of the matter, the argument which would settle it without trouble.

'No, sir, I wouldn't.' Max's voice was firm. Ellie looked at him nervously.

'Then you must know without any doubt that you cannot marry my daughter. I have nothing against the Jewish people, you understand, but Elena is a good Catholic and apart from anything else she will marry someone of the same faith.'

Conrad went on to express his views strongly. Elena, of course, pleaded the way she had done when she wanted anything as a child, but this time her father adamantly refused to be persuaded.

'I can still be a Catholic, Papa. I'll always be a Catholic—nothing can change that,' she insisted. 'And Max will still go to the synagogue.'

'What of any children? In which religious faith would they be brought up?' Sibylla ventured to join in the discussion, though she had promised to let Conrad speak for them both.

'Such a matter would be decided in the future,' said Max.

'There will be no future for you and my daughter. There will be no marriage. The matter is closed,' said Conrad. 'Now, Mr Berman, I must ask you to leave and not try to see Elena again.'

Ellie broke into a storm of weeping. 'Papa, I shall die.'

'At your age you will recover in no time,' said her father briskly. 'This infatuation will soon be forgotten. Lionel will be bringing his friends home for summer vacation next week.'

To his credit, Max Berman didn't make a fuss. He behaved with dignity, thanking Conrad for giving him a hearing, then he took both of Ellie's hands and made her look at him.

'Your father only wants what's best for you, Ellie, and so do I,' he said.

'Oh, Max!' Ellie threw herself into his arms and sobbed the louder. 'I'll love you forever. And I won't let them ruin our lives.'

Max extricated himself after a few damp seconds, but kept eye contact with her. 'Goodbye, for a little while,' he said.

'You will never set foot in this house again,' stormed Conrad.

'No, sir,' said Max. 'I never will.'

'Nor will you see Elena again.'

'That, sir, is another matter.'

Sibylla was relieved when her husband reached for the bell-pull, summoning the butler to show out the unfortunate suitor. But she had an uncomfortable feeling that they were not seeing the last of him.

When Max had left, Ellie was completely devastated. He hadn't asked to speak to her alone, nor had he given a hint of his future intentions. She felt bereft, frightened, and so very much alone. He wouldn't even be able to get a letter to her, for Papa would be more vigilant than ever now, and leaving the house by herself would be quite out of the question.

There was only one person to whom she could turn, and that was Drew. He was always generous in his support, and he would help her now. She waited until he was alone in the conservatory the following evening and crept in to sit on the stool at his feet.

'I must talk to you, Drew.'

'If it's about Max there's nothing I can do.' He was lighting a cigar and he looked at her over the match flame.

Ellie wrung her fingers together and tried to summon up some courage. She swallowed hard. 'If I tell you something, will you swear never to speak of it to a living soul? Especially not to Papa or Mama.'

'Sounds dramatic.'

'I mean it,' she said. 'Will you swear on oath?'

'I swear on oath,' he repeated, but there was a teasing tone in his voice. Then he saw her distress and became serious. 'What is it, Ellie? You know you can trust me.'

She hesitated, searching for words, and tears glinted in her eyes. 'I've *got* to marry Max, quickly, whatever Papa says. Do you understand? I'm having a baby. You've got to help me.'

Drew's reaction was different from anything she had expected. He stubbed out the cigar he had just lit with furious stabbing movements.

119

His face became dark and angry, his lips tightened into a hard line, and the pupils of his eyes dilated.

'I'll kill him,' he said, through clenched teeth. 'He's taken advantage of your innocence and I'll kill him.'

Ellie cried out. 'No, Drew! He didn't do anything wrong.'

'What was it then?' He got up, took hold of her shoulders and shook her. 'If you're pregnant he must have harmed you.'

'Oh Drew, please hush! I love him, you know I do.'

'The bastard—he defiled you. I'll make him pay if it's the last thing I do.'

'Drew...' Her brother wouldn't listen. She hardly recognised him as he strode out of the conservatory like a warrior about to do battle, anger apparent in every line of his body. 'Where are you going? Drew, don't hurt him. Drew—'

'I thought you didn't want Father to know anything,' he called over his shoulder. 'The whole house'll hear you.'

She ran after him, her skirt gathered up above her ankles. 'Wait for me. You can't go without me.'

Drew didn't look back. He snatched his gloves from the vestibule table and swept out through the back entrance to the stables. The air was sultry and stormclouds were gathering in heavy thunderheads over the lake. Ellie was close on his heels. She climbed into the gig while the groom was still harnessing it, and when Drew tried to lift her down she kicked his shins.

'I won't *let* you go without me!'

'You're mad, Ellie. Get back indoors.'

'I won't.'

He rubbed the fronts of his legs. 'All right then, come with me and see the bastard get a thrashing.'

'He's your friend, Drew.'

'Not any more.'

A stable-boy opened the gates and Drew drove the gig out into the avenue at frenzied speed. Ellie clung to the seat to keep her balance as they swerved round a corner.

'How do you know where to find him?' she cried.

'I'll try every bar in Kensington.'

'He's staying with his parents in the city.'

'At this time of the evening Max Berman will be in some shady bar-room talking workers' rights. He's a trouble-maker.'

'And so are you,' she countered. Her face was flushed, her hands clammy with fear and the heat of the August evening. 'You've no right to judge him.'

Flying hoofs pounded the streets and scattered pedestrians as Drew urged the horse on. They travelled along Cottage Grove Avenue, crossed 103rd Street and 111th Street at the southern part of Pullman to reach Kensington, a shabby district which straddled the Illinois Central line a mile west of Lake Calumet. It was known as 'bumtown' for very good reason. The tenements were slums, the streets smelt of decaying vegetation, and grog shops abounded. Saloon-keepers had grown rich on the men from Pullman who had no bars of their own to frequent, George Pullman only allowing the sale of alcohol in the Florence Hotel.

Drew threw Ellie a tartan cover and she put it round her shoulders to hide her gown.

'Drape it over your head and try not to look conspicuous,' he warned, as they slowed to walking pace beside the long row of saloons on 115th Street. 'Men come here through alleys so as not to be seen.'

'I'm scared,' she said.

'Too late for that.' He stopped at a place called Downey's. 'This is where he'll be.' Drew climbed down and hitched the horse to a post. Ellie scrambled down after him but he forced her back against the gig. 'Women don't go in these places. Stay here.'

She was terrified. There was very little light in the street and men were starting to take an unhealthy interest in the smart vehicle foreign to the area. Shaking, she cried: 'You can't leave me.'

Drew looked around and saw the danger, and at last he was contrite. 'You're right. I can't.'

In his frockcoat and silk cravat he was equally conspicuous, and she was afraid of him being jumped on at any moment by thieves. Drew was no weakling, but against a gang he would be overpowered.

The door of the saloon opened and a group of men spilt out, laughing and singing as if they were celebrating. Ellie shrank against her brother in consternation, fearing they were drunks who might see sport in the gentry trespassing on their territory, but they were too intent on ribald jokes directed at the tallest of them whose head was bent to ward off slaps and friendly punches.

'Never thought I'd see the day when a woman caught you,' one was saying.

'How'll you like being married like the rest of us?'

'Tamed at last, Max Berman.'

Ellie shrieked. Max raised his head, and their eyes met. She wanted to run to him but Drew anticipated the move and restrained her.

'Stay where you are,' he commanded.

The mood of the men changed and they became dangerously quiet, staring at the newcomers. One tied his scarf round his knuckles as though expecting trouble. Then Max strode forward and faced Drew angrily.

'What the hell do you mean by bringing Ellie here? Are you out of your mind? Have you any idea of the danger you put her in?'

Drew retaliated. 'What do you care? You've harmed her enough already.'

'Who will you be marrying, Max?' asked Ellie, her voice stronger than she was feeling. She would faint right away if he had taken Papa's word as final and settled for some other girl.

He was instantly reassuring. 'Why you, of course. Who else? Our child must be born in wedlock.'

'Oh, Max! And Drew was coming to kill you.'

Ellie broke free and threw herself on him, as if to protect him with her body, yet Drew had made no belligerent move or gesture. The men moved forward and surrounded him, full of menace, but they underestimated him if they thought he would be intimidated. He had worked with rougher than these.

'Is this the truth, Berman?' he asked, his jaw jutting. No one touched him.

'I'd planned to marry her tomorrow,' Max said. 'I didn't know how to get her here, but you've solved the problem, my friend. Now we can get married tonight instead.' His arms came round her and the strength in his body brought renewed vitality to her own.

'Father's forbidden it,' shouted Drew. '*I* forbid it.'

'You can't,' cried Ellie. 'It's my life. I'm going to marry him.'

'Shouldn't you be glad I'm doing the honourable thing?'

'This is no place to be discussing rights and wrongs. We must go somewhere private.'

Ellie was no longer afraid. She heard her brother and her lover arguing heatedly, but she was too excited to pay heed. Max's protective arm gave her courage. The men had been joined by others drawn to investigate the commotion and he turned to face them.

'Wish us well, my friends. This is my bride. We're going back to Pullman to get married.'

Drew dragged Ellie to the gig, out of earshot. 'Is this really what you want, Ellie? You know Father will never speak to you again.'

'He'll understand.'

'Never.' He handed her up into the carriage. 'I can drive you straight home.'

124

'My home's going to be with Max from now on.'

Max escaped from his jostling friends and sprang up into the seat beside her just as Drew pulled on the reins and guided the horse round to face the way they had come. There was hardly room for three in the gig but Ellie didn't mind the squash. It helped to quell her wild joy which made her want to stand up in the moving vehicle and shout to all the world that she was going to be Max Berman's wife.

But there was still plenty of argument in Drew. 'If you think you're going to get your hands on some money by marrying my sister, you're wrong,' he said, raising his voice to be heard above the noise of wheels on the cobbled road. 'Father will cut Ellie off without a cent.'

'I'd never accept his money.'

'Have you thought what it'll mean to *you*, Ellie, living without any luxuries?' Drew persisted.

'I don't need them.'

'I can support a wife without help,' said Max scornfully. 'Ellie must get used to my way of living, that's all. And had I really been mercenary, I could have made you persuade your father to take me into the family.'

'Impossible!'

'I think not. You wouldn't like him to know about the letters you wrote inciting men to strike, would you, Drew?' Max reached forward and touched the hand on the reins. 'Don't worry, I'm not going to blackmail you. You're my friend.'

125

Drew was not won over and his disapproval was still evident as he urged the horse to greater speed and turned towards Pullman. 'I guess if you're the one Ellie's set her heart on I'll have to put up with it,' he said finally, but without enthusiasm. 'I could probably do worse for a brother-in-law.'

'Drew, I love you,' cried Ellie, hugging his arm.

An hour later Elena Harvey became Max's wife at a ceremony performed by a Justice of the Peace in the main lounge of the Florence Hotel. The witnesses were her brother Drew and a stranger who happened to be staying there.

Hedda Berman looked at the beautiful creature in her living room and wished she could howl like the wolves which had prowled near her home when she'd been a girl. So gracious and poised was the young woman her son had brought home. So young, yet so worldly. At first glance she could have been Jewish with her glossy black hair, but her skin was like pale porcelain, her eyes the blue of a summer sky, and her nose small and straight. Hedda knew instinctively that she was not a child of Zion. Her clothes were of fine quality, even though she was dressed plainly, but such things were not important. She had expected that when Max chose a young lady, she would be homely like Laban's Elizabeth.

And then came the ultimate shock.

'Momma, Poppa, this is Ellie,' Max said,

drawing her forward. 'We were married this evening.'

'I'm so happy to meet you,' the girl said, smiling and extending her gloved hand. No one responded and her smile faded like the sun going in.

Hedda trembled and looked to her husband for support, knowing that his feelings must be akin to her own. Jacob stood at the head of the table laden with kosher food which would have pleased a Jewish girl, and the candlelight shone on the front of his balding head on which, as always, he wore his yarmulke. His expression was solemn.

'Forgive us, we are totally unprepared for this moment,' he said. The Bermans' house in a Jewish area of Chicago was open to anyone in need, the bell above the door of Jacob's tailoring shop ringing as often to admit friends as customers. Never before had they been so slow to offer hospitality. 'Do we know your family?'

'My father is Conrad Harvey,' Ellie answered.

Jacob's beard flicked as his mouth went into a spasm which he immediately controlled. He said: 'Not only an important railroad man but also a respected member of the Catholic Church, I believe?'

'That's right.'

Hedda felt faint. She'd known from the moment the girl came in the room that something else dreadful was happening, but this was worse than she could have possibly imagined.

Max was anxious for approval which he had no right to expect.

'Have you no words of welcome, Poppa? I told you I was planning to get married. It just came about a little sooner than I had intended.'

'You have always been impulsive, my son. This time you have acted without any consideration for your family.'

'I'm sorry if this upsets you, but please have respect for Ellie's feelings.'

'I love him, Mrs Berman,' Ellie declared. No doubt it was the truth. Her eyes glowed with it, her gaze rarely straying from Max's face. 'I'll make him a good wife.'

Life was continually cruel to the Bermans. Sometimes they had thought they wouldn't survive, but having escaped from Russia with little more than their lives they had found enormous strength to cope with misfortune. Now they faced yet another evil blow, so soon after the death of their beloved daughter Katrina. Hedda braced herself, determined not to let anyone see the depth of her misery, but the inward pain was dagger-sharp.

Yesterday Max had said he would be bringing home someone special and she had thought it would be to ask for their blessing and their permission to become betrothed. She remembered when Laban had introduced them to Elizabeth and how happy they had all been, so she had looked forward to welcoming another good Jewish girl into their midst—perhaps one she could love and eventually accept as God's chosen substitute for Katrina. Not for a moment had she suspected that Max would disappoint them like this.

For seven days following the death of Katrina they had been in deep mourning. They hadn't left the house after the funeral, but had sat on low stools receiving help and consolation from neighbours who brought them food. Now they had taken up the threads of life again with hearts heavier than at any time since the barbaric loss of their unborn child which had prevented Hedda from ever again conceiving, but it was far from easy. Sometimes she wondered how to find patience and strength, for it had fallen on her and Jacob to look after the infant Galina while the gentile Katrina had married was wallowing in self-pity in Philadelphia, too weak to accept his domestic responsibilities.

Ellie saw the cradle and went over to it, looking in with joy. The baby still had slight breathing problems from the smoke and gas fumes which had filled her tiny lungs, but she was strong and progressing well.

'She's growing,' she exclaimed. 'And she's so beautiful.'

'Ellie saved Galina's life after the fire,' said Max. 'Momma, for that reason alone can't you make her welcome?'

Hedda's eyes filled with tears. 'For that reason she has our eternal gratitude, but I cannot let another gentile bring destruction to our family. I do not wish to embrace her. I do not want to see her again. You must take her away, my Max.'

He was her wayward son, but her favourite. She had jealously guarded his love for herself and had dreaded the time when he would take a wife, but she had been prepared to sacrifice him to someone wisely chosen. She remembered standing with Jacob under a splendid chuppah to make their vows, and how important she had felt in her bridal white, drinking wine from the goblet of joy. Jacob had put the gold ring on her finger, saying, 'Behold thou art consecrated unto me by this ring according to the Law of Moses and Israel.' Now she would never hear Max saying the same words to his bride.

'Tell me,' said Jacob to Ellie. 'Will your father approve of this marriage?'

She flushed. 'He's going to be very angry.'

'While we are heartbroken. You have lured our son away from his faith.'

At that Max flared up. 'Katrina married out of the Jewish faith, and you accepted it. What right have you to judge me differently?'

'Think what has happened!' cried Hedda, in sudden hysteria. Her voice rose in a crescendo, ending in a sob. She raised her arms as she swayed back and forth in torment. 'Katrina has lost her life!'

'Her death had nothing to do with Oliver.'

'God has punished her, and us, for allowing a gentile into the family. They were not married according to the Law of Moses and Israel. Now it has happened again.'

'Momma, be calm,' pleaded Jacob, as his wife continued to wail. He faced his son. 'She is right, of course. We can never give our blessing

130

to another mixed marriage.'

The girl looked close to tears and Max went to her. The candles fluttered. 'Ellie, I'm sorry.'

'Leave us,' Jacob commanded. 'There's no home for you here.'

Max took his wife out into the night, and Hedda was too distraught to care that they had nowhere to go. She rocked Katrina's baby in her arms and continued to weep.

SEVEN

No one in Chicago could remember such a terrible winter as the one of 1893–4. Following on from a bad autumn, it was the coldest ever known, and the depth of the Depression added to the appalling misery, bringing starvation and death. On the same day in late October that the World's Columbian Exposition closed, Mayor Carter Harrison was assassinated outside his Ashland Avenue home. Widespread unrest followed. The number of homeless multiplied and hundreds of people marched south to Washington with the Commonwealth of Christ Army, hoping to find help. Those who stayed suffered increasingly from hunger, and the unbearable cold seemed as if it would go on forever.

For Ellie Berman the winter was worse than any horror she could have imagined.

The night of her marriage to Max was spent at the Florence Hotel, an extravagance which she accepted as normal, and in spite of the upsetting visit to his parents it became a romantic experience she would always remember. Max was an exciting lover and she responded to him in a way that would have been shameful had they not been man and wife. It didn't occur to her until she saw Max counting out money next morning that he might have difficulty finding enough to pay the check.

The following morning they went to Prairie Avenue, Max having been given one day's leave of absence from the shop. Ellie hoped that her Papa might have a change of heart once he realised that the deed was done and she was legally married, but she was told that Mr Harvey had gone early to his office and Mrs Harvey was not well. A trunk containing some of her clothes had been left on the doorstep and instructions given that on no account was she to be allowed to enter the house.

'May I just see Prudence then?' Ellie begged.

'I'm sorry, Miss Elena,' said the butler, his face expressionless. 'I'm afraid no one is available to speak to you. Good day.'

'I'm not Miss Elena,' she shouted. 'I'm Mrs Berman.' The door was shut in her face.

Tears sprang to Ellie's eyes, and Max rang the bell again with angry persistence but no one came to answer it.

'I won't have my wife treated like this. Have they no feelings?'

'It doesn't matter, Max,' said Ellie shakily. 'I

have you now. That's all that matters.'

After a few minutes he calmed down. 'Very well, we'll take the trunk and go.'

'I don't want the trunk. I don't want anything from here.'

'We're accepting nothing else from your family. Have these before I change my mind.'

She agreed reluctantly. He hoisted the heavy trunk on his shoulder and they walked down the road to take a trolley into the city. It was Ellie's first lesson in economy. Back in Pullman Max went to the agent's office on the second floor of the Arcade to apply for a single-family house at a rent of eighteen dollars a month. The houses had five rooms, a basement kitchen, fireplaces and a water faucet on each floor. But the agent was apologetic.

'Mr Berman, I regret I can't offer you a house until you have paid for the repairs to your tenement in Fulton Street which is now habitable again.'

'I can't possibly find that much money,' Max exclaimed, looking at the detailed document handed to him. 'The damage was caused by a fault in the gas system. My sister died.'

'I'm sorry, sir. The lease is in your name and if you read your contract you will see that you are responsible for all repairs.'

It was grossly unfair but there was no way out of it. As soon as they had left the office Ellie voiced her indignation loudly.

'It isn't right, Max. They can't make you pay for that terrible accident. I shall speak to my godfather about it and he'll see that we get one of the nicest houses in Pullman.'

Max rounded on her immediately. 'You will do no such thing. I forbid you ever to speak to Mr Pullman about our affairs. There'll be no favouritism, no charity. Is that understood?'

'But, Max...'

'Ellie, if I ever hear of you going to your godfather for a single cent I'll never forgive you. You will live on what *I* can provide from now on.'

'Then why did you make me bring my clothes?'

'We didn't ask for them. They were thrown out.'

They had been married only a few hours and already they were having a row. It was so awful Ellie decided she must fall in with whatever Max wanted, rather than risk escalation. A short time later they climbed the wooden stairs to their tenement home and she experienced another pang of anxiety. She didn't want to live in the place where poor Katrina had died. And she was afraid of the gas stove, but as there was nowhere else for them to go she knew she would have to get used to it.

The rent was raised to pay for the repairs in instalments so there was no money to buy furniture to replace what had been destroyed in the fire, but Max used his talents to make a sofa out of boxwood and upholstered it so cleverly it could have come from a rich home. Soon there were two chairs to match, simple in design but comfortable and elegant. Neighbours who saw them exclaimed over the originality and Max took orders for more. After a few weeks his evenings were taken up with furniture-making at home and he had no free time at all.

Ellie found housekeeping hard and quite dreadful. Menial tasks which other women took for granted were horrid chores which made her back ache and spoilt her hands, and when Max came home he often had to finish cooking the evening meal. At first he made allowances for her inexperience.

'It doesn't matter. You'll get used to it,' he said, when she failed to get his shirts clean. 'There are men wearing far worse than these.'

She cut herself trying to peel potatoes, scalded her hand draining vegetables, had to be told she was responsible for keeping a section of the staircase clean, and there were no potted geraniums as there had been in Katrina's day.

'I want things to be nice for you, Max, really I do,' she wailed against his shoulder. 'I try but everything goes wrong.'

'You do your best,' Max consoled her. 'And you must rest. Getting too agitated won't do the baby any good.'

The days were long, and though other wives in the block-houses were friendly she found it hard to mix. They had hordes of children, and their main topic of conversation was how to exist on Pullman wages, which were getting smaller all the time. Ellie's frilled, expensive gowns were so out of place she took the scissors to them in an effort to make them simpler, but she was no needlewoman and the result was disastrous; by November, when none of them would fit her

135

expanding figure, Max had to buy her a frock from an Arcade shop. It made her look fat and shapeless, and it had cost him a week's wages.

She hated her altering shape. She hated the tenement and the hard work. But most of all she hated the cold. At night Max would hold her close and warm her with his body, but during the day she shivered so much the tension made all her muscles ache.

Loneliness and homesickness prompted her to take a train into Chicago one day at the beginning of December. She walked towards Prairie Avenue dreaming of the warmth inside her old home, but as she approached it she came upon the dispossessed huddled together in doorways, their faces blue and pinched as they trembled uncontrollably in the bitter cold. She looked at them, and someone moved over to make room for her. Tears filled Ellie's eyes and spilt onto her cheeks where the frost made them sting her skin. She looked no different from these poor homeless creatures, yet only yards away was the home she had given up to make a new life with Max. Self-pity threatened to engulf her, but she had the strength of will to push it aside. She loved Max just as much, if not more than ever. For his sake she would survive. Bracing her shoulders she started back to the station, passing a long queue for bread on the way, and was thankful that at least she had enough to eat.

On 9 December the steamfitters and blacksmiths went on strike for higher wages, but it was over in a few days.

'Why didn't they succeed?' Ellie asked Max. It had become important to take an interest in what the working men of Pullmen did, now that it affected her.

'They're only a small group against the company,' Max explained. 'If every shop went on strike it might be different. The craft unions ought to form an alliance.'

'Would *you* go on strike, Max?'

'Yes, if I thought it would do any good. But Harvey Middleton's made a list of men who're still out and they're barred from working for the company again. That doesn't help anyone.'

Harvey Middleton was in charge of all the Pullman shops and his main objective was to cut costs, which made him unpopular, especially as he favoured the foremen.

'But we need more money,' protested Ellie. 'I can't manage on so little.'

'You did very well last week.'

'That was because Drew came and gave me some.'

Max was so angry she backed away in sudden fright. He caught her by the shoulders and shook her until she felt faint. 'You will *never* take money from your family. You know I've forbidden it. Don't ever do it again.'

'Oh Max, stop, please stop.' When he let her go she sank onto a chair, holding her stomach and swaying back and forth. 'I didn't mean to upset you.'

He was contrite, sinking to his knees beside her. 'I'm sorry, Ellie. Forgive me. I'm too proud, I know it. But I'm doing well making furniture after work and we're not nearly so badly off as most people.'

'I'm so cold,' she cried. 'So cold I could die.'

He sighed and took her in his arms, comforting her until the shivering stopped. Then he went out and didn't come back until the early hours of the morning.

Above the noise of the machines in the upholsterer's shop the scream of a worker with a needle through his hand was like the cry of an animal in pain. There was an immediate rush to help him but Warren, the foreman, cracked down on it.

'Get back to work,' he yelled, his voice like a whiplash. 'It doesn't need an army to see to one man with a cut hand. Meddons, you're out. Berman—take over his work.'

'You can't do that, Mr Warren,' Meddons gasped, holding a cloth to his hand where blood spurted from the piercing between the bones. 'I'll be fine shortly, soon as the bleeding stops.'

'Carelessness can't be tolerated. I've got to stand off three more men by the week's end. You're the first.'

'But Mr Warren, how'll I pay my rent?'

Max wanted the work, but not at the expense of Charlie Meddons. It was an awkward situation. He looked around at the others and saw support for Meddons on every face.

'How much extra will you pay me?' Max asked.

'You heard me say three men must go. That means there's no extra money for anyone.'

'Then I'll do my own work and nothing more,' Max said, risking his neck.

A cheer went up. Warren was lower management and liked the feel of power, but the men were becoming increasingly hostile. Many were left with only a dollar on which to feed a family for two weeks after the rent was paid, and many more were so badly in debt they'd had to give up their homes, yet it was said that Warren and those like him had suffered no wage cuts, George Pullman being afraid of losing his better men.

'You could be the second laid off,' Warren threatened, though he knew he had to tread carefully with Max Berman.

Work had stopped in the shop. 'We're on piece rates,' someone said. 'We want fair payment.'

'Let Charlie Meddons report sick or I'll take the matter to the ARU,' said Max.

'That'll get you nowhere.'

'It'll let Gene Debs see we need a union of all the shops in Pullman.'

The upholsters were ready to strike, but while Max kept an argument going with Warren, another man had stopped Meddons' hand bleeding and within an hour he had been reinstated. That was not to say he wouldn't have to go anyway at the end of the week, but a stand had been made. A small battle had been won and Max's popularity soared.

Yet he trudged home in the snow to Fulton Street with leaden feet. Every day he took less

139

pleasure in returning to his wife since he knew that as soon as he opened the door she would be complaining about the cold, the lack of money, and her discomfort. He felt sorry for her, having to cope with the hardship of this dreadful winter as well as her pregnancy, but other women were having to endure it in the same condition. Of course it was so much harder for Ellie who had been spoilt, but she didn't seem to be trying to accept the changes in her life.

Sure enough, he smelt burnt food as soon as he climbed the stairs. 'Max, the soup stuck to the bottom of the pan again,' she wailed, before he'd hardly crossed the threshold.

He lost patience. 'You're useless, Ellie. You can't do anything properly.' She quivered from head to foot with shock but his nerves were so strained he felt impelled to go on. 'Why the hell did I have to marry you?'

He scraped the pan, cut up the last of the turnips and set them boiling with potatoes and onions to make some more soup while Ellie sobbed. For the moment he didn't even feel guilty. It had been a bad day and he needed to unburden his problems on someone, to be able to talk about the fracas at work as he could have done with Katrina, but Ellie only had room for her own troubles.

After supper she took off her pinafore and stood in front of his chair pitifully. 'I know I'm a failure, Max, and I'm so sorry. I don't deserve you.'

He suffered remorse immediately. Her gaze trapped him, just as her persistence and her desirable body had trapped him last summer, and he cursed himself for his weakness. Even now she could arouse him physically at the first touch. If anything, privation had improved her looks and she was more beautiful than she had been six months ago. The contours of her face were sculpted to show the fine bone structure, and the way she drew her hair into a tight chignon at the back of her head gave prominence to her features. Her neck was long and graceful, her shoulders sloping, her chin honed to perfection now that all trace of the fat of rich living had vanished. Even the thickening of her waist suited her.

'When I make my fortune you can have servants and a big house of your own,' he said. 'Until then I'm afraid you'll have to put up with what we've got.'

She wound her arms round his neck. 'I'll put up with anything for you and I'll *try* not to grumble. I love you so.' She put her mouth to his and trailed her tongue along his lips until he groaned and held her close. 'If only you'd let me take some money from Drew.'

'No.' So this was what it was all about. He put her away from him. 'I've told you we don't accept charity.'

'Just once, Max, so that I can buy a new gown.'

'Not ever. I buy your clothes now.'

'But I look so ugly. Look at me! I'm hideous in this dreadful dress.'

'A beautiful woman still looks beautiful in rags.'

141

'I hate living here.' She buried her face in her hands. 'I hate having a baby.'

She needed consoling regularly and he blamed himself for not being able to give the kind of love which would have soothed her and made her happy. The physical side of marriage was fine, but Ellie wanted more. She wanted to be told that she was the most important person in the world to him, and he couldn't give that assurance. He couldn't say the words she longed to hear because he was not in love with her.

He went out, ignoring her plea not to leave her. Usually he went via a dark footpath to Kensington and spent an hour or two at Downey's, but this evening he stood in the shadows while his frustration simmered. He was desperate to escape from the cloying, obsessive love with which Ellie bound him to herself. It was like soothing oil being poured over him with a perfume that made him sick.

After a few minutes he turned away from Kensington and took the train into Chicago. He hadn't seen his parents since his marriage and he missed them unbearably, but though he yearned for his mother's love he couldn't face her while she still nursed bitter disappointment over his choice of a wife. He had hurt them both too much. Perhaps after the baby was born they would accept what had happened.

He gripped his coat collar tight round his neck and pulled his felt hat over his ears to keep out the freezing cold. The doors of the City Hall were open and hundreds of people were already sleeping in the corridors. An old man begged for money to buy bread and Max gave him the last cent in his pocket before turning in the direction of the Jewish quarter. It was just as well his pockets were empty. He'd been tempted to venture instead into the First Ward where gin-mills flourished and dime hotel rooms were available for cheap pleasures.

For the first time in many months he knocked on Mariette Schuman's door, and the warmth of her welcome assured him that he would find the comfort he needed inside.

On a blustery April day Ellie went into labour, and after several hours of the hardest, most painful work she had ever done she gave birth to a lusty boy child. She was strong and healthy herself and there were no complications. The midwife gave the baby to her as soon as he was clean and well-wrapped, and she gazed in wonder at the tiny replica of Max, marvelling that she had at last produced him.

Someone went to the upholster's shop to give Max the news, and a short time later she heard him running eagerly up the stairs. She had never seen him so emotional as when he held the baby. There were actually tears in his eyes.

'He's perfect, Ellie,' he breathed.

'I can't believe he's ours,' said Ellie, with awe. 'Our son. He'll bind us together forever, won't he?'

Max handed him back to her.

The baby was called William Isaac, though there were no plans to have him baptised. The names had no family significance but seemed to embody both cultures, and Ellie liked the ring to them. In a few days she was up and about again, revelling in her new slimness and eager to show her child to the block-house women as if she were the only one clever enough to have achieved motherhood. They admired him and teased her.

'Wait till you have half a dozen,' one girl said.

'You'll be cursing you're a woman and praying your husband stays away,' nodded another.

'Never,' cried Ellie. 'I never want Max to stay away. I don't even like him going out of an evening.'

There were more jokes at her expense, but they were not unkind. Young Ellie Berman had endeared herself to them over the months, once she had stopped giving herself airs. It was common knowledge she had married beneath her, but she didn't think anyone knew she was Conrad Harvey's daughter, and certainly not that George Pullman was her godfather. Max had told her never to speak of it.

William was three weeks old when someone completely unexpected knocked on the door. It was a Sunday and Max was out. Thinking it was a neighbour, Ellie merely patted her hair and left her pinafore on, but the caller was a man with sandy-coloured hair and freckled skin whom she had seen just once before. He was of average height and build, broad in the shoulders and slim-hipped. His eyes were the colour of green olives and they widened with admiration as he stared at her.

'I'd heard my brother-in-law picked himself a peach but I'd thought the tale exaggerated,' he said. 'My name's Oliver Devlin. Can I come in?'

'Max isn't here at the moment but I'm sure he'll be pleased to see you when he gets back.' Ellie held the door open for him and he appraised her as he passed. Then he looked around the living room and when he saw William's cradle he drew an involuntary breath. 'It's brave of you to come here,' she said gently. 'This apartment must be full of painful memories.'

'Max will have told you what happened.'

'I was here that day. I'd come with Max to visit Katrina. It was so dreadful...' Reliving the tragedy brought a lump to her throat even now and wisely she didn't continue. Instead she removed a shawl from Max's chair. 'Do sit down, Mr Devlin. Have you seen your little daughter recently?'

'Galina is being brought up in the Jewish faith by doting grandparents who have shown me the door, just as I believe they did to you. We have much in common.'

'Do they know that Max has a son?'

'A friend of his told them.' Oliver went to the cradle and moved the covers aside. 'He's awake. May I pick him up?'

She wasn't sure what to make of her visitor. He had a way of talking which charmed her, an Irish brogue that caressed every word and gave it warmth. She studied him while he held William, noting that the sandy lashes didn't hide the way his eyes moved over every item in the room and finally came to rest on herself. He had hardly looked at the child in his arms.

'You deserve a better place than this to live,' he said.

'We'll move when Max can afford it. I don't mind as long as we're together.'

He accepted the offer of coffee and cold meat and bread. While he ate he questioned her about herself and her life before her marriage, about her family and the sacrifices she had made. She found herself telling him how she had suffered through the terrible winter, and how she could never do things right even though she tried so hard.

'Max obviously doesn't appreciate you,' said Oliver sympathetically. 'I'd give my eye-teeth, so I would, to have a wife as beautiful as you. I've been so lonely without Katrina.'

She felt sorry for him, though his glib tongue proved he was not in need of too much sympathy himself, and she preened at the compliment. It was a long time since anyone had commented on her looks.

'We're here if you need company,' she assured him.

'Thank you—but I came to tell you both that I'm going to Ireland to see my mother and my sister, should anyone be asking after me.'

'What about Galina?' Max would be angry if his brother-in-law still intended leaving the child with his mother. 'Will you be staying away long?'

'Momma Berman's happy to keep her. Now,

if I could persuade you to come with me to Ireland it's likely I'd settle for good.' His eyes were twinkling and the corners of his mouth quirked up.

Ellie blushed crimson. 'Oliver Devlin, what a thing to say.'

She heard Max's step on the stairs and was glad. His brother-in-law had great charm, but he had no business flirting with a married woman, and she wished she hadn't been quite so open in her talk with him. She hoped she hadn't said anything rash, and it worried her that she might have been unfair to Max. She ran to meet her husband at the door.

'We've got a visitor,' she cried. 'Come and see who it is.'

Max was restrained in his welcome. He wanted to know what Oliver had been doing over the past nine months, and the rogue gave evasive answers with such good humour it was easy to think he was being frank.

'I've been doing this and that since the Pullman shops were closed in Detroit. Didn't fancy coming back here to work.'

Ellie nursed her son in the bedroom and listened, frowning every now and then as a vague sense of unease stole over her.

Oliver left late in the evening, refusing their offer of the sofa to sleep on overnight. When he had gone the room still rang with the lilting Irish voice boasting of recent money-making ventures in Philadelphia, which Ellie had found hard to believe. Perhaps if he had shown a desire to have his daughter with him she would have been

147

more convinced, and Max would have been less hostile, but he'd hardly mentioned Galina and she had the feeling that once he was in Ireland the child would be forgotten.

'I suppose I'm glad he came,' Max said, later. 'At least he hasn't cut himself off from us.'

'I'm glad too, for your sake,' said Ellie. But it was a long time before the unsettled feeling Oliver had created would go away.

EIGHT

Max's sideline, the making of cheap furniture, did well for a while. He'd taken small items to Chicago where a dealer was willing to buy everything he could produce, but it wasn't long before he discovered that the dealer was making a vast profit while paying next to nothing for the workmanship, and complaint brought an end to the association. There was nothing Max could do about it unless he could start a business of his own, which was impossible without resources and in a recession. But risks had been taken before and great companies had sprung from little more than great ambition.

It was with this in mind that he began investigating the wealth of the Pullman Company through contacts in the finance department. What he discovered shocked and angered him, and for a while his own dreams were shelved. That winter, fifty-two thousand dollars worth of car contracts had been lost and employees' pay-cuts totalled sixty thousand dollars. Men had been laid off for weeks and some like himself worked on reduced pay, yet the company had added another two million dollars to its surplus funds and stockholders had received eight per cent dividends the same as usual.

The more he delved, the more incensed Max became. He took his findings to Eugene Debs but by then many of the facts were general knowledge and there was talk of action being taken. In the spring, the American Railway Union held meetings at which resolutions were passed to get George Pullman to reduce the fixed rents of Pullman property, to cut the high charges for gas and water, and to restore wages to their former level. All these requests were refused, however, on the grounds that profits were down and the money was needed for the company's new car-building works. At two meetings between workers and officials it was agreed that the men's complaints would be looked into, but nothing could be done about wages or rents.

The troubles in his model town affected the health of George Pullman and he retreated to his holiday home at Long Branch, but when talk of a strike became serious he hurried back to Chicago, and on 4 May he went to see for himself what conditions were like in Pullman. After inspecting the workshops he turned his attention to accommodation, and many tenants were surprised to find the great man himself on their doorstep, impeccably dressed in a black suit with silk revers on the jacket and a heavy gold watch-chain across his waistcoat.

On his agenda was a visit to the tenement in Fulton Street where a young woman had lost her life. The tragedy had stayed in his mind and he wanted to see for himself that there was no danger of such a thing happening again. With accompanying officials, he entered the main door of the building and was greeted by the occupants of the ground and middle-floor apartments who followed him with a mixture of awe and aggression. By the time he rang the bell of the Bermans' home quite a crowd had gathered, filling the landing and the stairway in order to see and hear what transpired. It was not what anyone had expected.

Ellie Berman came to the door, her face flushed and her sleeves rolled up. She looked tired and was obviously unprepared for a visitor, especially one as important as George Pullman, and they felt sorry for her. Her eyes widened. And then, to everyone's astonishment, she gave a delighted gasp and reached out to touch his arm with extraordinary familiarity.

'Why, Mr Pullman! Oh my, what a wonderful surprise,' cried Ellie. 'I'm so pleased to see you.'

The man appeared to be shaken. He pulled on his beard and it was as if the action made his jaw drop. His eyes flicked over her in bewilderment.

He spoke. 'My dearest god-daughter, what on earth are you doing here?'

'It's my home.'

'Then why was I told that you had gone to live in New York with Frederick and his family almost a year ago? Surely I had a right to the truth from your father! Have I not always taken my duty towards you seriously?'

'Dear Mr Pullman, of course you have.'

'This can't go on. You can't continue living like this. Where is your husband?'

'Max is at work in the upholstery shop.'

'I must arrange for you to have a proper house for a start,' George Pullman went on. 'Had I known...'

'Please, please—come inside.' Ellie Berman became aware of the silent witnesses to this most unexpected meeting and she interrupted quickly. 'You must see my baby, and I want to hear everything that Florence has been doing.'

To everyone's disappointment the door closed on any further revelations. There followed a murmur of speculation. Of course, no one heard Ellie telling her godfather that her husband had adamantly refused to let her contact him and would never countenance favouritism of any kind whatsoever.

It wouldn't have been possible to keep George Pullman's visit a secret from Max even if Ellie had wanted to. It was the talk of the town, and in the block-houses word had travelled fast to every family on a fierce wind of gossip, so he already knew of it before he arrived home.

'I've never been so surprised,' Ellie said, unable to keep the excitement out of her voice. It had been such a joy to see someone who was

151

almost family. 'And do you know, Mr Pullman thought I was in New York with Frederick and Henrietta. Fancy Papa telling such a lie!'

'Why did he come here of all places?'

'He remembered the fire. I thought it was very kind of him. Oh, I was so pleased to see him, and he was very taken with William.'

'Do you swear you accepted nothing from him?' Max said urgently.

She was indignant. 'Of course I didn't!'

'I'm sorry. It's just that I wish he'd gone to any other place but this.'

'Max Berman, I hope I'm an obedient wife. Why don't you trust me?'

'I do...'

'Then please don't question my good sense. We could have been given one of the best houses in Pullman, and you could have been elevated to a high position in the company just because you're married to me. I refused everything.'

The degree of his relief seemed out of all proportion as he drew her close in a rare display of affection. Then he explained: 'I want you to understand, Ellie, why we can't accept any help from George Pullman. These are difficult times. If the strike materialises it could be dangerous if we were seen to be favoured by the management.'

'Well, we won't be,' she said brightly. 'I told my godfather that you can provide everything William and I need.'

'Good girl.'

The reassurance pleased Max and he was particularly attentive. He even discussed some

152

of the strike politics with her so that she would know what was in the air. Many men were now members of the American Railway Union and Max was part of a committee of forty-six elected to try negotiating with the Pullman Company over wages and conditions, but as he told Ellie, it was impossible to reach agreement.

'I'm afraid it *must* come to a strike,' he said. 'There's no other way.'

The weather was pleasantly warm and Ellie carried William down to the Arcade stores on Thursday 10 May, 1894. It was several days since she had been that way and she was surprised and puzzled to see a wall being built along the eastern end of the workshops. When she questioned a young woman she knew slightly she had her first taste of antagonism.

'What do they want a wall for?' she asked.

The girl looked at her and sniffed. 'It's so as the likes of you can be safe from the likes of us,' she said.

'I don't know what you mean,' said Ellie. 'Why am I any different from you?'

'*You* can ask that when you're related to George Pullman!'

'But I'm not.'

'That's not what I heard.' The girl walked away and Ellie was left feeling uneasy. The brusque exchange had been unlike anything she had experienced since coming to live in the town and she kept thinking about it long afterwards.

She entered the vast iron and glass Arcade which contained over thirty stores and was always bustling with people who congregated as much to gossip as to buy, and saw several groups holding animated discussions. Voices were loud and it appeared that three committee men in the ironwork shop had been told there was no work for them.

'It was rigged,' she heard a man say. 'They were told to come back Monday but we all know they were discharged and it was a cover-up.'

'Discrimination, that's what it is,' said another. They all sounded angry.

That night Max was called to an urgent meeting and he didn't come home until the next day's sun had risen. Ellie was sick with worry.

'What can you have found to talk about all these hours?' she said, when he finally came into the bedroom where she had spent an equally sleepless night. 'You'll be so tired. You can't go to work this morning.'

Max shrugged off her fussing. 'I'll be there as soon as I've had some breakfast, but I doubt it'll be for long. We passed a resolution to strike.'

She knew that to withdraw labour was serious, but she had no idea of the full implications. The blacksmiths had gone on strike in December and the action had only lasted a few days: it hadn't affected anyone. So she cooked food for her husband and fed her son before settling down to what she thought would be the routine of just another day.

Soon after ten-thirty she heard the sound of cheering coming from the direction of Florence Boulevard. It was repeated a few minutes later and Ellie went to the window to see the women of Fulton Street hurrying towards the sound. She picked up William, strapped him against her chest with a shawl, and joined the flow.

At Florence Boulevard she saw men arriving at the gates in an orderly fashion from their respective shops to join the freight-car workers who had come out first, and as each group came there was a fresh burst of cheering. The embroidery girls earned particularly loud applause when they appeared.

'Ain't a machine operating in the whole damn place,' a man cried. 'Let's see how long it takes management to get 'em working again.'

There was a lot of jovial banter and by the mood of the crowd it could have been a holiday. Someone started singing and a chorus was taken up. Wives began running to their menfolk, but it was some time before Max appeared and Ellie knew he wouldn't want to be distracted while he was involved in union business so she watched at a distance and waited until he came.

'The walk-out's nearly a hundred per cent, Ellie,' he told her. 'We *must* succeed. Only the foremen are left in and they're at the root of the trouble.'

'It'll soon be over though, won't it?'

'It'll be over when your precious godfather listens to the workers instead of the foremen, and realises he doesn't own *us* along with all his property we're forced to pay nearly all our wages to rent. His model town might have been a good idea but it's grown too big.'

'The town means everything to him,' Ellie

said. 'He's always wanted what's best for his workers.'

'Sure he has. So perhaps he should take a look at those closest to him who don't share all his high ideals. At the meeting it was promised there'd be no retaliation against committee men, but there has been, and now the company faces the consequences.'

That night the Strike Committee called a rally and organised day and night guard duty round the works which would protect property and also be a picket line to ensure no new labour was recruited by the company.

On Saturday Max and Ellie took a picnic to the Arcade Park and sat on the grass listening to the Pullman Band. It made a wonderful change from the scrubbing and cleaning which never made the apartment look any better, and the seemingly endless washing a baby made. William gurgled happily on a rug and kicked against the restraining shawls which made him hot in the sunshine. It was like a public holiday and people who came from Chicago to witness the effects of the strike on the community were puzzled to find no outward sign of suffering or hardship.

But the apparent tranquillity was short-lived. On Monday Ellie found that the Arcade stores were no longer giving credit.

'If only you could make some extra money with your furniture, Max,' she said that evening.

'No one has money to buy furniture!' he replied sharply. He was so edgy these days that

156

she was half-afraid to say anything.

He'd hoped to rent a shed behind a store in Roseland, a town on a ridge west of Pullman, where he could work late on his designs, but now it was impossible. Instead he spread sheets of paper on the kitchen table and covered them with drawings of elaborate sofas and revolutionary armchairs which would have been the ultimate in elegance had he been able to produce them. He could no longer afford the materials. The drawings were filed away between two plywood boards and tied with cord before he stored them under the bed each night. The saloons in Kensington seldom saw him any more.

Days became weeks and the workshops were still closed. Those who had predicted the strike would crumble in a few days were proved wrong, but the Chicago newspapers reported with sympathy on the unusually dignified industrial struggle. The *Chicago Dispatch* spoke of a model strike in a model town, but like most other papers it thought the men were making a grave mistake in staying out. The *Tribune* called it suicidal. Indeed, conditions in Pullman were becoming more and more difficult as money and supplies dwindled, and a Relief Committee was set up to help those in need. Towards the end of May potatoes, flour and meat were distributed, and assistance came from many of Chicago's charitable organisations.

At the end of the month, Drew turned up on one of his periodic visits to see Ellie. He came at midday when not many people were about so no one in the tenement block saw his arrival. Ellie hugged him fiercely and he had to force her away, laughing as he did so.

'Anyone would think you were pleased to see me,' he joked.

'Oh, I am. I'm so happy,' Ellie babbled. She always longed for news from home, and there was so much to tell him about developments in Pullman.

'I came to see how my favourite nephew's progressing,' he said, taking the baby from her. 'And to let you know Clarissa and I are getting married.' He had put on weight and matured over the last year. The rough edges acquired during his rebellious years on the footplate had been smoothed away and he was now a self-assured man with a distinguished air. But he was still a champion of workers' rights, often to his father's frustration.

'That is just wonderful,' she cried. 'I always hoped you'd ask Clarissa. She idolises you.'

'I wish you and Max could be at the wedding but Father won't hear of it. When I suggested it he nearly threw a fit. I'm so sorry, Ellie, I keep trying to get him to forgive you but it's become an obsession. Mama says *he* is the loser and he ought to at least compromise, but he just bellows that he is head of the house and no one is to go against his wishes.'

Ellie sighed. 'I miss you all so much.'

'And I worry about you,' Drew said. 'Every time I read about the strike I fear for you and wonder if you've enough to eat. That's why I've

158

brought you some money. This time you must take it.'

'Max will be so angry if I do.'

'Then don't let him know. Keep it hidden and use it sparingly. I beg you to have it, Ellie, for William's sake.'

The temptation was too great and she succumbed. After her brother had left she found a pin box and rolled the notes until they fitted inside it. Then she tucked it into the bottom corner of her untidy sewing basket.

It was noticed that Ellie Berman was still able to afford most necessities.

'No chance of *you* getting thin, or your kid either,' said a woman with a tartan shawl around her bent shoulders. Ellie was buying cereal and eggs, and William was looking over her shoulder, his large brown eyes alert to everything going on around him. 'Does your husband wear a flag or a ribbon, tell me that?'

The strikers were pinning white ribbons to their lapels these days while company men sported tiny United States flags. The barb hurt Ellie, but she continued to provide the best food she could for her family, particularly since she'd heard there was the threat of a malaria epidemic in the town.

Conditions were deteriorating fast. Sickness due to hunger and worry became commonplace, and Nell Frencham who lived in the apartment beneath the Bermans' became so weak she had to take to her bed. Hearing of it, Ellie went down with hot soup which she fed to Nell and the three children, but when she would have

159

done the same the next day she was stopped at the door by Dan Frenchmam, Nell's husband.

'We don't want your help,' Dan said. 'We don't want company hand-outs.'

'What are you saying?' Ellie demanded. 'This is food I bought myself. Isn't it good enough for you?'

'Bought with money from George Pullman. We all know you're kin to him.'

'I'm no relation to Mr Pullman.'

'God-daughter, he called you. Near as kin since he's your father's friend. Oh yes, we know you're one of the Harvey clan, though what you're doing here God alone knows. Spying, I don't doubt.'

Ellie was shaken by the bitterness in his voice. Not long ago she had thought they were friends. And she was furious at the accusation.

'I am Max Berman's wife,' she stated. It did her case no good when her own cultured voice became arrogant. *He* and our baby are my family and I won't have anyone judging me by any other standard. He's a good committee man.'

'How do we know that everything said in committee isn't taken back to George Pullman through you?'

'I refuse to listen to such wicked talk,' said Ellie, and she stalked away with her head held high. But when she was alone she wept at the unfairness and decided not to tell Max. He already had enough to worry about.

She became increasingly aware that she was being ostracised. Women who had previously

160

stopped to chat and to make a fuss of William began to pass her by, some smiling faintly, other going so far as to cross the road rather than risk having to speak. Ellie was desperately lonely, and guiltily yearned for some of the company she had once kept. In particular she longed for a heart-to-heart talk with Clarissa.

Various events were organised by the union to keep morale high in the town, and one of these was a dance to be held on the second floor of the Market Building. Ellie begged Max to take her and after much coaxing he reluctantly agreed, but when he tried to find someone to look after William for a few hours everyone had an excuse.

'They're not all going dancing,' he said, after the fourth refusal. 'What's going on? What have I done?'

Ellie came out of the bedroom in a blue satin gown which had been put away for almost a year and she looked so lovely her husband caught his breath. Her hair was elegantly knotted on top of her head, elbow-length gloves covered her forearms, and her slender neck was exposed in all its beauty by the low cut of her bodice. She could have been going to dinner at the Richelieu.

'You haven't done anything, my dearest,' she said. 'I'm the one no one will speak to. I don't fit in here any more. Everyone thinks I'm on the side of Mr Pullman.'

Max stared at her. 'You can't go dressed like that.'

His sudden anger was explosive and so

161

unexpected Ellie recoiled, but in a few seconds her surprise turned to indignation.

'There's nothing wrong with the way I'm dressed,' she retorted. 'I've gone to a lot of trouble and I'm sure none of your friends' wives will look any better.'

'That's just it—none can possibly match up to such finery. You look like a Chicago socialite. You look like Conrad Harvey's daughter instead of a striker's wife.'

'If I can't wear this gown I'm not going,' Ellie said. 'I *am* different from the women here and if they want to shun me I'll give them even more reason.'

'Go and take it off,' Max commanded.

'No, I won't.'

'Then we'll stay at home.'

He pushed her roughly into the bedroom and began to disrobe her, ignoring both her protests and William's frightened cry at the sound of raised voices. He wrestled with her and when she fell back on the bed he pinned her arms above her head, holding her wrists in one of his strong hands while he pulled off the dress with the other. She struggled violently, but when she was wearing only her chemise he kicked off his trousers and took her with a force that shook the bed until it moved towards the cradle. And Ellie responded. Since William's birth, Max had rarely touched her and she had longed for a spontaneous, uninhibited union like this to put some spark back into their marriage. Now his passion roused her to ultimate excitement. He had never been such a demanding lover and he awakened a wild joy in her which was pagan in its intensity. Her fingernails clawed his shoulders and drew blood which stained his shirt. Her body throbbed with a tumultuous climax which made her cry out.

She was sure he would say that he loved her—how could he not when they had just shared such an ecstatic experience? But when he was spent, Max simply rolled away from her and lay on his back with his eyes closed, his lips set firm as if he were still angry.

'You've the looks of a countess and the appetite of a kitchen skivvy,' he said.

Emotional pain cut short the euphoric aftermath. His cruelty was incomprehensible and Ellie wanted to strike him, but even as she contemplated it she was held back by the love which enabled her to forgive him anything. All the same, he couldn't go unchallenged.

'Is there no way I can please you?' she demanded. 'What must I do, cover myself in grey cotton and pretend to be a prudish Puritan? Well, I can't do it.'

William was now crying loudly and insistently. Max jerked himself off the bed and replaced his clothes. 'I'm going to Downey's,' he grunted. 'See to the baby. He needs you more than I do.'

When he had gone Ellie allowed tears to fall unchecked as she covered herself with a wrap and lifted William out of the cradle to feed him.

She didn't understand why Max continually found fault. So often he used complaint as a

163

whip to humiliate her, and she had excused him by admitting that she was a poor housewife. She had blamed herself and made allowances for his impatience, but this time it was the shared intimacy of love-making he had found distasteful and she could find no reason for it. Had she been frigid he would have had cause to reproach her, but she was far from that; she could match him in passion whenever he came to her. She'd thought his self-control since William's birth had been out of consideration for herself, but it seemed the reason was deeper and more worrying.

There was something else which disturbed her much more profoundly. Max was always too involved with the union, his meetings and his furniture designs to take an interest in his son.

It was no wonder Ellie couldn't understand her husband when he had difficulty understanding himself.

Ever since their wedding, Max had been trying to come to terms with the enforced marriage. Sometimes he looked at Ellie and told himself how fortunate he was to have such a beautiful wife who declared her love for him at every opportunity, but the more she strove to please him the less he liked it. He was caught in a situation which became more intolerable as she failed to adapt to her new station in life. Yet he ought not to expect her to change completely. If he was truthful he didn't want her to.

He walked through the alleyway to Downey's in a confused mood. Ellie had looked so lovely in her blue gown. The sight of her in it had aroused him even before he'd lost his temper, and they could easily have come together peaceably. Instead, he had seen her flaunting the remnants of her rich background and it had enflamed him.

His resentment was increasing since the strike had worsened. No matter how hard she tried, Ellie would always be different from the other wives, and it set him apart as well. He knew there was talk behind his back, especially since George Pullman's unfortunate visit. Men who had trusted him to speak for them were now more inclined to turn to someone else, and he could feel their suspicion growing. It was unjust. Nothing had changed his attitude towards the company or lessened his enthusiasm for the workers' cause. He was as resolute as ever to see justice done and he was a good orator. It was his wife who was the trouble.

He walked on, keeping in the shadows beside the wall. The evening sun shed too much light on his problems and exposed another unpleasant truth. His resentment of Ellie was spilling over to affect the way he felt about William, who was the sole reason for this unsatisfactory alliance. Without him there would have been no marriage. To his shame, Max held his son responsible for his fate and could find no great affection for him. Ellie had set the seal on his rejection when she had talked of William tightening the bond.

He reached Downey's. Inside, the malty smell of alcohol filled his nostrils and tobacco smoke stung his eyes, but the saloon was quieter than usual. Even the honky-tonk piano was silent. The evening was damp and warm, and a fan revolving close to the ceiling was like a lazy hover-fly.

'Thought you'd be at the meeting,' the barman said.

'What meeting?' Max hadn't been told of one.

'Strike Committee's gone to the usual place a half hour ago.'

This was so surprising it aroused suspicion. Max sniffed the air as if to get a scent of what was going on. 'Thanks for telling me,' he said.

'Drink, Mr Berman?'

'Later.'

He left the saloon quickly. The store where meetings were held was not far down the street and he got his feet wet in the gutter having to avoid a group of drunken strikers from the brickyards who jeered at his pace. When he pushed open the door of the store Dan Frencham was at the head of the table addressing the committee, but he stopped in mid-sentence. There was an awkward silence.

'I take it I wasn't expected,' Max said.

'I'm sorry, Max. We thought you'd be over at the Market Hall.' The chairman, a man called Blake, spoke after a pause and he was plainly embarrassed. He cleared his throat. 'This ain't gonna be easy. You see, we ain't happy about the relationship between your wife and George Pullman. Means there's—'

166

'My wife severed all contact with her family and with George Pullman when she married me,' Max interrupted. 'The fact that he came to our house was pure coincidence and nothing changed as a result of it.'

'All the same, it don't seem right that a man with your connections should be on the committee. We've taken a vote on it and agreed we must ask you to resign.'

Several of the men looked down at their hands. Others nodded.

'This is infamous,' Max protested. 'Haven't I served you well? I've been a member of the ARU longer than any of you and I'll fight for the rights of the workers with my last breath.'

'It's the risk,' said Dan Frencham. 'Information's been leaked lately.'

'Not through me, I swear.'

'But who knows what talk there is between man and wife that could be passed on?'

'I never discuss union matters with my wife.'

The heated exchange went on for some time with Max defending himself so strongly there were several who actually changed sides, but the majority were still of the same mind and the decision stood.

'I'm sorry, Max, we all are,' Blake concluded. 'But for the security of all those we represent we must ask you to step down from this committee. You've served us well, but there's real trouble ahead and we need to be sure that every man, and his family, gives solid support.'

Max did not accept the decision with good grace. His face was white and he spoke between gritted teeth. 'You'll be sorry for this, make no mistake.'

He didn't return home that night, but went to Mariette Schuman because he was afraid of what he would do if he had to face Ellie while his emotions were so fevered. He couldn't trust himself not to lay a hand on her.

The strike continued into June, when the mood changed. Neither side gave any ground, the company refusing to go to arbitration and the strikers determined to hold out for their demands whatever the cost. A boycott seemed the only way, though Eugene Debs tried to avoid it, and at a convention on 26 June instructions were given to American Railway Union members not to handle any Pullman sleepers or diners.

The effect of the boycott was like a prairie fire spreading from the east coast to the west. There were twenty-four railroads centred in Chicago, and most hauled Pullman rolling-stock. The first men who refused to switch Pullman cars were fired, but this provoked a general walk-out and within hours the yards in Chicago became immobilised by jammed trains. To make matters worse, crowds gathered and the *Chicago Tribune* carried pictures of rampaging mobs.

Ellie read a report in which the general managers predicted a reign of terror, and her heart jolted at the mention of riot guns. What had started out as a peaceful protest in Pullman was now affecting the whole of America, and she feared for those who had started the strike.

'Why can't we leave Pullman?' she asked Max, soon after he had told her of his rejection by the committee.

'Because we need the Strikers' Relief money,' he said impatiently. 'We've nothing else to live on.'

She didn't know why he was no longer a committee member. Rumours reached her ears about it being to do with her godfather's visit to Fulton Street, but she couldn't believe there was any connection, and Max refused to discuss it.

The money Drew had given to Ellie was gone, and as he didn't come with any more she was reduced to accepting bread and potatoes from the Relief Committee the same as everyone else. There were queues for the hand-outs which she had to join, but often pointed elbows forced her back, and being the last to receive anything she had to make do with what was left. Privation meant her milk was drying up and William, now three months old, was continually crying with hunger. Max hated it and stayed out for hours. She never knew where he went.

At the beginning of July there were 50,000 men on strike across the country and the disruption to transport caused further serious problems. No mail was being carried, food became scarce and very expensive, and Chicago was like a city under siege. Newspapers began calling Eugene Debs a dictator and their sympathy with the strikers was evaporating.

Independence Day on 4 July was marked by violence; in the city there were numerous fires, one huge one disposing of many of the now-deserted Columbian Exposition buildings. Damage to railroad property was estimated at more than 300,000 dollars. The strike was beginning to paralyse the nation, and it looked as if the workers had won, until President Cleveland ordered troop reinforcements to restore order, clear tracks and ride shot-gun on trains into Chicago.

Pullman company men armed themselves with revolvers and took to walking in pairs. Federal troops made their headquarters at the Florence Hotel, and soldiers camping on the lawn, with Gatling guns pointing down the wide streets in case of trouble, were a sight to chill the hearts of all who lived there.

Late one night Max brought a man home with him, and after looking in the bedroom to make sure Ellie was asleep he closed the door. The pair settled to a whispered discussion, but Ellie hardly ever slept until Max was with her and she was well aware of what was going on, though she didn't know the identity of the other man. She tiptoed to the door and put her ear against it, trying to make out the conversation.

'There'll be mayhem...' she caught.

'It would demolish the clock tower.'

'...dynamite.'

Her stomach churned. They were hatching a plot which would do untold damage to the workshops and probably destroy a fleet of Pullman cars. The wickedness of it and the terrible danger petrified Ellie and she longed to rush out and beg Max not to be so foolhardy.

Had she done so, his anger would have been equally frightening.

The two men were talking all night and sometimes there was argument, but just before dawn the visitor left stealthily. Max came to bed but lay there in the pale light with his hands behind his head, and when Ellie turned towards him he looked at her with bleak eyes.

'Things are going too far,' he said.

She pleaded with him. 'Please, Max, don't get too involved. Promise me you won't take unnecessary risks.'

'I can't promise anything. I have to do what I think is right.'

She admired his sense of duty. He had never shirked responsibilities in favour of an easy option, as he had demonstrated when she fell pregnant, but surely in this strike, there was right on both sides? She knew enough about her father's company to know that there was never total unfairness. In bad times such as this recession, it wasn't easy to keep paying high wages when there was less money coming in, so something had to give. Surely Mr Pullman was doing what was best for the men he employed, because if he had to pay out too much there would be nothing for new contracts, resulting in even fewer jobs. She had tried to get Max to talk about all this but he had no regard for her opinions.

Early the next morning, he left home without having had any sleep. His clothes were creased, his hair combed only by his fingers, and two days' growth of beard made his appearance forbidding. One look at him would put the authorities on their guard and she feared more than ever for his safety.

By mid-morning she could no longer bear to be alone with her fears. She dressed William, picked up her shopping basket and left the apartment, walking towards the Florence Hotel which had become the hub of daily activity. A marquee for the Illinois First Regiment was like a huge mushroom filling one side of the front lawn, and the usual women and children had congregated to watch the soldiers drill, some calling out friendly comments, some actually flirting with them, others jeering.

Suddenly the sounds of a riot could be heard coming from the direction of the workshops, raucous hate-filled voices lifting into the tension-filled air. At once the soldiers stopped drilling and primed their rifles. The women turned with a swish of petticoats and set off towards the barrage of shouting, bonnets slipping, skirts hoisted. Ellie went with them, jostling to get to the front of the running crowd. William was like a lead weight against her chest, giving her lungs no room to expand, but she had to keep going. Instinct told her that whatever trouble had erupted, Max was at the centre of it, and she was desperate to reach him.

Panting, gasping, she crossed 111th Street and saw an ugly mob outside the barricaded workshops entrance. Sentries had been posted there for several days now and no one was admitted without a pass signed by the military or Thomas Wickes. Sure enough Max was in the

172

forefront, but incredibly he was on the inside of the barrier with the company men. The rioters were howling for his blood.

Ellie pushed forward. 'What're they doing?' she cried.

'That bastard betrayed us,' a woman yelled. 'Can't trust nobody.'

'He wouldn't do that.'

'Bloody traitor!' she heard men shouting. 'Get him!' they chanted.

Somewhere behind her, rifles were fired into the air to disperse the crowd and there was further pandemonium. Ellie was crushed against a wall. She couldn't go forwards or back and it took all her strength to protect William. Her feet were trodden on, her basket was swept away, and she couldn't escape from the seething mass of people.

She screamed to her husband. 'Max! Max, help me!'

It was the worst thing she could have done. Max Berman's name on her lips attracted the attention of those nearest, and the women found a new outlet for their inflamed passions.

'She's the one we should be after! She's the root of the trouble!'

'George Pullman's girl.'

'Conrad Harvey's daughter. Too bloody proud to be one of us.'

They were like harridans pointing at her and deriding her, but they were not content with words. With cruel vindictiveness, the first blow was aimed at Ellie's shins and she cried out with pain. Within seconds she was being beaten.

Someone snatched the screaming baby from her just before she fell to the ground, and she tried to protect her head with her arms as blows rained on every part of her body.

She attempted to roll over, groaning and imploring the Holy Mother to protect her. Blood was soaking her clothes and pain blinded her, but she still found her voice. 'What have I ever done to you? You bitches! Leave me alone.'

But they had found a scapegoat on whom to vent their anger against the establishment and they wouldn't let go of their quarry. The last thing she remembered was being kicked in the stomach. She was unconscious when Max scattered the women in a terrible fury, gathered up his wife and carried her to relative safety.

NINE

Ellie struggled to open her eyes but her lids were so swollen she couldn't see enough to make out where she was. The room was dark. Shadowy figures hovered round the bed talking about her, but she couldn't understand what they were saying.

She knew Max was there. Love made her aware of his presence in every situation, and because he was there she wasn't afraid, even though the pain in her body was excruciating. Sometimes she heard a strange language. At others she recognised voices and thought one was her mother's, but they faded away and she was left with only a roaring in her head.

Dark curtains were drawn across the window making it seem to be perpetually night, and footsteps were soft so as not to disturb the quietness cocooning her. Water was spooned into her parched mouth a drop at a time by a woman she couldn't see and she drifted away again into unconsciousness which lasted until the following morning. This time a beam of daylight cut across the room and shone on the righthand door post, illuminating a small mezuzah with a seven-branched candlestick design on it. A silk tallith with knots at each corner hung over a chair. Painfully Ellie tried to work out the significance of these things and a gradual picture built up in her mind of the house where Max's parents lived. She had been here before, on the night of their wedding.

A stranger with a black beard, whose worn coat smelt of antiseptic, bathed her forehead with cool water.

'She will never be able to have another child,' she heard the man say.

Max's voice answered. 'It was a miscarriage. Surely another time...'

'She is lucky to be alive. The damage to her internal organs is extensive and another pregnancy is out of the question.'

Who were they talking about? Ellie wished they would go away and talk elsewhere.

The next day the swelling over her eyes had gone down and she awoke fully to see Hedda Berman beside the bed with William in her arms

175

and a small child tugging at her skirt. She smiled through dry lips.

'You're better,' Hedda said. 'We have been very worried about you.'

Ellie tried to speak but it required all her strength just to murmur one word. 'Max?'

'Max will come.'

She knew she must have been very ill for the Bermans to have relented and taken her into their home, yet she could remember little of what had happened to make it necessary. Garbled voices echoed through her head but it was only by the high-pitched tone that she could tell they were angry. Sometimes her body jerked as if she were trying to ward off blows.

Two days later, when she had recovered enough to be given broth and was alert and questioning, Max told her about the women of Pullman who had beaten her because she was George Pullman's godchild. He was deeply moved by her suffering, compassionate and full of contrition. Recollection came to her slowly as vivid pictures pieced together until she could remember almost everything.

'Ellie, please forgive me. I couldn't get to you,' Max said, his eyes pleading with her. 'They were like savage animals wanting to tear you apart. It was dreadful.'

'You were going to blow up the clock-tower.' She remembered him talking through the night to a man he had brought home.

'No, I wasn't. I was told of the plot and we managed to prevent it—that was what caused the riot. What good would it have done to destroy the workshops? It would mean less work than ever once the strike is won.'

'But that was going against the Strike Committee!'

'I am no longer on the committee,' he reminded her.

'So they called you a traitor.' Weak tears welled up. 'Oh Max, it's all my fault. I'm so sorry.'

'Dear Ellie, the blame must lie with those who can't see reason.' He smoothed the damp hair from her forehead. 'Rest and get well, and try to put it out of your mind.'

'How can I? I have to go back there.'

'We'll talk about it when you're stronger.' He drew her into his arms very gently so as not to hurt her. 'It's *my* fault you're lying here injured. I've brought you nothing but pains and trouble. You would've been better off if we'd never met.'

'Don't ever say that, Max. You know I couldn't live without you.'

'You've sacrificed your home and the love of your parents...'

'They don't matter.' She wouldn't let him torture himself.

He cradled her silently for several minutes and she was more contented in his company than she had been for a long time.

'Your mother came to see you while you were still unconscious,' he said, after a while. 'She was very upset.'

'And my father?'

'He didn't come.'

She brooded over the news after Max had left, happy yet unhappy at the reaction of her parents. She wished Mama would come again, but more than anything she longed for Papa to relent and understand that she had chosen the path her life was to take and had no regrets, even now.

Sometimes Hedda Berman brought her needlework and sat with Ellie. The curtains were pulled back now and the dark wallpaper didn't look so depressing, once she could see the pattern of roses trailing across it. One day Hedda put William in her arms while he was sleeping, and the little girl who was always there would curl up on the bed to be near them. She was the most beautiful child Ellie had ever seen, with red-gold curls which shone in the sunlight like a halo round her head. Pale and cherubic, she could have been the model for a painting of the Madonna and Child.

'Galina, take care,' Hedda warned the year-old child when she fidgeted.

'Galina?' Ellie was suddenly alert. 'This is...'

'Our dear Katrina's daughter. You saved her from the fire. We owe you so much, Ellie.' Hedda's expression was loving. 'Galina idolises the baby. She won't leave him for a minute and I have to put his cradle beside hers. I don't know what she will do when you take him away.' She touched the infant head nestling against Ellie's breast and a lovely smile lit up her lined face. 'I, too. Our grandson has brought us peace.'

Hedda was different now from the woman who had been so hurt on the night Max had introduced her to his gentile wife. Jacob, too, was caring and considerate. He came to the bedroom diffidently to ask after her health, and kept his eyes averted if she was not covered to the chin with shawls. They were kind people, gentle and God-fearing, and Ellie's heart warmed to them more each day.

It was a while before she recalled the strange conversation she had heard whispered between Max and the man in the black coat. The next time her husband came to see her she asked him about it.

'Max, will I be able to have any more children?'

It was a moment before he answered. Then: 'You had a miscarriage,' he said. 'Dr Harris said you must have been about six weeks pregnant but you lost the baby when you were kicked. There can never be another.'

Ellie thought back to the evening when she had worn the blue gown and knew that was when she had conceived. She bit her lips to stop them trembling, but nothing could stem the flow of tears. Max sat on the bed and drew her into his arms, holding her while she sobbed. He stroked her hair and tried to comfort her with soothing words, but she was inconsolable. Grief for the child she had lost overwhelmed her, and the knowledge that she could never bear him another son was the bitterest blow of her life. How could other women have done this to her?

The doctor came once more and was satisfied with her progress. The pain in her body was easing, the bruises fading, and she was able to stand without help. In another week, he told her, she would be able to go downstairs.

Time had become static and she could hardly believe that it was already the beginning of August. She had been ill for four weeks, and in that time the strike had ended. The call for a general strike had failed and the boycott had gradually broken down as men sought re-employment, while the American Railway Union had lost many of its members through disillusionment. Little had been achieved. Eugene Debs had been jailed for a week for contempt, and when the Pullman Palace Car Company posted notices advertising for workers, those on strike feared for their future. Rallies were still being held to try to revive men's spirits and their passion for the cause, but empty bellies and empty pockets had already dictated the outcome.

Max didn't go back to the upholstery shop. He stopped paying rent for the apartment, collected the folder containing his designs, and every day he took them out to show Chicago furniture manufacturers. Every night he came home with them rejected, and his face grew longer.

It was raining the second time that Sibylla Harvey came to see her daughter. The carriage pulled up outside Jacob Berman's Tailoring Emporium and Melksham helped her down, holding an umbrella over her as she crossed the sidewalk. Even on a fine day she would

180

have disliked being in the area. In the rain it was so depressing she almost decided to postpone the visit, but Drew had been insistent that something must be done to help Ellie.

'What a pleasure, Mrs Harvey,' Jacob Berman said. 'Welcome to our home.'

'I wish to see Elena and her husband. I trust they are here.'

'Please come through.'

The narrow passage between the shop and the house would hardly accommodate the width of her hat and leg-of-mutton sleeves. Everything was spotlessly clean, yet Sibylla lifted her purple damask skirt as if afraid it would be soiled, and she kept her bead handbag clasped against her waist. The living room behind the shop was dark and dreary, colour seeming to be non-existent except for the brightness of the red-headed child who looked like an angel asleep on Hedda Berman's lap.

At once there was activity. The woman stood up and disturbed the child, Jacob called his son, and Ellie appeared on the stairs at the back of the room which were shrouded in shadows.

'Mama!' Ellie cried. She was painfully thin and wore a dress of grey checked wool poplin which sapped what colour she had left. The dowdiness of her daughter shocked Sibylla almost more than her fragility. 'Oh Mama, this is wonderful. I'm so pleased to see you.'

'Can I offer you some refreshment, Mrs Harvey?' asked Hedda.

'Thank you, no. I wish to speak to Elena and Max alone.' Sibylla removed her gloves. A fire was burning in the grate and the humid heat made her feel quite faint. 'Is there somewhere private?'

The bedroom was the only place. It was where she had last seen Ellie lying still and bruised, and unaware of her presence. The visit had distressed her so much she'd put off coming again. Had Conrad known anything about it she would never have been allowed to come at all.

'Dearest Mama, if only you knew how much I've missed you,' Ellie said, holding her mother's hands as soon as they were alone. Her cheeks were damp.

'I've missed you too.' Suddenly Sibylla realised that they had hardly touched in years, and the feel of Ellie's fingers clutching her own, unleashed emotions she had kept in check since her own unhappy girlhood. In those days she had learnt not to show her feelings for fear of being hurt. 'Oh Ellie, I've been so worried about you. I can't tell you how distraught I was at what happened to you.'

She undid the veil tied beneath her chin, removed her hat, and drew Ellie into the first embrace they had shared in a very long time.

Max appeared. He greeted his mother-in-law coolly. 'To what do we owe this honour, Mrs Harvey? As you see, my wife is almost recovered.'

It surprised Sibylla to see that he was the master in his marriage. Ellie had always been so headstrong she had thought that anyone who married her would be left trailing in her wake, but Max was dominant. Sibylla couldn't help but recognise the sexuality of the man. Those smouldering eyes must surely inflame every woman he looked at, and it was no wonder Ellie was still plainly besotted.

'I'll come straight to the point,' she said. 'You can't return to Pullman and it appears you can't get work in Chicago. What do you intend to do?'

'I shall find work,' said Max.

'We're deeper in recession than ever. There *is* no work. My husband won't employ you, though I've asked him and so has Drew.' Sibylla sat on the edge of a chair and waved her gloves in an effort to feel some cool air. 'So I've come to offer you a solution and if you refuse I shall know you have less sense than a baboon.'

'Mama, how rude you are,' protested Ellie.

Surprisingly Max smiled. 'You're not expecting me to swing from trees, I hope?'

'I'm expecting you to pack your things and take your wife and child to England,' said Sibylla. She twisted the gilt catch on her handbag and opened it. 'The money in here represents some of the dowry Elena should have had ... and before you remind me that your pride forbids you to accept anything from Conrad Harvey, let me tell you that the money is mine, not his. I don't need it—you do.'

'But, Mama, what would we do in England?'

'There'll be an opportunity for you to make a new start. My father, Sir Robert Cromer is a very rich man with a good deal of influence. I've written to tell him you'll be arriving early next

183

month and asked him to see that Max is given a good job.' She brought an envelope out of the bag and handed it to Ellie. 'Your grandfather's address is in here. So are tickets and reservations on the steamship *New York* which will take you to Southampton. I've spoken on the telephone to Dr Harris and he assures me you will be fit to travel in a week's time.'

Max took the envelope from his wife before she had a chance to look inside and, as expected, he tried to give it back. 'You cannot run my life, Mrs Harvey. We both thank you for the offer but we can't accept it.'

'But Max...' Ellie cried.

'I make the decisions,' he said. 'We're not leaving Chicago.'

'Your pride will be the ruin of you,' sighed Sibylla. 'No one can go through life without accepting help sometimes. How do you think Presidents are made? They need support. At the moment you need money to help you out of this intolerable situation and I'm giving it because you are family.'

'The money is my wife's.'

'I want you to have it,' Ellie put in immediately.

Sibylla felt sorry for them. Ellie was still only eighteen but by her own choice she was locked in a marriage which had brought nothing but trouble and deprivation while her contemporaries still danced the night away without a care. And Max was too unyielding and too honest to see that opportunities were there for the taking, if you wanted to succeed in this life! Where would

184

Conrad have been without *her* father's money? She would never say that Conrad had been unscrupulous, but thinking back she could see that he'd had a dual purpose in marrying her and she had always suspected that the advantages of her dowry had figured larger than love.

'Think of your son,' she said to Max. 'He deserves the best, just as Elena does. What can you do without money?'

'I can provide.'

'With what?' she was fast losing patience. 'You are responsible for my daughter. I'm not saying you are totally to blame for the situation she is now in, because I know how she plagued us to give our consent, but I'm saying that you ought to allow for the fact that she was not born into poverty and cannot be expected to exist in it permanently when there is an alternative.'

'I'd love to go and see Grandfather Cromer,' said Ellie. 'And I want to see England.'

Max was too tall for the low-ceilinged room and he had been standing with his neck bent. He rubbed it vigorously while he deliberated. Sibylla was afraid Ellie's enthusiasm might jeopardise her chance and reverse the faint sign of weakening, but surely Max was no fool. He would know that by refusing he would be destined to remain at the bottom of the pile while others who had not been blacklisted took the work he sought.

'Very well,' he said at last. 'For Ellie's sake I will accept, but it will be a loan. One day I shall repay it.'

'I never want to hear of it again,' said Sibylla.

185

She gave the envelope to Ellie and handed a package to Max containing more banknotes than he had ever seen. 'Open a bank account and when you get to England you can transfer it. There will be enough money to last until my father settles you in business.'

She embraced Ellie again before leaving and was surprised at how emotional she felt. Briefly she regretted the action she had just taken because it meant she would not be seeing her daughter again for a very long time, but at least she had the satisfaction of knowing she had rescued her from degradation.

It had stopped raining when she left the tailor's shop.

'Drive home, please,' she instructed Melksham. 'Thank goodness we won't have to come here again.'

Ellie and Max talked about their changed circumstances well into the night. The money and the steamship tickets had been put into Jacob's safe, but the letter with Sir Robert Cromer's address had become creased with scrutiny.

'Why go to England?' Max asked. 'The money would set me up in business here. I could make furniture from my designs.'

'And who would buy it? You've already been round all the manufacturers, and if they don't like your ideas no one else will. That would be throwing the money away.'

'We could go to New York.'

'No.' Ellie's return to health was marked by a

spirited revival of obstinacy. 'We have the tickets to England—why waste them?'

'The money's yours,' he said with bad grace, after she had discarded several more suggestions. 'It seems I must go where my wife wishes.'

'It's *our* money, Max, and we're going to do wonderful things with it.'

She was cross with him. He was showing no gratitude for her mother's generosity, yet they were living in his parents' house for nothing, relying on them for food and a roof over their heads when the Bermans could ill afford it. He was behaving stupidly and it was time he learnt to be a little more flexible.

'We'll be together, that's what matters most,' she said later, curling up against him in the lumpy double bed. She longed for him to kiss her like a lover, but he refrained from any overture which might signal the start of a renewed physical relationship. Until now she hadn't wanted it, but since the excitement of her mother's visit she felt revitalised and the first quiver of desire disturbed her body.

'Go to sleep,' Max answered. 'Tomorrow we'll go over things again.'

'And I shall insist we go to England.'

Two weeks later, Max and Ellie Berman with their son William occupied a stateroom aboard the USMSS *New York* when it sailed to Southampton, England, and they were treated according to the importance of their hundred-dollar tickets. They had deckchairs hired in advance, ate at the Captain's table, and were obliged to change into full evening dress for dinner. A portmanteau labelled 'Hold' and containing new clothes had been delivered the day before they left, along with a small one with items for William and there was a selection of small flat boxes marked 'Wanted' which could be stowed away for use in the cabin. Sibylla never did things by halves and she had ensured they would want for nothing, either on the voyage or in their new life. Max had agreed to use the suits and shirts carefully chosen for himself, but nothing would stop him wearing the long green coat his father had made for him.

The ship cut through the choppy Atlantic water causing a swell which spread out like a white lace fan beyond her stern. In the moonlight Max could trace it back almost to the horizon and his eyes focused on the most distant waves, wishing he could ride them back to New York City.

Leaning on the deck-rails, he compared this voyage with the one he had made from Russia with his parents. Then there had been disease and overcrowding, yet everyone had been united in the belief that America was the land of plenty where they would no longer be refugees. They'd been right to hope for good things. He loved America and had no wish to leave it. What hope was there of happiness on an island where every road must lead to the sea? He was used to vast open spaces.

The night air was chilly and he huddled deeper into his coat. It wasn't that he objected to the preferential treatment. It was just that he had done nothing to earn it except marry a wealthy man's daughter. It would have been enough for some men, but Max wanted to be accepted on his own merit.

Ellie, of course, was quite at home amongst the upper class who professed friendship because they dined at the Captain's table. She was at ease with them, in her element holding long conversations on subjects about which he knew nothing, and he could see how she blossomed in her own environment. The effects of her illness had disappeared. Ellie ought never to have been plucked from her rich background where she was so comfortable and contented. And Max was growing more and more *un*comfortable in the presence of these people with whom he had nothing in common. He didn't fit in. He never would.

He pondered over the letter Sibylla had written about her father. Sir Robert Cromer was a self-made man, a contractor. He'd built elegant railroad stations in two British cities, laid countless miles of track to link almost every town in the country, and had been knighted for his work. He employed agents, sub-agents, navvies in their thousands, lawyers, advisers and secretaries. His headquarters was his home in London, a grand mansion on the scale of Prairie Avenue property but without the surrounding gardens. Land in London was at a premium. He also had a country house and more money than he knew how to use. Max thought of him with grudging admiration, but with no wish to be beholden to him.

On the sixth day of the voyage, when eyes were trained westward in the hope of catching a first glimpse of the Irish coastline, Ellie began unfolding her plans for the future.

'One of the first things we must do is enrol William for a public school,' she said. 'I'm told Eton is the best. Mrs Faber's son went there.'

'William is only four months old,' Max protested. 'It'll be time to talk about school in another five years.'

'Oh no. We're already late. Apparently we should have enrolled him when he was born.'

'I will not have my son brought up to be soft.'

'He must be educated like a gentleman,' she insisted. 'He is the great-grandson of Sir Robert Cromer, a peer of the realm.'

'And the grandson of Jacob Berman, an honest Jew.'

'Are you saying my grandfather didn't come by his money honestly?'

'I'm saying that William is just an ordinary child and all I want is for him to be wise enough to make a living and strong enough to defend himself.'

'You're impossible, Max. You don't appreciate anything.'

Angry words flew between them and both were determined not to back down. It was one of many rows that developed in the confined cabin space and Max frequently left abruptly, walking round the deck to cool off.

Ellie's ideas were becoming more fanciful by the hour, partly because Mrs Faber had lent her a magazine featuring London's social life which advised on where it was fashionable to be seen and with whom, and what to wear on each occasion.

'We shall have to go dancing, Max,' she said. 'I love dancing, don't you?'

'I've never danced in my life. When would I have learnt?'

'Well, I shall teach you. I'm sure Grandfather will have a ballroom in his house. We'll be invited to all the important functions, and I *must* be presented to the Prince of Wales. Mrs Faber says the Queen just never goes out, but perhaps we'll be able to go to Windsor Castle, or wherever it is she lives.'

'Ellie, you're expecting too much. You're living in a dreamworld.'

'No, I'm not. Mama wouldn't have sent us all this way if she hadn't known that it will be absolutely marvellous.'

As her plans became more far-fetched so Max's dread of arriving in England increased. It wasn't that he was entirely opposed to the good life she envisaged, but was sure he was going to feel like an interloper. He could imagine the reception he would get from Sir Robert when he knew he was merely the son of Russian immigrants.

He'd talked a lot to his father before leaving Chicago, and Jacob had tried to persuade him not to accept Sibylla Harvey's help.

'It's good to make money, my son,' Jacob had said, 'but you will have no pride in it if you haven't made it yourself. You will lose your

191

self-respect if you live on your wife's dowry. Stay here, my son. Work on your furniture designs. I've great faith in them.'

'Then I'll leave them with you,' Max had answered. 'I must go to England, for Ellie's sake. She's been through a lot and now she's set her heart on seeing her grandfather. But I shall insist we only live with him until I can support us independently.'

Grand resolutions he had made, but Ellie's ambitions were grander and she was becoming impossible. The thought of setting foot on English soil filled him with morbid dread.

On the final day he stood on deck with William in his arms as the ship took on a pilot to navigate the last stretch of seaway which he was told was Southampton Water. Like those around him he ought to have been thrilled at arriving in a new country, but as he looked from side to side at the grey view blurred by misty rain he was filled with a great hatred for this land. It gnawed at his spirits.

He thought back to New York Harbour which they had left in perfect weather. How right he had been to have regrets as they sailed from the dock on North River. The impressive landmarks they had passed, like the Bowling Green Building, the spire of Trinity Church and the square Florentine tower of the Produce Exchange were engraved on his memory. The sun glinting on the gilded dome of the World Building had been as bright as a jewel, and he had marvelled over the statue of *Liberty Enlightening the World* on Bedloe's Island, which hadn't been there when he'd arrived from Russia. There was simply nothing to compare on the Southampton skyline; only dock buildings and shed-like constructions beckoned as the *New York*'s graceful bows nosed towards the quayside between a conglomeration of steam and sailing vessels.

He had left Ellie in the cabin arranging her hair so that the new hat she had been saving for the occasion would sit on it at exactly the right angle. When she joined him on deck she was splendidly arrayed in a matching silk coat of royal blue her mother had chosen and which was quite unsuitable for the cold, miserable weather. She clasped his arm and cooed to William.

'Isn't this the most exciting day of our lives? Why didn't you wait for me? I'm just longing to be on our way to London,' she babbled on with childlike enthusiasm. 'I've checked I've got Grandfather Cromer's address safely in my handbag. Are you sure you've the letters of credit and the money?'

'Ellie, calm down.'

'Why should I? We're making a new beginning and I'll never again have to live in a dreadful tenement apartment like the one in Pullman.'

These days she was careless with words, not stopping to think how cruel they could seem when she was so disparaging about the life they had left behind. She no longer hid her dislike of all things low-class and this latest effrontery wounded him like a knife-thrust. They were surrounded by other passengers, otherwise there would have been another row. It was

193

willpower which stopped him from making a caustic reply.

'I'm going to get the boxes out of the cabin and up on deck,' he said coldly, handing her the baby.

'The cabin boy does that.' She shuffled William into a more comfortable position, then went on imperiously, 'I've already tipped him more than he deserves, considering the service he's given us—though I suppose you are partly to blame. You really must get used to leaving menial jobs to those who are paid to do them.'

He gritted his teeth. 'Thank God I was never drawn into your background before this. The inequality makes me sick.'

'Stop thinking like a peasant, Max.'

'I *am* a peasant!' He was livid.

His nerves were still raw when they were at last in the disembarkation hall along with the portmanteau, boxes and the rest of their luggage. Ellie, who had been flitting amongst the friends she had made on the voyage to say her last farewells, had to be made to stay in one place with William.

'I have to go to the immigration office,' Max told her. 'Don't move from here until I get back.'

'Hurry, Max,' she urged. 'The London train leaves quite soon.'

He turned up the collar of his green coat and strode out into the drizzling rain towards the office which had been pointed out to him, head down and emotions simmering.

It was then, without warning, that the most extraordinary coincidence occurred. Had he not been so exasperated with Ellie and her new airs and graces, and so frustrated with the way he no longer seemed to be in charge of his own life, Max would never have been tempted by this opportunity, so suddenly presented. Given time to reflect, he would have realised that such an extreme step was wicked and cowardly, but he was required to make an instant decision—and the one he made was destined to affect the lives of everyone close to him.

As he opened the door of the immigration office and was about to step inside, he collided with a man who was just coming out. Both steadied themselves and launched into apologies. Then they gaped at each other in amazement.

'Oliver!' gasped Max.

'Max, you wonderful boyo!' cried Oliver Devlin, throwing his arms round him. 'By the saints, what're you doing here?'

'It's the last place I want to be.'

'And here's me wishin' I could stay.'

The two men laughed and went outside, Oliver firing questions at his brother-in-law faster than peas from a pea-shooter. There was so little time. In the few minutes available, Max tried to fill him in with what had been happening in Chicago, and how Ellie's connection with George Pullman had led to violence and suspicion of his own loyalties.

'I ought never to have married her,' he said. 'Ellie and I were wrong for each other from the start. And now I'm stuck with being the poor relation of a British peer. All I can do is take what job he offers me and pretend to be grateful.'

'And so you should be, you old devil. Haven't you just landed in clover!'

'I'd rather be in Chicago making my own fortune.'

'Then you're a fool,' Oliver told him. 'I'd change places with you any day, so I would.' Suddenly there was a glint in his eye and he felt in his pocket. 'Tell you what, you can have my steerage ticket for the *Paris* which sails on the tide, and I'll take your beautiful wife to the comfort of her grandfather. How does that sound?'

They both laughed at the absurdity, but suddenly fell silent as the suggestion took root.

It was impossible. Max clenched his fists and controlled his erratic breathing with difficulty. He couldn't desert Ellie. He couldn't deposit her on the other side of the world and return alone to Chicago. Besides, there was William...

With a flash of insight he saw himself trying to adapt to the rich, well-bred society with which Ellie was so familiar and he knew he would be only a hindrance to her. He had no breeding—hadn't she just called him a peasant? All he knew about was upholstering furniture for railcars, and he would be made to feel inferior. In America he could try again to market his furniture, and without family responsibilities he could use every dime he made to start up in business on his own. He'd be able to hold his head up and be proud of his achievements, like Poppa had said.

It wasn't as if he would be leaving Ellie stranded. In another hour or two Oliver would have seen to it that she was safely with her grandfather, and she would be able to do all the things she had daydreamed about on the voyage. He would write to her as soon as he landed back in the States and beg her forgiveness. Somehow he would have to make her understand that she would be so much better off without him.

The rain was settling in droplets on Oliver's sandy-red hair. Never had Max been so pleased to see anyone.

'It'll work,' he said. 'I know it will.'

'Here's my ticket,' said Oliver.

Max took a packet from the inner pocket of his coat. 'And this is Ellie's money that her mother gave us. Give it to her and tell her to let her grandfather handle it. She'll never want for anything.'

'You're a fool to leave her, boyo, but you know your own mind.' Oliver stowed the packet away carefully.

'Sir Robert Cromer'll pay for a first-class ticket for you to replace this one and I'll see you back home in a few weeks.'

'That'll suit me fine.'

They embraced once more and parted in haste, Max seeing by the steam coming from the black and white smokestack of the *Paris* berthed opposite that he had little time to lose. His heart was hammering as he crossed the quayside and he closed his mind to rational thought. He would have seven days and nights alone on the return crossing to agonise over what he had done.

In another five minutes he was striding alongside the New York's sister ship with a single roll of luggage which had been Oliver's. It could be stowed beneath his steerage bunk. His tall, handsome figure attracted the attention of some American girls leaning over the rails, and they waved to him daringly, giggling behind their hands the moment they had done so. But Max was not interested. He was the last passenger to board and there was a lightness to his step as he climbed the gangway.

He was free.

PART TWO

OLIVER

TEN

The shock of Max's desertion was worse than anything Ellie had ever experienced. Even her beating by the Pullman women couldn't be compared with this. She rocked back and forth with her face hidden in William's shawls as he cried again in dismal sympathy.

The porter was still standing in front of her. She saw his booted feet shuffling uncomfortably. If only he would *do* something... With a great effort, Ellie found her voice.

'What am I going to do?'

'Don't rightly know, ma'am.' What a mercy she was in a country where English was spoken. 'You can't stay here, that's a fact. Reckon we'll have to tell the coppers so they can find you somewhere to doss down with the kid.'

'A place to stay, you mean?'

'That's what I said.'

She was shivering in the blue silk coat, and the ribbons on her new hat were limp and bedraggled in the damp. Her clothes felt wet, but she hadn't been out in the rain and she realised that though she was cold, she was sweating heavily. Her mind felt numb and she couldn't seem to think coherently. Every nerve was jangling, every mental effort fearful.

In a little while she would have to think about Max, but at the moment she dare not.

It required all her strength and sanity to cope with what was happening now, and she forced herself to stay calm.

What did one do without a cent in the world? Everything cost money. She stood up and straightened her shoulders, taking a deep breath as Drew had taught her to do when things went wrong, though the effort pained her ribs.

'My grandfather is Sir Robert Cromer. Here's where he lives,' she said, producing Mama's letter from her handbag. 'If there's some way I can let him know what's happened, I am sure he will send transport to collect me.'

The porter glanced at the address. 'London— hm, it'll take time.'

'Could I perhaps leave my jewellery as a collateral at some hotel while I wait?'

'The South Western, maybe...'

'If you can please take me there I know my grandfather will pay you well when he comes.'

It was then that another man appeared at the far end of the building and came hurrying towards them, his hair plastered down by the rain and his shoes squelching. There was something familiar about him and Ellie took a tentative step in his direction. When he was close enough for her to recognise she stopped in astonishment. It was Oliver Devlin.

'It's all right,' Oliver said in a rush to the porter. 'I've come to look after her.' He felt in his pocket and gave the man a bright coin which was gratefully accepted. 'Ellie, my dear girl, what can I say?'

Ellie was beyond speech. She was cold and tired and miserable, and she had got to the pitch where nothing was surprising any more. Soon, no doubt, she would be able to ask questions, but all she could do just then was stare bleakly at Oliver over the top of William's head.

'Where do you want the luggage then, sir?' the porter asked deferentially.

'I've a cab waiting. We'll be taking the next train to London from the West Station. If you'll be so kind as to move the cases, I'll look after the lady.'

'Is that all right, ma'am?' The porter turned to Ellie for confirmation. 'You do know this gentleman?'

'Yes,' she said. 'I know him.'

The man driving the hansom cab got down and helped her into the vehicle while Oliver held the baby. Ellie moved mechanically, straightening her skirt as if it mattered, while the rain, beating down on the cab roof, had a mesmerising effect. The horse snorted and clopped across the wet cobbles, bearing Ellie Berman towards the next stage of her life.

As they turned the corner into the street the steamship *Paris* was still visible in the far distance, taking Max back home to America. She closed her eyes tightly and wished the ship would sink.

They were well on their way to London before Ellie had recovered sufficiently to question Oliver.

The countryside she had looked forward

so greatly to seeing slipped by unnoticed. Somewhere over to the left she vaguely saw the cathedral at Winchester, but it didn't register. The jolting of the train was making her feel sick and she longed to get off, but there was still a considerable journey ahead of her with this Irishman in the seat where Max should have been.

Oliver had paid for two first-class tickets and now they sat alone in a compartment which boasted sepia photographs of British seaside resorts above the comfortably upholstered seats. Buttoned leather padding covered the lower half of the door to the outside, and the strap to open the window hung over it. Once, when they had picked up speed, Ellie had been tempted to pull on the strap, open the door and throw herself on the track. Life without Max was inconceivable. But then William had stirred on the seat opposite and opened his dark eyes at the very moment when the thought flashed through her mind and she abandoned it immediately, ashamed of having entertained it for a second. For her son's sake she had to come through this nightmare. He went to sleep again as though reassured.

'I want to know what part you played in my husband's absconding,' she said, surprised that her voice sounded so firm.

'None whatsoever,' said Oliver smoothly. 'I couldn't believe my eyes when I saw him. There we were in the immigration office, both with tickets for home in our pockets, and I said how grand it was we'd be travelling together.'

'What did he say about me?'

'He said he'd brought you over here to stay with your grandfather and I thought he must have seen you safely into his care, but no. There wasn't time because the boat we were sailing on was due to leave sooner than he'd expected. "Thank God," says he when he sees me. "I've not been knowing what to do. It's urgent I get back to America and I've left Ellie sitting on her luggage." I was appalled. "If you'll do me a favour I'll be indebted to you for the rest of my life," says he. "Look after Ellie. Tell her I'm sorry." ' Oliver rubbed his nose and scratched it. The window was open a fraction and soot had landed on his freckled skin. 'Now I could never leave a lady to cope on her own, especially in a strange country, so I told him. I said: "If your business is so important, I'll do it. What's another few days to me?" He fell on me with gratitude so he did, and the next minute he was gone.'

'I don't believe you.' It was so incredible Ellie couldn't take it in.

'I swear on my mother's name, God rest her soul, it's the truth.'

'He had a return ticket, you say?'

'In his pocket.'

It corresponded with what the porter had said: she had to believe it. Yet Max had said nothing about important business, and if the porter hadn't told her that a man by the name of Berman had boarded the *Paris,* she would have gone on contradicting Oliver's story. As it was she had to accept it until she could prove otherwise.

'And what about our money?'

'Money? Now he never mentioned that.'

'Surely he must have given you a package for me—he *knew* I have nothing.'

'It must have slipped his mind,' said Oliver. 'He was so concerned with asking me to see that you got to your grandfather's safely...'

'Oh, was he!' She had recovered enough from the shock for there to be a shift in her emotions as anger took over. Where she had been numb there was new pain, like the thawing-out of frosted fingers in hot water, and her blood which had been ice-cold now began to boil. 'So Max Berman is on the high seas with my dowry, heading back to America where he can spend it any way he likes.'

How much worse could things get? She was livid. On the voyage over Max had been tense and uncooperative, unwilling to fall in with any of her plans for the future. She had complained at his lack of interest, his unwillingness to put aside his pride, and all the while he had been scheming to rob her and desert her. She would never, never understand what she had done to deserve it.

'I thought you knew he was returning on the next boat,' Oliver said, his expression puzzled and concerned.

'Of course I didn't know. Would I have let him leave me there like that?' She stood up. Her fury was like a fuse burning. 'And I don't believe a word of that trash you told me. You've got a glib Irish tongue, Oliver Devlin, and I'd say you were in league with him. You'd planned it between you. It's too much of a coincidence, you being there at just the same time as Max.'

'It was coincidence right enough. May God strike me down if it wasn't.'

She stared at him, waiting for God's vengeance, but nothing happened. Oliver looked up as she swayed with the motion of the train, and his eyes were innocent of subterfuge.

'I'm sorry,' she said. 'Perhaps I misjudged you—but you must admit I have good reason.'

'Ellie, my heart goes out to you.'

'Why didn't you try to talk him out of it? Why didn't you make him see what a terribly wicked thing he was doing? How could you let him treat me like this?' Tears gathered in her eyes, mainly because she couldn't find enough words to express her anger. 'I'm destitute. You bought my train ticket and I can't repay you.'

'I don't want repaying. I'll do anything for you.'

'What am I going to tell my grandfather?'

Oliver got up and took hold of her hands. She was gesticulating wildly as she talked and he tried to pacify her. 'We'll think up something suitable, so we will. I'll be there to give you all the support I can. Trust me, mavourneen.'

'I must go to the lavatory. I don't even know if I can trust you with my baby and my belongings while I'm gone, but I'll have to.'

She felt like screaming as she passed along the corridor, but it would have achieved nothing.

Like it or not she was dependent on this Devlin man for the time being and she had to be strong, but as soon as she got to Grandfather Cromer's she would make sure he didn't stay around. He had been likeable enough when he had come to the apartment in Pullman, but even then she'd had an uneasy feeling. No matter what he said, nor how many times he swore on his mother's name, she didn't believe he was innocent. He and Max had been close. There'd been collusion between them, she knew without doubt, but for what purpose she failed to understand.

She washed her hands in the rose-patterned porcelain basin, letting cold water over her wrists to cool her feverishness. It was hot on the train. The rhythm of the wheels played on her nerves, drumming out repetitive phrases which were like torture. *Max has left you ... Max has left you ... Max has left you...* Steam drifted past the window in clouds, and when they went over some points the wheel rhythm changed. *He'll never come back ... he'll never come back ... he'll never come back...*

'I don't want him back,' she cried to her reflection in the mirror above the basin. 'I never want to see him again. Not ever!' Then she sobbed in earnest. 'Yes, I do. I want him right now.'

There was hardly room to move in the enclosed space. She took off her hat and smoothed her hair back from her forehead so that she could bathe her tear-stained face. It was only a few hours since she had dressed so carefully for their arrival, yet it seemed like another age. Perhaps she was still ill and hovering on the brink of consciousness.

The cold water on her skin had a stringent effect, and she pulled herself together. This turn of events was only too real and had to be met with courage if she was going to survive.

First of all she had to face up to the fact that Max was not the man she had always thought him to be. She had put him on a pedestal, loving him unreservedly and making allowances for any shortcomings. Now she knew that she had made the gravest mistake of her life and the consequences had caught up with her. Max was heartless. He had never loved her, and the only thing that could be said in his favour was that he had not tried to take advantage of her rich family. It might have been better had he done so... Then he wouldn't have found it necessary to rob her.

His desertion was the most wicked, the most contemptible act imaginable. In anguish, Ellie realised that her precious love had been killed at a stroke, supplanted by disillusionment and wrath which already threatened to turn to hatred. She could find no sympathy for her husband's actions, no excuse or validity. What he had done was criminal and she wept afresh.

Suddenly all the problems of the last few months took on new significance. She thought back to when Max had first found fault with her, and realised it was from the beginning of their life together. Instead of helping when she'd found things difficult, he had told her to try harder. He had wanted to bring her down to his level, never raise himself to hers, and his refusal to accept monetary help from Drew had been a way of punishing her for trapping him in a marriage he had never wanted. He had turned against George Pullman because he was her godfather, forgetting how kind he had been to him in the beginning. He had an outsized chip on his shoulder which made him resentful of his betters, and now he had shown himself for the villain he really was.

How blind she had been. How utterly stupid not to have listened to Papa. She couldn't say she hadn't been warned.

There could be no dissolution of the marriage, of course. The teaching of the Catholic Church ensured she was tied to him forever. She had no clear idea what the Jewish laws were, but imagined they were the same. For good or evil she would always be his legal wife, which meant that he, too, was tied. Putting an ocean between them made no difference.

She longed to reach the comfort of Grandfather Cromer's home. He would advise her what to do next. One thing was certain—she was not going to rush post-haste back to Chicago to face her husband with his crime. Max was not the only one with pride. Ellie replaced her hat and tilted it at an angle which gave her confidence, then retraced her steps to the first-class railcar, and Oliver Devlin.

Mama's letter gave a vivid description of her old home. *'The house is a mansion in Chesterman Court, off Curzon Street, and you will love it.*

The interior is so gracious, suitable for every occasion, and I remember wonderful parties held in the music room which has a parquet floor ideal for dancing. There are paintings on the walls which your Papa drooled over and would love to own, and exquisite miniatures of myself, my sister Beatrice and my brother Julian which my father specially commissioned. The china is as colourful and beautiful as anything you can imagine, and inlaid tables set with it are indeed a joy to the eye. The ceilings are all painted a delicate blue with intricate white stuccowork edging them. The mantelpiece in the drawing room is genuine Chippendale with a carved canopy, and the Sheraton cabinets are full of porcelain and silver which you must see to believe. I could go on all night describing everything. It brings tears to my eyes just remembering.

'Ask your grandfather to let you have the bedroom on the second floor, which has a four-poster bed once used by Queen Elizabeth at Hampton Court, I believe. Conrad has never forgotten how it felt to be so close to history dating back farther than anything we can lay claim to over here. The bed has cream tapestry hangings and the drapes have been made to match. From the window you may just see a glimpse of Hyde Park.'

Ellie didn't show the letter to Oliver. She knew it off by heart and had built up mind-pictures of the palatial residence to which she was going. The grandeur may have frightened Max but Ellie had thrilled to the thought of it every time she had reread the descriptions.

London had promised to be the mecca of

all things sublime and she had imagined it a city of grace and beauty like Paris, but on her arrival at Waterloo station with Oliver she hardly looked around to see if the reality matched up. It was an oddly planned terminal, with a maze of platforms and throngs of people bustling through the steam from screaming engines. Without Max there was no beauty anywhere.

'Stay here while I get a porter for the luggage,' Oliver instructed, when he'd helped her down from the train with William.

Ellie panicked, terrified of a repetition of what had happened at the dockside. 'Don't leave me! Please don't leave me,' she cried. Oliver Devlin might be an unwanted companion but at least he was a link with home. Not another soul knew her in this great metropolis.

Luckily a porter came along, loaded Ellie's luggage on a trolley and wheeled it to the station entrance where elegant carriages were drawing up in quick succession to meet weary travellers.

'I should have sent a telegram to tell my grandfather what time we were arriving,' Ellie fretted. 'He would have sent his carriage for me and I wouldn't have needed to trouble you further.'

'I'll not be leaving you till I'm sure you're expected,' replied Oliver suavely. 'I gave my word to Max.'

'Of course I'm expected!'

All the same she was nervous, and she was glad of his concern. Two fashionable young women carrying tennis racquets walked by in conversation just then, and their accents sounded so aristocratic it filled Ellie with an unaccustomed sense of inferiority. These relatives whom she had never met might not accept her. Ellie hadn't thought to ask her mother what reply she'd had from Sir Robert Cromer. Supposing they looked down their noses at her and made her feel unwelcome...

'I've secured a hansom,' said Oliver. Anxiety made her hold back and seeing it he put a hand beneath her elbow. 'Come on, my dear, the worst's over.'

'Somehow I doubt it.' She couldn't rid herself of the spectre of Aunt Beatrice, Uncle Julian and their respective offspring peering at her as if she had crawled out from under one of the Sheraton cabinets. For the first time, she feared that the rich of Chicago were quite unlike London's nobility. Then she remembered that Mama was one of them, and as her daughter she had every right to hold her head high. 'Five, Chesterman Court, please,' she told the cab driver.

In spite of everything her spirits rose as they crossed Westminster Bridge in the hansom. She gazed at the Houses of Parliament and Westminster Abbey with awe, and when the journey took her past Buckingham Palace it was like a photograph from one of Mrs Faber's magazines coming to life. They had left the rain behind in Southampton and the sun shone on stretches of green either side of Constitution Hill. A right turn at the top brought them into Park Lane, a wide thoroughfare with luxurious residences facing the park, and a few minutes later they were in Curzon Street, leading from which was Chesterman Court.

Ellie looked up at the large mansions lining the street, all but one a dazzling white. Each had a portico balcony and bow-fronted windows through which lighted chandeliers could be seen twinkling now that evening approached. But what surprised Ellie was the flight of steps leading up to each door straight from the street, little different from the entrances to tenement buildings in Pullman. She had thought there would at least be some ground in the front.

'Number five, lady,' said the cabby, drawing the horse to a standstill outside the only house requiring a fresh coat of whitewash. The paint was flaking round the windows and the ironwork on the balcony was crumbling with rust. No light shone in the drawing room.

'You must be mistaken,' said Ellie. 'This isn't the home of Sir Robert Cromer.'

'No mistake, ma'am. That's where the old geezer lives, up them apples and pears.'

'I beg your pardon?'

'Stairs,' said Oliver. 'It's Cockney rhyming slang.'

Ellie was dumbfounded. While Oliver got down and paid the man she blinked hard and looked again, wondering if her eyes were playing tricks, but still the dilapidated mansion crouched between its pristine neighbours like some shabby joke. It was far from funny. She could only suppose that the interior would put all the others to shame.

Holding William tightly she went up steps

which obviously hadn't been cleaned for weeks, and when she pulled an iron rod at the side of the door a bell clanged inside the house. Twice more she jerked it, by which time the hansom had left and Oliver was behind her with the luggage.

'I don't understand this,' she said. 'It can't be right. Where is the footman?'

Her heart was beginning to thud painfully, the way it had done while she had waited on the quayside for Max, and a new and terrible dread took hold. Surely nothing else could go wrong, nothing on the scale of what she had already suffered.

Oliver, too, was looking mystified. He stood back and looked up to where a light flickered in a second-floor room. 'There's someone upstairs. Ring again.'

Once more the bell jangled, and this time it brought a response. Unhurried footsteps echoed on what sounded like a tiled floor. A bolt rattled and the door was opened by an elderly manservant who regarded them suspiciously with cold eyes. He wore a black tailcoat and trousers which were shiny with age, a black tie with a white wing collar, and his shoes turned up at the toes from constant wear. He would be the butler.

'Can I help you?' he asked. His sparse grey hair, brushed and pomaded, had receded either side of a centre tuft which peaked on his high forehead, and his beak of a nose overshadowed his pursed mouth.

'I wish to see Sir Robert Cromer,' said Ellie.

'I am afraid Sir Robert is unavailable at present. May I relay a message, madam?'

'I should like to be shown in. Will you please tell Sir Robert his granddaughter, Mrs Elena Berman, has arrived from America.'

The impassive face dropped. The fixed expression, conditioned to show no surprise, creased into disbelief. 'The master has said nothing. Is he expecting you, madam?'

'My mother has informed him of the date of my arrival by letter. It was impossible to let him know the exact time.' By now Ellie was irritable. 'I am not accustomed to being kept waiting on doorsteps. Please let us in and have someone come to deal with my luggage.'

'Yes, madam.'

The grand entrance was only dimly lit by a single electric fitting, showing two staircases at the far end curving up to meet at a central landing on the next floor. The carpet was grey with dust, the carved wood balustrades dull and unpolished. Ellie set foot inside the house, showing nothing of the trepidation she felt at the state of things.

She and Oliver were shown into a reception room on the right which was furnished with a set of upright chairs, a small occasional table, and a cabinet which certainly wasn't Sheraton and contained very little in the way of costly trinkets. A few etchings of railroad terminals hung on the wall, but it was obvious by the oblongs of lighter coloured wallpaper that several pictures had been removed.

'If you and Mr Berman would care to wait

in here I will inform Sir Robert,' the man said. His accent was exaggeratedly cultured.

When he had gone, closing the door behind him, Ellie seated herself on the edge of a chair with the sleeping baby in her arms; she kept her back so rigid it made her shoulder-blades ache.

'All will be well in a minute,' she reassured herself aloud.

Oliver went over to the window and looked out. His bright hair seemed to be the only source of colour in the cold room and Ellie tried to take comfort from it. After all, he should have been on his way back to the States with Max, but he'd had enough compassion to put her welfare before his own interests.

He turned round. 'How long is it since your Mama saw Sir Robert?' he asked. 'Has she been back to England since she married your father?'

'No, she hasn't.'

'Then it must be over twenty years. Have they kept in touch?'

'I don't think so. Mama didn't speak of my grandfather much.'

'He'll be an old man now,' Oliver said. 'Things change.'

'Everything will be different upstairs.' Ellie refused to be discouraged. All the same, she couldn't help being truthful over one matter. 'I'm glad you're with me, Oliver.'

'And I shall stay, so I will, until I see things in the light of day.'

It was unnervingly quiet. There was not even

a clock to break the silence so she couldn't tell how long they were kept waiting. The damp feeling in the room was getting into her bones.

At last the butler returned. The knot of his tie was loose, but when he saw her eyes go to it he hastily put it in place.

'Sir Robert has been indisposed for some time, madam, and does not receive visitors,' he said. 'He sends his apologies and has asked me to have a bedroom made ready for you and your husband. Tomorrow he may be a little stronger and feel able to see you.'

Ellie's temper was roused. She stood up and faced the man, who was no taller than herself, and her imperious tone when she spoke was exactly copied from her mother.

'What is your name? I like to know whom I'm addressing.'

'Frobisher, madam.'

'Then, Frobisher, shall we establish something from the start? First of all, I am here to stay—and I want to see my grandfather immediately. I'm sure the state of his health can't be so bad that he won't wish to welcome me. I'm not afraid of a sickroom.'

'Sir Robert...'

'Secondly, this gentleman is not my husband so we shall require separate rooms. Mr Berman was not able to accompany me, after all.'

'Yes, madam.'

'Thank you. Now if you will show me to the room where my grandfather is I shall be much obliged.'

Frobisher bowed courteously, his manner the essence of all that an English butler should be, but she could tell it didn't please him to take orders from her. He tarried still, the back of his hand to his mouth as he cleared his throat.

'Forgive me, Mrs Berman, it isn't that I am unwilling to take you to Sir Robert. The fact is, I think you will be shocked by his ... er ... illness.'

'I'll come with her,' Oliver intervened. 'This lady has had enough shocks for one day.'

There was no sign of any other servants as they followed the butler up the stairs and turned left at the top and along a landing which overlooked the lower hall. Several heavy oak doors led off it, and at the last of these Frobisher stopped and knocked loudly.

'I must ask you to wait,' he said, and went inside, careful to mask any view of the interior. Ellie didn't look at Oliver. She stood facing the door, her teeth gritted to stop the slightest quiver of anxiety from showing, and her hands clutching the baby's shawl so tightly it almost tore. For a moment there was no sound. Then a tremendous bellowing burst forth, like some zoo animal roaring.

'BLAST YOU, MAN, CLEAR TO HELL OUT OF HERE. I DON'T WANT TO SEE ANY BLOODY PEOPLE.'

There was certainly nothing wrong with Sir Robert Cromer's lungs. Nor his fists either. They thumped a hard surface to emphasise each word, and this was followed by the shattering of some glass.

'Begorrah, the man's on the bottle,' said Oliver.

William was frightened by the noise and started crying lustily, at which point Ellie had had enough of waiting. She pushed open the door and marched in, her skirt rustling, her chin thrust forward. The scene which met her eyes was so appalling she recoiled. She had seen nothing worse, nor smelt anything so bad, in the Pullman tenements. Not even the inhabitants of the hovels near the brickyards had lived like this.

The room was obviously used to live and sleep in at all times, and judging by the state of the unmade bed at the farthest side it looked as if the occupant rarely left it. Books and papers were stacked round the walls, bottles littered the floor, and clothes lay where they had been discarded.

The old man half-lying across a table was as disgusting as his surroundings, his white hair matted and his velvet dressing-gown stained with the residue of food and various liquids. He was reed-thin. Claw-like hands gripped a bottle of brandy as if it were a lifeline. His parchment skin was colourless where it stretched across the bones of his forehead, but his nose was a mottled purple and his cheeks a network of broken red blood vessels. If there had ever been anything noble about him it had long since been obliterated by dissipation.

Somehow Ellie managed to regain her composure.

'Grandfather Cromer, your illness is of your

own making,' she said. Shock and anger made her voice shrill. 'How dare you refuse to see me!'

He looked up, his hooded, bloodshot eyes rheumy. For a moment he stared at her, propping himself up on his forearms. Then he began to cry.

'My little Sibyl's come back to me,' he murmured drunkenly.

Tears ran down Ellie's face. Oliver Devlin took the baby, put an arm round her and led her away.

ELEVEN

Annie Hovringham had come to 5 Chesterman Court as a scullerymaid in 1860. In those days there had been more servants than she could remember, and she had been so lowly no one had spoken to her except to give orders. But Annie had worked hard, found favour with the cook, and progressed to parlourmaid within two years. The position of housekeeper had come much later. Now, thirty-four years on, she was all these things put together.

Her marriage to the coachman, the late Albert Hovringham, had not been blessed with children, but the youngest child of Sir Robert Cromer had filled the need, and she had doted on him. Master Julian had been a year old when Annie had been given employment, and she had felt sorry for the little mite whose birth had cost his mother her life. His two sisters, so much older, had not shown him much love, and he had been left in the care of various nannies who rarely stayed longer than a few months. Julian had sought affection like other children craved sweetmeats, and Annie had supplied it wholeheartedly, spoiling him from the first. The boy had spent more time with her and Albert in their room above the stables than ever he'd done in the big house.

In caring so much for Master Julian, Annie had found little time for his sisters. Both had resented the child for robbing them of their mother, but while Beatrice had mostly ignored his existence, Sibylla had made that existence intolerable at every opportunity. It had been hard to forgive her unkindness. Now, when Mr Julian came and helped himself to his father's possessions, Annie closed her eyes and told herself it was the old man and his daughters who were to blame for the way things had turned out.

Now Miss Sibylla's daughter had arrived unannounced while Annie had been out trying to gain a little more credit at the grocer's, and it had fairly taken the wind out of her sails.

When Mr Frobisher had filled her in with details of how Mrs Berman had been so demanding, it had been in keeping with her memories of Miss Sibylla, and she had been prepared to make things difficult in turn. But the young lady had been so overcome when she'd got to the bedroom it had been impossible not to feel sorry for her. That was why Annie had relented and brought her a breakfast tray.

'Good morning, Mrs Berman,' she said. She put the tray down and carefully pulled aside the plum velvet curtains so as not to disturb the dust. 'I trust you slept well.'

'I'm afraid I didn't sleep at all.' The girl looked lost in the enormous bed with dull cream hangings. The baby was beside her, his blue eyes wide and inquisitive. 'I should like a personal maid to see to my clothes, Mrs Hovringham. Can you send someone to me, please.'

Annie came round the bed and placed her hands on her hips. 'Mrs Berman, there's only me and Mr Frobisher to run this house and we only have one pair of hands each. So if you're staying, you'll need to learn how to do things for yourself.' It was going to come hard on her but she might as well know straight away.

Surprisingly there was no show of tantrums. The newcomer looked resigned to anything.

'Never mind,' she said. 'I'm not helpless. In fact, I probably know more about hard times than you.' She pushed back the bedcovers, swung her feet to the floor, and padded to the table where the tray had been deposited. 'Thank you for bringing my breakfast. I prefer coffee to tea, but tomorrow I'll be down in the kitchen to make it myself.'

The morning was bright, which was a mixed blessing since it showed up the shabbiness of the room. Mrs Berman was caught in the shaft of sunlight which made her look pale and fragile, but that was probably due to tiredness after her

223

long journey, and the lack of welcome she'd received at the end of it. She was certainly not behaving in a helpless fashion. Annie was intrigued.

'Surely Miss Sibylla made a very good marriage. Mr Harvey was always a very ambitious gentleman.'

'My parents are among the wealthiest people in Chicago,' said the girl. 'My husband is one of the poorest, or he was until he made off with my dowry yesterday. He's deserted me.' She poured tea and sipped from the Dresden cup, one of the few that remained. 'I'm telling you this from the beginning so that there's no need for any falsehood.'

The disclosure was so unexpected it robbed Annie of words. She said, 'Oh!' on a startled breath, and remained rooted to the spot. This was like one of the melodramas in the novelettes she read avidly to lift her depression. How could anyone speak so brazenly of such shame? She longed to know more, but was forestalled.

'And now,' the deserted wife went on, 'I want to know how things have got into this dreadful state. My mother would be horrified if she knew.'

'Your mother has never cared.'

'She wrote to my grandfather to say I was coming—did he not tell you?'

'Sir Robert has little idea of what goes on around him these days, as I'm sure you'll understand now you've seen him. If there was a letter I doubt if it was opened.' The baby started to whimper and Annie was drawn to him. 'He's a beautiful child. May I hold him?'

'Of course.'

The first bond was forged. Truth to tell, it was good to have another woman in the house, Annie thought, and it seemed as if the situation was going to turn out different from what she had feared. There was a mystery to be unravelled for a start—and that promised to liven things up. Then there was the child... Annie picked up the warm baby and held him against her ample bosom, revelling in the feel of his small body and the milky smell of his breath.

'How could any man leave a mite like this?' she murmured.

'I've been tormented by the same question all night.'

'I'm very sorry.'

'Yesterday I had every intention of leaving this house before I'd been in it an hour. I was horrified, truly horrified. It was Mr Devlin who reminded me that I'm penniless and in a foreign country so I have no option but to stay for the present. Mr Devlin is my husband's brother-in-law and having come to my rescue at the dockside he kindly insisted on seeing me safely to London. What he must think I just don't know.'

'He's down in the kitchen, ma'am, eating breakfast, and I don't think he's too shocked or unhappy.'

'I must see him before he departs.'

'Yes, Mrs Berman.'

'Perhaps you should call me Miss Elena,'

said the girl. 'I've taken a great dislike to my husband's name.'

Shouting commenced along the corridor. Annie sighed and handed the baby back, yet her heart was not quite so heavy as it had been at the same hour yesterday.

She spoke evenly. 'Master's awake, Miss Elena. There'll be no peace now till he's drunk himself into the next stupor. Come down to the kitchen when you're dressed and I'll have a bowl of warm water ready to bathe the little one.'

When the woman had gone Ellie took William over to the window and looked out. Once there might have been a glimpse of Hyde Park; now there was only a view of more grand buildings which must have been erected since Mama's day.

'What we have to remember, my darling, is that we're living in Chesterman Court for the moment, not Fulton Street, even though there seems little difference.' She kissed the top of the baby's head and let him look down at a passing carriage and pair. Then she pressed her cheek urgently against his infant face. 'Oh William, what *are* we going to do?'

The night had seemed neverending. Through the long, sleepless hours Ellie's emotions had ranged from darkest despair and disbelief to repressed anger, and she had tossed around on the pillow until her head hurt. Coming on top of her suffering and humiliation over Max, the discovery of her grandfather's condition had actually caused little pain at all. She had been too numb to feel the full impact. It was as if, deep down, she had known that the high expectations she had carried euphorically across the Atlantic were bound to be false, and that after losing Max nothing would go right. Now, in the light of a new day, many grievous problems had to be faced.

There was nothing she could do about Max, no matter how much she fumed and fretted. Having had him on her mind all night it was now time to let the torment rest and think about her future. She wouldn't be staying here longer than was absolutely necessary, of course, but she could see no immediate alternative until she had made some investigations. Planning the best course of action would be good therapy.

First of all she had to make Sir Robert Cromer understand that she was his granddaughter and not his 'dear Sibyl'. It would have been a waste of time pressing the matter last evening, even if she had felt up to it, and after a few minutes she had left him to his pathetic ramblings. Today, however, it would be interesting to discover the reason for his inebriated state. The house couldn't have become so run-down, nor its owner so degraded, without there being some primary cause.

'He's a dreadful old man, William,' Ellie said aloud, 'but he's my grandfather, and your great-grandfather, so I guess we'll have to put up with him until we can do something about it.' Her son gurgled and smiled as if there was nothing wrong, and his innocence brought a lump to her throat. She hugged him tighter. 'I don't think I'll ever trust a man again after what your father's done to us.' Then: *'You'll* never let me down, will you, my darling?'

Downstairs, Annie Hovringham relieved her of the baby while Ellie went to the dining-room. Here at least there were a few signs of former glory, though again, various shapes on the walls denoted the removal of pictures. The long table had fourteen chairs round it, six along each side and at each end, one with arms. Oliver Devlin sat at the head of the table, eating a cooked breakfast.

'Will you be having some?' he asked, without getting up. He indicated the sideboard behind him. 'There's more under the silver cover.'

'I've had mine,' she said. 'What time are you leaving?'

'I'll not be going until you ask me to. I'm thinking you'll need a friendly face around for a while and I've no definite plans.'

'Thank you. It won't be for long. I'm going to find out where my Uncle Julian and Aunt Beatrice live—one of them will surely take me in.'

'Now that sounds sensible.' He wiped his mouth on a napkin. 'Will you be occupied this morning, only I've a few bits of business to attend to in the city.'

'Please do whatever you want.'

Ellie left him to finish his meal. She was grateful for his support but didn't want him to feel obliged to be with her every minute of the day. Besides, she had things she wanted to do herself.

She found the kitchen. Mrs Hovringham

looked in her element letting William splash his feet in a china wash-stand bowl in front of the fire. A towel covered her lap, and she held his chubby body round the middle with capable hands which would give him confidence. William found it the greatest fun. He was laughing the way he had done the last time Hedda Berman had bathed him, and seeing it Ellie experienced a wave of homesickness which had to be hastily thrust aside.

'It's a long time since I did this,' the woman said. 'But you never forget the knack.'

'Mrs Hovringham, what does my grandfather have for breakfast? I'd like to take it up to him.'

'Bless you, he never eats anything.'

'Then he will today.'

'Mr Frobisher always goes up to him in the morning. He washes and shaves him.'

'But doesn't take him anything to eat. I shall see to it that he gets something this morning.'

Annie Hovringham looked horrified. 'It wouldn't be wise to try. Likely he'll throw something at you.'

'It's all right, I'm not afraid of him.'

A few minutes later, after further remonstrations from the housekeeper, Ellie was once more at the door of the lion's den, steadily holding a tray appetisingly arranged with a bowl of steaming porridge, a folded napkin, and a glass of freshly squeezed orange juice. If she wanted to get any sense out of the old man she knew from hearing some of the Pullman women talk

229

about drunken husbands that it had to be early in the day.

She listened for a moment, but there was no sound so she knocked loudly and went in. Mr Frobisher wasn't there, but had obviously left only recently. Grandfather Cromer was in bed, his head back against the stacked pillows, his face cleanshaven and his eyes shut.

'Good morning, Grandfather,' Ellie said, approaching the bed. His eyes flicked open They were bright blue like her own. 'I've brought you some food and I'm going to sit here while you eat it.'

He didn't look as bad as he had done last night. There was something pathetic about the bony shoulders hunched in a striped nightshirt, and his hands fluttered on the sheet like birds frightened to settle.

'Sibyl, I'm so glad you've come home. You must have known I needed you,' he said, in a normal voice.

'I'm not Sibyl. I'm Ellie, Sibyl's daughter.'

'You haven't changed, girl. Does that Yankee treat you well?'

'I want you to eat some porridge, Grandfather.' Ellie sat on the edge of the bed and put the tray across his lap, keeping hold of the handles in case he decided to swipe it to the floor, but he merely stared at it blankly. She plucked up courage and put a small spoonful to his mouth. 'This is what you need to make you strong again.'

He meekly swallowed the first offering. The second he spat out. 'I don't want that filthy stuff. Get me brandy.'

'You're not having brandy until you've eaten every bit of this,' she said, undiscouraged.

'Damn you, Sibyl, you know I hate porridge.'

'Then what do you like? I'll bring you something else but you must eat it. How long have you been living like this?'

'Since Beatrice died,' he said. 'She looked after me when you'd gone.'

He was lost in memories for several minutes, during which time Ellie popped in several more spoonfuls without him objecting. It was like feeding a child. And she was equally preoccupied, having learnt that one of her considered options could come to nothing as there was no longer an Aunt Beatrice. Clearly her mother knew nothing of her sister's death or she would have mentioned it. The news made Ellie a little more sympathetic towards the old man. It must have been a terrible shock to him and could account for his reliance on drink.

She saw the need to humour him if she wanted his cooperation. 'And where is Julian these days?' she asked, as if talking of a brother rather than an uncle.

The effect of his son's name was fearful. Grandfather Cromer's knees shot up, spilling the orange juice, and he pushed Ellie away with such strength she landed on the floor beside the bed. He looked down at her, hawk-eyed, and prodded the air with a claw-like index finger.

'Don't ever mention your brother's name again. Don't you know how he's treated me? He's taken everything—*everything!* And he only

231

comes here to bleed me to death so that he can have the house as well.'

Ellie scrambled up, by which time Grandfather Cromer was lying back again on the pillows with his eyes shut, as if exhausted. She was so taken aback by the onslaught it took a moment to get her breath, and she was furious.

'I don't wonder your family all left you if this is the way you treated them,' she stormed. 'I was trying to show you a little kindness.'

'You came here thinking I had money. Well, I haven't any!'

'So you *do* know I'm not Sibyl.'

'I'm not senile.'

'And I'm not a gold-digger. What I'd hoped for was some affection and comfort but you're obviously not capable of giving either. Goodbye, Grandfather.'

She took her skirt and smoothed it, then marched towards the door with her head tilted so as to stem the threatened tears. The old devil could live in this squalor for the rest of his life and grow more and more sour on his grievances. She need have nothing to do with him.

But Uncle Julian was not likely to help her either. Well, she was glad she knew so that she was saved the embarrassment of approaching him. Unfortunately, that left her with only Oliver Devlin but he was infinitely preferable to anyone she'd come across yet in this country.

She was turning the flowered porcelain doorknob when her grandfather called her.

'Don't go,' he pleaded. She turned to see him with his feet over the side of the bed

232

as he struggled to stand. 'Why do you need comfort?'

'Yesterday my husband left me.'

'I'm not surprised. You're the most bullying female I've ever met.'

'And you're a rude, ungrateful old man.' Her words were harsh, but tears filled her eyes. She dashed them away hurriedly, but not before he'd noticed.

'I didn't mean to be so wretched.' She got a surprisingly half-apology. 'What did you say your name is?'

'Ellie.'

'Have you got any money?'

'No, my husband took it.'

'Then what the hell's the use of you staying here? I've not got enough to feed myself, never mind you.'

'I'm not asking you for any. And you could afford to feed yourself better if you didn't waste so much money on brandy. It's killing you.'

'I please myself what I do.'

'So it's no use trying to help you. I've got enough problems of my own without taking on yours.'

'Get out of my house then.'

They faced each other with hostility, continuing to shout cruel words which could not be retracted. And then they stopped. Ellie saw his eyes shining with emotional tears which he would hold in check as fiercely as she was doing. Deeper than that she saw his unvoiced cry for deliverance from the enemy which gripped his thin body and ruled his life. He needed her as no one else had ever done; not Papa or Mama or Drew; certainly not Max. He was as helpless as William, and she was turning her back on him.

The silence was profound for several seconds. Then: 'You're the first person who's cared anything about me in years,' he quavered. 'Don't go.'

She was slow to answer. He was too unpredictable to be trusted. 'If I stay I shall make you eat porridge.'

'It'll make me sick.'

'What *do* you like then?'

'Onion soup,' he said. 'For breakfast.'

Her lips quivered at the humour. 'All right. I make a very good onion soup.'

She went to the tall, gaunt man in his nightshirt, and kissed his cheek. He was trembling. Arms which were unaccustomed to holding another closed round her, and they stood together, drawing strength from each other.

'You'll stay then?' he asked anxiously.

'Yes, Grandfather,' she said. 'I'll stay.'

'It's a mistake you're making,' said Oliver, when he heard of her decision to remain at Chesterman Court.

It was evening and the fire burning in the drawing room did nothing more than provide an occasional flame. There was no warmth in it, nor any cheer, and September seemed like midwinter in the chill house.

'What choice have I got?' asked Ellie. 'Julian Cromer sounds cruel and insensitive, and I doubt if he'll want to know me. Aunt Beatrice is dead, and my grandfather needs someone to look after him. I'm going to break him of his dependence on alcohol.'

'You'll never do it.'

'I will. He's already promised he'll give it up if I stay.'

'A drunk will promise anything. Oh, he might make an effort right enough, but if you threaten to leave he'll blackmail you with talk of taking to drink again. You'll be tied to him, so you will, and that's no life for a girl like you.'

She sighed. 'Then tell me the alternative.'

Oliver poked the meagre blaze and the soot-covered fireback became studded with glowing red sparks.

'You can take your chance with me,' he said. 'I can offer you better than this.'

The sparks glittered like jewels, then one by one died out.

'It's kind of you, but I think not.'

'There's been no chance to tell you that my dear old mother died while I was in Ireland. I was blessed with being able to see her at the last.'

Ellie's warm heart went out to him at once. 'Oh Oliver, I'm sorry.' She touched his hand. 'And here am I burdening you with my troubles when you've enough of your own.'

'She left me her money. I'm a wealthy man, Ellie. I'll be more than happy to look after you, so I will.'

'I won't go back to America.' She emphasised it. 'I won't. And I can't keep you here. You

235

must be longing to get home to Galina. I haven't told you that she's the most beautiful child.'

His expression changed, as if a cloud passed over his sunny nature. He looked down, his spirits dampened by sadness at the mention of his daughter, and Ellie understood him better than she could have done a short time ago.

'I can't see Galina,' he said. 'It's why I went to Ireland. She reminds me too much of Katrina.'

'But surely that's good?'

'To some it would be. To me it's unbearable.'

They talked intimately for a while, the consolation of shared confidences washing over them, but Ellie knew that this was a friendship of convenience and she couldn't impose on him any more.

Presently Frobisher announced that dinner was ready.

'Does Sir Robert come down for dinner?' Ellie asked.

'No, madam. I take it to his room.'

'Then please take mine there as well. I'll be eating with him.'

'Very good, madam.' The man's training guaranteed no show of surprise, but a slight sniff betrayed his disapproval.

Her grandfather had been drinking again, but he was not in the dire state of the previous evening. To her surprise he was dressed, and she saw that he had once been a distinguished man, even though his clothes were old and hung loosely on his emaciated figure. He was sitting at the table in a high-backed chair, a decanter and glass beside him.

'Where have you been?' he demanded. 'I've been waiting for you.'

'I thought we'd eat together as Oliver is out tonight,' she said, sitting next to him. 'In a few days I shall expect you to come down to the dining room.'

Frobisher had followed her in. He placed the tray in front of her, flicked a damask napkin out of its folds and tucked one corner in the buttonhole of Grandfather Cromer's lapel.

'The young lady insists, sir.'

The dinner was roast duck. Ellie felt no more like eating than he did, but in coaxing him she found a small appetite herself, and though it took a long time the two plates were cleared. While they ate she asked him questions. She found out that Aunt Beatrice had died of consumption five years earlier, and that her death had left him heartbroken.

'Bea was a good daughter,' he said. 'She stayed by me, which was more than Sibyl did. Sibyl never forgave me for not being a gentleman. Called herself "Sibylla".' He put on a different accent to mimic Mama's airs and graces. Ellie laughed at the accuracy. 'When that Yankee came along she couldn't get away fast enough.'

Tales of her mother went on until the next course came.

'Now tell me about my Uncle Julian. Where does he live?'

'Southampton.'

The very name of the place made Ellie shudder, and Grandfather Cromer's monosyllabic answer hung in the air waiting for modification. None came.

She continued to probe. 'What does he do?'

'Do? DO? Julian gets fat on my money, that's what he does. Him and his prissy little wife and precocious brats.'

'He went into the business you started, then. Surely you must have been pleased about that?'

'My son would never have lasted five minutes in my business. He hasn't got the guts.' He made to pour himself another drink, but Ellie moved the decanter just out of reach. 'Give me that damned brandy.'

'When you've finished your dinner you can have it—but not to get drunk on.'

'I'll do what I like.'

'Not if I'm here to look after you. Now tell me more about Julian.'

'You're an interfering, nosy creature.'

The old man was obstinate, but after a while she was able to piece together the reason for his antipathy, and the more she heard the more she was inclined to think he had every right to feel the way he did.

Sir Robert Cromer had made his fortune by taking risks which would have made lesser men quail. He had become a contractor at a time when the railway industry was at its height and he had employed so many men he'd lost count. On one deal alone he had made enough money to buy this house and furnish it like a palace.

'I suppose I behaved badly,' he chortled. 'On

238

that one deal I put in a tender for seventeen thousand pounds, then thought I'd round it up to twenty.'

'You're a wicked old scoundrel.'

'That wasn't all. Overnight I decided the job was worth double that, so next day to be on the safe side I doubled it again. Would you believe I finally got eighty thousand for that contract? Those were the days, right enough!'

'How could you do it?' said Ellie.

'The laugh was I hadn't a penny in the bank when the contract was signed. It was all bluff, but it paid off.' He stabbed a piece of meat with the point of his knife. 'Julian had everything on a plate.'

'Is he connected with railroads too?'

'Owns a company building rolling-stock— Court Carriage Works.'

'Where?'

'Southampton, where else? The company belonged to that sanctimonious Millicent's father, and Julian stepped right in.'

Bit by bit Ellie pieced together a picture of her mother's brother, and it was not pleasing. Money had been lavished on him as a child; nothing denied him as he grew up and went to public school. He had taken wealth for granted, and when contracting became less lucrative, he'd had no good word to say for his father. Sir Robert Cromer had always run his business from 5 Chesterman Court with hardly any books, relying mainly on his retentive memory, so the only way Julian could learn to carry on in the same line would have been by word of mouth, and for that he'd had no patience or interest. By 1880, when he came of age, the great railways of Britain were mostly completed and there remained only smaller projects for which to contract. It was the end of an era, but Julian had seen it as the personal fall of a man for whom he'd always had scant respect, and the subtle persuasion had begun.

He'd met Peter Farling one January day at Cannon Street Hotel, the financial meeting place for everyone connected in any way with the railways, and he had discovered that he was the founder of the largest rolling-stock building company in the south. Peter Farling also had a beloved only child called Millicent who would inherit everything, and Julian had seized his opportunity. An introduction to Millicent had led swiftly to marriage, and following the sudden death of her father two years later, he had become joint owner of the Court Carriage Works in Southampton, only to discover that it was not financially sound. Large sums of money had been needed to keep it going, and when he could no longer rely on his father's generosity he had taken to acquiring funds from the sale of priceless paintings and anything else he could pilfer from his father's house.

'I gave that boy everything,' Grandfather Cromer said bitterly, 'wealth and education, a position in life—and how has he repaid me? I'll tell you how. He despises me because I'm self-made, and he hasn't been near me for months now there's nothing left worth taking to line his pockets. He's ashamed of my poor

240

background—my own son! Peter Farling had breeding so it was no sin he let his business slide but because I made money when I could hardly read or write, *I'm* dross. That's what he thinks of me.'

Ellie reached out and covered the gnarled hand with her own. 'Well, I don't think you are, Grandfather, and I'm going to look after you.'

She welcomed the challenge. It would save her sanity by helping to take her mind off Max.

Although Oliver went to stay in an hotel after the first few days, he came regularly to Chesterman Court to check on Ellie's situation and she was glad of his support. He was kind and humorous, and concerned about her, which was a comfort. She needed all the help she could get to cope with the ever-changing moods of her alcoholic relative, and it was good to know Oliver was there in the background to give encouragement and light relief. He took her out sightseeing while Mrs Hovringham looked after William, and he made himself endearing in countless ways. Ellie didn't know what she would have done without him.

At the end of the first week she wrote to her mother.

'*My dear Mama,*' she began. '*You sent me into a lion's den. The state of your papa and his household would shock you beyond measure, but I am staying to try and bring a little order out of the chaos. Your brother Julian, whom I have not yet met, has practically bankrupted your father and left him to exist with barely enough money for*

241

the next bottle of brandy. The treasures are gone from the house, along with all the servants except Frobisher and Mrs Hovringham. I know you shared Uncle Julian's opinion of Grandfather Cromer, but if you could see him now you would surely weep with pity.

'*I must tell you, Mama, that I have been deserted by my husband. I doubt if he will show his face in Chicago, but should he do so and you happen to see him I trust you will say nothing of my life here. I don't intend to return to America. I couldn't face the scorn of my friends at the failure of my impetuous marriage. You and Papa were right to try to discourage me. I should have listened, but it is too late now, and I am needed by my grandfather.*

'*William is thriving. Give my love to Papa, if he will accept it, to Drew and Clarissa, Lionel and Jefferson. I miss you all.*

'*Your ever-loving daughter, Elena.'*

She said nothing about the money with which Max had absconded. It was shameful enough having to admit she couldn't keep a husband, and if her parents knew she had also been left penniless they were likely to call in the American Consul. They would urge her to return home, and Papa wouldn't rest until Max was caught and prosecuted. That could mean coming face to face with her husband again, and Ellie went cold at the prospect.

Max would be back in America now. Where would he head for, with his stolen wealth? Every nerve was raw as she tried to fathom a reason for what he had done, and she suffered continual agony. It was like trying to penetrate a solid wall. No matter how hard she tried there was no answer, not a single factor which could in part exonerate him, and she had to admit that she had loved a heartless villain. In the depths of her soul it was hard to come to terms with such a terrible truth, but it couldn't be denied. He was an abomination.

Her bitterness grew daily as she tried to reconcile herself to a lonely future. She was well rid of him, and she prayed to be spared any further contact; prayed he had gone forever. She wanted neither sight nor sound of him ever again.

With these emotions consuming her it was understandable that when a letter arrived from her husband at the start of her third week in London she threw it straight into the fire unopened.

Thanks to Ellie's care, Grandfather Cromer's health began to improve, and by the beginning of October she had managed to coax him downstairs to the drawing room in the evenings. However his battle with the bottle was far from won. With great difficulty she had restricted his intake of alcohol considerably, but his moods could be unbearable. Sometimes he became aggressive, at others maudlin, and he was too preoccupied with his own misery to show any curiosity about the life of his grand-daughter.

William contributed greatly towards his improvement. From the moment Ellie had put the baby into the old man's arms, Sir Robert seemed to take a new hold on life.

'This is your great-grandson,' Ellie told him. 'He's going to be someone important one day but he'll never achieve anything without a good man to influence him, and right now there's only you to fill that role.'

She had told him about Max but couldn't be sure whether he understood what had happened. He never questioned her presence in his house, or showed any curiosity about her disastrous marriage. But William became the pivot of his existence.

'He's a fine boy.' The baby gurgled and squirmed in the sinewy arms, smiling at the old rogue as if there was a conspiracy between them. 'But it's the school of life he'll be learning from if he stays here. I've no money to educate him like I did Julian.'

'Things will get better, Grandfather.'

'It'll take a miracle.'

She didn't believe him, but as the days went on she became aware of tension in the kitchen and a reduction in the standard of living. Meals were becoming so plain they were little better than the ones she had cooked in Pullman before the strike had reduced them to bread and potatoes, and twice she heard Annie Hovringham having words with a tradesman at the door.

'Mrs Hovringham, I wonder if I might see the household accounts, please,' Ellie said, after the second occasion. The woman was reluctant, but Ellie insisted. 'My grandfather is incapable of managing his affairs at the moment, but if

I think it necessary to speak to the bank for more money then I can persuade him.'

'I doubt the bank will help you.'

'Things can't be that bad.'

'They couldn't be much worse, Miss Elena. If any more bills come in we could paper the kitchen wall with 'em.'

Ellie was horrified to learn that neither Mrs Hovringham nor Mr Frobisher had been paid for two months, and it was only their loyalty to Sir Robert that had kept them from finding other employment. Added to this was the drastic rise in the pile of unpaid bills and the fact that tradesmen were threatening to cease delivering.

'Something's definitely got to be done,' Ellie said. 'Sir Robert *must* be made to understand the situation. I'll speak to him today.'

That evening, for the first time since she had been there, Grandfather Cromer was found in the study adjoining the drawing room, sitting at an oak desk covered in papers. She approached him boldly and tackled the problem from the angle which would affect him most.

'Grandfather, there is only one more bottle of brandy left in the cupboard. When it's gone there won't be another. We've no money.'

He didn't lift his head. The mountain of letters and bills hid the green leather top of the desk, and when he thumped both fists into the middle of the pile they scattered everywhere.

'Do they have brandy in the debtors' prison?'

'I'm sure they don't.'

'Then I'd better get used to water because that's where I'm heading. You'd have been better off not coming here, girl.'

The following day the bailiffs arrived.

TWELVE

Oliver Devlin didn't tell Ellie that he was going to Southampton. First he wanted to see for himself the calibre of Julian Cromer. The supporting of Sir Robert Cromer, now that he had been evicted from his home in Chesterman Court, was his son's responsibility, and he had to be made aware of it. Oliver had found temporary accommodation for them all in Clerkenwell, paying the rent for it himself, but it was no good waiting until the Chesterman Court house was sold to see if there would be anything left to live on.

'You're the most generous man I have ever met, Oliver,' Ellie told him emotionally, clinging to his hand. 'We'll see that every cent of your money's repaid, you know we will.'

'And how will you be doing that? The old man's debts are colossal. I doubt there'll be a brass farthing left after settling the bills.' The feel of her fingers curling round his drove the Irishman wild with longing. He disengaged them. 'Your uncle should be told.'

'Grandfather's forbidden me to get in touch with him. You know how proud he is.'

246

'What alternative is there?'

'I'll write again to Mama,' she said.

'And that will take time. My money won't last forever.'

'Oh Oliver, I hate having to use it at all. You're doing so much for us.'

The tall Clerkenwell house was sparsely furnished, but Oliver felt warmer here than he had ever done in Chesterman Court. It was not only physical warmth. Ellie's gratitude and her nearness had as much to do with it.

'It's for you I'm doing it, mavourneen,' he said. 'No one else.'

Two days later, in late October, he was travelling down to the coast by train from London, this time in a second-class carriage. He was impressively dressed in a city suit, his sandy hair oiled smooth and covered with a bowler hat set at an elegant angle. His shoes gleamed from polishing, and his reflection in the carriage window pleased him so much that he repeatedly glanced at it, on the pretext of admiring the scenery. He was a man of many parts, none of them irredeemably wicked, but all geared to improving the lot of Oliver Seamus Devlin, who had started life in a mud-and-wattle dwelling on the edge of a field in County Cork. Today he intended to be seen as the advocate for Sir Robert Cromer and his grand-daughter, Mrs Elena Berman, and he wouldn't be allowing any excuses to let Julian Cromer escape his duty.

His concern for Ellie was the most genuine thing about him. He daren't even let himself think where his feelings for her were leading. She bewitched him. Ever since he had called at the tenement in Pullman he had been unable to get her off his mind. The fortuitous meeting with Max on the dockside at Southampton had been quite amazing. Every time he thought about it he couldn't believe his luck, and he blessed the saints who had put the right words into his mouth to persuade his brother-in-law to head back to America alone. The fool had actually trusted him with more money than Oliver had ever dreamed of holding, and it had only taken a second to decide that it would go into no pocket but his own. Ellie, to all intents and purposes, had been on her way to relatives richer than the family she had left behind and wouldn't need it, and Max would be too far away to find out where it had gone.

But what a disastrous turn things had taken. He would never forget Ellie's face when she'd discovered the appalling mess which had greeted her in London. His privation-hardened heart had almost melted with pity. It wasn't fair of Fate to be so hard on one person and he had never admired anybody more than Ellie Berman for the way she had handled the situation. He didn't think he could have been so strong himself.

The crux of the matter lay in Ellie's totally unexpected need of the money Max had left her, but without incriminating himself there'd been no way of returning what was rightfully hers. He couldn't produce it from his pocket and say, 'Oh, by the way, Max gave me this to give to you.' She would know by the delay that he had intended to keep it. The only solution had been to use it for her benefit, and that had led to enormous expenditure in the last few weeks which had to be stopped or there would be nothing left. Oh, it had raised Ellie's opinion of him a hundredfold. Her gratitude was sweet and he wallowed in it, dreading to think what would happen if she were there to discover his poor old mother had actually died in the workhouse. He didn't think he could bear it if she were ever to find out the enormity of his deception.

His thoughts turned guiltily to Katrina, the wife he had loved and so tragically lost. Katrina wouldn't have approved at all. He had met her through a Jewish friend who had invited him to some celebrations during a Shavuot festival. She'd been sweet and gentle, possessing all the attributes lacking in the women he had previously known, and he'd been irresistibly drawn to her. It had meant pretending great piety to win her, but it hadn't been difficult. Her influence had made him a better man. How sad she would be, to know he had slipped back into the old ways...

The railway carriage jolted and swayed at speed, causing Oliver's stomach to revolt, but the feeling of sickness was more to do with his emotions. He wished Ellie was sitting opposite so that he could feast his eyes on her exquisite face. Max must have been out of his mind to leave such an adorable creature, but Max's stupidity was going to be Oliver's gain.

He loved Ellie; she had now taken Katrina's

place in his heart. He wanted her esteem. He wanted her body. She was still too mentally bruised to be rushed into anything, so he had cultivated a brotherly attitude that wouldn't frighten her, and hoped she would soon see him in a different light.

He was glad when he arrived. The *boom-boom-boom* of the wheels had oscillated in his ears. To his surprise he discovered that his destination was within walking distance of West Station. As the train came out of the tunnel at the west end of Southampton he looked out to his left and saw a collection of workshops grouped around a square white office building of two storeys which had COURT CARRIAGE WORKS emblazoned in large brass letters between the ground and first-floor windows. Had he noticed it previously, it would have meant nothing. Now it set his nerves tingling.

The autumn day was bright and warm. Sun glinted on Southampton Water and waves lapped up to the Western Shore alongside the railway line where a small crowd was watching corporation horses bathing up to their bellies. The light had that golden tinge so typical of England in autumn, and industrial buildings were reflected in the calm water further along the bay. Within minutes Oliver was alighting at the station, and in spite of the short distance he had to go he hired a hansom. He needed to make a good impression.

Judging by Pullman standards the office building was not large, but the inside reception area amazed Oliver. There was every sign

250

of luxury, from the marble floor to the chandelier and plush furnishings. It was more like an hotel.

No wonder 'Uncle Julian' also had financial difficulties, Oliver mused.

Gilt-framed photographs on the walls showed distinguished-looking people in royal regalia; among them, Oliver recognised the Prince and Princess of Wales. Others looked foreign. Above the oak reception desk hung a painting of a royal train arriving at Kings Cross station, and there were several other pictures showing the interiors of rail-coaches, more elaborate even than anything George Pullman had yet designed.

A clerk in black trousers and frockcoat appeared from a side room. He had a carnation in his buttonhole.

'May I be of service?' he asked.

Oliver removed his hat. 'I've come to see Mr Julian Cromer.'

'Ah yes, we're expecting you, sir. May I say what a pleasure it is to welcome you to Court Carriages.'

'But...'

'I regret that Mr Cromer has been unavoidably delayed. He sends his abject apologies and has asked me to see that you are looked after by our senior manager, Mr Wilkinson. Would you care to step this way?'

Oliver raised his eyebrows in surprise and did as he was told. There was obviously a mistake, but it could prove useful.

He followed the clerk from the office building

and across a rail siding leading to the main line where a locomotive crouched in an open-fronted shed in readiness for harnessing to repaired or completed cars. In the timberyard, mahogany logs were stacked up everywhere in readiness for making panels, and there were strips of oak in all shapes and sizes.

'We let the wood season for three years here,' the clerk said conversationally. 'Of course, being so near the docks is ideal for receiving imports of teak which we use in great quantity, and we're experimenting with Padouk wood from South Australia. Have you had experience of it?'

'Er ... no,' said Oliver. 'I'm more familiar with the use of steel. How close are you to a foundry?'

'I'm afraid steel frames have to be sent down to us from Crewe, but it isn't a great problem, I assure you.'

'And how many shops are there here?'

'Twenty, sir. Over seven thousand vehicles pass through these shops each year for repair, and then there are the special cars which are a feature of our company. Mr Wilkinson will be in the body shop, I imagine.'

Inside the shop where a fifty-foot carriage was under construction, the clerk again aired his knowledge. 'You'll recognise the cantrails of this model are oak, and yellow deal is being used for the roof and floor and partitions. We strengthen the outside mahogany panels with a strong canvas glue, which you can probably smell. Not too nice, I'm afraid.'

Oliver was intensely interested. He had held

a good position at Pullman, being in charge of the fitting shop there until Katrina's death, so he made keen comparisons, and approved of what he saw. The car body had curved ribs of channel steel spanning the roof, and this was to be a corridor coach in the latest style.

'How many coats of paint does the wood receive?' he asked.

'Let me see... There are three coats of white priming, four to fill up and one of red stain. Then there are three coats of lead, one of Kremnitz white, one enamel, and three of varnish. That makes sixteen. On the chocolate body it's slightly different. We use carmine, and that's very expensive.'

'You know all about the job, Mr ... er...' The smell of the varnish caught in Oliver's throat, but it was a heady reminder of Pullman and he felt a momentary tug of nostalgia.

'Carew, sir. Thomas Carew. I'm only just learning, but I want to know everything so I can rise to management.'

'A man after my own heart, so you are.'

'I'm so sorry, I don't know where Mr Wilkinson can be.' Thomas Carew was becoming agitated. 'I'm afraid you arrived a little earlier than we expected. Perhaps the upholstery department... There's a lady there Mr Wilkinson rather admires.'

Oliver smiled. The young man might be quick at learning construction details but he urgently needed lessons in diplomacy.

The high-ceilinged body shop echoed with the sound of hammers, but for a company with such

253

potential there didn't seem to be enough going on. It needed someone like George Pullman to come along and get things moving. The men doing the hammering worked in a desultory fashion and seemed to have no motivation.

'You know, of course, that some of our customers are the highest ranking nobility,' the clerk said, with a certain awe.

'Very impressive,' said Oliver. 'Are your books full?'

'That's something you must discuss with Mr Cromer, sir.' The young man's boyish shoulders rounded with deference to Oliver, who enjoyed the fawning. It gave him a feeling of power. 'You'll not regret buying into this business, sir. It is truly an expanding company. We receive orders from European royalty all the time, and there is talk of an Eastern gentleman, a Sultan, I believe...'

'I think you're under a misapprehension,' Oliver interrupted.

At that moment a tall man with receding fair hair strode into the workshop, immaculately dressed in a grey suit of the finest cloth with every crease pressed to perfection. A diamond pin held a black cravat in place, and the gold watch-chain across his waistcoat weighed enough to have graced one of the royal personages pictured in the reception office. He had a high forehead and a silken beard lightly covering his deep chin, giving his face an elongated appearance. As he approached them he was obviously trying to conceal anger.

'Mr Carew, just what do you think you're

doing, bringing Mr Kendall into the workshops?' he demanded of the clerk. His eyes were as grey as his suit, and ice-cold.

'But sir, you asked me to find Mr Wilkinson to look after him!'

'In the comfort of the reception office. Return to your work at once and I will speak to you later.' He turned to Oliver, his mouth expanding into a tight smile. 'My dear Mr Kendall, I do apologise for the inefficiency of a very new clerk, I'm sure you understand how difficult it is to get good staff these days. Allow me to introduce myself. I'm Julian Cromer.'

'I found your Mr Carew very helpful,' said Oliver. 'It would have been better, however, if he had asked my name beforehand. I'm not Mr Kendall, so I'm not.'

'Not...'

'No, sir.'

'Then please explain who you are and why you're here.' Julian Cromer's gracious expression slipped. 'If you're an industrial spy for the opposition in Eastleigh I'd be obliged if you'll leave now before I have you forcibly removed.'

'My name's Oliver Devlin and I'm here on behalf of your niece, Mrs Elena Berman. Is there somewhere we can talk in private?'

The fair eyebrows rose, the smile again in place. 'Elena,' he said, letting her name linger as if with affection. 'I had heard, of course, that she is staying with my father.'

'Had you heard also that Sir Robert has been evicted from Chesterman Court? If so, I feel you could have shown some concern. There is too

255

much to discuss standing here. Do you have a personal office?'

The man inclined his head. 'Forgive me, of course we must talk privately. And what is your relationship to my niece, Mr Devlin?'

'I am brother-in-law to Mrs Berman and financial adviser in her present straitened circumstances.'

'I trust you are not looking to me for financial help. Perhaps she should have stayed in America.'

'That's as may be.'

Julian Cromer indeed had an office. It was more like a salon in an exclusive club, the bookcases filled with leather-bound volumes, the paintings rare and beautiful, the floor richly carpeted. He invited Oliver to sit on the chesterfield while he took the high-backed leather armchair himself which had been strategically placed so that sunlight played on his face and shoulders, making his grey eyes more penetrating. The dark background accentuated the lightness of his appearance and gave him a strangely menacing air.

'Now, Mr Devlin, let me assure you I had no idea my father had come to such a pass. Why was I not told? Has my niece got through what was left of his money in the short time she has been living off him?'

Oliver was not intimidated. 'The old man drank away his fortune, as I'm sure you know. Ellie has saved his life. And with my own money I've re-housed him, so I have, after the bailiffs laid claim to everything. But I need

256

reimbursement now, and the responsibility is yours, not mine.'

'If I could afford to support my father, do you think I would be looking for an injection of money into my business?' Julian Cromer's fingers clawed at his knees. He had spoken hastily, almost to himself, and a nerve twitched at the corner of his mouth.

Oliver cast his eyes round. 'You've some beautiful paintings here, Mr Cromer. They would have looked very fine gracing the walls at Chesterman Court.'

'If there is a family matter to be discussed I would prefer to do it with my father or my niece personally.'

The clerk returned in a state of new agitation, and crossed to his employer, braving the look of disapproval shot at him like a barbed dart.

'Mr Cromer, sir, I've just had Mr Kendall on the telephone. He asked me to tell you he's changed his mind. He won't be coming after all.'

'Changed his mind. About—?'

'Yes, sir.'

Julian's pale face became flushed. He stood up. 'You must excuse me, Mr Devlin. I've no time for you right now. I'll order a hansom to take you to the station, and if you will leave the address with Mr Carew I'll try to get up to town at some future date. Good day to you.'

Oliver's dismissal contrasted baldly with the effusive welcome he had received earlier, but it didn't worry him. When the hansom arrived he cancelled it, and walked instead to the South

257

Western Hotel which was only a few minutes away. There he booked a room and installed himself for an indefinite number of nights so that he could do some quiet thinking, make some discreet inquiries, and seek advice from the Southampton branch of the bank in which he had deposited Ellie's money in his name.

Ellie was very worried. It was six days since she had seen or heard anything of Oliver and his desertion awakened new fears. She had come to rely on him. Surely he hadn't walked out, after all he had done to find them somewhere else to live? He wouldn't leave her without word. Each morning she awoke with a deepening fear that once more she had been deserted.

His absence made her think of Max, something she tried never to do, and she prayed that this wasn't a repeat of what had happened at the dockside in Southampton. It wasn't the same, of course, because she had no emotional ties with Oliver Devlin, but over the weeks his friendship had been invaluable and the debt she owed him was more than monetary. The only consolation stemming from the amount she and Grandfather Cromer owed him financially was that if he wanted repayment, he wouldn't abandon them. He was under no obligation to tell her where he was going, but it surprised her how much she wished to be taken into his confidence.

Ellie took William out regularly in the perambulator Oliver had bought for him, but she rarely left Grandfather Cromer for long. He was recovering well from his addiction to alcohol, but there was no knowing when he might lapse. And whenever she was away from the house he sulked.

'What am I supposed to do in this rat-hole?' he would ask testily. 'Ain't room to move.'

'Be thankful you're not in the workhouse,' she admonished him. 'If you want some exercise, come out with me and William.'

'In Clerkenwell? No—it stinks.'

She didn't like the place much herself, but there were far worse parts of London. Mainly she disliked it because it was a community where strangers were not welcome, and she distrusted the people with their Cockney dialect that she couldn't understand.

The tall house Oliver had found for them was not far from St John's Gate. It belonged to a watchmaker who lived like a recluse in one room at the back of his shop and was willing to rent out the rest of the building for a reasonable sum. The furnishing was sparse, the outlook depressing, but at least they had a roof over their heads for the time being. Sadly they'd had to dispense with the services of Mr Frobisher, but there was a room for Mrs Hovringham, who still cooked and cleaned. When he was there, Oliver occupied a garret which was cold and cramped, but he insisted it was all he needed. This sacrifice added to Ellie's guilt. They had become too dependent on him and she didn't know how to alter the situation while Grandfather Cromer insisted on keeping his son Julian in ignorance. It was too early yet to go against his wishes.

They had only been in the new accommodation two days when Oliver had left.

'I've business to attend to, mavourneen,' he'd said. 'It'll only take the one day, then I'll be back.'

And here it was, nearly a week later.

As Ellie pushed the perambulator along Clerkenwell Green, she admitted to herself that she was frightened. There would soon be another week's rent to pay, but she had no money with which to do it. The nightmare was starting all over again.

'Your Uncle Oliver can't be as bad as your father, William, can he?' she said to the baby, who gazed back at her with eyes as blue as the fine autumn sky. His likeness to Max, except for the colour of his eyes, was sometimes so disturbing she wanted to cry. 'There can't be two men who would treat me so despicably.'

She remembered that on the day Max had left her, Oliver had been at the docks intending to return to America on the very same ship himself. According to him he'd said, 'What's another few days to me?' But he hadn't bargained for Grandfather Cromer's unexpected condition delaying him even further. The few days had become weeks, but surely he wouldn't have bought another ticket and left the country without telling her... The mere thought made Ellie go cold.

Mrs Hovringham was preparing dinner when she got back.

'There are times when I think Sir Robert was

easier to live with when he depended on the bottle,' she grumbled. 'He won't eat stewed beef now. He wants pheasant, if you please.'

'Stick a feather in the beef and tell him to use his imagination,' said Ellie. 'He's got to make do like the rest of us.'

'Oh, and Mr Devlin's back. He came just after you went out and he's been up with Sir Robert ever since, talking private.'

Relief swamped Ellie. She dumped William in the poor woman's arms, lifted her skirt and ran up the stairs to the living room with tears streaming down her cheeks. The door was shut but she burst in, breathless.

'Oliver, I really thought you were on your way back to America,' she cried. The two men sat at the table studying papers, their chairs close, heads almost touching, but Oliver got up as soon as she entered and she ran into his arms. 'I'm so pleased you're back.'

His arms closed round her, holding her imprisoned. It was the first time she'd been so close to a man since Max had left, and elation turned to panic as she freed herself.

'I've some good news, mavourneen,' said Oliver. 'And I've not wasted my time away from you.' He led her to the table.

'He's a man after my own heart, this one,' nodded Grandfather, making room for her.

Oliver pressed her into the chair he had vacated. 'I've been to Southampton...'

'Oliver, you'd no right!'

'I'd every right to look after me own interests, so I had, and that meant enlightening your

261

uncle as to his responsibilities. He has a fine business, and an extravagant wife. Expensive tastes himself too, begorrah, and they've been leading him into difficulties.'

'So he can't help us.'

The smile on Oliver's thin lips was puckish. He seemed very pleased with himself, and he crouched beside the chair so that he could look into her eyes.

'How would you fancy seeing me a director of Court Carriages, Ellie?'

'You're talking in riddles.'

'I've bought shares in the business. All of forty per cent, would you believe. Sure and that entitles me to a large say in the running of the company.'

He was going too fast for her. It was impossible that Julian Cromer would allow a stranger to buy up more than a third of his business in such a short time. He surely couldn't be *that* desperate.

'We're moving to Southampton,' Grandfather said. 'Can't say I'll enjoy the provinces, but anywhere's better than this.'

'No, I won't go to Southampton.' Ellie was horrified. She never wanted to see the place again.

'We need to be where our livelihood is,' said Oliver firmly.

'Yours, not ours.'

'I made a stipulation that you are to be involved in the business. A house belonging to Julian Cromer is to be made over to me, for Sir Robert's use and yours. You'll have no more worries, so you won't.'

This was quite unbelievable. Oliver Devlin, who had no real connection with them, was suddenly taking their future into his hands, and Ellie shivered. It wasn't that she didn't appreciate him. What she feared was the hold he was gaining.

'In what way could I possibly be involved?' she asked. Her tone was sharp. 'And I don't understand how Uncle Julian could have let you buy up so many shares.'

'Twenty-five per cent, he offered. The rest I've secured through a solicitor from shareholders who were happy to get rid of them. The company's ailing badly, Ellie. It needs new blood.'

'But why should I have anything to do with it?'

'Because you are Conrad Harvey's daughter, and you told me once that he said you had a very good head for business.'

'He's right, girl,' urged Grandfather. 'Accept the challenge. You're capable enough.'

There was very little else she could do. If she refused, Oliver might well withdraw his support—and then where would they be? But it was not simply a matter of agreeing; there were a number of important issues at stake. After a lot of further discussion she made up her mind.

'Very well,' she said. 'It's true I learnt a lot from Papa, and I know what makes or breaks a company. But I won't consider anything unless I have a salary which will allow me to pay rent for the house so that I can support William and Grandfather myself.'

'Fair enough.'

'And where will you be living?'

'That, mavourneen, I haven't yet decided,' said Oliver.

The move to Southampton took place two weeks before Christmas. It was easy, as there was scarcely anything to pack, Sir Robert having no possessions left. Ellie's portmanteau and boxes were pressed into holding her grandfather's clothes as well as her own and William's, and Mrs Hovringham had managed to salvage her favourite cooking utensils which were packed and sent on separately. Oliver had escorted the housekeeper to the new home a few days earlier to prepare it, and had stayed on himself.

The train took them to Southampton West Station. Grandfather Cromer weathered the journey well, though he objected to travelling second class. To Ellie's embarrassment he had insisted on buying a 'secret travelling lavatory' at Waterloo, even though they were only to be on the train for two hours, and she hoped no one else in the railcar was aware of the strange rubber appliance strapped to his leg.

A carriage had been sent to meet them on arrival and they were driven to Julian Cromer's residence in an outlying district of the city. It was in a leafy lane called Lances Hill and a toll for the vehicle had to be paid before they reached Fortune Cottage, which was nothing like any cottage Ellie had ever pictured. Luxury was evident from the first glimpse.

'So this is where my son hoards my treasures,' said Grandfather. Julian walked across the drive to meet them. 'Don't exert yourself, boy! Why weren't you at the station?'

'Father, it's good to see you.'

'The feeling isn't mutual.'

Grandfather Cromer allowed the coachman to help him down, and Ellie moved forward from the protection of the hood to see her uncle for the first time. She was quite unprepared for the impact he made. She had expected him to resemble her mother, but Julian was so fair it was hard to believe they belonged to the same family. She had also forgotten that he was much younger than Sibylla and would be no more than thirty-five.

It was obvious that he, too, was surprised. Ellie had travelled in a gown of maroon water-marked taffeta, the dark colour relieved at her throat by cream silk ruffles which were flattering to her complexion, and her wine-coloured hat supported a bunch of cherries on the narrow brim where it tilted over her left eyebrow. Julian blinked his eyes rapidly when he saw her, and his mouth opened slightly before he uttered a word.

'You must be Elena,' he said. His voice was smooth and light, and pleasant on the ear. 'How could I have neglected you all these weeks?'

'I'll forgive you if you'll be so kind as to help with William,' she answered, holding out the sleeping child for him to take so that she could alight herself.

The move disturbed William and he started to cry the moment he was in Julian's arms. The noise brought two children, a boy and a girl, from the house like eager puppies, but their enthusiasm to greet the new arrivals was cut short by an authoritative command from a woman at an upstairs window.

'Children, behave in a proper manner, if you please!'

'Their nurse is rather strict,' Julian said apologetically. 'Francis, Charlotte, you may greet your American cousins indoors when I've introduced them to your mama.'

Millicent Cromer was a small woman, but what she lacked in stature she made up for in presence. She was cool but gracious when introduced to her niece by marriage, and practically ignored her father-in-law.

'You'd think the cow might make an effort,' Grandfather muttered, and was about to say more until silenced by Ellie's scandalised glance.

'We'll take tea in the drawing room,' Millicent said.

'Tea! Is that all you're going to give us after the journey we've endured?'

'Tea will be very welcome,' said Ellie.

Millicent's clothes were as fine as anything that could be bought in London, the bead embroidery on her pink bodice probably having cost as much as Ellie's entire outfit, but the colour didn't suit her. She had the type of brown hair which went with sallow skin, and she should have worn brighter tones to lift the yellowish pallor. Her fingers were heavy with rings, her ears studded with diamonds. Clearly she had dressed to impress her visitors, but Ellie's reaction was to make a mental note of the expense involved in her aunt's adornment, and she resolved to question it as soon as she had some say in the running of the financially-ailing Court Carriage Works.

The children, who were aged seven and five, were given a few minutes in which to unleash their excitement and bombard their Cousin Ellie with questions, then they were taken off by the nurse, who also took charge of William.

A parlourmaid appeared with a trolley laden with silver and fine porcelain which overshadowed the offering of tiny iced cakes. The teapot fitted a description Mama had given of one used in her childhood, and was not the only recognisable object in a room rich in paintings and priceless works of art.

The scene of upper-class elegance washed over Ellie as if it had no substance. She sipped tea, delicately ate a cake, and took part in polite conversation, but a strange prickling sensation affected her skin like a multitude of ants on the march. Her grip on a rose-patterned plate tightened in an effort to stop her hands trembling, and the crumbs of cake were dry in her throat. These curious feelings were due to a vibrant awareness of Julian Cromer's eyes fixed upon her. She felt as if a snake was uncoiling, swaying, hypnotising her, and there was nothing she could do to keep it from striking; there was nothing she particularly wanted to do. No previous experience had quite prepared her for this, and she foolishly allowed a purely physical attraction to take hold.

She kept her own eyes downcast as much as she could, but her normally strong willpower was insufficient to resist an overwhelming urge to meet her uncle's gaze. And each time she did so, she felt as if an invisible force was propelling her towards something new and frightening, something she must take all steps to avoid if her life was to remain bearable.

THIRTEEN

Ellie now resided in a house in The Polygon with Grandfather, William, and Mrs Hovringham. Grandfather Cromer approved of the air of gentility. The sea could be seen from the second-floor windows, the drawing room on the first floor opened out onto a narrow, iron-railinged balcony, and carriages passed frequently along the road curved round the attractive buildings.

It had been decided that a small staff was necessary, so a parlourmaid and scullerymaid were employed to help Mrs Hovringham who still did the cooking. A nurse for William was the next necessity when Ellie became actively involved with the company, which was to pay for such luxuries.

Oliver Devlin took permanent rooms in a nearby hotel.

'It wouldn't be seemly for us to live in the same house,' he said, when Ellie questioned the expense. 'Though there wouldn't be any impropriety, of course, unless...'

He didn't finish the sentence, and the incident left Ellie feeling uneasy. She didn't press him again to share the house.

Her first Christmas Day in England was spent with the Cromers at Fortune Cottage, at Julian's insistence. Ellie would have preferred to stay at home with only Grandfather and William, but Oliver was all for forging a stronger link with the family now that they shared a common interest, and he persuaded her to overlook any past grievances. He himself was not invited, but seemed content. Julian made no secret of his dislike of the man who had so underhandedly acquired shares in his company, and even at work there was little harmony between them. Each took responsibility for different sections, an arrangement which suited both.

The season of goodwill passed without incident, with the children given precedence, and William, at nine months, old enough to enjoy all the attention from his older cousins. Only Ellie's acute awareness of Julian and the certainty of her attraction for him, caused inner turmoil, but that was successfully hidden. She refused to give any importance to the traitorous stirring in her body whenever he was near. It wasn't as if she even liked him! On the few occasions they'd conversed at any length she had found him pompous and unreasonable, and had come away convinced that the effect he had on her was revulsion. He was cold, calculating, and dangerous.

By the following spring, Ellie had regained her self-confidence. Winter evenings spent with Grandfather Cromer had become history lessons in the background to the British railway system, and she had absorbed every detail avidly. At first he had reminisced about his own success, in particular his most important achievement, the construction of the line from London to Brayminster. This alone had given employment to over 2000 navvies, and was also considered a major engineering feat, since it spanned a gorge in the Mendips which the experts had said was impossible. He knew the history of nearly every line in the country, and his contract experiences gave Ellie knowledge of gauges, locomotive power, speed and comfort—in fact, everything she needed to know to enable her to speak with authority.

'Ain't no good though, less you know about money too,' Grandfather cautioned. Her enthusiasm was contagious and he had benefited from it. The gaunt features had filled out and there was evidence of the handsome man he had been before alcohol had taken its toll. 'Julian only knows how to spend it. You have to know how to *make* it, girl, else you'll go under with him. That's what'll happen to Court Carriages, if you and Oliver can't use your influence.'

Oliver was turning out to be surprisingly businesslike. Ellie had been afraid that his inexperience might mean he had invested his mother's money unwisely, the shares having been bought so hastily, but her brother-in-law was no fool. He had put his own ideas before the Board at the first opportunity, with the result that output had increased over the first two months of the new year. Having learnt from George Pullman the importance of good working conditions, he had justified the expense of a recreation room for the men, better ventilation, and a bonus scheme to encourage more initiative.

Ellie was given an honorary seat on the Board, at Oliver's instigation, and her first contribution to the financial recovery of the Court Carriage Works was daring. She attacked what she saw as the biggest flaw in the company—the extravagant décor in the main offices. A meeting between Julian, Grandfather Cromer, Oliver and herself was called before Easter. The venue was Oliver's office, a plainly furnished room with a plan of the Works on the wall, an oak desk, upright chairs and good drawer space.

'There's no need for opulence,' Ellie stated firmly. 'The paintings in the reception office and your own must be sold, Julian.' He had asked her to drop the prefix 'uncle' when she addressed him. 'There's enough money hanging on your walls to pay all one thousand seven hundred employees a year's wages and more. That is a wicked waste.'

'Ridiculous! Many of our customers are royal—it's important to make a good impression.'

'The quality of the finished product is what

271

matters. An office like this is all that's necessary.'

'I will *not* lower my standards.'

'The impression given to ordinary people is enough to put them off, so it is,' Oliver was equally vehement. 'We won't survive on royal patronage alone—it's more rail company orders we need.'

Grandfather poured himself some water. 'I suppose the Prince of Wales pops in every now and then,' he said scathingly, then: 'And anyway, the paintings are mine, removed from my house without my permission. Ellie's right, they must be sold.'

The discussion became heated. Julian's anger increased, his eyes narrowed and his mouth was grim as he fought to hold onto his ill-gotten possessions. The minute hand of the clock made two complete circuits and still they argued.

'This must be a matter for *all* shareholders. You can't dictate from a minority position,' he stormed.

'Call a meeting then,' Oliver insisted.

The outcome of consultation with all shareholders a few weeks later was a unanimous decision to raise capital as suggested, and Ellie had won her first battle with Julian Cromer.

On 3 April 1895, William had his first birthday. He was developing into a sturdy little boy who could walk quite well, and his adventurous spirit necessitated Nanny Simmons having to watch him every waking minute. There had been several frights since he had found his feet.

On one occasion he had discovered the French windows open, and was out on the balcony before anyone knew what he was doing. Ellie had found him excitedly jumping up and down as a water-car trundled by.

'Horsie!' he had cried, pointing to the poor animal pulling the vehicle. 'Horsie, Mama.'

His birthday brought back painful memories for Ellie. Thoughts of Max inevitably played on her mind, and in spite of her resolution not to think of him she wondered what he was doing. She stroked the head of their son as she cuddled him during a lunch-time nap. Her fingers slid through the black hair growing thickly from a peak on his forehead, and it was so much like his father's that she couldn't stop a forbidden longing for the past of a year ago.

One big surprise had been a card and money for William from his Grandmama Harvey in Chicago. Ellie had written to her mother to tell her of the move to Southampton, and had received one of her carefully worded replies. Sibylla didn't write often, and her answer to that first letter from London had avoided the use of Max's name.

'Dear Ellie,' Mama had written. 'We are very sorry to hear of your misfortunes and wish you would reconsider your decision not to return home. You know that you and William would be welcome here in your changed circumstances.' How delicately she phrased things. 'The news of my father's problems is not too surprising, remembering the man he was, and I'm afraid I wouldn't shed tears even if I could see him. I'm just sorry that

273

you've had to become involved, but there is no need for you to stay.'

There'd been a page about Frederick whose family had further increased, and a large paragraph about Lionel who had decided to take up a good job offered him in Canada. Drew and Clarissa were well, as were Jefferson and Papa.

'Your Papa is concerned about you. His condemnation of your husband is unrepeatable and he says it was wicked of him to have taken you to England in the first place without the means to support you.' The underlining in a different coloured ink told Ellie that Papa was still in ignorance of Mama's gift and was a warning not to mention it. *'He loves you and misses you, Elena, and he wants you to come home.'*

Ellie's reply had been brief. *'If Papa really loved me he would not have turned me out when I decided to marry Max, so I'm afraid my return is out of the question. I have become very fond of Grandfather Cromer and would rather look after him than live on Papa's charity.'*

Mama's cold reaction to Grandfather Cromer's plight had made Ellie angry, and strengthened her own affection for the old man.

There were no more letters from Max. Not once had she opened the ones which had come to the London address. Now that she was in Southampton she hoped any correspondence from him would be returned to sender, address unknown. All links with him were broken. She didn't know where to contact him in America, and he had no knowledge of her whereabouts in England. That was the way she wanted it.

All the same, after the birthday tea at which Millicent, Francis and Charlotte had been present, Ellie felt too depressed to spend the evening alone, so she was very grateful when Oliver came with an invitation.

'I thought we might dine at the Dolphin,' he said. 'I know it's the boy's birthday, but I've a feeling it's his mother who needs cheering up, so I do.'

'Oh Oliver, you're right!'

The Dolphin was one of the oldest hotels in the city, and Ellie liked being surrounded by so much history. Lord Nelson had once stayed in one of the bedrooms, but the building went back much earlier than that, and it had the feeling of still being inhabited by its earliest residents. One of the things she liked most about England was its antiquity.

'You're thinking of Max, aren't you?' Oliver said, when she picked at her food. 'It's natural, Ellie darlin', but it's doing you no good.'

'I know.' She toyed with her spoon. 'Why did he do it to me, Oliver, when he knew I loved him so much? I would have given him as much of the money as he wanted—*all* of it. We could have been happy.'

'Faced with temptation, who knows what any of us will do?'

'I don't know what I would have done without you. I owe you so much for the time we were in London. How can I ever repay you?'

He made her put down the spoon and took

both her hands. 'You could let me help you to forget,' he said.

Ellie's back stiffened and she firmly withdrew her fingers. She knew how he felt. The signals had been getting stronger for weeks now and she had been silly to let him see her weakness. It was going to be difficult to hold back without hurting him, and that was something he didn't deserve.

'You help me enough.' Her tone was gentle.

'Enough is it, just to settle for words when my heart's aching for you?'

'I'm still a married woman,' she reminded him.

'With a husband you'll never see again. What kind of life is that?'

'We're both Catholics.'

'And I am a widower, so I am.'

'But I'm not a widow. I'm sorry, Oliver. There can never be anything but friendship between us.'

He reached for her hand again and this time raised it to his lips. His eyes held hers. 'I've been tormented with love for you ever since we first met. You're so beautiful and intelligent—you're all a man could want. Don't let Max keep you from everything that makes life worthwhile.'

'Are you suggesting I become your mistress?' Once more she broke contact, this time pulling her hand away sharply. 'Because if you are, I take exception to it.'

'You can't live like a nun.'

'I would rather be a nun than ever trust another man.' The evening was spoilt. Oliver

276

had ruined their relationship. Ellie gathered up her bag and gloves and stood, smoothing her skirt. 'I'm going to the ladies' room. When I come back I don't want any further personal discussion. The matter is closed.'

But Oliver didn't leave it there. When the hansom drew up in The Polygon he made no effort to get out, and barred Ellie from touching the door.

'I want access to this house whenever I fancy it, mavourneen.'

'No one has ever denied you access.' She leaned back in the cab as far as she could, dismayed by the change in his approach. 'It was by choice you took rooms elsewhere.'

'To give you time. Now I can't wait any longer.'

He leaned over and pressed himself against her, his thin lips seeking hers with obsessive persistence, even though she tossed her head from side to side. Finally his mouth stopped her protestations. She felt sick. The feel of his tongue trying to force entry into her mouth revolted her and she continued to resist with all her strength. But when he cupped one of her breasts and squeezed it so that the pain almost made her cry out she kicked his shin until he let her go. And all the while the cabby up on his seat kept his back towards them.

'Don't ever touch me like that again,' she said, through clenched teeth.

'Next time you'll want me as much as I want you.'

'Never. Our door will be locked against you.'

'I have a right to come in whenever I want, so I have.'

'The house belongs to Julian. He lets us use it rent-free.'

'No, my darlin', *I* pay the rent. It was part of the agreement.'

Ellie felt as if she were suffocating. The revelation shocked her beyond measure, for she had believed their dependence on Oliver had ended with the move to Southampton. Now it seemed he was still supporting them. Well, it couldn't go on.

'You'll regret this evening, Oliver, because everything's changed. Tomorrow I shall see to it that Julian puts me on the payroll at Court Carriages and I shall earn my own keep.'

That night she couldn't sleep. The shock of Oliver Devlin's behaviour had upset her more than anything since Max's desertion and she couldn't stop trembling. She felt unclean.

Of course, she should have known that a price has to be paid for everything, and generosity on the scale of Oliver's would come very expensive. From now on there would be no more dependence on him, and she would see that every cent he had spent was repaid with interest.

Over the next year, Ellie became increasingly involved in the Works, having first persuaded her uncle of her capabilities.

'Just because I'm a woman doesn't mean my only accomplishments are sewing and socialising,' she said. The interview took place in Julian's office a few days after Oliver had shocked her into making changes. 'I learnt a lot from my father, and from my godfather, George Pullman. I even lived in Pullman. My husband worked there.'

The tips of Julian's fingers traced the edge of his finely-bearded chin with such sensuality that she shivered. 'You never speak of your husband, Ellie. I find it hard to credit he left you so abruptly.'

'So do I. And I don't intend to speak of him now. He no longer exists in my life.'

'And Oliver Devlin?'

'He has been a friend—no more.' The use of the past tense was deliberate, and Julian smiled as if he could guess why she used it. 'I'm not here to discuss my private life. I need paid employment, Julian. As from now the rent for your Polygon house will be my responsibility.'

'I am willing for you to live there rent-free.'

'Until the other night I was under the impression we already did so,' she said. 'I foolishly thought you had enough concern for your father to provide him with a roof over his head but obviously, that was too much to expect.' She was never at ease with him. Always suspicious. 'It's too late to make amends. I wish an agreement to be drawn up straight away stating the rent I must pay. And I want an official job here. I'm not afraid of hard work.'

'I could make you an allowance.'

'No. I'll not be under any obligation to you. Or to Oliver.'

He came to the window where she was

standing looking out at the road, and she could see his reflection. For several moments he stood behind her, his left thumb moving back and forth within his left shirt-cuff, showing that he was not as calm as he appeared. Her own emotions appalled her. A short time ago she had been angry and repulsed by Oliver's advances; now here she was with electrifying sensations coursing through her body at the nearness of Julian Cromer, her own mother's brother! It was disgraceful—wicked. But acknowledging it gave her no greater control over her feelings.

'You're very proud, Ellie.'

'I'm independent.'

She was relieved when he moved away. Had he touched her, she might have lost that independence.

'Very well, we'll discuss work,' he said. 'I need someone to reorganise the women in the sewing room. I'm sure you can find a way to cut costs and improve output in that area.'

'Don't patronise me, Julian. You might as well relegate me to the laundry.' She faced him angrily. It was ironic that he should suggest the sewing room. Part of Max's job in the upholstery department at Pullman had involved supervising the women who stitched cushions and handrests, and stuffed seats and backs with horsehair. 'I'm capable of more than that.'

'I suppose you want to start by designing a new royal coach!' scoffed Julian.

'I might just do that,' she countered.

He made a joke about it, but Ellie was determined not to waste her talents. Since he wouldn't let her start anywhere better than the sewing room she made herself unpopular by ordering new steam sewing machines which were more efficient, enabling her to reduce the staff of thirty women to twenty-five. But in her favour she also improved the lot of those in the stuffing department by introducing methods she had learnt from Max to minimise the effects of the horsehair on their hands.

In her spare time she took up drawing, and it seemed only natural to begin sketching car interiors. She let her imagination run riot, embellishing her designs with improbable luxuries and using exotic colours. But quite unconsciously the form her ideas took became less original, and she recognised Max's hand in the colours and inventions she had thought to be completely her own. She had been relying on memory of his genius rather than being inventive herself. For a while she put the drawings aside, hating this new reminder of Max, but they were so striking that after a while she felt compelled to take up her pens again to finish them, seeing no harm in it. Thousand of miles separated her from the husband who had robbed her of everything.

The only person to see the drawings was Grandfather Cromer. 'Fit for the Queen of Sheba, no less,' he teased her.

Drawing became an important part of her spare time, and an attic room with good light was turned into a studio where she could display her work on the walls. It was here that Julian found her one summer evening in 1896. He had taken to visiting his father once a week, but Ellie was well aware that his motive was not filial concern for the old man. He came when he knew she would be at home, though varying the day and the time to ensure she didn't anticipate the visit and go out.

He knocked sharply that evening, and thinking it was Nanny Simmons and William she sang out an invitation to enter. The sight of Julian in her workroom caused instant panic, but she managed to conceal it.

'You're trespassing, Julian,' she said.

His eyes flicked round the room in amazement, taking in the large plans and scale drawings she had made of dining and sleeping compartments, intricate and perfect in every detail.

'Why have you never shown me these?' he demanded.

'They're personal. I didn't think you would be interested.'

'They're incredible.' He walked round slowly, studying each one. 'Where did you learn such technique? And who gave you the inspiration?'

She kept her hands clasped to stop them trembling. His praise surprised her.

'I did remind you I come from a railroad background. I used to take a lot of interest in my godfather's company. Max worked for him.' She had used water-colour paints to complete the plans, delicately picking out the detail on floral tapestries and wall coverings.

The sloping ceiling made it difficult for Julian to stand straight, and he had to lean towards her to look closely at the drawings. His nearness was suffocating. There was a faint smell of pomade on his hair, and she was conscious of his eyes straying from her work to the hands which had created it. She had long, tapering fingers with almond-shaped nails buffed to a bright shiny pink, and her wedding ring gleamed in the evening light through the attic window.

'Why did Max go back to America without you?' Julian asked.

'I refuse to talk about him.'

'Because you miss him?'

'No.'

He touched her beneath the chin. Where his fingers rested, it felt as if there would be a scorch-mark. She flinched and backed away.

'You're a very sensual woman, Ellie. I'm sure you must miss the love of a husband.'

Her cheeks coloured. There was no mistaking the underlying meaning to his remark and she was afraid he would notice the rapid rise and fall of her breast as she tried to regulate her breathing.

'Why don't you speak plainly?' she said. Better to shock him and clear the air than allow intimations to linger. 'You want to know if I'm physically frustrated without a man in my life. The answer again is no. I don't need anyone.'

His arm brushed hers. 'You're wasted in the sewing room.'

'I told you I would be.'

'I could have you moved to the draughtsman's office tomorrow. You can have a small room of your own so that you don't have to sit with the men all day.'

'That would be very nice, but if there's a string attached I don't want to know.'

'Ellie!' His eyes drew her gaze, but she was able to look away, showing him she was in control. 'All right, you want plain speaking, then let's acknowledge the attraction between us. No other woman has ever made me feel as you do. I'll give you everything you want if you'll let me spend time with you.'

'Be your mistress? But we're closely related, Julian. It's a despicable suggestion.'

He inclined his head in acknowledgement of the fact, and had the decency to take a step back. 'So be it,' he said, and went to the door where he paused with his hand on the knob. 'I need you to work with the draughtsmen, Ellie, all the same. I've just accepted a very important order from Ezbania and from what I've seen this evening, there's no one else can do the interior designing so well as you. I give my word there'll not be a single string.'

Ellie had won another small victory, but this one didn't give her the same satisfaction. She was not given to lying even in the smallest degree, but it hadn't been the truth when she told him she had no need of physical love. Her body ached for a long time after he had gone.

And now there were two men desiring an illicit relationship with her.

She tried not to see too much of Oliver Devlin, but it would have been impossible to avoid him altogether, even had she wanted to. His behaviour on the night of William's first birthday had brought an apology the following day, but the damage had been done and her trust in him suffered. She still needed his friendship, but made sure there was no opportunity for it to be abused.

He had bought up more shares in the company, making him the second biggest shareholder next to Julian. It didn't surprise her. Oliver had found his feet when he'd invested in Court Carriages, and most of the new contracts were due to his efforts. He was becoming a rich man, and had bought a house for himself in the fashionable Brunswick Place. Pillars flanked the front door, which was opened to visitors by a butler, and the furnishings were costly, though somewhat lacking in taste.

'You'll always be welcome here, Ellie,' he told her, as soon as he had taken possession of the house. He was alone with her in the garden at the rear, Grandfather Cromer having said it was too cold to venture out. 'In fact, it could be yours.'

'I'll come when I'm invited, but only with company.'

'You won't need a chaperone—I promise you'll be quite safe with me.' His eyes narrowed. 'Safer than with Julian Cromer.'

'Julian is my uncle,' Ellie protested. But her heart raced unexpectedly with the shock that he had noticed.

'I've seen the way he looks at you. He's like a

hungry boy with his eyes glued to a candy-shop window, so he is.'

'Don't be ridiculous.'

'Ridiculous is it, to care about you! I don't like it.'

'There's no need for you to be jealous,' she said.

Oliver guided her towards a gazebo at the end of the path, putting a hand under her elbow to steady her when she almost tripped over the crazy paving. Beneath a riot of trailing plants he turned her to face him.

'I love you,' he said. 'And I feel responsible for you. I promised Max I'd look after you, and I'll go on doing it no matter how you feel about me.'

His gaze was innocent of guile, and she would have been foolish to take exception. Truth to tell she had missed their easy friendship since the split, and knew it would be sensible to renew it.

'You're good to me, Oliver. If I can trust you I'd like us to be friends again.'

'Mavourneen, all I ask is to be guarding over you.' He took her hand and held it against his chest. 'I swear I won't frighten you or make you angry again, so I do.'

The pledge made Ellie so happy she reached up and kissed his cheek. He made her feel safe.

Plans for the Ezbanian train progressed rapidly and there was great excitement at the Works. It was the most ambitious project so far undertaken and promised to generate fresh interest in the company when it was shown. Ellie's part in the success could not be underestimated. At Julian's insistence she had used the plans which had so impressed him in her workroom, and the ideas she had seen Max developing at his drawing board in their tenement kitchen were incorporated in her reclining chairs and the draped bed which remained level no matter how great the swaying motion of the car. She felt no compunction about claiming Max's work as her own. He'd had none for her when he left her destitute.

When the train was finally unveiled in 1897, photographs of the Crown Prince of Ezbania seated in the smoking room appeared in all the leading newspapers and magazines, and every detail of the luxurious and revolutionary furnishing was described in minute detail. It was a triumph for Court Carriages.

One unforeseen development with success and a more competitive outlook in the Works, was increased antagonism between the men at Court Carriages and those working for the rival company at Eastleigh, which had transferred its carriage and wagon workshops there from Nine Elms in 1891. Frequent skirmishes were reported in Southampton's public houses, and at managerial level devious methods were now employed to win over contracts.

The unrest bothered Ellie. Vivid memories of Chicago during the strike made her nervous of industrial troubles and she wished the men would settle their differences amicably.

FOURTEEN

Interest in the Ezbanian train was not confined to England. Photographs and articles about it appeared in many parts of the world where railroads made news, chief among them being the United States of America.

It was several weeks before copy of the ceremony in Southampton, England reached Albany, the capital of New York State. The city on the west bank of the River Hudson where it met with the Erie and Champlain canals was built on hills, and had a large and thriving timber market. It was partly this which had brought Max Berman to Albany back in the spring of 1895.

He was the first to admit he didn't deserve the luck which had started on board the steamship *Paris* as it carried him back to America after he had left Ellie. From the moment the ship set sail he regretted what he had done, but it was too late to turn back. He was practically penniless, and having acted on terrible impulse he would have to live with terrible guilt for the rest of his life. For two days he drank and slept, eating nothing. On day three he met Jarvis Warding.

Jarvis was returning to Albany after a visit to his dying father in England. The reading of his father's will after the funeral had disclosed that he had inherited immense wealth, but grief at

288

his loss overshadowed the good news and he was still trying to drown it when he found a fellow sufferer at the bar in Max. The result was the beginning of a new friendship.

'It's good to find someone who understands,' Jarvis said, after pouring his troubles into Max's ear. 'Everyone else on board seems so intent on frivolity.' He looked at his companion with deep sympathy. 'You've lost your wife. That's a dreadful thing—even worse than losing a parent, I imagine.'

'She isn't dead,' said Max. 'She's in London, with her grandfather. She...' Suddenly the need to talk about his guilt was overpowering and he had to burden this stranger with it. He began: 'I've done something terrible.' And he proceeded to confess.

Luckily, Jarvis was a very understanding man, and he welcomed the chance to help his fellow traveller, if only to take his mind off his own problems; for the rest of the voyage, the two men were often in each other's company. On reaching American soil once more Max was invited to travel to Albany to meet Jarvis's family, but he declined, saying he was going to try for work in New York. He couldn't return to Chicago, and he'd no idea where he might settle.

'Well, if things don't work out you have my address. Like I said, I run a sawmill. No doubt I could find a job for you,' Jarvis told him. He was edging forty and excess fat showed he was used to living well. 'It's in the Lumber District close by the Erie Canal, but

I myself live near Washington Park. You can see the Catskill Mountains from my house and it's right pretty.'

As Max had never been to that part it meant nothing, but he thanked him warmly for the offer.

Winter in New York was very hard. Work was scarce and Max's depression deepened. Finally he realised the folly of not taking up Jarvis Warding's offer, and contacted him before it was too late. Soon afterwards he travelled on a steamer up the Hudson River to its confluence with the canals, and passed the time by reading a book about Albany. It was important to learn all he could about the place because Fate was beckoning him towards it more surely with every nautical mile. But he was not happy. His reading was disturbed by thoughts of Ellie, and illogically he found himself longing to share this new beginning with her. More than at any time during their life together he began to appreciate the wonderful qualities she possessed. The vast distance now separating them enabled him to see the sacrifices she had made for love, and he was so ashamed his eyes misted over, blurring his first glimpse of Albany. He looked down into the dark river water and in the depths he saw pictures of Ellie holding their son in her arms. The water seemed to draw him irresistibly, but a shout from Jarvis on the quayside brought him back to reality. There was no easy way out.

It soon became clear that the two men could help each other in many ways. Jarvis had money to extend his business: Max had talent and ambition. The opportunities opening to him over the next few months should have been cause for excitement, but the burden of his guilt became heavier.

The Wardings were good to Max. Ruth, Jarvis's wife, was a motherly soul who began including him with their brood of seven children as soon as he arrived, and straight away he shared a room with Henry, the only son. Jarvis was an astute man. On learning of Max's experience in the Pullman industry, and seeing evidence of his creativity, he knew he had stumbled on something as valuable as his newfound wealth. Within weeks he had established a new company which was to make exclusive furniture. Within a year he had found countrywide recognition, and by the winter of 1896, Warding Upholsterers was selling to the most exclusive shops in New York.

Max himself was the power behind the firm's success. He worked fourteen hours a day, sometimes more, and took no leave. He longed to see his parents, but shame held him back. Not only that, he couldn't face going to Chicago without Ellie.

He wrote to her often from New York and then Albany, longing for forgiveness. He poured out his heart to her, allowing her to see for the first time to what degree the difference in their backgrounds had affected him. He blamed his pride, but also admitted his inability to cope with the selfless love she had bestowed on him.

'Ellie, I didn't deserve you. You were far too

291

good for me,' he confessed in writing. *'I took everything with such bad grace it was a wonder you didn't leave me. How I wish that you had, then you would have been spared the final acts of cruelty I have inflicted on you. I can never forget that through me you have been denied further children. What plagues me incessantly is the similarity between what happened to you and what happened to my mother in Russia. Since I was a boy the horror of Momma's suffering has haunted me, yet I let you be led into danger which ended in another barren future. Can you ever forgive me? I am earning good money now and want to help support our son. Even though you have a rich family I hope you will accept what I send.*

'I plead with you, implore you, if you can find it in your generous heart to spare me the rejection I deserve, please write and say that you understand a little of what I do, too, suffer now.'

The letter was five pages long and written in such anguish it surely couldn't fail to move the reader, yet no answer came. He continued to write in spite of her silence, until his letters were returned because she was no longer at the same address. When he knew he had lost her completely, he spent every waking moment building up the business in which Jarvis Warding had made him a partner, and tried to banish Ellie from his mind.

It was on Easter Day 1897 that Max's life again changed direction. He was spending the day as usual with the Wardings, but in the middle of the celebrity dinner Jarvis collapsed

292

and died from a heart attack. It was a tragedy, as much for Max as for the family. The man had been both friend and father-figure, and Max felt his loss so keenly he had to get away to be by himself to mourn.

Jarvis had always regretted that Max had a wife. He would have been supremely happy to see one of his six daughters married to him. For one thing, the furniture business could then have been kept completely in the family. However, his disappointment didn't stop him from dividing Warding Upholsterers equally between Max and Henry in his will, and there was no ill-feeling. In fact, Henry had no interest in that side of his father's business and was agreeable to selling Max his own share, so that he himself could go off and concentrate on expanding the sawmill and timberyard.

As sole owner of a thriving company Max should have been content, but without Jarvis nothing was the same. To stretch his mind he turned once more to the designs he had once made for the most luxurious railcar ever envisaged—plans Ellie had said deserved recognition, but which the recession and the strike had rendered too expensive to contemplate. He put the senior manager in charge of the Works and left Albany for the first time since he had arrived three years ago, taking a train to New York, and another to Detroit.

The company to which he took his designs was so enthusiastic that Max was treated royally. He attended meetings with directors and the head draughtsman, all of whom were keen to use his ideas.

'These will set Pullman back on his heels,' he was told. 'Did you ever see such fine detail on car upholstery? And the suspension on those chairs ought to make travelling as comfortable as sitting at home in the drawing room!'

Such flattery was a balm for Max's spirits and he returned to Albany full of revived ambition, to await a contract for his work. None came. Instead, he received an official letter to say that the company took a very serious view of his attempt to pass off certain designs and inventions as his own, and had considered taking proceedings against him.

'However, we are prepared to be lenient in view of the fact that the deception was discovered before any expense was incurred,' the letter said. *'But should any further fraudulence be brought to our notice we will not hesitate to call in the Law.'*

He was amazed. There'd been a terrible mistake. Anger consumed him and he prepared to make another journey to Detroit to clear up the misunderstanding. How had it occurred? His designs had not been seen by anyone, not in Chicago or Pullman, certainly not in Detroit. They had remained in his possession, hidden away with other papers pertaining to his past, and he defied anyone to prove otherwise. The ideas were his, and his alone—inventions from his mind which were unique.

It was on the morning of his planned departure to raise hell with the Detroit company that Max received a copy of a newspaper from the manager, with photographs and detailed drawings of the Ezbanian train on view in Southampton. He couldn't believe his eyes. The car was identical in almost every detail to the designs he had shown in Detroit, and descriptions of revolutionary methods used to ensure travelling comfort corresponded exactly with his own carefully-worded notes.

For a few moments he was too stunned to seek an explanation. Then he realised that Ellie had taken her revenge.

FIFTEEN

In the June of 1897, Ellie returned to London for a visit together with Julian, Millicent and their children, and Oliver Devlin, to attend the Diamond Jubilee Celebrations of Her Majesty Queen Victoria. Julian had booked rooms for them all at an hotel in the Strand, outside which hung multi-coloured glass globes, and they arrived on Sunday, 20 June in time to attend the National Service of Thanksgiving at St Paul's Cathedral. The following day they took their places at a private viewing platform on Paddington Station by special invitation to watch the Queen's arrival in her own Great Western Railway train from Windsor. The Royal Standard was flying at the front of the engine and the Royal coat of arms were emblazoned on either side.

'Pity Court Carriages weren't asked to build a new car for the occasion,' remarked Oliver, who these days never missed an opportunity to do business.

At twelve-thirty the train glided into the station slowly with scarcely a puff of steam to pollute the air, and Her Majesty was helped to step down on the red carpet. Only the white egret plumes in her bonnet relieved the sombre black of her clothes.

'The Queen's an old lady,' cried Charlotte, with disappointment. 'Why does she look so dowdy?'

'She's still in mourning for her husband,' said Millicent.

'Did he die recently, then?'

'No, you goose,' said Francis. 'He died years before we were born.'

'Then she should be out of mourning by now. *I* shan't go into black for more than six months when *my* husband dies.'

Everyone laughed, and Ellie hugged her young cousin, for whom she had developed quite an affection. 'You might if you loved him as much as the Queen loved Albert,' she said.

'Or as much as I love you,' whispered Oliver in her ear, making Ellie blush.

Over the past few weeks she had been turning to him again with renewed confidence. He was honouring the promise he had made her in his garden and the warmth of his love was a great comfort. He was her shield against the harsh world, against painful memories of Max, and against the temptations Julian presented. She

296

was beginning to love him in return, not with any sexual longing, but with a gentle gratitude for his devotion.

When they left Paddington Station, Oliver suggested taking her to see the sights from the top of a horse-drawn bus, and Ellie accepted with alacrity.

'I thought you would be coming back to the hotel with us, Ellie,' said Julian disapprovingly. 'You should rest—you'll be tired.'

'Oh no!' she cried. 'I can't waste time resting when there are so many exciting things going on.'

'I'll hire a private carriage for us to tour the city later if you wait until I've seen Millicent and the children back to our rooms.'

'Ellie's coming with me, aren't you, mavourneen?' said Oliver, taking hold of her hand.

'Yes, I am. Thank you, Julian, but I'd rather see everything from the top of a bus.'

She saw the tell-tale twitch at the corner of his mouth denoting his displeasure at Oliver's interference, and she was stricken with guilt. After all, Julian had paid for her to come here, and she knew he had expected them to be spending time together. A treacherous increase in her pulse-rate signalled a desire for the same thing, so she was glad of the alternative. She had foreseen such dangers from the beginning, and had been on the point of turning down the invitation to come to London when Grandfather Cromer, who had initially been included as one of the party, had asked Oliver to take his place. It had been a great relief, she felt safer with Oliver around.

It wasn't as if she even knew Julian very well. They rarely conversed on any subject other than business, and inner feelings were never discussed. She didn't know how he felt about anything on a personal level, and she was afraid to find out. It was safer by far to remain distant. This attraction between them was pure chemistry, and could only be contained for as long as there was no physical contact.

'Very well,' he said, his winter-grey eyes boring into her. 'Mix with the riffraff if you must. I trust you to take care of her, Devlin.'

'Sure she's safer with me than anyone,' Oliver assured him. The double meaning was not lost on Ellie.

London was a riot of coloured decorations, the streets vying to outdo each other. Crowds of people from all parts of the world thronged the thoroughfares. St James's Street was probably the most lavishly decorated. Two Corinthian pillars at either end had real palms and flowers at their bases. Festoons of evergreens were laced between forty Venetian masts on either side of the street, and red, white and blue glass globes caught the sunlight. Serpentine trails of tiny gas-jets coloured the Mansion House, and buildings from St Paul's to Buckingham Palace were outlined with electric-light lamps. Draperies of every hue hung from windows. Errand boys wore Jubilee favours; bicycles sported red, white and blue streamers; whips of the hansom-cab drivers had pennants tied to them, and almost every city man had a button-hole in the national colours.

'It makes me think of Chicago at the start of the Exposition,' said Ellie wistfully, and a little of her good humour evaporated. 'Only this is so much grander.'

'I took Katrina there,' Oliver remembered, sadness in his voice.

'And I met Max for the first time since I'd grown up. Do you know, I already loved him when I was fifteen. I thought he was the most wonderful person in the world.'

He pressed her hand in sympathy, then directed her attention to the boarding round the Law Courts. 'Some wag in the *Daily Mail* wrote that barristers and solicitors have to dive inside as if they're going to clean out chicken-houses,' he said, and she laughed obediently. He was silent for a moment, then he took his wallet from an inner pocket and brought out a letter and a photograph. 'I heard from Momma and Poppa Berman a little while ago, but I didn't know if you would be interested. They sent me this picture of Galina. Isn't my daughter beautiful?'

'Of course I'm interested.'

Ellie took the picture with trembling fingers, the link with her past so strong it brought a lump to her throat. The dimpled child with freckles visible even on the sepia-toned reproduction was standing on a dais in the photographer's studio, a doll in her hand which Ellie had given her before leaving Chicago, and she was as petite and lovely as a doll herself. Last month she would have had her fourth birthday. Memories of the tenement fire, and all that had followed, sent shivers down Ellie's spine.

'You saved her life,' Oliver said quietly. 'I'll never forget. Don't you know that's another reason why you mean so much to me.'

She didn't want to go any deeper into emotional commitments. 'What did Momma and Poppa have to say in the letter?' she asked, handing the photograph back.

'Poppa is ill,' he said. Then he debated a moment before adding: 'They've heard nothing of Max.'

'So he hasn't been back to Chicago.' She took a deep breath. 'I wonder what great things he's done with *my* money. I hope it hasn't made him happy.'

'Don't think about it, my darling. I'm here to look after you.'

'I'm not your darling, Oliver. And I can look after myself.'

She didn't know why she was suddenly so irritated by his affection. It had to be the unexpected mention of Max. Only by conditioning her mind to reject thoughts of him had she been able to live at peace, but it was a fragile peace which crumbled easily with the slightest remembrance.

Tuesday dawned dull and overcast, a bad start for the Queen's triumphal procession through London. The Cromers, Oliver and Ellie were out early to take their fifteen-guinea seats in a specially constructed stand close by St Paul's. At eleven-fifteen the first gun of the Royal Salute in

Hyde Park boomed out to announce that Her Majesty had left the Palace, and the sun burst through as if pre-arranged.

'I wish I could see everything right from the start,' complained Francis. 'We've got to wait ages till she gets here.'

'Just be glad you're seeing it at all,' said Julian reprovingly. 'A lot of boys would change places with you.'

Scarlet-coated soldiers lined the seven-mile route being covered by the procession, keeping the standing crowds back from the road. Mounted guards rode by, children waved handkerchieves and cheered in anticipation, and it was possible to see down to Ludgate Hill where the splendour of a company of Indian Rajahs and oriental nobilities created a brilliant patch of colour. Time passed quickly with so much to watch.

Ellie's excitement was compounded by having Julian pressed close to her on the red plush seat. He hardly glanced her way; he didn't need to. The heat from his body inflamed her, and she knew instinctively that he was equally aware of the contact. To try to minimise the effect, she concentrated on Oliver who was on her opposite side, talking animatedly about everything that was to be seen.

When the head of the procession advanced towards St Paul's the splendour was breathtaking. A mass of colour filled the street as horsemen, ambassadors and princes came into view, wearing dazzling outfits of scarlet, purple, azure, emerald and white, each one embellished with gold. Ellie had never imagined a pageant could be so spectacular. Carriages bearing the royal family passed by, then the cheering rose to a roar as the Queen's own carriage, drawn by eight cream-coloured horses, came into view, entered the churchyard and drew up at the Cathedral steps. With her were the Princess of Wales and Princess Christian of Schleswig-Holstein, and on horseback, waiting to greet her were the Prince of Wales and the Duke of Cambridge. The sun shone brilliantly. The shouting and cheering swelled to a delirium.

'The Queen's still in black,' wailed Charlotte.

'But so distinctive,' said Millicent. 'Such beautiful silver embroidery on her gown, and look at the panels of grey silk.'

Ellie was completely absorbed now in the quiet, grave lady who was unmistakably a Queen. Her black bonnet was ornamented with jet and silver and trimmed with ostrich feathers and white acacia. She looked pathetically small amidst the multitude of foreign royalty and dignitaries. On the steps were bands accompanying 500 choristers who surrounded the Archbishops of Canterbury and York in their purple coronation copes. The Bishop of London's cope was yellow, and the Dean and Chapter were in green, gold and white. The Cathedral steps were ablaze with colour, like a field of exotic flowers.

Seeing so many important people all at once was so awe-inspiring that Ellie felt close to tears. 'How Mama would have loved this,' she breathed.

There was too much to take in all at once.

Oliver's fingers twisted through hers, and she was so carried away by the atmosphere she didn't disengage them. Encouraged by her lack of inhibition, he went a step further and kissed her cheek. She turned to him and smiled, not seeing the venomous look Julian bestowed on the man who not only controlled a large part of his business, but now appeared openly to have the affection of the girl he desperately coveted himself.

Julian had thought to shelve his problems at the Diamond Jubilee Celebrations. Industrial troubles were to be left behind while he used the opportunity to spend time with Ellie. For long enough now there had been this unacknowledged passion between them simmering below the surface, and he couldn't endure the agony and frustration it was causing him any longer. She was the most exciting woman he had ever encountered, the first he had wanted and not possessed almost immediately, and if he didn't possess her soon he was afraid he might do something rash in the extreme. The celebrations were going to provide the answer.

Things started to go wrong with his well-thought-out plans the day before the family's departure for London.

His generous invitation to pay for his father and Ellie if they cared to join the party had been given solely on the expectation of having Ellie to himself for part of the time. He had dissuaded Millicent from asking some new and rather special German friends, the Gottmanns, to go with them, saying it was to be a family occasion. His father's constitution would be unequal to all the sightseeing prior to the processions, and with Millicent's stamina also on the weak side it would surely not be beyond the bounds of propriety to offer to escort his niece on a tour of the city. It would be simple then to slip away to an hotel room he had booked in anticipation, so certain was he that Ellie wouldn't object.

His father was to blame when things went wrong. It was as if the old man sensed intrigue and was determined to thwart any attempted liaison. He'd always been a conniving old devil. Having initially shown enthusiasm for the trip, declaring himself fit for anything, he had then changed his mind at the very last minute.

'I'm too old to go gallivanting off to an hotel,' he grunted. 'I like my own bed too much.'

'So you're not coming?'

'No—I'll stay with William and Mrs Hovringham. Take Ellie with you, though.'

The decision pleased Julian enormously, and he congratulated himself on getting rid of one more obstacle. It was unforgivable that his father had then gone behind his back and arranged for Oliver Devlin to take his place. Devlin presented himself at the station as bold as brass, saying that Sir Robert had thought it necessary for more than one man to be looking after the ladies.

'You can't come with us,' Julian said rudely. 'We can't both be away from the Works.'

'No harm'll come of it. What do we pay senior managers for?'

'This is a family party—and you're not family. I'm sorry, I don't want you with us.'

'He's a part of *my* family,' said Ellie unexpectedly. 'If Oliver doesn't go then I won't go either.'

Julian hoped he knew why she did it. As usual she was fighting against the magnetism which drew them towards each other, and was seeking protection, but the day would soon come when she could fight it no longer. For the moment he had no option but to bow to her wishes, otherwise all would be lost, but he seethed inwardly. His disappointment festered.

Julian's dislike of the Irishman was growing to be an obsession. There were so many things about Devlin which jarred, like his knack of always being right in business arguments. There could be no denying that he had brought Court Carriages back from the brink of bankruptcy. Without a large financial injection the company would have gone under. But it was not only the man's money that had saved them. His knowledge of railway matters was impressive, and he had known how to make the firm competitive. Julian had gone blindly into the business, having inherited it prematurely before he'd had a chance to learn from Millicent's father, and he had no natural aptitude for it. Nor was he gifted with his own father's entrepreneurial flair for talking big and taking risks.

Oliver Devlin was very much like Sir Robert

Cromer, and there was an understanding between the two men which excluded Julian. Of course, Julian would never admit to jealousy. He had never respected his father, nor loved him, but it came as an unpleasant shock to find himself usurped in parental esteem by a stranger.

These were personality differences which had to be endured if the company was to thrive. More difficult to take was Devlin's hold on Ellie. The sight of him touching her and kissing her in public at the climax of the pageant outside St Paul's made Julian feel physically sick, and his interest in everything beyond their personal sphere evaporated. Colours became grey. The sound of bands and voices and cheering was a cacophony.

That evening he excused himself from the party and went out alone, unable to watch Devlin with Ellie any longer. His bitter resentment grew as he walked along through the milling crowds, and he was receptive to a current of unhappiness beneath the surface. It was as if he identified with all who were lonely or unhappy in this time of frenzied celebration, and eyes seeking comfort seemed to meet his too frequently. When he stopped on Westminster Bridge to look down at the activity on the water, he was joined by a young woman in a stained taffeta dress and crocheted shawl.

'On yer own?' the woman said. 'T'ain't right. Shall I keep you company?'

Julian looked at her and saw the curve of her breasts bulging from a too-tight bodice, the provocative movement of her hips, and the invitation in her coquettish glance. He thought of the hotel room he had booked which was still waiting to be used. Perhaps if he took a prostitute there his pain would be relieved. But then she coughed and he noticed the yellow tinge to her skin. Julian was a fastidious man who bathed twice a day, and spent a lot of time on his grooming. The thought of intimacy with such a creature was abhorrent, making his flesh creep, and he walked away from the woman without acknowledging her.

It wasn't that he was always faithful to Millicent. There would have been precious little sexual interest in his life if his morals had been sound, so he kept a mistress out at Swaythling whom he'd visited regularly until recent months. Now even she couldn't take his mind off Ellie Berman.

By the time he arrived back, Millicent had retired with the children and there was no sign of Ellie or Oliver Devlin. Suspicions filled Julian's mind and he was about to take his ill-humour up to bed to vent it on his wife when amazingly Ellie appeared, alone.

'Julian, I've lost my bag,' she exclaimed. 'I last had it when we were sitting in the lounge after dinner.'

'I'll help you look for it,' he said, beginning to smile at last. 'Seems I came back at just the right moment.'

She eyed him with curiosity. 'We missed you. Where have you been?' Then she blushed. 'I'm sorry, I shouldn't have asked.'

'I've only been walking.' How glad he was he could be truthful. Her nearness fired his blood and aroused him alarmingly.

The hour was late, the hotel quiet, and when the bag was finally retrieved Julian accompanied her in the lift up to their fourth-floor rooms, his mind racing on ahead with excitement. The trip was not going to be a disaster, after all.

At her door she stopped and apologised again. 'I'm sorry I've taken up your time. Thank you for helping me.'

He didn't want to linger with her on the landing so he took her key, opened the door and hurried her inside, following himself before she had a chance to realise his intention. He wanted her so desperately that he stopped her mouth with his before she could protest, locking the door while he was still kissing her. Confusion made her resist.

'What do you think you're doing, Julian?' she gasped, escaping. 'How dare you! Get out of my room at once.'

'You were waiting for me,' he said. 'Don't deny it.'

'I wasn't. *Please* go before anyone finds out you're here.'

He ignored the plea, coaxing her, following her when she backed away. 'This is a heaven-sent opportunity, Ellie. Admit we share a longing for each other. I know you feel the way I do.'

He pinned her against the wall, cupping her chin and lowering his mouth once more onto hers. She was shaking. The dream of possessing her had dominated him for so long he was

308

too impatient to employ his usual finesse. He dragged her against him roughly, his fingers digging into her arms, and the pressure he exerted on her tender lips brought a taste of blood. Never before had he subjected a woman to such a brutal onslaught.

He thought she was responding in like manner when she thrust her body towards him. He was exultant. But Ellie jerked her knee upwards, striking him where she knew she could inflict the most pain. He let go of her, doubled over with the agony of that cruel blow, and she stood glaring at him with her hands on her hips.

'You heard me tell you to get out. Why didn't you?'

Her lower lip was swelling and she had marks on her arms. Her violent reaction caused a masochistic excitement to flood through him, and the pain he suffered only added to it. This was going to be the most passionate night he had ever spent.

'You know how to drive a man crazy,' he gasped.

'I'm not playing games. I lived among women who knew how to protect themselves and I learnt a lot. I hate you, Julian. Get out.'

She went to the door. He lunged after her.

'How can you lie to me? I know what you've wanted every time we're together.'

'Yes, I've had feelings I'm ashamed of. Yes, you disturb me.' She was raising her voice. 'It makes me hate you as much as I hate myself. You're like a snake. You're cold and calculating, and you've been trying to take advantage of me ever since we met.'

'I've been responding to your signals.'

'That's right—blame me.'

He changed his tone. 'Ellie...' He turned his hands palm upwards and appealed to her. 'I love you. I'd leave Millicent for you.'

'Don't be a fool.'

'I'd give up everything for you.'

'Get out, Julian, or I'll ring the bell for someone to come.'

The embroidered cord for summoning room service was within her grasp but he prevented her from reaching it. Her voice rose higher as she cursed him. It was then that someone knocked loudly on the door.

'Ellie, are you all right?' It was Devlin. He tried the handle. 'Ellie, let me in.'

'Get rid of him,' hissed Julian, going white with anger and fear of discovery.

She took the key from him, straightening up with renewed dignity, her eyes flashing. 'If you try to hide you'll be shouting your guilt,' she said, unlocking the door. Devlin almost fell inside. 'It's all right, Oliver. Julian came to my rescue. There was a mouse running around and I was so scared I didn't know what to do.'

Julian composed himself and walked out. 'Good night, Ellie. I trust there'll be no more vermin troubling you tonight.'

'Not now you've left there won't be,' Devlin said.

He passed the Irishman without a word and went along to his own suite where Millicent was waiting at the door wrapped from throat to ankles in a blue silk robe. She too had been worried by the commotion. He pacified her and guided her back inside, but before following he was compelled to look over his shoulder. There was no one in sight along the length of the luxuriously carpeted corridor.

Devlin must have gone into Ellie's room.

It should have been memories of the pomp and pageantry in London which remained in Ellie's mind, but instead she found herself unable to forget the night Julian had tried to seduce her.

The family returned home on 23 June, a day earlier than planned, much to the children's disappointment. Julian was silent, Millicent was irritable because she had wanted to shop for souvenirs, and Oliver wouldn't let Ellie out of his sight. The atmosphere was so tense in the railway carriage that Ellie suffered with a headache and had to stand in the corridor by an open window because Millicent refused to let in a breath of air for fear of a draught.

She wished she hadn't raised her voice enough to alert Oliver last night. She was confident she could have got rid of Julian without all the fuss, and then there would have been no need for Oliver's suffocating protection. It was kind of him, of course, and she appreciated it, but she was not the helpless, wilting type who had to be cosseted, and his worrying irritated her. It had taken all her powers of persuasion to stop him from storming after Julian and creating a scandalous scene in the hotel, and the only way to dowse his fiery Irish temper had been to insist on the innocence of Julian's late visit to her room. Whether he finally believed her or not, she didn't care. She resolved to keep all men at arm's length in future, mindful to avoid every word and action which could be misconstrued.

Oh yes, she admitted inwardly that she was partly to blame for Julian's behaviour, but it would never happen again. She fingered the bruise on her lip which she claimed had been caused by falling against the wardrobe in fright when she saw the mouse. If anything good had come out of the experience it was the fact that she was cured of being physically attracted to her mother's brother. Julian's intimate touch had been repulsive.

It was good to be with William again. She had missed him so much. At three years old he was of above average intelligence and could hold a reasonable conversation, perhaps because she spent so much time with him. When he flung himself into her arms she held his little body against hers with a rush of love which threatened to swamp her, and he cried out to be released.

'Mrs Hovringham said you wouldn't be back till tomorrow,' he said.

'And now I'm back today. Are you pleased?'

'Yes, yes, yes!' He jumped up and down with excitement. 'When are we going to see the ships?'

'On Saturday.' She had promised to take him to see the Naval Review at Spithead, for which ships of every nation, and in particular the British Fleet, were already gathering. It was going to be the most wonderful naval spectacle ever seen, and William had been cutting out ship pictures with Nanny Simmons to paste in his scrapbook.

On Thursday and Friday things seemed to have returned to normal. Julian visited her in the draughtsmen's office to discuss a possible new contract following on from the Ezbanian success, and he was coolly businesslike. Oliver, too, was less intrusive. It was almost as if the excursion to London had not taken place, and Ellie settled down at her drawing board with an easier mind than she'd had for weeks.

It was the lull before a storm.

Saturday 26 June dawned fine but cloudy and Ellie set off for Southsea early with William and Grandfather Cromer in a carriage drawn by two black horses which wore plumes of red, white and blue. It had been loaned by Julian, who had also reserved seats for them in a stand on the sea-front so that they could see the Royal yacht pass between the lines. Ellie had been tempted to refuse both offers, but it would have been churlish when the arrangements were partly for her grandfather's benefit. Sir Robert was suffering with rheumatic pains which limited him.

Had it not been for William's promised treat, Ellie would have preferred not to be going to Southsea at all. There had been an incident outside the West Quay Tavern the evening before, between men from Court Carriages and a group of their Eastleigh rivals who had travelled to Southampton for the evening expressly to cause trouble. Oliver, whose plebeian origin often made him gravitate towards the waterfront bars, had unfortunately become involved. His fiery Irish temper had been roused by accusations of wage-cutting to finance luxury travel for the nobility in countries where peasants were fighting for crusts of bread. The implication that Court Carriage men were traitors to the working class had so incensed Oliver that he had joined in the scuffle, ending up with a bruised hand.

Ellie saw him on the Saturday morning before setting out for Southsea, and she touched the area round the bruise with caring fingers.

'Don't ever do that again, Oliver. I can't bear it,' she said—then hastily made the remark more general, lest he took it to be exceptional concern for his own safety. 'If anything like the Pullman strike started here I'd be terrified.'

'Don't worry, it won't,' he said. 'And I'll mend my ways. I've a meeting with Julian later today which'll change a few things. It's an important man you're looking at, mavourneen, so it is.'

She was intrigued, but he wouldn't tell her more. In spite of his optimism, though, she couldn't shake off a feeling of impending disaster, or some new upheaval in her life. It stayed with her all day, spoiling her enjoyment, and she wished she hadn't seen Oliver that morning.

The streets of Portsmouth through which they passed overflowed with blue-jacketed sailors and uniformed men from foreign ships. Thousands of people lined Southsea beach and the sea-front.

The viewing place reserved for Ellie and Grandfather Cromer gave the best possible land view of the four lines of ships stretching away into the distance. One hundred and sixty-five ships of the Royal Navy rode at anchor through Spithead, while innumerable merchantmen and pleasure craft decked with pennants and bunting were dotted on the water for as far as the eye could see.

'Why can't *we* go on a boat?' William wanted to know.

'Because I can't walk up the gangway,' said Grandfather Cromer.

Undaunted, William said: 'We could leave you here.'

At exactly two o'clock the lines were cleared and a salute from guns onshore proclaimed that the Royal yacht *Victoria and Albert* had set out with the Prince of Wales on board to carry out the inspection of the fleet. In its wake came other yachts carrying royal guests, but Ellie couldn't tell William any of their names. She was still preoccupied, still ridiculously on edge, and when a threatening storm finally broke over them just as the Prince of Wales had returned to harbour, she welcomed it as the reason for her tension. She had never liked storms.

They all got a soaking as the rain continued.

'We must get back to the carriage and return home,' she said, fearing for her grandfather's health.

315

'Damned weather,' the old man grumbled.

And William indulged in a tantrum. 'I want to see the boats light up! I don't want to go home!'

She had said they could stay a short time after dark when every ship would be illuminated, but that would not be for several hours yet, and her anxiety was growing.

'I'm sorry, William. You can go to the top of the house when we get back and perhaps you'll be able to see some of the lights in the distance. There's such a lot of ships. I'm sure the line must stretch nearly as far as Southampton.'

She didn't know what she expected to find when she returned: there was just this overwhelming apprehension which sat in the pit of her stomach and made her feel every jolt of the carriage-wheels on the return journey. Dreadful pictures of the Works going up in flames crossed her mind. Others of Oliver in danger made her realise how deeply she held him in her affection. Thankfully, not one of her terrible imaginings materialised.

However, something of equal gravity awaited her.

She was surprised when Annie Hovringham came to the door of their house in The Polygon as soon as the carriage pulled up. The woman was agitated and approached Ellie the moment she had been helped down.

'I'm so glad you're back. In your absence I tried to speak to Mr Devlin on the telephone but he's at a meeting with Mr Cromer so I've had to leave the gentleman without anyone to entertain him.'

'Who is it, Mrs Hovringham? What's happened?' The spirals of fear in Ellie's stomach became taut springs which almost stopped her heart.

'Your husband's here, Mrs Berman,' Annie said.

SIXTEEN

He was standing by the fireplace in the drawing room, his handsome head reflected in the heavy gilt-edged mirror so that she saw him twice over. Once was too much. She wouldn't have returned home, had she known he was here. His presence caused her excruciating pain and she thought she was going to faint, but the feeling passed.

'Ellie,' he said, her name uttered part in greeting and part question as he anticipated her reaction. He looked forbidding. Where were the humility and guilt she had every right to expect?

'Why have you come?' she demanded. Her voice didn't sound like her own.

'We have things to talk about.'

'I'm amazed you have the gall to face me. What can we possibly have to talk about?'

He moved. She flinched, and her legs felt as if they belonged to a rag doll, but she resisted the temptation to back away.

317

'It's all right, Ellie, I'm not going to touch you.'

She had to pull herself together, otherwise he would be in control. He had already had supremacy by virtue of his totally unexpected arrival. She straightened her back, pulled in her stomach to ease its surging, and stretched her neck like a swan about to challenge an enemy.

'Had I been here when you came, you wouldn't have got past the front door,' she said. 'After what you did to me I ought to call the police.'

'I'm not proud of deserting you. It was the most cowardly thing I've ever done. But you've had your revenge, haven't you, Ellie? If we're talking about bringing in the law let me tell you I ought to consider charging you with stealing my designs. Oh yes, I saw reports of the Ezbanian train. Did you think I would never know?'

Her cheeks were very pale. How dare he condemn her for anything when she was the one with legitimate grievances! The Ezbanian train was the least important issue.

'Is that why you've come all this way? To accuse *me!* Really, Max, your hypocrisy astounds me.'

'I came to see you, and our son. And I want to see Oliver, if you know where he's living.'

'Oliver? Why Oliver?' She was incensed. He showed not the slightest sign of diffidence. 'It was obviously too much to expect that you might have repented of your sins.'

318

His manner softened. 'I've repented and I've suffered, Ellie, believe me. It wasn't easy to come here, but Poppa made me see that the wrong I did you must be faced, otherwise there will be no peace for either of us.'

'You want *me* to absolve you, is that it? *Never!* What you did to me deserves only that you rot in hell.'

'I know that. Reckon I've been there since the moment I realised I couldn't get back to you when the ship sailed.'

'I've put you out of my mind and out of my life,' she said. 'I don't want to hear how you felt. You killed me, Max. You left me empty of everything except hatred. But now I've built a new life and you will never be a part of it.'

He looked down at the carpet where the Turkish pattern was a complexity on a par with the complications in their marriage. 'There aren't enough words to tell you how sorry I am.'

'And if there were, I still wouldn't want to hear them.'

'Then for now I'll change the subject. My father is dead and I need to see Oliver because he should accept responsibility for his child.'

'Oh!' She was speechless.

'My mother is too old and infirm to continue looking after Galina—'

'How can you even talk of responsibility when you provide nothing for *our* child?'

'My letters set down in detail how I planned to support William—but how could I do anything without knowing where you were? I explained it

319

all. I poured my heart out to you, Ellie! Were you not the slightest bit moved? Had you no understanding?'

'I didn't read your letters.'

'And you didn't let me have your address after you left London.'

She had forgotten how keen his eyes were. They scrutinised her deeply, his unblinking gaze not leaving her face for an instant.

He was dressed sombrely but well, his black serge jacket edged with silk on the lapels, and his high collar touching the lobes of his ears. A pearl-headed pin kept his tie in place. No doubt he had used her money to his own good advantage. His black hair was still worn quite long, but it was carefully groomed. His hands with their tapering fingers were not those of a labourer, and she couldn't help remembering how exquisitely he had used them in the past to caress her. She drew a sharp breath as an old familiar weakness had to be curbed. Her mind rejected him, but her body was fickle.

'I wanted nothing to do with you,' she said. 'You took everything I gave you and threw it back in my face.'

'I was blind.'

'And deaf, and completely insensitive. You're a thief, Max, a common thief and I—'

'Now just wait a minute—'

'Please leave.'

Grandfather Cromer came into the room, stooped and hawk-like, but a powerful presence. 'What's going on? Ellie, do you want help to get rid of him?'

She let out a sob of despair. 'No, Grandfather. Max is just going.'

'I'll not go until I've seen my son,' said Max. 'Where is William?'

Ellie had packed the boy off in Julian's carriage with Nanny Simmons on its return journey to Fortune Cottage, with a request that he might stay until she was able to collect him later. She'd been petrified in case Max planned to kidnap him.

'You left us,' she cried. 'You denied yourself the right to see him.'

'He is my flesh and blood.'

Grandfather Cromer thumped the floor with his stick. 'Procreation carries no guarantee,' he blared. 'We earn our rights, young man, and from what I've heard you deserve none. You discarded the finest jewel in the world when you deserted my grand-daughter. There's no one finer, or kinder, or more warmhearted than Ellie, but you were too wicked to see it.'

A shadow clouded Max's face. He bowed his head and closed his eyes momentarily, as if pain blurred his vision.

'I'm so sorry, Ellie.' His voice throbbed with remorse. 'I wish you'd read my letters. I'm not good at saying how I feel. I was too proud and too heedless to appreciate you until after I'd behaved with the ultimate stupidity. I'm not asking you to forgive me yet. All I want right now is to see our son.'

'He's not here,' she said.

Grandfather held the door open. 'And you're not welcome.'

The storm which had started in the afternoon had now passed over, and evening sunlight slanted through the long window. In the distance there was a sound like gunfire—more royal salutes, most likely, since it was too early yet for the celebratory fireworks.

Max recovered his composure. 'Very well. I won't stay now, but I'll come back when you've had time to consider my apologies. I'm sorry if I've caused you more pain.'

He passed close to Ellie as he prepared to leave. She couldn't wait for him to be out of the house so that she could indulge in a storm of private weeping, but there was another matter which had not been touched on, and she couldn't let him think it too unimportant to bring out into the open.

'Max! Where is my money? I suppose it would be ridiculous to suppose you intend returning it to me.'

'Your money?' he queried, with commendable surprise. He turned back.

'I'm talking about my dowry which went with you to the States. How *could* you do it?' Her tone was as bitter as aloes. It felt as if a festering wound had been lanced and further words spurted out like a poison released. 'You left me with nothing—nothing! I was destitute, Max, alone with a baby, wet and cold and penniless, while you took off with my fortune...'

'Now wait!' He stopped her. 'I took nothing except the clothes I was wearing. I was the one who was destitute.'

'That's a lie!'

'I swear to you it isn't. I've now got my own furniture business but I've achieved it without any help from you or your family. I wanted nothing of yours.'

Grandfather Cromer closed the door so that the servants wouldn't hear. Ellie stared at her husband.

'What are you saying? I *know* you had it, otherwise I wouldn't have been in such a terrible predicament. Do you think I imagined it?'

'I think you're out of your mind.'

'It's you who are the liar,' stormed Grandfather. 'Thief, wrecker...'

'Slanderer!' retaliated Max. 'Will you let me have my say!' He turned to Grandfather Cromer. 'My greatest sin was leaving Ellie. I acknowledge it, but I will repeat until my last breath that I didn't take her money, even though I knew that you, sir, were supposed to be as rich as Croesus and titled into the bargain. It was partly that which scared me. I'd never mixed with your sort of people.'

'She found me in no better state than herself,' the old man told him fiercely. 'I was an alcoholic.'

Ellie had no intention of listening to excuses, and she indulged her anger to the full. 'If it hadn't been for Oliver, God knows what we would have done. I can't find words to describe the agony you caused me, Max. Oliver stood by me through the worst time of my life. When the bailiffs came and turned Grandfather out of his home, Oliver took on the burden of looking after all of us. His generosity was overwhelming.'

323

'The man saved us,' agreed Grandfather.

'Yes, Max, Oliver supported us all with the money his mother had left him, while you were using *my* money to feather your own nest.'

'What!' Max spat the word out.

She rushed on. 'What a brilliant plan! You never wanted to marry me. It must have been the biggest disappointment when my father refused to give me a cent or even acknowledge you as my husband.'

'Ellie...'

She clasped her hands together so tightly the bones cracked. 'What a clever way to get rid of me. You went back to America rich and free, while I had nothing.' Accusing him was making her so distraught her voice shook, but once in full flow she couldn't stop lashing him with bitter words.

'Ellie, I DIDN'T TAKE YOUR MONEY.' Max moved swiftly to clasp her arms, shaking her so that she would listen. 'And Oliver's mother lived in a cottage not far removed from a mud hut, so where do you think she would have got a fortune to leave him?'

'He had inherited money.'

'*I* gave it to him: it was your own money. I trusted him with it. He promised to give it to you and see you safely to London. I didn't take it, Ellie, I swear on oath.'

She fell silent. The Ormolu clock on the mantelpiece chimed the half hour in its frivolous tinkling fashion while Ellie's heart thudded. It dawned on her gradually that he could be speaking the truth, and she was thrown into confusion. They faced each other, two deceived people who had been living in shadows of misapprehension, and the wounds went deep. She shrugged free of his hands.

'Are you really making out that the money Oliver's been spending is really my own?'

'It must have been: he had none.' Max's mouth was now set in a grim line and his anger had to be controlled. 'Does he still live with you? Did he buy you this house?'

'No, he doesn't live with us!' She was livid at the implication. 'I pay rent to my Uncle Julian from what I earn at the Works. Oh yes, I'm a businesswoman now. I've had to be.'

'If it's true about the money, why didn't Devlin make off with it instead of buying into the company?' Sir Robert intervened.

It would take time for her to adjust to this totally new state of affairs, but what she saw straight away, appalled Ellie. 'He bought shares in my uncle's company with my money. Everything he owns rightfully belongs to me.'

'Then it's time to get it back,' said Max. 'Where does he live? I'm going to see him now.'

'I'll come with you,' Ellie said.

But Max refused to let her become involved. 'Stay here,' he commanded. 'If there's going to be trouble between Oliver and me, I don't want you anywhere near.'

'It concerns me—I've a right to know what's said!'

'No,' said Grandfather Cromer with authority. 'You'll remain here with me. Let your husband sort this out.'

There was nothing she could say to change their minds. Her grandfather gave Max directions to Brunswick Place, and she watched helplessly, her thoughts in chaos, as he strode from the room. His arrival in England had opened up a new can of worms and she feared to look inside.

Max was in a towering rage. His steel-tipped heels clipped the pavement so sharply they threw out sparks as he hurried along. He would never have believed his brother-in-law could be so criminal, and as he made for Oliver's home the questions he had to ask scorched his mind.

He had gone to Court Carriages earlier in the day expressly to ask for Ellie. It hadn't occurred to him that Oliver might work there, and being Saturday the office staff had consisted of juniors with little knowledge of the family connections. Julian Cromer, whom he knew to be Ellie's uncle, had not been at the Works during the Diamond Jubilee week, and only through persistence had Max managed to obtain Ellie's home address. He'd been surprised that her house was not more opulent. Discovery of the reason why had shocked him to the core.

This visit to England was officially to interest London buyers in his furniture, which was beginning to make a name for him. In Albany he owned a store called simply 'Berman's', and he was in the process of opening a much larger one in New York. The popularity of his furniture was exceeding all expectations and he had been persuaded to make contacts in

England before he was really ready to take on any foreign commitments. Unofficially, and far more importantly, he had come to see Ellie.

In the last two months, since the death of his father, he had made a decision. The time had come to try to right the wrong he had done, and though he knew he didn't even deserve a hearing, he was taking the first step towards putting his family together again. Laban had managed to locate him in time to be at his father's bedside with his mother and brother until Poppa had drawn his last laboured breath, and he had deeply regretted the years of separation. Families belonged together.

The storm had left huge puddles, and a fast-driven gig sent a shower of spray over him. It did nothing to cool Max's temper though, which was directed as much against himself as Oliver. It was his own fault that Oliver had betrayed him and duped Ellie.

He had always cared a lot for his brother-in-law. Oliver's devotion to Katrina had been an inspiration, and his departure after her death understandable. Everyone had presumed the trip would be short and he would return to his child, but Oliver had stayed away. He had turned his back on Galina.

The child was beautiful. Her frizzy red-gold hair brushed out round her head like a halo of light, and her piquant face was as cherubic as a Michelangelo painting. But she was also a boisterous child, filled with boundless energy. Poppa had doted on her, even wanting her near at the last when noise had caused him pain,

327

and it had been a struggle for Momma to cope. Neighbours had been kind, but Galina didn't mix well with other children. Momma, frail with grief and the trauma of nursing her sick husband, had nevertheless said she wouldn't let her grand-daughter be cared for by strangers.

'Elizabeth's not fit to take on another child. I wonder she survived the birth of the last one,' she'd said, referring to Laban's sickly wife. Then with an edge to her voice: 'You must be responsible for Galina, Max, now that Poppa's gone. Though you're worse than Oliver, deserting your wife and son.' Enough had already been said on the subject to fill a book.

'I accept the responsibility,' Max had said.

Heavy clouds hung over Southampton and seemed to press down on his head. He was about to do battle with Oliver Devlin, who would doubtless remind him of his own guilt. Both had seized an opportunity for their own selfish ends, but which of them had committed the greater wrong? Oliver had robbed Ellie of her dowry, but he had used it to care for her. Max had left her to fend for herself.

He had come to England with only the newspaper report of the Ezbanian train to lead him to Ellie. Momma's correspondence with Oliver was always care of a London bank which would not disclose a forwarding address.

Not for one minute had he suspected that Oliver would still be with Ellie. His wife and brother-in-law had not been well-acquainted. No, Max was convinced that Oliver's native

Ireland had drawn him back. Now it seemed he had appropriated her money *and* stayed on in her company. The discovery was like salt to a wound, and jealousy was added to the emotions bedevilling Max as he strode along.

He found the house and pressed his thumb on the bell without releasing it. An unruffled butler came to the door.

'Mr Devlin said he would be working late this evening, sir,' he said. 'I'm afraid I don't know what time he'll be back.'

The matter was too urgent to be left. Max hailed a hansom which was drawing away from an adjacent house, and asked to be taken to Court Carriages. Sitting impatiently on the edge of the seat he was unable to forget the new Ellie he had seen.

He had prepared himself for the meeting with her. He'd known it would be an ordeal for both of them, but he'd certainly not anticipated this outcome. The change in her had taken him aback. She had acquired a wonderful grace. Her tall, slender body was as supple as a willow, her face more beautiful than he remembered, and sculpted with planes of maturity which enhanced the air of breeding. He had looked at her in the first few minutes, and a powerful longing had replaced the anxiety preceding the meeting. His reaction was so strong it had almost thrown him off-balance. And then she had attacked him in an ice-cold temper such as he had never seen before.

Now he knew the full extent of his folly in leaving her. All previous remorse was as a seed blowing in the wind. He had resented her pursuit and her manipulation of his life, but without her he was emotionally empty. Since his return to America he had been celibate. He'd told himself it was a penance for his crime, but seeing his wife again had opened his eyes to the fact that no other woman matched up to her. He'd had no hankering for Mariette Schuman, no interest in the daughters of Jarvis Warding who vied for favours even though they knew he was tied by marriage, and no wish to deceive any of the other women who thought him to be unattached. The jewel of them all was the girl he had spurned.

Damn Oliver. Damn him to hell. At that moment he wanted to kill him.

Max's expression was as thunderous as the weather when he entered the Court Carriage Works Office for the second time that day. Even though it was late the clerk was still there.

'I must see Mr Devlin,' Max said, in staccato tones. 'It's urgent and I'll take no excuse. Tell him Max Berman is here.'

'Yes, sir.' The clerk departed hurriedly, but returned within a few minutes, his expression puzzled. 'That's strange, sir. Mr Devlin informed me he had important work to see to and I was to stay on to take letters. Now it seems he's left without telling me.'

Max clasped his hands to his head in frustration. 'Where will he have gone? He's not at home.'

'There are celebrations all over town, sir. At a guess Mr Devlin will be joining in the entertainment down by the Town Quay.'

Max received further directions and set off once more on foot, following the crowd. He would search in every bar until he found him.

A short time earlier, Oliver had concluded an acrimonious meeting with Julian Cromer which had left him feeling elated beyond measure. A financial scheme on which he had been working had finally come to fruition and he'd visited Fortune Cottage that afternoon to inform Julian he was no longer the major shareholder in Court Carriages. By careful dealing Oliver had managed to secure the company holdings of a recently-deceased baronet whose widow was having to sell everything to pay his debts. The transaction had been secretive, the amount paid well above the market value, and the outcome presented to Julian as a *fait accompli*. It had given Oliver extraordinary pleasure to inform the other man that he no longer owned the company outright.

'I now have control of more than fifty per cent of the business,' Oliver gloated. 'In future it will be run by my methods.'

Julian was ashen; the hatred in his eyes had turned ice to fire. 'You will never run my company—never!'

'And what have I been doing these last three years? Without my money, where would you be now?'

'The money is irrelevant.'

'Oh, irrelevant, is it? And my knowledge of railways?'

'You are incapable of conceiving anything as ambitious as the Ezbanian train.'

'And how long can we survive on one spectacular order? We've only been asked to give one quote for another.'

'You've lowered our standards.'

'And increased our profits. Without me, Cromer, this company would have been taken over by Eastleigh two years ago, so it would.'

It had never been an easy partnership. The two men had no intellectual meeting point, and they talked only when business affairs necessitated it. All they had in common was a desire for Ellie Berman, and it was that which added to the friction.

Oliver had not been fooled for a minute by Ellie's excuse for the fracas at the hotel in London. It had only taken a second to assess the situation, and his Irish temper had been so inflamed he'd had the utmost difficulty controlling it. In any other place he would have not been so restrained. He hated Julian Cromer. Antagonism had marked their first meeting, and his obsessive urge to gain control of Court Carriages had largely been to overthrow him. Any man who could so heartlessly ruin his own father didn't deserve to succeed. Later, when Cromer's passion for his niece had become obvious, Oliver had laid plans to ensure the ruination of the son, and this latest acquisition of shares had tipped the balance.

Julian's anger was terrifying in its ferocity. He threatened legal action, while his cold, hard face gleamed with sweat, but he had no power to reverse the situation.

'You're a peasant, Devlin. You'll live to regret the day you invested money here,' he said, his voice cutting like a scythe. 'I hate your guts and I'll break you sooner or later.'

The threats were all hot air to Oliver. He knew how to stay in control.

He returned to his office in high spirits. The wealth he had amassed since coming to Southampton now exceeded his most extravagant ambitions, and it was only the beginning. Before long he hoped to be able to buy Julian Cromer out altogether, and then Court Carriages would be Devlin-owned. Devlin! Who would have thought it possible? And along with his possession of the company would come his possession of Ellie, for he also knew how to woo her. Ellie needed constant reassurance that his interest was only affectionate, but her dependence on him would eventually tilt her emotions. The competition Julian Cromer had presented was past. He had obviously overplayed his hand, in the same way that Oliver had done himself earlier, but Julian didn't have the character to patiently rebuild a shattered dream.

The future sparkled for Oliver as he reread the signed agreement which had enabled him to gloat over his enemy, and he started composing a letter to his solicitor asking for an appointment. There was something else to be done which could be delayed no longer. Deep in thought, he wandered to the window. It was then he saw

Max crossing the yard.

All Oliver's elation evaporated as if a tongue of flame had licked it dry. He went cold. Not once had he reckoned on Max returning to England, yet it had not been guaranteed. He saw his brother-in-law striding towards the office with the confidence of a man on a mission, and was seized by panic.

He couldn't face Max yet. He needed to prepare himself. God, what explanation was he going to give for the misappropriated dowry? In the space of a few seconds Oliver savoured the same kind of fear he'd rejoiced in inflicting on Julian Cromer. He had no respect for Julian and therefore no regard for his feelings, but Max was a different matter.

His heart raced as he left his office and quit the building by a side entrance which led through the brake shop and out onto Western Esplanade. The thought uppermost was to put distance between himself and Max, though he knew an eventual meeting was inevitable.

'I just need time,' he muttered to himself. 'I must make him see I've done everything for Ellie.'

Instinct made him want to turn in the direction of home where he could burrow deep and stay hidden, but the clerk would send Max to Brunswick Place when it was discovered the office was empty. He couldn't go there.

'I'll say I didn't tell Ellie about the money because the old man would have got it out of her for drink. Didn't I invest it for Ellie's sake?' He went over his options as he hurried through the

Bargate, forming excuses, looking for the least culpable. 'He'll know a woman isn't capable of handling a fortune wisely.'

Crowds jostled him as he threaded his way down the High Street. Sounds of revelry rang out from the numerous pubs and beerhouses along its length and looked set to continue well into the early hours as the last day of the Jubilee Celebrations drew to a close. Flags and bunting fluttering above his head mocked his plight. Oliver carried on past Smith & Lewis, the store where he had recently bought a brooch to give to Ellie to mark his success. The smell of baking potatoes on a cart turned his stomach, as also did the stench from an alley leading off the main road. He needed a strong drink and a corner where he could think and plan. He was within sight of the Town Quay, and the Sun Hotel was on his left. He went inside.

It was the luckiest chance that he had seen Max in advance. Had they come face to face without warning it could have been disastrous.

A special train had brought men from Eastleigh to Southampton for the festivities. They poured onto the platform at the Terminus, already in high spirits, and like a rising tide they surged towards the hotels and public houses at the southern end of the High Street. The Sun quickly became congested, and Oliver was pressed to drink with them. Refusal would have looked bad so his glass was refilled countless times until the momentous events of the day gradually became hazy. He thought of Max once or twice more but by this time, his head was pleasantly buzzing and he was able to laugh, ridiculing himself for having let the devils in his conscience scare him. Nothing scared him.

Yet as the crowd in the bar grew denser and the air thickened with tobacco smoke, Oliver had the strongest feeling that he was being watched. Faces merged; voices became a cacophony. It was ludicrous that amidst so many he should be singled out for scrutiny—unless Max had followed him. He looked round but saw no one he knew, yet the hair at the back of his neck seemed to stand out, and he rubbed his hand over it jerkily.

He downed another glass of whisky and tried to concentrate on the conversation around him.

'Who'd work for Court Carriages? No one with any sense,' scoffed a red-faced man in a cloth cap.

'Heard tell they'll be painting bloody posies on the sides of goods wagons next.' A roar of laughter greeted this scurrility. The speaker teetered against the bar and basked in his success. 'Posies the lot of 'em at CCW—eh, fellers.'

'Give 'em a year more,' said another, 'and they'll be under Eastleigh management. Everyone knows they can't match us for workmanship.'

It hadn't occurred to Oliver that he was drinking with Eastleigh men. He hadn't seen them arrive from the train. By now he had consumed enough to have reached an aggressive stage, and he staggered to his feet.

'Shut your bloody mouths, the lot o' you,' he shouted, in his thickest Irish accent. 'Bastards! Scum, so you are! Courts wouldn't employ a man of you.'

Shouting broke out. Oliver stood alone to fight for the honour of his company, but he was recognised as having been involved in the incident outside the West Quay Tavern, and all hell broke loose.

'It's the bugger who used his fists the other night,' the cloth-capped man yelled.

Oliver wasn't intimidated. He raised his voice above the rest to defend himself and wouldn't be silenced.

'Court Carriages will still be here when Eastleigh is buried under its own scrap iron,' he bawled.

'Who are you to talk such bloody rot?'

'I control Court Carriage Works,' shouted Oliver. 'As from today I'm the major shareholder, and I swear there'll not be better rolling-stock built anywhere in Europe, so there won't.'

'Any Works run by the likes of you is doomed for a start.'

The battle of words degenerated into another scuffle. Suddenly, Oliver was desperate to get out of the claustrophobic atmosphere, but the men hemmed him in, and the wall of resistance grew more menacing. He was completely outnumbered. No one from Court Carriages was there to take his side, and the stupidity of his bravado finally dawned upon him. Fear now brought an ice-cold paralysis to his limbs, yet he was sweating profusely.

It was then he caught sight of a familiar face reflected in the mirror behind the bar.

The hatred that Julian felt for Oliver Devlin bore no comparison to any emotion he had ever felt in his life before. It seemed now as if the devil himself had made an offer too good to refuse when Court Carriages had faced ruin after the failure of Mr Kendall to invest money. Devlin had come in the guise of good fortune, but he had been satanic in his drive for power once the door was opened to him. Julian had seen his men being swept along by new ideas, veering away from the tradition set by Millicent's father, and though the profits had soared he couldn't claim any credit.

The Board had proposed that Julian should concentrate exclusively on orders from heads of state and high office. Admittedly he'd had a great success with the Ezbanian train, but financially it had been close to disaster, since Ezbania had subsequently suffered a drop in its currency value and most of the bill was still outstanding. A few orders had come about through the publicity worldwide, but not enough to keep the company running, and Julian had ungraciously accepted that without the repair shop and wagon construction, there would have been the possibility of bankruptcy.

If there had been any rapport between himself and Devlin perhaps the matter could have been resolved and an understanding reached, but as it was, the thought of acknowledging his partner's superior business acumen stuck in Julian Cromer's throat. He recognised his own jealousy and was ashamed of it, but the realisation didn't alter the way he felt. He resented the man more every day, until dislike became hatred, and hatred made his temper rise to near boiling point.

All might have stayed calm if Ellie hadn't been involved. Ellie was the flame capable of torching the fragile link between these two men of totally opposing character. She was the essence of femininity, yet as intelligent as either of them, and antagonism spilt over into a mutual craving for this woman who could belong to neither. Julian adored her. She was everything Millicent was not, and he desired her to the point of recklessness. The affair in London had shown him the result of such impatience, but he couldn't help himself. And every time he saw Devlin near her he felt sick.

Now had come the final humiliation. How could the Irish bastard have contrived to acquire a majority holding without wind of it reaching Julian's ears? He'd made a furious telephone call to his solicitor with no satisfaction. The deal had been so quietly done there'd been no leakage of information until after the signing, and shares which Julian had believed would remain in the widow's possession had changed hands in sly secrecy.

His hatred boiled over. He couldn't stay at home, even though his wife had invited Hans and Clara Gottmann to dinner. First this other matter had to be challenged. There was a lot more to be said, more proof required that the outcome was legally correct before he would finally accept Devlin's claim. He suspected fraud, and if he could prove it he would get rid of the usurper once and for all. Prison was too good for him. He'd have him deported to Ireland where he could sink in his own rotten bogs.

Julian set out that evening with the intention of going through Devlin's books, but as he approached the Works he saw the Irishman leaving with a distinctly suspicious air. He was hurrying as if a demon were after him, and Julian, intrigued, followed to observe him at a safe distance. Along to Above Bar, through the Bargate and down the High Street he scurried, as furtive as a thief, and only his red hair enabled Julian to keep him in sight as he mingled with the crowd. The street was jammed with carriages and wagons making for the Town Quay, and horse-droppings had been trodden onto the pavement, making it so slippery he almost tumbled. Then Oliver Devlin entered the Sun Hotel.

There were so many people crowding in the bar it wasn't difficult to stay out of sight. Someone thrust a tankard of beer in Julian's hand, and though he would never normally partake of the vulgar drink he held onto it as reason for his presence. He witnessed his prey quickly becoming loquacious and edged as close as he dared, to listen. To his consternation he discovered that most of the crowd drinking with

Devlin comprised railmen who had come down from Eastleigh.

This was a new development—something completely beyond all the previous problems which had threatened Julian's control of his company. He'd believed Oliver's meddling and plotting to be centred internally, but here was proof the treachery extended beyond that. Devlin was courting the opposition, and there could only be one reason for doing it. He wanted amalgamation and eventual control himself of the Eastleigh Works as well.

Julian's fury rose to a crazed height which robbed him of any further rational thought. He no longer concealed himself on the edge of the crowd, but pushed forward with the strength of Goliath, the need to put a stop to the traitor's scheming uppermost in his mind.

A barman had been opening a box containing a fresh supply of glasses. The knife he had used was lying on the corner of the bar. Julian's gloved hand closed round the handle and gripped it hard. He saw his enemy passionately involved in a scene which smelt of violence, but his ears were deaf to the cause. Rage blinded him, so he didn't see Devlin glance in the mirror and recognise him with what seemed to be a look of thankfulness.

Julian used the knife with uncontrollable fury at the very moment a blow was levelled at the Irishman's chin which sent him reeling backwards into the crowd; the blade embedded itself in his spleen. He would have collapsed on the floor if the crush around him hadn't supported his body for several minutes.

In horror at what he had done, Julian backed away and managed to reach the door unobserved while attention was focused on the terrible scene. Amazingly, there had been so many people compressed together it would have been impossible to see whose hand had used the weapon. With a bit more luck he would get away with it.

He reached the street and took a gulping breath to calm himself and rid his lungs of the smoke. The festive crowd milling around him sang patriotic songs, and arms were linked as men, women and children danced on this night for temporarily forgetting life's cares.

Julian Cromer was jeered as he thrust the merrymakers aside, but he heard nothing except the clamour within his own head as he set about fleeing as far as possible, as quickly as possible, from the place where Oliver Devlin's life-blood was draining away...

SEVENTEEN

That same evening, Max took the Western Esplanade route to the Town Quay. He, too, got caught up in the throng, and as he was a stranger to the town he could only go along with it. Children were climbing over the Stella Memorial and played around the Russian cannons along the front which had been

342

fired earlier in celebration of the Jubilee. Isle of Wight steamers sporting bunting were tied up at the Royal Pier, and he could hear music coming from the bandstand and the pavilion, but these distractions which beckoned the revellers were not for him.

He stood by the pier entrance for several minutes, depressed by the futility of looking for Oliver amidst such crowds. It would be almost impossible to find him. Nevertheless he didn't intend to give up, so he walked on further. There were plenty of beerhouses and pubs at the corner of the High Street. He would start with those.

It was about a quarter of an hour later that he was pushed by a man in an elegant grey suit emerging from the Sun Hotel, and he was struck by his manner. Even on an evening such as this the gent looked out of his province. The Sun had no appeal. Advertisements for wines and spirits, lead glass and rope adorned the white-washed walls, and the raucous sounds from within came from working-class voices.

But it was not merely the man's elegance which attracted Max's attention. It was the haunted look which gave his light-coloured eyes a piercing wideness, as if he had just witnessed something unspeakable. A second later he was gone, lost in the multitude, and the encounter slipped to the back of Max's memory.

He was about to move on when he noticed that an uncanny silence had descended on the hotel, but even as he paused, the silence was replaced by a different clamouring, an urgent blending of voices. A man in a striped jacket dashed out.

'Find a doctor,' he cried. 'Where's there a doctor? A bloke's been knifed!'

Max was not a medical man, but during the Pullman strike he had gained enough knowledge of first aid to help in an emergency. He forced his way through the door and edged between the crowd of men with their backs towards him, gaining access to the long bench where the victim had been laid. Amidst the shouting and arguing, the landlord was appealing for calm.

'He's dead,' said the man nearest. 'Ain't no use going for help.'

'Bloody big-mouth Irishman,' another muttered. 'Deserved what he got.'

'Who did it?' someone else demanded. 'By hell, I never saw anything happen quicker.'

The questions and recrimination increased in volume as Max looked down in horror at the body of his brother-in-law, Oliver Devlin.

The death of a senior director of Court Carriages in a celebration-evening brawl at the Sun Hotel was the talk of Southampton the next day. Eastleigh men were questioned for hours by the police, but none would confess to having used the knife which caused the fatal wound. No one had seen it used. It was a mystery which the newspapers claimed was a vow of silence to protect the guilty, but as the majority present at the time of the killing had been the worse for drink, it was deemed unlikely that the truth would ever be known.

Ellie Berman heard of the tragedy soon after it happened. William had been disappointed at not seeing the fireworks at Portsmouth and she'd promised to read to him after Nanny Simmons had settled him in bed, but before she could go up to his room a policeman came to the house, asking for Oliver Devlin's next-of-kin. The terrible news he brought drained Ellie's face of all colour and she went to Grandfather Cromer's room instead, as if in a trance.

'Max murdered him,' she said, her voice tight and toneless. 'Max has killed Oliver.' Then as the fact sank in she let out a cry. 'Oh my God, what's going to happen next?'

It took the old man several minutes to quieten her. She sobbed in his arms, repeating garbled questions.

'You don't know that's what happened,' her grandfather said, stroking her hair with his gnarled hand. 'A crowd under the influence of drink can become mindless—I've seen it.'

'Max went after him and he was in a killing mood.'

'No, child. He was angry, but not that. He didn't strike me as a killing sort.'

'A man who can desert his wife and child the way he did is capable of anything.'

'I've dealt with a lot of men in my time and I'm a fair judge of character. Max may have let you down but I'd say he's suffered for it and come out stronger. Don't go condemning him before he can defend himself.'

'You're excusing him!'

'No, I'm repeating he's no murderer.'

She thought about it for a minute and conceded that he was probably right. Whatever else Max was guilty of, surely he wouldn't take another man's life, and certainly not that of his brother-in-law. But she wouldn't allow that he was blameless.

'They say Oliver was drunk,' she said. 'That wasn't like him. Max must have had something to do with it.'

'Perhaps—who's to know?'

Events were moving too fast for her. She hadn't been able to absorb the completely unexpected return of her husband before having to face this new and even more terrible trauma.

'What am I going to do, Grandfather? I can't take it in.'

'You've got guts, child. Nothing beats you.'

But it was going to take more than guts to come to terms with all these new developments.

She had loved Oliver. Oh, not the way she had once loved Max—she would never again be foolish enough to love like that—but Oliver had earned a special place in her heart with his seeming generosity and understanding. Even now she was still not completely convinced of his duplicity. Not once in three years had he given her grounds to be suspicious of his wealth. And now he couldn't answer for himself.

She couldn't think straight. If Max was to be believed, Oliver, whose kindness she had accepted as a declaration of love, had been deceiving her from the moment he had appeared as her saviour on the quayside the day Max had sailed out of her life. Had he really been greedy, selfish, heartless, and clever? Whatever else he had done, he could never have been accused of neglect. Oliver, with his Irish charm, had looked after her. He had cared for William and Grandfather as if they were his own family. If he had embezzled her money she could never say that he'd been wholly wicked, for though it had changed his own life he had used it to improve hers also. She had often wondered where she would be now if Grandfather Cromer had been able to get *his* hands on it.

Max returned not long after the policeman had left. One look at him was enough to tell that he was deeply upset, but Ellie was not yet prepared to retract her suspicions. She came into the room where they had so recently exchanged bitter words, but offered no greeting.

'I've heard about Oliver,' she said. 'Were *you* the last to see him? What did you say to him?'

'I didn't have the chance to say anything. He wasn't at the house and he'd left the office—' he stopped abruptly, his expression changing. 'Ellie, you can't be blaming me!'

'Why shouldn't I? Oh, I don't think you killed him, though it did cross my mind at first. Grandfather talked me out of it.'

'Oliver was like a true brother. What he did to you was partly my fault, so how could I have loved him any the less? Oh, I admit I was angry, but I would never have killed him.' He rubbed his hand across his eyes. 'I found him too late. He was already dead when I got to the place where he'd been drinking. I'll never forget it, seeing him lying there.'

He was so genuinely affected that tears sprang to Ellie's eyes. Two steps separated them as she crossed the barrier to briefly put her arms round his shoulders with an urge to share their mutual grief. The feel of him was so powerfully evocative she gave a little groan, but when he returned the affectionate gesture she hastily retreated.

They talked for a time, debating the tragedy but unable to find a single valid reason for it. Oliver had been well-liked at the Works. To Ellie's knowledge no one had borne him a grudge. The only possible solution was that he had again antagonised the Eastleigh men with his vociferous Irish talk, and maybe one of them the worse for drink had acted on impulse.

'I don't believe it was premeditated,' said Max. 'Every man there was scared.'

She acknowledged the conclusion with a weary inclination of her head. The effect of Oliver's death was taking its toll and she was desperately tired. So much had happened since yesterday she could hardly believe it was only a short time ago that she and William had been enjoying a happy day in Portsmouth.

There was a commotion out in the hall and William could be heard thumping downstairs in defiance of Nanny Simmons's command to return at once to his room. The boy had a temper, and even at three years old he could exert his will.

'Mama said she would read to me,' he was shouting. 'I want to see Mama.'

Ellie went to the door, and as he rushed into her arms his little pyjama-clad body was warm and wriggling like an excited puppy's. He scolded her as he hugged her.

'I'm so sorry, madam,' his nanny apologised. 'I just couldn't keep him quiet any longer.'

'It's all right, Nanny,' said Ellie. 'I'm afraid I was delayed.' She had half-closed the door behind her so that it was impossible to see in. 'There's someone here to see William. Would you mind leaving us, please?'

'Of course, madam.'

Ellie picked him up. He smelt of lavender-perfumed soap.

'Who is it, Mama? Who's here? Is it Uncle Oliver?'

'No, sweetheart, it's not Uncle Oliver.' She returned to the drawing room with him in her arms.

The tall man with jet-black hair came slowly towards them, but in spite of the gentle smile she sensed that Max was nervous. The child with equally dark hair, and so like the man about the nose and mouth, stared in disappointment because he was unfamiliar.

'Hello, William,' Max said. 'I'm your Papa.'

The expression on his face as he beheld his son was difficult to read. It was as if a blind had come down over those discerning eyes to hide his inner feelings, and Ellie's spine tingled. She had never known what went on in Max's mind. He was an introvert who shied away from sharing personal thoughts, and to William he must have seemed very solemn. The little boy buried his face against his mother's neck.

'It's all right, darling,' she said. 'Papa has come all the way from America to see us. Don't you think you should say hello?'

'No,' William cried. 'Go away!'

Max booked an hotel room for that night, but the bed was merely a place to rest his head. He couldn't sleep.

His mind was churning. The revelations and tragedy of the last twenty-four hours had left him dazed and he had to put his thoughts into some sort of order before the morning. Suddenly events from the past were boiling over to stain the future with problems he had never envisaged.

A gaslight outside the window cast a greenish glow on the ceiling and tree shadows moving over it gave an impression of the sea. It was hypnotic, but there was no peace. Images of Ellie and William crowded in to twist the knife already piercing his conscience. His desertion of them had taken on a new and even more damning significance, now that he knew the true state of affairs she had encountered in London. Only her strength of will would have seen her through—and her capacity to love. Old Sir Robert Cromer would have probably been incurable if she hadn't loved him.

Love, too, had probably weakened Oliver. No doubt he had intended making off with the money once he had deposited Ellie with her grandfather. It must have come as a great shock to discover what awaited her, and he would have stayed initially out of sympathy and guilt. And now he was dead.

Max closed his eyes but the shadows still danced across his lids. He cupped his hands over them to bring darkness, his head aching badly as he peered into the black cavern within his palms.

Ellie's love for himself had been full and unconditional. How could he have rejected it?

Oliver's death was a blow of the greatest magnitude. The violence of it caused mystery and questions, and added pain. The suddenness, before personal grievances and reasons for his duplicity could be aired, made it doubly tragic. And it left Galina without a father.

'You're the one, Max, who should have responsibility for the child now,' Momma had said, even before this had happened. 'Oliver would want you to be her guardian in his absence now that Poppa is gone.'

He knew he would now have to accept that responsibility, but it was difficult to know in what practical capacity he could care for his small niece. He didn't find it easy to communicate with children.

He had been avoiding the one great test of his emotions which had left him feeling even more devastated, and that was the meeting with his own son. Not for one moment had he expected to be so moved. Remembering his antipathy towards the baby in Chicago, he hadn't anticipated any strong reaction in himself now, so it had come as an added shock when he'd experienced a powerful feeling of love and pride. The boy was exceptional. He was obviously very advanced for his age, and his looks were a combination of the best features in both parents, which made him a handsome child indeed. Max had stared at him incredulously, aware of his own stupidity as never before in denying himself the privilege of being with his son through the early years.

He dug his fingers into his temples until the pain was agony, but inflicting it brought no relief. He had wanted to take William out of his mother's arms and draw him into his own with fierce possessiveness, but there would have been noisy resistance. William had looked at his father with mature antagonism, as if he knew everything about his betrayal. Any overture would have been rejected, and Max could only accept that he deserved nothing else.

He was a broken man.

The funeral of Oliver Devlin attracted an exceptionally large crowd, the mourners at St Michael's Church overflowing into the square outside. Curiosity brought many to the scene, but there was a genuine feeling of sadness in the town that a businessman of Oliver's calibre should be the victim of such a callous attack.

Ellie, dressed in black moiré silk, arrived with her husband to walk with him down the aisle as chief mourners. They alighted from the carriage drawn by two black horses and stood at the church entrance to await Grandfather Cromer, Julian and Millicent. Max was an elegant figure in an immaculate dark suit. Ellie was studying him, surreptitiously when the occupants of the second carriage arrived and stepped down, so she saw his expression. It was the first sight of Julian which disturbed him.

He turned to Ellie. 'Who is that man?' he demanded urgently.

'My Uncle Julian,' she said. 'Why? What's the matter?'

'I saw him leaving the Sun Hotel at the time Oliver was killed.'

'You couldn't have done. Julian would never go to such a place.'

'I know it was him.'

Ellie glanced behind her to where Julian was talking to a group of senior men from Court Carriages. Black didn't suit him. It took away what colour he normally had and gave him a drawn appearance, but he was animated in his conversation. He didn't give the impression of a man with something shameful to hide.

'Tell me how you're so sure,' she said.

Max didn't hesitate. 'He's too distinctive for there to be any doubt. The high forehead, the light hair, the eyes...'

'I'll introduce you,' said Ellie.

She put a gloved hand politely through the crook of his arm and they walked over to the group. Her uncle stopped in mid-sentence as she approached, and came towards her with a sympathetic expression.

'My dear, this is a very sad day,' he said, taking her hand and lifting it to his lips. 'Millicent and I are full of sorrow for you.'

It was the first time she had seen him since

the killing. He had sent a letter of condolence expressing his deep sorrow at her bereavement, and saying how much he regretted losing a business partner and a friend, but he had asked her to forgive him for not calling in person. The loss of Oliver at the Works meant he was now having to undertake double the responsibility, and there would be no time before the funeral to visit her. Ellie had read between the lines. The excuse was the shelving of an awkward encounter.

'Julian, I'd like you to meet my husband,' Ellie said. 'He's over here on business. Max, this is my mother's brother, Julian Cromer.'

'It's an honour to make your acquaintance,' said Julian.

The two men shook hands, and to his credit Julian was the more friendly. He asked after Max's journey and whether he intended to stay long in England.

Max was brusque in reply. 'A week would have been sufficient. Now I'm not sure.'

'Of course, Oliver was your brother-in-law. How sad that you arrived just too late to see him alive.'

Ellie listened to a brief exchange between them, and was sure Max had been mistaken about seeing Julian coming out of the Sun.

'I was there when he died,' said Max. 'If I ever find the man who did it, I'll ruin him.'

'He deserves to hang,' agreed Julian.

People were moving into church. Millicent came to her husband's side and drew him into his place behind Max and Ellie. Grandfather

Cromer, who grieved for Oliver as if he had been a son, walked between the two couples.

After the burial it was only necessary for these same five people to gather in the drawing room of Oliver's house in Brunswick Place at the request of his solicitor, Mr Richard Cresswell of Messrs Radham Cresswell & Son. There were no other relatives or close associates to hear how Oliver had wished to dispose of his wealth. The day was sunny. A shaft of light from the long window was filled with dust specks, and it illuminated the photograph of his daughter which Oliver had shown to Ellie with such pride only recently in London. He had bought a silver frame for it. Poor Galina would never now know her father.

They sat on high-backed chairs. Ellie looked from one to the other with curiosity, wondering what their thoughts were. It was unlikely any one here except herself would benefit from Oliver's will, unless it was Max. She was fairly confident of her own expectations. Oliver had told her on more than one occasion that should anything happen to him, her financial future would be assured. How noble of him in the light of Max's revelation! There would be provision made for Galina, of course, and Ellie wouldn't begrudge it to the child. After all, Oliver had invested the money well and there would be far more than her original dowry.

Mr Cresswell undid the catches on his case with a loud clicking noise.

'Ladies and gentlemen, I will not take up much of your time,' he said. 'The business I have to carry out will be very brief.' He took a single piece of paper from the case and closed the lid again. 'There is only a single beneficiary following the death of my client.'

The room was warm and Millicent held a crystal bottle of smelling-salts beneath her nose. Max's expression was inscrutable, and Grandfather Cromer's head was lowered as if he was trying not to show interest in the proceedings. It was Julian who commanded Ellie's attention, and for the first time she considered what this was going to mean to him. He looked anxious. There were indentations at the sides of his mouth from drawing his lips into a tight line, and by watching the rise and fall of the jet-headed pin in his cravat she could tell that his breathing was erratic. With Oliver dead and Ellie the inheritor of his wealth, Julian would have to accept her as his new partner in the business. The situation intrigued her.

'I shall only be getting back what has always been rightfully mine,' she mused. 'Though I won't tell Julian that.'

The solicitor seemed reluctant to disclose the information. He was a young man with curly brown hair and pimpled skin, obviously the 'Son' in the legal partnership, but his junior status in no way detracted from the shrewd light in his eyes. A fly buzzed annoyingly against the window pane.

'I always advised Mr Devlin to the best of my ability,' Richard Cresswell said at last, clearing his throat. 'He was keen-minded and issued business instructions which never failed to improve his standing. He mainly relied on his own judgement, but he also took advice from me, on all matters except one. Mr Devlin was strangely reluctant to arrange for his wishes to be known in the unlikely event of his demise. I frequently reminded him of the necessity, with so many assets to be disposed of should it occur, but he always deferred the moment.'

There was a stunned pause.

'Are you saying Oliver didn't make a will?' asked Max, sitting forward in his seat.

It was as if no one in the room drew breath. The fly stopped buzzing.

'There is no will,' said Mr Cresswell. 'Mr Devlin's entire estate passes to his immediate relative, his only daughter living in America. Miss Galina Devlin inherits everything.'

All eyes turned incredulously to look at the photograph in the silver frame.

The revelation that a four-year-old girlchild had inherited a major part of one of Southampton's chief industries came as a shock to the business community. It temporarily damaged trading with the company and caused rejoicing at Eastleigh. Mercifully, thanks to Max, the setback was short-lived.

The day following Oliver's funeral brought the three people most affected together again for an urgent meeting in Julian's office. Only Max was forward-thinking. Ellie, who now had even less than before, was too exhausted to contribute anything at the beginning, since whatever the outcome she would be the loser. Julian was pompous and full of furious resentment which had no doubt festered throughout the night.

'I'll sell everything I own to regain control,' he stated. 'Millicent will have to resign herself to getting rid of Fortune Cottage, the pictures will have to be sold, and the children will forego luxuries.'

Had it been left to Ellie he might have been successful in his bid, but she had lost all right to any say in the matter. Max was the one who could call the tune.

'As Galina's guardian I shall be looking after her interests,' he said.

'You'll sell out her shares in Court Carriages, of course,' said Julian smoothly. 'You'll want to realise the capital.'

'No, she won't need it. There'll be enough money with Oliver's own capital to provide everything my niece is going to need, but should it not be enough, I can sell the house.'

'There's no one to take Oliver's place at the Works,' said Ellie. Fatigue clouded her vision. She could see nothing beyond the spectre of Court Carriages falling into the hands of the receivers. 'He was the drive behind every new idea. I'm sorry to have to say it, Julian, but if it hadn't been for him there would have been no company to argue over.'

'We'll take over together, Ellie.' Max spoke quietly and with confidence.

Julian protested by thumping his fist on the desk and declaring the suggestion an outrage.

Ellie stared at her husband coldly, amazed

that he could even voice such an idea. Her answer was succinct. 'Never!'

'It's the only sensible solution.'

'It's preposterous,' shouted Julian. 'A woman issuing orders!'

'My wife is as capable as any man of running a business. She was brought up among railroad magnates and probably knew as much about the system in childhood as you do now, Cromer. She's got knowledge and ability, and above all the courage to succeed against all odds.'

This was Max defending her, giving exceptional praise. Ellie listened with surprise. In Pullman he hadn't even taken her into his confidence when the troubles started. How had he rated her intelligence then? Oh, she knew why he was being so lavish. He wanted her help now that so much responsibility had been put on him, but she had no intention of giving it.

Throughout the night she had tossed in sleepless confusion, tormented by the unfairness of everything. Just when she had begun to feel settled there had come yet another powerful shock to rob her of her security. It was like trying to climb a sandhill. There was no sure foothold in her life, and all she could do was look up from the bottom once more with determination not to stay there.

Max was full of plans. Galina would be brought over to live with them and they would be a family together in Oliver's house. William would like having his cousin for company. He made it sound idyllic, but she offered no comment.

The men began arguing again forcibly while she sat in passive contemplation. Their heated words went over her head and she let them discuss the pros and cons of her merits as if she wasn't there. Then Max addressed her.

'An official document will be drawn up then, Ellie,' he said. 'I know Galina will be glad when she's older. You'll be a partner in the company and you'll be consulted at all levels. When there are decisions to be made you will have an equal say.'

Ellie got up slowly. It was another bright day and the sun shone on her black hair which was drawn severely back from her face so that her beautiful features were accentuated. Her mouth relaxed into a gentle smile, the fullness of her lips moistened by the slow rotation of her tongue over them. Her eyes rested on Julian first with cool disinterest before moving on to her husband. She stood tall and straight.

'I'm sorry, Max, I won't be here to accept any of the consolation prizes you're offering. I won't stay in the same country as you, never mind the same house.' She used the imperious tone of her pre-marriage days. 'I shall return home to Chicago on the first available ship, and I'm taking William with me. Grandfather too, if he will come.'

A week later, clothes were packed for the three of them in the trunk which had accompanied her on that fateful voyage to Southampton, and she brushed off the dust of England from her shoes without a tinge of regret.

Ellie was leaving Max in an unenviable situation.

He called it desertion.

PART THREE

WILLIAM

EIGHTEEN

After she had been back in Chicago a few weeks, it almost seemed to Ellie as if she had never been away. The Prairie Avenue mansion became her home once more. Papa had at last forgiven her, and she settled down to a renewed social life which helped to ease the pain of all that had happened since she had quit the family home in the belief that love would compensate for everything. It wasn't exactly the life she wanted but it was preferable to being in a state of perpetual turmoil, which she would have been, had she listened to Max.

She went shopping once more with Mama, choosing new gowns as if she were a girl again at the start of her first social season. And she looked at Chicago with new eyes. She had forgotten how impressive the tall buildings were: they appeared to touch the sky. The new Root's twenty-storey Masonic Temple at State and Randolph had fourteen elevators which went from bottom to top and back again in three minutes, and there were hanging gardens on the roof. Where else in the world was there anything so impressive? Good entertainment, too, was something she had missed, and a visit to the Auditorium Theater at Michigan Avenue and Congress Street with Drew and Clarissa brought back so many memories she could have cried.

Ellie had no regrets at leaving Southampton. It had been her home for three years but she hadn't put down roots. The place had never inspired any great affinity, and it wouldn't sadden her if she never saw it again. Mainly though, it had been important to leave so that Max would know he couldn't walk back into her life and expect her to resume any kind of relationship, business or otherwise. She wanted nothing to do with him.

Mama welcomed Grandfather Cromer with caution. It was so long since she had seen her father. The once dynamic and overbearing character had become an irascible old man, but it was impossible not to admire the courage which had enabled him to set out at the age of seventy-six to start a new life in a new continent.

'I'm pleased to see you, Father,' Sibylla said. 'Elena seems to have reformed you, though how she's done it I just don't know.'

' "Elena"? Why don't you call her Ellie like everyone else?' he demanded.

'Because she was christened Elena. Now, do you want to live with us, because if so I hope you will try to fit in.'

He smiled wickedly. 'I bet you've told your posh friends they'll be meeting a titled Englishman. Oh, I'll behave myself, don't you worry.'

For the first time ever Ellie saw her mother discomfited and realised the effect Grandfather Cromer must have had on her in her youth.

Papa, to his credit, remembered the early help

366

Sir Robert had given him, and tried to make the transition easier. It was, as Grandfather said, no great thing really. Since the coming of the bailiffs he hadn't called anywhere home.

It was William who won the hearts of everyone and set the seal of approval which Ellie sought. He was a great delight to his maternal grandparents, so different from Frederick's boys. Clarissa was unfortunately still barren after several years of marriage, and Jefferson, who had disappointed his father by becoming involved with theatre work, showed no sign of wanting a wife.

'Nothing is the same,' lamented Papa. 'John Harlan ran for Mayor on the strength of being a Princeton footballer, and Carter Harrison tried to outdo him by posing for posters on a racing bicycle. I ask you, where has the dignity gone? Trying to catch the imagination of the young voters who don't know enough about politics to fit in a flea's ear! Whatever is the world coming to?'

'You must admit, Conrad, that the photograph made us laugh,' Mama reminded him. 'There was Harrison with his moustache and sweater and knickers, sporting a pendant with eighteen bars hanging from it to represent his runs with the Century Road Club. It was quite ridiculous.'

Jefferson produced a copy of the picture for Ellie and Grandfather to see. It proclaimed: *Not the Champion Cyclist, but the Cyclists' Champion.*

'It looks more like a music-hall porter,' laughed Ellie.

'The Germans swung the vote in favour

of Carter Harrison, of course,' Drew said. He had become staid and serious since his advancement in the Union Atlantic Railroad Company. 'Harrison speaks their language and drinks their beer.'

'Well, at least he's Chicago-born,' said Papa. 'It remains to be seen if he gets the eight-hour working day, the garbage improvements and the immigration support he's promised.'

Yes, it was good to be home indulging in the kind of conversation she had grown up with, and Ellie was happy.

It was good, too, to see her godfather again.

'My dear Elena, how I've missed you,' he greeted her, and hugged her warmly. 'I would have come to see you on one of my visits to England, had I known where to find you.'

'I'm afraid your name isn't very popular at Court Carriages,' she told him, after a long discussion about the business. 'My Uncle Julian objected strongly to the American competition.'

'He'd better pray, then, that the Wagon-Lits organisation doesn't get a foothold over there. It's prevented *me* expanding into Europe.' And the talk went fascinatingly on.

George Pullman arranged a special reception in his garden to celebrate Ellie's homecoming; it reminded her of her eighteenth birthday party. Florence was there with her husband, Frank Lowden, and their son George Mortimer Pullman Lowden who was the apple of his grandfather's eye. The earlier rivalry between Ellie and Florence still lingered.

'Don't you think my son is far more handsome

than hers?' Ellie asked Clarissa.

'Without doubt,' came the expected answer.

Mr Pullman himself looked tired and much older.

'Poor George hasn't been the same since the strike,' said Papa. 'Pullman City is now annexed to Chicago and there's talk of getting a Supreme Court Order to make him sell the houses to workers. He never wanted that.'

It came as a great shock to everyone when George Pullman died very suddenly on 19 October, at the age of sixty-six. He'd had a massive heart attack. All Americans were shocked at the news and there was speculation as to who would take over as head of the Pullman Company, none of his children having shared their father's passion for it. The late President Lincoln's son, Robert T Lincoln, was favoured as the most suitable, and indeed that was what happened. The Harvey family grieved over the loss of their good friend and neighbour, Ellie most of all. Her godfather had meant so much to her, and at the interment at Graceland Cemetery she broke down when the dear man who had been a precious link with her childhood was laid to rest.

The days breezed by, carrying Ellie from one activity to another like a bee from flower to flower. It was wonderful to renew old friendships, and she had so many invitations she couldn't accept them all. Her sojourn in England had wiped away the stigma of her failed marriage and she was once more the toast of the town.

There was one visit, though, which she undertook as a duty early on, and that was to see Max's mother. Ellie had warm memories of Hedda Berman and it was only fair that she should get to know William. The meeting was difficult, however. Hedda took her grandson into an emotional embrace which upset him for the rest of the time they were there, and wariness marked her attitude towards her daughter-in-law.

'My son is a good man. Why can you not live together?' she asked, after the formalities had been dispensed with. 'I do not understand.'

'He left me, Momma Berman. He didn't want me,' said Ellie.

'But he wants you now. He has repented. Why can't you forgive him? Surely they teach the law of Moses in your Catholic Church.'

'Love is the most important Commandment, and Max has never loved me.'

'I'm sure that isn't true.'

'Well, until the day he proves his love I shall not be living with him. We're tied for life by our marriage vows, but that doesn't mean he can drop me and pick me up again just as he pleases.'

The conversation bored William. He began to misbehave, and was so busy tugging at Ellie's skirt and grizzling that he didn't see a little girl come and stand in the doorway. She stared at him with disapproval.

'Grandmother, I don't like boys like him,' the child said, pointing.

The two women turned. William stopped crying.

'Galina, come and meet your cousin,' said Hedda, drawing the girl to her side.

Ellie stiffened as she looked at Galina, seeing her now in a different light from when she had saved her infant life. She was so like Oliver. Her flame-coloured hair was as bright as polished copper, her mouth small and determined, the chin pointed to give her a heart-shaped face. Only her eyes were different. They were as dark as Max's, and were the only indication that she came from Berman stock. She was dressed in a plain black dress which came to her knees and showed the white broderie anglaise frills on her pantaloons. Black stockings covered her thin little legs which seemed too fragile for the black buttoned boots. The sombreness of her clothes gave her a drab plain appearance, but the signs of future beauty were unmistakably there, though William was too young to appreciate them.

'You've got hair like a scarecrow,' he said to her, scornfully.

'And you've got a big nose and big feet,' scoffed Galina.

William was not standing for that. He set about his cousin with such ferocity that it took Ellie several minutes to disengage him, but he didn't come off best. Galina had used her fingernails to scratch his face and she had drawn blood. It was as much as Hedda could do to hold her, so eager was the child to continue the battle, and even then tongues and grimaces were used to display their sentiments about each other.

The visit was a fiasco which Ellie didn't repeat. Galina Devlin was not a likeable child, which made it even harder to accept that she was rich at Ellie's expense.

Just before Christmas, Max came back to Chicago. He telephoned the Prairie Avenue house to say that he would be visiting his wife at four o'clock in the afternoon so that she wouldn't be able to say she'd known nothing of the arrangement. Ellie hadn't answered either of his recent letters so he presumed she was still disregarding any mail from him, disposing of it unopened.

It was only the second time he had been to this house, and he vividly recalled the interview in the anteroom on the previous occasion. This time he was shown to the luxurious drawing room where the red, blue and gilt painted pipes of a huge organ dominated the décor. This was a great improvement on his previous reception, which he took as a sign that he now had a position of sorts in the Harvey family.

When Ellie came in, he was captivated anew by her loveliness. Today she wore an expensive gown of midnight blue, and with jewels decorating her throat and ears she looked every inch a Chicago socialite. He could hardly believe she was married to him, but he saw with relief that she still wore her wedding ring.

'If you've come to try and make me change my mind about Court Carriages you're wasting your time,' she said. 'This is my home now. It's where I'm staying.'

Her pride was another mantle, cloaking her in an impenetrable aloofness. He longed to shake her free of it. Into his mind came pictures of her in the cotton frock she had worn in Pullman when she was pregnant with William and he wished it were possible to have that time over again. How differently he would use it.

'I came partly to give you this,' he said, handing her a long white envelope. 'I was afraid that if I sent it through the mail, you might burn it without examining the contents.'

She took it. 'I read your last two letters. They don't alter anything.'

'This is a cheque to cover the dowry money you were deprived of,' Max told her. 'I've sold my furniture business in Albany.'

Surprise rendered her silent for several seconds. She held the envelope as if it were red-hot and studied it while she drew breath. Then she attempted to hand it back.

'I don't want it,' she said. 'It was Oliver who stole my money, not you. It isn't your responsibility to repay it.'

'Take it. I was as guilty as Oliver and it's only right that I should try to make amends.'

'You can never do that as long as you live.'

'Won't you at least let me try?'

'It's too late, Max. The wrong you did me was unforgivable. If you'd left me while we were in Pullman I might have been able to consider it. I might even have understood if you'd gone away with another woman, and perhaps forgiven you. But to desert me in a foreign country was like taking an unwanted dog onto the plains and

373

dumping it. You had no compassion whatsoever, and now I have no feelings for you.'

'It was done on the spur of the moment. I didn't have time to think.'

'That is the weakest excuse I have ever heard. I loathe you now, and I shall go on loathing you forever.'

Her sentiments were expressed with cold conviction, but he noted that the envelope she gripped was fluttering slightly. However, she was gracious enough to invite him to stay for tea. Neither of her parents were at home. Max talked of Court Carriages and gave Ellie news of Julian Cromer, who was at the Works from dawn till dusk and making himself unpopular with the men by expecting too much. Her uncle was driving himself hard and expecting others to do the same, with little reward.

'You and Julian ought to get on well,' she said, pouring tea from a silver pot. Cream lace ruffles at her neck gave her skin a softness he longed to touch. 'His main interest is in luxury cars, the kind you design.'

'On the contrary, the man won't work with me. He wants me out, but the harder he tries to get rid of me the more I dig in. I learnt a lot when I established Berman's. I did damn well out of it. Now I've given up everything else to take over Oliver's position and I intend to see Galina's inheritance is managed well.'

'How ironic. If you'd stayed with me, the company might one day have been ours instead of Galina's.' She was understandably touchy about anything to do with Court Carriages.

Prudence brought William downstairs to join them a short time later. Max's heart jolted at the sight of his son, this time dressed in short turquoise knickerbockers and a white frilled shirt. The boy eyed his father with the same suspicion as before, but behaved impeccably, and was treated as if he were much older than his three years. Max wanted to take the child out to the garden and play with him as any normal father would do, but at the first overture William shrank against his mother. She picked him up and held him straddled across her hip like the child of any tenement-dweller. Max felt a throb in his loins. She was all woman, a creature to make any man excited.

'He's settled well,' Ellie told him. 'Everyone spoils him, though.'

'I heard about his meeting with Galina and their instant dislike of each other.'

A smile lifted the corners of her mouth. 'Your mother and I had to hold them apart like squabbling puppies in the park. It wasn't funny at the time, but now...' William was fidgeting and she put him down. He ran off alone. 'Galina is very precocious.'

'Life hasn't been easy for her, living with old people. I'm taking her to England straight after Christmas. Nanny Simmons has agreed to look after her.'

'I'm glad,' said Ellie. 'Nanny could have come with us, of course, but she has family in Southampton. You need have no worries. She's a very caring woman, and well-qualified.'

'I also employ Mrs Hovringham. She misses

375

you very much—talks of you all the time. Everyone speaks so highly of you, Ellie.'

'Whereas you had no use for me. It's a pity you had to discover my worth from others.'

'Ellie, come with us.'

'No, Max.' She had melted slightly, but her attitude remained the same. 'Didn't you listen to a word I said earlier?'

The time had come to tell her of the other purpose of his visit. Persuasion was obviously having no effect so he would need to be firm.

'There's something important you must know, Ellie,' he said. 'I want my son to be brought up in the Jewish faith. In order for that to happen he must be with me, so whether you agree to come or not I want to take William back to England.'

Ellie's face became ashen. She was completely unprepared for such a demand and he hated having to be so cruel. But her refusal was instantaneous.

'Never! Never, do you hear?' she cried. 'I won't countenance even the suggestion. William has already been baptised into the Catholic Church and goes to Mass on Sundays. And as for him going anywhere with you... You must be out of your mind.'

'Then I repeat, come with us.'

'I will not.'

'I'm your husband. I can insist on it,' he said.

She was trembling, and she wrung her hands together. Her voice was like ice. 'Don't ever try to claim any rights to me. You have none.'

'But I have rights to William.'

'Get out of my home, Max, and don't ever come back. I'm going to issue orders that you're never even to see William.'

'Ellie, listen to me—'

'You, a railroad waiter, think you can dictate to me!'

Her arrogance incensed him. 'We'll see, shall we?'

She moved towards the bell-pull to summon the butler, but he forestalled her, dragging her away from it. His arms closed round her masterfully and his mouth found hers, silencing her outraged protests. The feel of her full lips beneath his own was fuel to the fire in him, and he continued to kiss her even when her teeth brought the taste of blood to his mouth. In her fury she had never been more desirable.

She kicked and struggled for several minutes, but he tightened his hold. His fingers dug into her back between her shoulderblades, and the weight of his broad chest kept her own hands pinioned between them so that she was helpless. She tried to toss her head, but the backwards tilt of it ensured her mouth remained captive until he was ready to release her, and his longing for their complete union was almost overpowering. Now he knew why he had been celibate.

Finally, he let her go. Deep, sharp breaths escaped him; shame engulfed him. He had used his physical strength to prove she couldn't insult him and get away with it, but there was no satisfaction. On the contrary, he had now added to the complexity of their relationship by antagonising her further, and by proving to himself that his growing appreciation of her fascination and virtue had not been idle fantasy. She was everything he wanted.

Ellie didn't back away. She stood with her feet firmly planted in the luxurious pile carpet, and she didn't touch either her lips or her dishevelled hair.

'Don't expect an apology,' he said.

She, too, was regaining her breath. With a jerk she thrust out her chin, and she spoke between her teeth: 'If you ever come near either me or William again you'll regret it forever. I swear I'll prove that you knifed Oliver to death, and in England you'll hang for it.'

'Ellie! Damn you, there's no way you can do that. You know it would be a lie.'

'Do I? You thought you saw Julian near the Sun Hotel. He would testify if I asked him to.'

'Perjure himself?'

'Perhaps he wouldn't need to. Perhaps he also saw *you*. And you had enough reasons to commit murder.' She swung round and this time he didn't stop her tugging the bell-pull. 'Remember that, Max, and stay away. We don't need you.'

Max departed, knowing he had made the second gravest mistake of his life. He strode back along Prairie Avenue with the crisp winter air filling his lungs, but it was not through fear he decided to honour her wishes. His innocence over Oliver's death made him immune to her threats. He would stay away from her now

378

because he had discovered the only truth which mattered. He loved her. For the first time he admitted it, and in loving her he found he had to put her feelings before his own.

It was not long before Ellie tired of the everlasting round of frivolous activities which filled the lives of other women of her class and age. She was in a difficult position, being neither spinster nor widow, yet without a man at her side. There were some who began to resent her, or saw her as a threat to their own marriages since husbands tended to think she was available and gave her too much attention. Not that Ellie wanted it. She had to be discouraging to the point of rudeness at times, and frequently refused invitations in order to avoid the problem. Jefferson was happy to escort her on occasions, but more and more often she preferred to stay at home.

She was disillusioned with the lives her contemporaries led because she saw the shallowness. Having shared poverty and suffering in Pullman City she knew how degrading it could be, and how terrible when there seemed to be no way to get free of the downward spiral. She had shared Grandfather Cromer's degradation when there was no money left to pay off debts, or even to buy food. Her understanding of poverty made her impatient with the extravagance of her wealthy friends, and she no longer had time for their petty jealousies.

But there was more to it than that. At first after Max's visit she had thrown herself into the

379

social whirl with all her energy, becoming the talk of fashion writers and gossip columnists. She had attended every function, every party, and was seen at every important occasion in the Chicago calendar, until she was exhausted. None of it could erase Max from her mind.

He hadn't come to see her again before leaving for England with Galina after the Christmas of 1897. The cheque he had insisted was hers remained in the envelope for several weeks while she considered returning it, but after a long talk with her mother it had been invested, to be kept for William's education.

In the spring of 1898 Ellie received the first of many letters from Max.

'Ellie, I swear again I had nothing to do with Oliver's death. Believe me, because it is the truth. You asked me not to visit you again in Chicago and I respected your wishes, though I longed to be with you,' he wrote. 'Momma blames me for William's baptism into the Catholic Church. She is full of pain. Naturally you chose your own faith for him in my absence, but when he is old enough he must decide for himself. All I ask is that you remind him as he grows that he is half-Jewish.

'Ellie, I implore you to come to Southampton. Galina needs a mother, not a nanny. We should be a family, and I offer you everything I have if we can just be together.'

It was a long letter, deeply remorseful yet flawed. Ellie read it over and over, trying to understand why it offended her. The truth came when she realised his aims were selfish. Basically, he wanted a reconciliation to salve

380

his conscience and to make his own life more comfortable. Nowhere did he express a desire to do anything for *her* sake, or ask what would make *her* happy—but arrogantly assumed that she ought to absolve him from his sins and agree to his proposals. She could not do either.

She wrote back to him. *'It seems you are putting Galina and her needs before your son. Even if I was tempted to consider your offer, which I most certainly am not, I would have to think first of William. He is settled here now and I wouldn't uproot him. I made my feelings quite clear—my threat was not an idle one. If ever you attempt to force yourself upon us I shall inform the English authorities of my suspicions.'*

She was ashamed of the threat. She didn't doubt his innocence in the Devlin affair, but maintaining the pretence gave her a weapon to keep him at bay.

She hoped there would be no more correspondence. She wanted to forget him, but memories of the way he had kissed her tortured her mind and inflamed her body. Had he held her with such passion just a few seconds longer that evening she would have been lost, and they might well have been reunited, purely to gratify their sexual needs. That wasn't what she wanted at all. It would have been wrong, and against all her principles. Only love could change things. If he had said he loved her she could perhaps have forgiven him and smoothed the path to a new beginning, but love which was one-sided would inevitably lead to a repeat of the past, and that was no basis on which to build. In spite of all her harsh words, she did still love him. All it would have taken to reverse her protestations would have been for Max to admit the same. If he had done that they could have been together now.

Sadly, Hedda Berman died suddenly of pneumonia in the spring. It meant severance of all connection with the family, since Ellie hardly knew Max's brother, and William became a Harvey in every way.

There being no solace in frivolity, and even less in dwelling on Max, she wanted to do something more useful with her life, but could find no worthwhile occupation until she was introduced to someone with similar feelings. That summer she met a lady by the name of Mrs Ursula Fenden.

'My dear, we could do with you at Hull House,' Mrs Fenden said. 'We need all the help we can get, and believe me it's very rewarding.'

Ellie had heard of the place. It was a charitable settlement on South Halstead Street, one of the lowest areas of Chicago, established in 1889 by two ladies named Jane Addams and Ellen Gates Starr. They had originally intended the house to be simply a community service project, but with many willing helpers it had gradually become a shelter for the destitute, the homeless and the abused, a place where the sick could be cared for, and children could be protected.

'I wouldn't know what to do,' Ellie protested.

'You would soon find out.' Mrs Fenden had

a wonderful enthusiasm for everything, which would carry her through into old age still looking younger than her years. 'Mrs Berman, forgive me, I know you are living apart from your husband. My own situation is somewhat the same. My husband is in a mental institution.'

'Oh, I'm so sorry.'

'I don't tell everyone, of course, but I feel we have much in common. It would be so nice if we could work together.'

'I really believe it would,' agreed Ellie.

So, armed with her own experiences she went to Hull House and offered herself in the service of those less fortunate. She was received joyously, and quickly became one of the women who gave unstintingly of their time and resources. There was so much to be done, the days were not long enough. At the beginning she helped to teach English to the multi-racial population crowding close to its doors, but there was more satisfaction in caring for the sick, and Ellie was soon rolling up her sleeves and tying an apron around her waist to do the most menial tasks.

'You spend more time at that hostel than you do at home,' grumbled Mama, who had been against her going there from the start. 'Goodness knows what infections you might bring back. You should have more consideration for William.'

'William is strong, and so am I. I'm not afraid of illness. I love doing nursing.'

In fact, Ellie seemed to have a natural vocation for it, and as the months passed her interest in all things medical took priority over her drawing and painting. By learning how to care for the disabled and understand a little about mental illness she was able to help many people. Those whom she nursed and counselled began to call her 'Sister Ellie', and she was very contented working with the immigrant families. She enjoyed being with these people because she was reminded of the early days of her marriage when she'd been so happy with Max.

More letters came from him. In the first he spoke of his grief at losing his mother, and his regret that he'd been too far away to attend her funeral. In the next he offered to sell out Galina's share of Court Carriages if it would make any difference.

'*I know I said I would work to protect Galina's inheritance, but if it is standing between us then I am willing to sell her interests in the company and bring her back to the States,*' he wrote. Then, on an impatient note: '*You accuse me of putting my niece before my son. May I remind you it was your decision to forbid me any contact with William. The remedy is for us to be together, then I can be a proper father to him.*'

Ellie's reply kept up the antagonism. It was difficult to carry on a row on paper, especially when letters took so many weeks to reach their destination, but she was not going to let him get away with placing blame in her corner.

'*Selling the company would make no difference whatsoever to our relationship,*' she told him, pressing so hard on the hand-made writing paper the nib made indentations through to

384

the next page. *'Rightfully, those shares in Court Carriages should belong to William since they were bought with my money. Your sins were the cause of his loss, but I will keep the truth from him for as long as I can—for his sake, not yours.'*

By return of post came an indignant response. *'Are you forgetting I reimbursed the money Oliver embezzled so I am no longer in your debt, or William's.'* There was much in the same vein. Then he made another appeal. *'Tell me what I can do to put things right between us. I have pleaded with you for forgiveness. I have told you repeatedly how much I regret what I did to hurt you. I have offered to give you everything I have. What else is there I can say or do? What is it you want, Ellie?'*

The only word which could have altered Ellie's determination to stand firm was never used. *Love.* If he had said that he loved her she would not have written her final reply.

'I want you to stay out of my life forever.'

NINETEEN

One of the most surprising friendships within the family sprang up between Sir Robert Cromer and Jefferson. The youngest of the Harveys practically usurped Ellie's place in their grandfather's affection, and Jefferson found an unlikely ally for his theatre work in the old man from England whom no one had known about before Ellie's defection. Grandfather Cromer developed a great love for the theatre. He would go to see everything, be it opera, ballet, an orchestra, or a play, and the lighter the production the more he enjoyed it.

Just after Christmas 1903, he celebrated his eighty-second birthday, and when asked what he would like more than anything, he chose to see a performance of *Mr Bluebeard* at the Iroquois Theater.

'It must be a matinée,' Mama insisted, when Jefferson said he would get the tickets. 'Your Grandfather's chest is troublesome and he mustn't be out in the cold night air.'

To suit Jefferson the outing was arranged for the afternoon of 30 December, much to William's disappointment as a prior invitation to a big Christmas party at the home of one of his schoolfriends fell on the same day and he was told it would be ill-mannered not to attend. Ellie couldn't go at the last minute due to the wintry weather having decimated the staff at Hull House. Nor did the date, or choice of play, suit Sibylla or Conrad, so Jefferson was Sir Robert's sole companion on that day.

Sir Robert Cromer, wearing his long grey overcoat with the black velvet collar, his kid gloves and his top hat, looked very distinguished as he settled in his seat in the front row of the stalls. He removed the hat as the curtains went up and applauded as loudly as anyone.

The star of the show, Eddie Foy, was giving a remarkable performance in his grotesque costume, and laughter was echoing up to the gallery when an open arc light high up began to splutter dangerously. No one in the audience saw a strip of gauze on the proscenium arch catch fire until a small flame developed and spread to one of the velvet drapes. In horror and sudden panic, everyone in the theatre began to move.

'Be quiet, please,' called Eddie Foy, stepping forward. 'There isn't any danger.'

He nodded to the orchestra and music temporarily calmed the audience. But burning strips of muslin began to fall on the stage. Jefferson Harvey was torn between looking after his grandfather and rushing to the assistance of Eddie and the rest of the cast who were trying to restore order.

'Get to the side exit, Grandfather, fast,' he ordered. 'I've got to help them get the asbestos curtain down. Looks like it's jammed halfway.'

Jefferson jumped onto the stage. A stampede for the exits started, and Grandfather Cromer put his top hat back on.

'Come with me,' he said to some small children nearby who had been separated from their parents and were shrieking with fright.

He took hold of two little hands and pushed along with the fear-crazed crowd as flames billowed out from the orchestra pit. The balcony caught alight. Suddenly, at three-fifteen in the afternoon, the Iroquois Theater was engulfed in flames. Some of the exits had been locked and the fire spread so fiercely and with such terrifying speed that those inside stood little chance of escaping.

After only fifteen minutes it was brought

under control, but 596 people had died.

Chicago went into mourning, hardly able to comprehend the terrible tragedy which had struck at the heart of almost every family. In the gutted auditorium it was not even possible to identify some of the victims, but a gold pocket-watch engraved with a presentation date to Sir Robert Cromer was found on a body near one of the locked side exits. Jefferson Harvey escaped with his life, but was so badly burnt he would need many months in hospital.

Ellie was devastated by the loss of Grandfather Cromer. She had loved the old man so much, and memories of the time she had arrived in London kept returning to her mind like a cracked photograph record. Her grief was greater than her mother's. Sibylla took a philosophical attitude to her father's death.

'It's the way he would have wanted to go, Ellie,' she said. 'He would have hated to be confined to bed with a lingering illness. My father was a man who got the most out of life, and he died while doing something he really enjoyed. I consider it a blessing.'

Ellie had to agree, and took comfort.

William made up his mind at an early age that he wanted to be an engineer. Not the kind that his Uncle Drew had been, though he would have liked to ride on the footplate of a locomotive. No, William wanted to do great things like building bridges and roads. He had been very attached to Grandfather Cromer and the old man's death had left a void in his young life which nothing could fill except ambition to be like him. Grandfather's tales of the contractors' heyday in England had fired his imagination, and he wanted to be equally successful.

At sixteen he said: 'I want to go Harvard, Mother. I won't go anywhere else. I'm going to get the best engineering degree I can.'

He didn't see it as a problem. Ever since he could remember there had been money for anything he wanted and he presumed his mother had independent means. It came as a shock therefore when he overheard his mother and Grandfather Harvey talking about his education in financial terms.

'So the boy wants to go to Harvard University,' Conrad was saying. They were in the library and William couldn't resist listening unobserved. 'I'm glad. But who will pay, Elena? Are you expecting me to find all the money, since you have none of your own?'

'Papa, when are you going to let me forget I made a disastrous marriage?'

'Max Berman should be providing for William. Heaven knows I don't begrudge the boy a cent, but I do have other grandchildren. I couldn't keep digging into my pockets for all of them.'

'No one's asking you to.' Mother was the only one who could speak to Grandfather Harvey in such a manner. 'The others don't need it anyway. Frederick's tribe have no worries—he's richer than you are. And Drew's daughter is so spoilt she wants for nothing.'

'I ought to have sent you back to your husband. I was too soft. You married him

389

recklessly and you should have been made to live with the result of that recklessness.'

'Papa, dearest, you know you were glad when I came home.' William watched through the crack in the door and saw his mother reach to kiss Conrad. Her tone was teasing. Then she straightened up. 'Anyway, I'm not going to ask you for anything. I have the money invested for William's university education.'

How he loved her. She was the most wonderful mother in the world and he was so proud of her. That lovely voice was like music to his ears and he still remembered how he had fallen asleep as a child to the gentle sound of her reading to him.

'Money invested? Where did you get it?' demanded his grandfather.

'Max left it with me.'

'You never told me! Was that so you could go on scrounging?'

'No, Papa. It was because I never intended to touch it. I didn't want anything from Max, but when he refused to take it back I decided the best policy was to keep the money for William.'

William didn't stop to hear any more. He rushed out into the garden and down as far as the gazebo, where he retched. After a few minutes he sat on the stone seat to recover and sort out his emotions, thankful that he had discovered what was going on in time. It put paid to his hopes of Harvard, but that was better than finding out later that he was being paid for by his father. He would forfeit everything rather than be in that man's debt.

His hatred of Max had no actual foundation. It was as if he had been infected with it in infancy and the disease had become chronic. He had never even tried to find a cure. When he'd been old enough to ask questions, his mother had been charitable. She hadn't actually condemned his father, but she had been evasive, and being a boy with a vivid imagination he had put his own interpretation on her lack of straightforwardness. He didn't know what Max Berman had done but it was obviously something pretty terrible. His mother was the kindest, most caring person he knew, and she wouldn't have banished her husband from her life without the best of reasons. As he matured, William decided it must have been a problem with other women. That was what always seemed to go wrong with adult relationships. Bigamy occurred to him, but Mother still called herself Mrs Berman and had never remarried so that notion had been discarded. But there was nothing else bad enough that he could think of.

It wasn't as if he knew the man. All he had were vague memories of two brief meetings which had taken place when he was very young, but he vividly remembered his reaction. Max Berman had seemed so incredibly tall, and there had been harsh, bitter words exchanged between his father and mother which had created an atmosphere. Whenever William had read about the devil he had pictured his father. Max had instilled fear in the heart of the small boy, yet he had neither done nor said anything directly to cause it. All his feelings had come about subconsciously through his closeness to Ellie, whom he adored.

That evening he decided the time had come to insist on being told the truth, and to do that he also had to be truthful. He gathered his courage and joined his mother in the conservatory after dinner when he knew she would be alone for a while.

'William.' Her face lit up. 'Am I to have the pleasure of your company?' She put down the book she'd been reading and patted the chair beside her.

He continued to stand, clearing his throat and wondering whether this had been a good idea after all. He couldn't bear to upset her, but the matter couldn't be put off any longer.

'I'm sorry, Mother, I don't want to go to Harvard after all,' he said, gritting his teeth. There was nothing he had ever wanted more.

'Stop teasing,' Ellie said. 'And don't stand there like a disgruntled giraffe. I can't talk to you with your head up in the roof.'

He was already as tall as his father and his hair was just as black, but the lightness of his eyes gave him an added handsomeness which guaranteed him the heart of every eligible girl in town. He was so popular it was a wonder he had any time to study, yet his academic progress was phenomenal.

'I'm serious,' he told her. A puzzled frown creased her brow as he dropped down heavily into the cane chair. 'I heard you talking to

Grandfather. I won't be paid for with my father's money. I'd rather not go.'

Ellie sighed deeply. 'So that's it.'

'I know I shouldn't have listened.'

'You know nothing about your father.'

'Then it's time I did.' William faced her. 'I mean it, Mother. I won't be fobbed off any longer with the excuse that I'm too young to understand. No one ever talks about him. Why?'

His mother looked down at her hands. Her wedding band was the only ring she wore. 'I loved him too much,' she said, quietly. 'That was the root of the trouble.'

'Then why did you leave him?'

'I didn't. He left us. He abandoned us on the quayside at Southampton and returned to America on the next ship. You were only a few months old and I was deserted in a foreign country with no money, nothing. It was the cruellest thing anyone could do.'

Gradually the story was told. William listened avidly, but couldn't fully comprehend the tragedy. It was not until she got to the part about his Cousin Galina's inheritance that his blood began to boil. He remembered Galina as a scraggy kid with carroty hair who had scratched him, the only time they had met.

'You're saying this company in England which belongs to Galina, and which my father runs, was bought with your money!' he exclaimed. 'That means it should rightfully be yours.'

'Not according to English law. Your Uncle Oliver bought shares in it legitimately and when

393

he didn't leave a will everything he owned went to his daughter.'

'But you could have contested it. You could have proved the money was yours.'

'How, William?' his mother asked. 'Remember, my father didn't know my mother had given me the money. I could never have gone through the courts. Think of the humiliation. And who would have believed me?'

He understood that. What he didn't understand was how she could have continued to accept the situation all these years without doing anything to avenge herself. She had even claimed it was her fault. If that was loving too much he vowed he would never fall into such a trap.

'The way I see it,' he said, 'my Cousin Galina is sitting on a fortune which would in time have been mine, and I don't take kindly to that. She has no right to anything, and my father is a thief.'

Ellie covered his hand with one of hers to stop him when he would have gone on. Even when she spread her long, tapering fingers they scarcely met the edges of his own broad palm.

'What should or should not be Galina's is debatable,' she said. 'And your father is not dishonest. When he came here back in ninety-eight he returned to me all the money your Uncle Oliver had embezzled, so in effect Galina only inherited the profit Oliver made out of what had been mine. Do you follow?'

William inclined his head. 'Yes, I think so.'

'Which means you can go to Harvard without

394

any qualms because the money to pay for it, and for anything else you may need, has always been mine.'

He needed time to digest the facts. In some ways things were not quite so bad as he had always imagined and he found he could live with the truth more easily than he had anticipated. What galled him was the unfairness of it all, and his mother had every bit of his sympathy. And yet... He thought of the way Ellie had always kept him close and fussed over him. Sometimes, lately, he felt smothered. Was that how his father had felt? Ashamed of his disloyalty, he concentrated on the guilt. If Max Berman hadn't left them stranded their lives would have been different now, and Galina Devlin would still have been in the Jewish quarter where she belonged.

From that moment, Galina Devlin took equal place with his father in the hatred stakes, and with all the impetuosity of his sixteen years he planned revenge.

'All right,' he said to Ellie. 'I'll go to University and I'll be the top student of my faculty. Then, when I'm one of the most powerful men in engineering I'll put Court Carriages out of business.'

His mother only smiled.

By the time William Berman was due to sit for his degree, a great many things had changed in the world and his priorities were altered. He had far more important matters to think about than a carriage-building company in England.

Ellie became interested in the American National Red Cross soon after 1905 when the second Congressional Charter was granted to it, and she quit Hull House in order to broaden her knowledge of nursing and community work. There was a section of the organisation in Chicago where she could learn about public health, and how to assist victims of natural disaster. She took training in water-safety programmes, and it wasn't long before she was training others. Elena Berman was a woman of note in Chicago, not for giving lavish parties or trying to outdo the spending of her contemporaries, but for her charitable work As well as her social studies she had a gift for management, and she took great exception to a remark made by W.I Thomas in his book *Sex and Society*, when he said that women were incapable of becoming scholars.

Her activities didn't meet with the approval of her family.

'It's unbecoming,' Sibylla clucked. 'Whoever heard of a girl of your class being more interested in the sewage works and the city's water than a new season's wardrobe?'

'Expensive too,' complained Conrad, though he was rather proud of his unconforming daughter. 'With your membership fees to this society and various other subscriptions it seems as if you're paying for the privilege of working. Can't understand it.'

Ellie took no notice. 'It's my money,' she reminded them. 'Mr Pullman left me a legacy to spend wisely and that, I hope, is what I'm doing.'

Her godfather's multi-million dollar estate had not been settled until 1903. Most of his fortune had gone to his family, of which he had often said she was a part, but a very generous amount had been left to Chicago charitable institutions so Ellie knew he would have approved.

Work with the Red Cross kept her increasingly busy over the following years, but Mama insisted on a certain amount of socialising, and without ever intending to, she broke several male hearts. In the summer of 1909 Randolph Sale reappeared in her life, still tall and thin, and now a barrister of repute. He declared he had never forgotten her.

'Ellie, I've never married because of you,' he said. 'I've not found anyone to compare, and that's the truth.'

'Tosh,' Ellie replied, teasingly. 'It's because no one will have you.'

'That's not the case. I'm quite a catch, you know, and plenty of mothers try to interest me in their daughters.'

He was still pompous and conceited, as boring as ever. All the same, she knew her own parents would have approved if he had been her choice. Now, because of her religion, there was no question of re-marriage, and in the case of Randolph she was glad of it.

On the whole she enjoyed her independence. Two years later, in 1911, she went on a tour of Europe with William to broaden his outlook, but England was not on the itinerary, and neither was romance, though there were plenty of gentlemen anxious to persuade her that she needed it to brighten her life.

It was the outbreak of war in Europe in 1914 which suddenly made her very aware of Max again. He would be too old for active service, but British civilians were suffering from privation and industrial problems with so many men being mobilised. She hadn't seen her husband in sixteen years. He would be nearing forty-five now and she wondered if he was ageing well, or whether prosperity had led to dissipation. It ought not to have mattered, but she found herself dwelling on him to the point of sleeplessness some nights, though all correspondence between them had finally ceased and she didn't even know if he was still in Southampton.

Sometimes Ellie cursed her pride. Long ago Max had given her the opportunity to forgive, and as a good Catholic she ought perhaps to have been generous. Since talking openly with William she had questioned whether that single unpremeditated act of desertion should have resulted in a lifetime's separation, especially the separation of father and son. Without conscious thought she had poisoned William's concept of Max. That was a sin for which she asked repeatedly for absolution when she went to Confession.

The European war brought the International Red Cross into prominence, and Ellie attended meetings at the headquarters of the American branch in Washington where she met members of the governing board. Many volunteers were already in France helping the wounded and the French homeless, and she longed to be allowed to join them.

'Mrs Berman, your enthusiasm for fieldwork is commendable, but you are much more valuable to us here,' she was told.

She went back to Chicago greatly disappointed, but keener than ever to work for the cause. In 1915 she would be forty, but she seemed to have more energy than she'd had in her youth, and she was never tired.

That year the American people were horrified and alarmed by the torpedoing of the unarmed British ship *Lusitania* with much loss of life, and it gradually dawned on them that German policy was to dominate the world. The National Security League tried to arouse them to awareness of their own potential danger, but it was clear that the United States was not militarily prepared for active intervention, and the movement gained no encouragement.

The war was already in its third year in February 1917 when President Wilson broke off relations with the German Empire because, amongst other things, it refused to restrict submarine warfare. There was much opposition to the decision.

Jefferson Harvey was one of many pacifists who tried to bring pressure on the government to remain neutral. He organised demonstrations in Chicago, and on the eve of the President's speech to Congress on 2 April he took part in a march through Washington with other pacifists

399

calling for peace at any price. Their voices went unheard. The President announced: 'We will not choose the path of submission,' and on 6 April the United States declared itself to be on the side of the Allies. On the whole those who had voted him into a second term of office agreed that in the interest of national security the move had been necessary, but there was still no enthusiasm for the involvement, and most thought it could have been avoided.

For Ellie it was different. She had been reading everything available about the conflict on the other side of the Atlantic and was glad that something was at last being done to help. The authorised war loan of seven billion dollars was just the beginning. No army had ever been mobilised so quickly, and she suddenly found herself in charge of a team recruiting nurses to serve in military establishments. From that time on she hardly had a spare moment to think of anything else.

It was Drew who shocked her into facing the possibility of William being conscripted. He was then twenty-three and came within the age limit set by the Senate.

'He's written to me already,' Drew said. 'A Reserve Officers Training Corps has been set up at Harvard under French officers sent by the government, but William wants to volunteer straight away.'

'He can't!' exclaimed Ellie. 'What about his studies?'

'Nothing beats the school of life. I came to no harm.'

She couldn't deny it. Three years ago, Drew had taken over from his father as President of the Union Atlantic, and was now one of the most respected men in the city. But she would not allow William to jeopardise his career.

'You must stop him being so foolhardy,' she fretted.

'Your son's a man now. My advice is to let him make his own decisions, or you'll lose him the same way as you lost Max.'

The suggestion staggered her. She had never thought of herself as an over-protective mother, but clearly that was the way Drew saw it, and she trusted his judgement in all things. He was actually laying the blame on her... She ignored it.

'Why hasn't William said anything to me?' she asked. 'I visited him only a few weeks ago.'

'I think he was afraid of opposition,' said Drew, with a wry smile. Then he went on to explain his plans for his nephew. 'William is a brilliant scholar. He's going far. Now, the Railway Committee of the Advisory Commission wants nine regiments recruited from the railroad, a thousand men in each, for an expeditionary force in France, and I've been asked to supply men. Each regiment will be headed by engineer officers of the Regular Army, but commissions are being given to civil engineers. I can get one for William without any difficulty.'

Ellie went deathly pale. 'You can't let him go to France.' It was unthinkable that her son, her baby, was going to war. 'I won't let you do it, Drew. He'll be in terrible danger.'

'And so will thousands more. It's what he wants. Be proud of him! He's got guts.'

William was headstrong, a trait he had inherited from his mother as she knew only too well, and if he had made up his mind to be among the first American engineers, then that was what he would do if she didn't intervene. Two days later she took the train to Boston and met up with him.

'This is madness,' she protested. 'Why can't you wait for officer training at University? The war might be over before you would have to go abroad.'

'Mother, I wouldn't miss this for anything,' William declared. 'Harvard men have already sailed with a unit of the Medical Corps and I'm green with envy. I want to be involved in the action.'

He had stopped growing at six feet two, and had become broad in the shoulders. She could hardly believe she had produced him, and the mere thought of perhaps losing him was more than she could bear. She tried everything from coaxing to emotional blackmail, but to no avail.

'I love you so much, my darling. You're all I've got,' she said finally.

He tucked an arm through hers and took her into a fashionable Boston tearoom where the cakes had become plainer, the portions smaller, and the customers fewer since Mr Hoover, the Food Administrator, had appealed to the people to cut out four o'clock teas. As a nation they were asked to eat less, to have no second helpings, no food at parties and none between meals. Life had changed rapidly in so many ways.

'Tell me,' William said, drawing out a chair for her. 'Is it right that you asked to be sent overseas with the Red Cross?'

She met his eyes. 'Yes.'

'And if you get a chance in the future, will you go?'

'Yes, but that's different. I'm older than you. You've everything to live for.'

'What crap!' he exclaimed rudely. Then he took her hands in his. 'Do you think I wouldn't worry just the same about you? Mama, I love you too—more than anyone in the world. But I wouldn't try to stop *you* doing what you believed in, and *I* believe in the right to fight for peace. The Germans have got to be beaten and I'll be there doing my bit, the same as you.'

'Oh, William,' Ellie sighed. She had to accept she'd lost out to Drew and the Harvey spirit of adventure.

In July, Lieutenant William Berman was drafted overseas with a group of Engineers who were to pioneer the building of piers, docks, and roads ready for an American army of two million men to launch its offensive against the Germans. There were not the facilities in France to handle such a vast number of men and machines, and as the Americans intended to be independent of other armies they would need to build new ports for their ships, warehouses for the food which would

403

have to be brought over, arsenals and foundries for the artillery, towns for salvage work and repairs, and new rail-links between the Atlantic coast and the battlefields which were about 400 miles away.

William went first to England, landing in Liverpool on a day full of sunshine. He stepped off the ship onto English soil and was aware of a feeling of antipathy towards everything British, yet the welcome extended to him and his comrades couldn't have been warmer or more enthusiastic. Somewhere in this country was the man who had fathered him, then deserted him, but it wasn't fair to judge a nation simply because it had become Max Berman's adopted home.

The feeling stayed with him on the special train which carried him south to a camp at Winchester which was being set up for the use of American forces. It disturbed his concentration when he attended the first conference with men of the Royal Engineers to discuss the difficulties confronting them.

'Some of you are railway men,' said the engineer detailed to spell out the problems. 'When you study the situation over there, you'll see that French railways aren't going to cope with the strain of transporting munitions and provisions for two million troops.'

The man had an aggravating accent and talked as if he had a golf ball in his mouth. William found his mind wandering. He had discovered that Southampton was only a few miles away, so his father and his Cousin Galina with her ill-gotten gains were within easy visiting distance.

'The Frenchies go in for safety rather than speed,' said one of his own number.

'Just so. We can carry fifty per cent more over a line than they can.'

'We plan to build new sidings and terminals,' the American officer in charge told the meeting.

'You'll need new tunnels too if you're bringing your own freight cars,' said the plummy Englishman.

'Twenty-ton freight cars and a hundred-and-fifty-ton locomotives,' said William. 'Union Atlantic already have some at the docks ready for transportation.'

It was a warm day and flies buzzed round the low-ceilinged rooms with its black-out curtains for drawing at night. Two weeks earlier there had been a raid on London by the German Gotha twin-engined bombers. Fifty-seven people had been killed and nearly two hundred injured. Air raids were becoming more frequent. William tried to centre his hatred on the Germans, but he couldn't keep vague memories of his father from surfacing. As the meeting dragged on he knew he'd have no peace of mind until he had delivered a few well-chosen words to Max Berman in person. He had to find out for himself the calibre of the man who had almost destroyed his mother.

The contingent of Engineers was due to sail for France before the end of the month, but two days' leave was granted beforehand. William decided to use it to visit his father. He remembered him as a frightening, angry giant of a man who had been too rapt in the quarrel with Mama to take any notice of a small boy. If he tried hard, William could recall the scent of his mother's skirt when he had hidden away in fear. Twenty years separated that day from this but he was still curiously reluctant to arrive at a possible meeting.

Timetables could no longer be relied upon, but there were frequent trains to Southampton. It was the premier port for military embarkation and the train was so crowded he had to stand in the corridor, but it was only a short journey and there was much to interest him. New sidings had been laid out at a place called Eastleigh. The railways here, he'd been told, were carrying everything from men and horses to tanks and ammunition. At one point there was a delay while an ambulance train travelling northwards with a large red cross painted on the side took precedence at a junction.

'Some more poor buggers copped it,' commented a British Tommy who was sitting on his kitbag next to William.

'Guess they're the lucky ones,' William said. 'At least they're alive.'

The Tommy's ears pricked up at the American accent and he looked at William's uniform, from his gaiters buttoned from the instep to the knee to his round-brimmed khaki hat tilted at a rakish angle. 'Thought you Yankees were sending a bloody great army over. Are you it?'

The British sense of humour might have caused trouble if William hadn't seen a roguish gleam in the other's eyes.

'Advance guard,' he said. 'Two more are coming.'

With a roar of laughter the soldier thrust out his hand. 'Glad to meet you, mate. We can do with you.'

William was on the left-hand side of the train. When it entered a longish tunnel on the outskirts of Southampton he pulled on the leather strap to raise the window and keep out the smoke, but once in daylight again he let it fall in surprise. The first thing he saw as they slowed down to draw into Western Station was a sign in brass letters across one of a collection of buildings which said *Court Carriages*. His heart jerked.

Half an hour later he entered the main office of the company his family had been involved with since before the turn of the century. He removed his hat. A girl clerk was dealing with a difficult telephone call, but she looked up when he came in and her mouth opened slightly.

'Can I help you?' she asked, holding the candle-stick mouthpiece against her shoulder.

'Mr Berman, is he here?'

'Who shall I say wants him?'

'His son.'

The girl gave a dazzling smile and replaced the telephone while a blurred voice could be heard calling for her attention at the other end of the line.

'My goodness, I just knew you had to be related,' she said, and went off in a hurry,

407

leaving William alone to prepare for the coming meeting.

The telephone jangled. A large railway clock ticked the minutes away with a heavy beat which was at odds with the drumming of his pulse. It was an austere room, the only light touch being a framed cartoon of the Prime Minister, Mr Lloyd George.

A few minutes later the girl returned, her cheeks dimpling as she smiled at the handsome American. 'Come with me, please, sir. I didn't tell Mr Berman who you were. I just said I'd got a big surprise for 'im.'

William didn't know whether to be angry or grateful. At least he still had the advantage. As he followed the girl through the administration block he tried to retain his air of confidence, but inwardly he quaked. It was ridiculous. She opened an oak-panelled door across the corridor.

'Mr Berman's waiting for you, sir,' she said, and tactfully disappeared.

The man across the desk stood up, and it was as if William looked at a mirror image of himself, though one which had grown slightly older. The likeness between them was incredible, and they stared at each other in silence while William closed the door. He was the first to speak.

'Hello, Father.'

Max Berman slowly recovered from the shock, came round the desk, and held out his arms.

'William,' he breathed.

Afterwards, the unexpectedness of his own reaction never ceased to astonish William. He took two steps towards the other man and they embraced so tightly that each was aware of the other's trembling.

'Tell me about your mother.' Max could no longer keep the request at bay. 'How is she? Is she still as beautiful?' His voice throbbed with emotion.

He couldn't think of a time when he had been more overwhelmed. Seeing his son in the doorway had been the biggest, most wonderful surprise of his life, and he felt light-headed. He'd longed to bombard him with questions straight away, to hear of everything that had happened over the intervening years, particularly to Ellie, but it had been necessary to talk first of generalities. They were strangers meeting virtually for the first time.

They'd talked of William's journey to England, the task before him, his time at Harvard, his rank in the army. Max had spoken of the changes in Southampton and the movement of troops through the docks. The Court Carriages repair sheds were overloaded with work, women were making munitions, and where construction of royal cars had once been carried out there was now a full-time crew of workers building and converting trains for use as ambulances.

Now, at last, he dared to breathe Ellie's name.

'She's more beautiful,' said William. His son used the same adoring tone when speaking of her. It was obvious he loved his mother.

'Tell me everything she's been doing,' Max

begged. 'Does she still keep the fashion writers busy?'

'Not any more. Her charity work seems to be the most important thing in her life. It has been for years.'

'She doesn't give parties, then.'

'Only in aid of the Red Cross. She's quite a leading light. Went to Washington and met the President when there were Red Cross meetings there at the start of the war. She wanted to be sent to France but apparently she's too useful at home.'

Max sighed, his eyes clouding with memories. 'I can imagine how dedicated she'd be. She's got a lot of courage.' He leaned across his desk and offered his son a cigar from a carved wooden box. William declined. 'Did you know that in Pullman your mother saved our Cousin Galina from a fire?'

William shook his head. 'She doesn't talk about you or Galina.'

'I can't blame her.'

The young American soldier got up and went to the window, his back ramrod straight. 'Where is my cousin?' he asked.

'In France.'

'Nursing?'

'No.' Max bit his own cigar and smoke curled into the suddenly charged atmosphere. 'She drives a motor ambulance. She's a very spirited young lady, and she decided to learn to drive a motor car before the war started.'

'I wonder she didn't want to stay, with so many women employed in industry. Shouldn't she be taking an active interest in her company?'

Max detected a hint of malice. 'Only half of it is hers,' he corrected. 'I'm afraid Galina and I have frequent disagreements over the issue.' He stood up. 'Come with me, I'll show you over the Works. We have to supply the War Department with everything from water-carts to eighteen-pounder gun carriages, and we've a new factory entirely staffed by women assembling shell-fuses. We're answerable to the War Office these days so everything is dictated by them.'

He took his son across the yard and into areas where construction sheds were ringing with the sound of hammers and drills, and welding sparks filled the air. In the paint-shop, a completed khaki-coloured railcar was having a huge red cross painted on the white roof, and Max showed him inside the vehicle which had been enamelled white throughout.

'This one is a conversion,' he told William. 'It used to be a parcels van. See, it still has the sliding doors. Now it's a ward-car and we'll fit three tiers of Furley-Fieldhouse cots along the sides, enough for thirty-six patients.'

'And is this for overseas?'

'No. We have to build larger ones to conform with French railways.'

'You'll need to modify the couplings and fit Westinghouse airbrakes, then. How many vehicles to each train? What weight are they?'

'Sixteen bogies. Four hundred and forty tons.'

Max embarked on a discussion with William which did his heart good. His son, the engineer, was obviously very knowledgeable in everything

411

to do with railways, and all his hopes were realised.

At the end of the tour he took William upstairs to a window which looked out on a view covering most of the workshops and yards; they were humming with activity.

'Take a good look, William,' he said. 'One day the other half of these Works will be yours. A few years ago I bought out Julian Cromer, and now Galina and I own equal shares of Court Carriages. My share is willed to you. I know now it'll be in the best of hands.'

William absorbed the information slowly, his expression changing. 'Shouldn't my mother be the beneficiary in any will of yours? Don't you owe it to her?'

The wonderful camaraderie faded, replaced by accusation, and Max responded to it with truthfulness.

'I owe Ellie for everything, don't think I don't know it. But she made it absolutely clear twenty years ago that she didn't want me, or anything of mine. I've respected her wishes because I love her.'

'Does she know that?'

'I hope so. I've lived a bachelor existence here ever since I came back with Galina because I've always hoped your mother might one day forgive me. But the next move, if there ever is one, must come from her. I tried and failed.'

'I guess you're both too proud,' said William. Then: 'You betrayed her. In my opinion you'd have to do a god-damned lot to prove you loved her before she'd ever let you near.'

Long after William had returned to camp Max mulled over what had been said, but he didn't know of any way to prove how he still felt about Ellie after all these years. In the past, all attempts had resulted in a strengthening of her resistance, and clearly she hadn't changed.

TWENTY

Ellie was devastated by William's departure for Europe, and she blamed Drew for encouraging him. Surely there was a need for highly skilled engineers in the States, now that the railroads had been taken over by the government?

'There's need for manpower, you're damned right,' said Drew, 'but William is fresh from University with all the most up-to-date knowledge, and that has to be put to use in the field, not in the backwoods. He'd be wasted here.'

Once her son had sailed she devoted more and more time to the Red Cross so that she wouldn't have to dwell on the danger he faced. It was ridiculous, but she couldn't even read reports of the war without feeling that every gun was pointing directly at William, and she knew she had to become more involved with the war effort herself, if only to feel that she was doing everything she could to support him.

Letters she received spasmodically from France told her nothing of significance to

413

do with his work and nothing at all of his whereabouts, but at least she had the assurance that he was safe. The first contained only news of his visit to Southampton.

'I've seen my father,' he wrote. *'He looks prosperous and told me he has bought out Julian Cromer. Apparently his share in the company will one day be mine, though Galina, who is driving motor ambulances in France, doesn't seem to approve. The meeting went off well and I've revised my opinion of Father, not because he's put me in his will, but because he has remained faithful to you in spite of your refusal to forgive. He's a good man, Mama. He genuinely regrets leaving you. Things are clearer in my mind now and in a way I can understand how he felt the need to escape. You are very strong-minded and perhaps a little too determined sometimes to have things your own way. I know because you've tried it with me so often, and until our differences over my joining the army you always succeeded. Dearest Mama, this doesn't mean I love you any the less.'*

The letter hurt. It made her angry. She ought to have been pleased that William was no longer so bitterly against Max, but the criticism of herself was unkind and it stirred up new resentment. Max must have put on an impressive performance to bring his son round to his way of thinking. She imagined them in close conversation, discussing her faults. It was impossible to put up a good defence on paper, but she stored up her wrath in readiness for a confrontation with her husband if she eventually got the chance to go to England again.

The news that Julian Cromer was out of the business came as a surprise, and it was another source of disquiet. No part of Court Carriages belonged to anyone in her family now, and it was all Max's fault. Ellie hadn't heard anything of Julian for many years. The last communication had been after Grandfather Cromer's death when Mama had written to inform him, and there had been only a short, uninteresting letter back. She had hoped he would regain control of the company, but it seemed Max had been the more powerful. She should have known he would succeed, if only to prove he didn't need her. Only the fact that he hoped to leave something for his son was in his favour, but her experience of promises like that left her cynical.

Subsequent correspondence from William contained only permitted references to his life in France. *'There's so much to do I hardly have time to grab a few hours' sleep,'* he grumbled. *'Refrigeration is the key to feeding the troops well and there have to be rail-links with the plants. I've been working on the largest of these. Now I'm moving on to another town and taking charge of several hundred men engaged in track-laying. Speed is essential for getting to the front line, and to join up with the British and French troops.'*

Mention of the front line terrified Ellie, but all she could do was pray for the continued safety of her son and trust that nothing would happen to him. She just had to be thankful that he was not in the trenches.

In the autumn of 1917 she went to

415

New York to join in the great Red Cross Demonstration. Crowds lined Fifth Avenue to view the contingents of nurses in their white uniforms, stretching back as far as the eye could see, who met with a rousing reception as they marched past. The Old Glory flags and Union Jacks flew side by side from windows along the route. Women throughout America were taking up Red Cross work with enthusiastic dedication and they were applauded wholeheartedly. Many would soon be going overseas to nurse the wounded, and affection and gratitude was voiced by every parent and every wife in the land who had someone in France. To Ellie Berman the shouts and cheers were a most gratifying sound, but more important was the fund-raising, and she hoped there would be a repeat of the twenty million sterling raised in one week at a previous rally in June.

It was summer of the following year before she was finally sent to Britain. She was to help in the organisation of an American hospital just outside London. It had been previously decided to provide large hospitals in France for the American wounded, but King George V had graciously offered land on which to build one in Richmond Park. It was erected and equipped with 500 beds, and offered as a gift from the British Red Cross, to be handed over before the autumn. The gift was gratefully accepted, and Ellie, as a senior administrator, was among the first to arrive there with a group of American nurses.

It felt strange to be in England again. So

much had changed, and though she had been prepared for the austerity, Ellie found it hard to realise this was the same country where she had once watched the extravagant celebrations to mark Queen Victoria's Diamond Jubilee. Another monarch had come and gone since she had last been in London, and now it was the grandson of that old lady she had seen in her widow's black who sat on the throne. This made Ellie feel old.

She didn't look in the least bit old, however. British newspapers printed a picture of the American nurses on their arrival at the hospital, and Ellie appeared no older than girls in their twenties who posed with her for the photograph. A straight grey skirt showed the neatness of her ankles, her cape with the small red cross stitched below her left shoulder had a mandarin-type collar which emphasised her long, unlined neck, and a dark felt hat covering her elegantly coiled hair was worn at just the right angle to display her flare for fashion. She still had a sophisticated air which made her stand out even among a group of women all dressed the same.

The caption under the photograph read: *Mrs Elena Berman of the American Red Cross with nursing staff at the Richmond Hospital which is a gift to the Americans from the British Red Cross and the Order of St John.*

The outcome of the publication was exactly what she had expected. A week later Max came to Richmond. He had seen the article and followed up the news of her arrival, and she was forced to admit she had courted the

417

publicity in the hope of it happening. Not for anything in the world would she have given him the satisfaction of knowing she wanted to see him. The newspaper report had been an opportunity. Published news of her had brought him to her before and somehow she had felt sure it would do so again.

Ellie was in the hospital grounds when a junior nurse came running to tell her he had arrived, and she was glad of the chance to compose herself before coming face to face with her husband after so many years.

'Send him out here, please,' she instructed the nurse. Much easier to meet him in the open air.

Her legs trembled as she waited, and she pressed her hands together against her breast as she tried to still the much greater trembling within. For days she had been rehearsing a speech but now her mouth was dry and she couldn't remember a word of what she'd been going to say. She walked towards the hospital so that she would see him come down the steps, but kept close to the shrubbery so that she would be just out of view. What a fool she was. Surely she'd no reason for wanting to see him, other than curiosity.

The little nurse returned to the door with him and pointed towards the place where she had left Ellie, then she went back inside, leaving him to make his own way across the garden. My goodness, how handsome he was still. It could have been William. He wore a black lounge suit with a dark blue striped tie. His shoes were black patent leather and he carried a trilby hat and a cane. The years seemed to melt away as she watched him approach and she was almost tempted to run towards him as she had done when she was a girl.

She walked out into the path and waited. His step slowed. When they were a few paces apart he also stopped.

'I guessed you would come, Max,' she said.

'Why didn't you write and tell me? I would have met you. Did you sail to Southampton?'

'No, Liverpool.'

His hair was still thick, and still black apart from wings of grey at his temples which suited him. Thankfully he hadn't grown a moustache which would have been aging, but now he was closer she could see there were fine lines at the corners of his eyes and mouth.

'I've been hoping to see you,' he said. 'Ever since William told me about your Red Cross work I've kept an eye on the news. I even went to a rally of American nurses in London in case you were there.'

'I'm surprised. I thought from the way you swayed William into seeing your point of view you still thought of me as too dominating to be worthy of your time.'

'Oh, Ellie.' He sighed with exasperation. 'I haven't come all this way to embark on yet another analysis of my past sins.'

'Then what have you come for?'

'I could give you a whole list of reasons.'

'I don't want to hear them.'

'You haven't changed. You're still as beautiful,

419

and obviously just as infuriating as ever.'

'Am I? Perhaps it's because I am so angry that you got at William.'

'I said nothing biased.'

They sat down on one of the new wooden seats placed where wounded patients would get a good view over the parkland. Deer were grazing in the distance.

Ellie sat with her back very straight, but her primness hid inner turmoil. 'After he had seen you William wrote a letter criticising me. It was cruel.'

'And you're blaming me.' In contrast Max relaxed against the seat, a wry smile curving his mouth.

'He's never said anything like that before. How dare you run me down to our son and...'

'I did nothing of the kind. He must have come to his own conclusions.'

It was a cool day and the wind caught them. Max reached over to draw Ellie's cape closer round her shoulders, but she shrugged off the brief contact. His fingers had brushed her neck. Had she allowed the physical response to spread she would have been weakened.

'And another thing,' she said. 'I was shocked to hear you've run my uncle out of his own business. You're callous, Max. You only ever think of yourself. The company was Julian's life.'

'Stop judging me, Ellie.' Max's attitude changed. He was no longer so amiable. 'Julian Cromer is sick in mind and body. It'd been coming on for years and he was no longer fit to make even the smallest company decisions. He was also in financial difficulties and agreed to me buying him out.'

'You could have let him retire and keep his shares.'

'No. He was ruining us. As it was I had to work damned hard to bring us out of trouble.' He leaned forward to look into her eyes. 'I didn't come here to talk about Julian or the company, or even William. I came to talk about us. I want the past to be buried.'

The tug at Ellie's heart was so painful she put up her hands as if to ward off further assault. Her shoulders pulled inwards as she closed her eyes momentarily.

'Don't,' she begged him. 'For me the past is already buried and I won't resurrect it.'

'Then we can start again.'

'Never.'

'Ellie, I love you.'

She drew a sharp breath. The words she had longed to hear over the years had at last been uttered, but they had come too late and now she didn't want to hear them. She couldn't understand herself. All she knew was that she needed more than a casual declaration.

'That's easy to say.' She was aloof. 'No doubt William put you up to it, but it's not enough. My life is full without you and I won't let you walk back into it thinking all is forgiven and forgotten.'

'It all happened so long ago,' said Max. 'I've done as you wished and stayed away, but I've kept faith with you. Call it penitence or what you will.'

'Are you expecting me to reward you for it?'

'I think you still love me.'

She was incensed. His presumptuous arrogance touched her pride.

'You can think what you like,' she stormed, getting to her feet. 'It changes nothing.'

He also got up. Standing so close she was afraid he would see the throbbing pulse in her neck. She covered it with a tense hand, aware that he, too, was under stress, but rejection of him had become a deeply ingrained habit which made no allowances.

'Don't you think I've served a long enough sentence for my crime?' he asked. 'I've said I love you. What more can I say?'

'Words. They're just words, Max. When you can prove their worth I'll listen.'

At the end of the afternoon she sent him away. Then she went up to her room and wept at her own foolishness.

It was not only Max who saw the account in the newspaper of Elena Berman's post in England. Julian Cromer saw it too, but unlike her estranged husband he didn't do anything about it. Just seeing her name revived a host of memories which added to the strain he had been under since her departure back in '97, and after looking at the photograph for several minutes he tore it out of the newspaper, screwed it into a tight ball and threw it across the room. But the action didn't bring relief. For the rest of the day he shut himself in his study with a bottle of spirits and tortured himself anew with recriminations and accusations.

With typical human frailty he needed a scapegoat, someone to blame for all his misfortunes over the past twenty-five years, and after the death of Oliver Devlin he had transferred that blame and laid it at the feet of his niece, Ellie. From the moment she had come into his life it seemed things had started to go wrong, and they had continued to do so ever since.

He thought of the first few years after he had married Millicent as the golden period of his life. Court Carriages had become his, he had moved into Fortune Cottage, and his father had been the source of many beautiful, valuable possessions. And then *she* had come, the loveliest creature he had ever seen, and bit by bit he'd lost everything. Now all he had left was a waspish wife and Fortune Cottage stripped of all its treasures. In moments of deepest gloom he knew it was his punishment for having lusted after his sister's child. Even if they'd both been free they would have been forbidden by law to marry.

It was Ellie's fault he hadn't been able to complete his acquisition of the works of art gracing his father's house in London. She had come along and cured the old man of his drinking so that he'd known what was going on. Ellie had brought Oliver Devlin on the scene, too. Ellie had so bewitched Julian he had become obsessed to the point of risking his reputation to have her, and in the end he had killed for her, or so it seemed in his troubled mind. No one had ever found out that his hand had held the knife. Sometimes he wished he could have hanged for it. It might have been preferable to the private hell he had suffered ever since.

Ellie was the reason why he now drank too much himself and incurred bills he could barely pay. He'd needed the alcohol at first to help him stop thinking about her. Ellie was the cause of Max Berman's arrival and the reason for him eventually bringing over the objectionable brat who had stepped so unfairly into a fortune. *Ellie, Ellie...* Her name was engraved on his heart. Ellie, no doubt, was behind Max Berman's vendetta towards himself. Julian hated the man, even more than he hated Devlin. And he never wanted to see Ellie again.

Max had treated him like an imbecile. In the last few years he'd used humouring tactics in an attempt to get him out of the company, but Julian had held on for as long as possible, until his financial problems had forced him to make a deal. Berman had tried to make out he was mentally unstable, which was plain slanderous! Admittedly, there were days when he could only find peace in brandy, but he was not an alcoholic like his father had been. He could stop as soon as he had blotted out the spectre of Oliver Devlin falling to the ground with the knife in his back.

'You're a danger to us all when you're in that state,' Max had said. 'We're doing vital work here. A word from your drunken mouth dropped in the wrong ear could be damaging to the war effort, to say the least.'

'Who are you to speak to me like that?' Julian had demanded. 'A bloody Russian Jew. Who knows where *your* loyalties lie?'

Come to that, Julian couldn't be quite sure of his own feelings towards the enemy. Their good friends the Gottmanns had become like part of the family when Charlotte married Johann Gottmann in 1912. She had gone to live in Germany with him and only spasmodic news had been smuggled out since the outbreak of hostilities. The Gottmann parents in England had been interned at the beginning of the war.

Perhaps it was the German connection which caused the Cromers' circle of friends to dwindle. Or it could have been Julian's heavy drinking. He could carry his liquor well, but by the end of an evening's entertaining he was usually in an unpleasantly argumentative mood. Certainly, many began turning down invitations to Millicent's parties when Francis became a conscientious objector, and she'd been devastated. But a new group of people had taken the place of the old, and Millicent had been in her element once more. The wives of Naval and Military officers living in the district had been pleased to accept her lavish hospitality, until Max had suddenly clamped down on the expense.

'We can't afford to entertain the whole of His Majesty's forces,' he'd complained.

'Where's your patriotism?' Julian had re-taliated. 'Hospitality to the troops is of major importance. Their morale has to be kept up.'

'Then why isn't Millicent opening Fortune Cottage to the boys off to the trenches?'

Millicent entertaining common soldiers! Julian wouldn't have dared to suggest it.

From then on Max had increased the pressure to get him out, ending in a showdown which Julian would never forgive or forget. It had happened on a day when the first ambulance train actually built at Court Carriages was on exhibition to the public. A long queue of people had been waiting in the street outside to file through after local dignitaries had finished their preferential viewing. Julian had needed a little extra brandy to see him through the ceremony, though not by the slightest sign was it noticeable. He'd stood beside the Mayor of Southampton with Max, in absolute control, when suddenly a simple comment from the Mayor's wife had affected him strangely.

'It's a really beautiful train for our boys,' the little woman had simpered. 'You're doing a wonderful job to help us win the war.'

'It's not a beautiful train,' Julian had shouted. 'It's bloody awful. Beautiful trains are what we *used* to make—and we ought to be making one now to present to the Kaiser as a peace offering, not bloody ambulances. We could stop the war in no time.'

There'd been a horrified silence. Then calmly Max had come up with an explanation.

'Your Worship, ladies and gentlemen, my partner, Mr Cromer, has a wonderful sense of humour,' he'd said. And everyone had started to laugh. Laughter had echoed round the shop, gaining strength until those outside crowded against the doorway to know what was going on. Every town dignitary had laughed at Julian, but he had been unable to laugh at himself. He had been publicly humiliated.

The day after that Max Berman had issued an ultimatum. Either he accepted Max's offer to buy him out, or he faced medical and security investigations which would cause a scandal for people to remember long after the war was over. Julian had taken the money but now, two years later, there was scarcely any left. It had gone in gratifying Millicent's unabated craving for social prestige, and in quenching his own ever-increasing thirst. And after the demise of his position at Court Carriage Works he developed an unhealthy loathing for everything to do with it.

Soon after seeing the report about Ellie, Julian had a visitor at Fortune Cottage. He was alone at the time, and tempted to ignore the doorbell, but the caller was persistent. He walked slowly through the hall, his shoulders stooped, his knees painful with gout, and when the evening sun shone on him through the open door it was obvious the years had not been kind to him in other ways. His fair hair had turned white and receded, leaving him with a high bald dome, and his pale skin had become lined and sallow.

An open-topped Alfonso motor car with red wheels and a smart white body was parked in the drive, and a young man wearing a leather flying helmet still rested his finger on the bell, looking up at the windows as he did so. When he saw Julian his face was wreathed in smiles.

'Mr Cromer! I'm so glad you're in. My name's Walter Goddard. You won't know me, but I'm related to friends of yours and they asked me to look you up if ever I was in Southampton.'

'Friends?' queried Julian.

'May I come inside?' Once he had gained entry and the door was closed the stranger's manner changed. He became conspiratorial. 'Is there somewhere we can talk in private?'

'My study.'

Walter Goddard removed the helmet and put it in the pocket of his coat. His leather gloves he took off and held. Julian went ahead of him down the corridor and showed him into the book-lined room where these days he did his drinking undisturbed. Once satisfied there could be no eavesdropping, Walter went to the desk and poured himself a glass of brandy. The liberty astounded his host, but for some reason he remained silent.

'Not easy to afford brandy like this these days, is it?' the fellow said. 'I'd say you'll soon be finding it very difficult indeed.' He paused. 'Unless you'd like to earn enough to keep you supplied indefinitely?'

'Tell me more,' said Julian.

Walter scrutinised him unnervingly. Then: 'I know I can trust you. I'm Hans Gottmann's nephew. Gottmann is my real name.'

Now it was Julian's turn to smile. He was

surprised and delighted to welcome a relative of Hans, and began plying him with questions.

'Have you seen them? More important, have you heard anything of Johann and my daughter?'

'I've not seen Johann—he's in the front line fighting the French—but I've seen Charlotte.'

'Oh, that's wonderful,' breathed Julian. 'Is she well? What's she doing?'

'She's well at the moment,' the young man told him. He slapped the leather gloves against the palm of his left hand. 'It really depends on you whether she stays healthy.'

It took a minute for the truth to dawn on Julian. He had opened his door to a German spy, and it seemed he was about to be drawn into something he definitely wouldn't like.

'Are you blackmailing me?' he asked, his voice level in spite of the shock.

'Let's say there is a job we would very much like you to do,' said Walter Goddard, who sounded so completely English it seemed incredible that he was not. 'It will be in your own interest to agree. More specifically, it will be in the interest of your daughter. I'm sure you'll understand when I say her life depends on your cooperation.'

William's platoon of engineers was with the American First Army in the battle to recapture the French town of St Mihiel after four years of German occupation. The weather couldn't have been worse. Heavy rain and wind swept across the hillsides, and when they moved forward each night the lorries became bogged down in mud.

429

It was worse for the infantry and artillery men. When they were within a kilometre of the line the sky became red with flashes from enemy guns, and exploding shells caused an immense number of casualties. The road was littered with dead soldiers, but like everyone else William had become immune to the sight, and he no longer shuddered.

His head throbbed from the incessant pounding of the shells. Every village and promontory had been hard-fought for along the way, the engineers repairing bridges and keeping open light rail-links which were working to capacity to supply guns and ammunition. He had watched planes bombing the highways ahead, leaving a carnage of men and horses, and a jumble of twisted vehicles, carts and guns to block the Boche escape route.

The German garrison was attacked mercilessly for four hours, and at five in the morning the American assault troops went over the top while French tanks pressed ahead at the same pace, crossing trenches and destroying enemy positions. By eight in the evening, thirteen thousand German prisoners had been taken, and the rest had left St Mihiel by the only route left to them. The following morning, French troops rescued the remaining population of mostly women and children, all of whom wept and sang with joy at their release, and the American engineers crossed the bridge into town to resounding cheers, the Old Glory flag flying.

There was no rest. They had to deal with the

havoc to communications left by the retreating Germans. Old tracks had to be reconstructed, and new lines to take extra rolling-stock through to the advancing armies had to be laid down in record time by men working continuously day and night.

Their most vital task was to reopen the main Paris–Nancy trunk line a few kilometres beyond St Mihiel which had been cut off throughout the German occupation. William had been ordered to take his men southwards towards Commercy where the rail-link had been under constant barrage from hostile batteries for years, but around the hamlet of St Baussant huddling in the shadow of Mont Sec, a natural fortress the Germans still held, they were targeted by German artillery positions sheltering in the heights above them. Casualties mounted. Motor transport ferrying vast numbers of wounded French and American troops from the front to the nearest field hospitals had to come to the aid of the engineers.

After many gruelling hours, William moved away from the platoon for a brief respite to consult new instructions from headquarters, but when he sat down at the roadside for the first time in hours, he was overcome with fatigue. He put his head in his hands. The war for which he had volunteered nearly eighteen months ago with such patriotic enthusiasm was more terrible than anything he had ever imagined. He now held the rank of Captain, but it gave him no satisfaction. He felt as if he had only ever known mud and filth and blood and death, and he was so tired his limbs moved mechanically. His eyes burned, his skin was sore and flaking and his throat was parched.

He felt rather than saw yet another Red Cross vehicle negotiating the road through the rubble which had once been a village. Grit showered into his matted hair and rattled on the tin helmet he had removed. It smelt of sweat that had collected on the inner leather rim. He didn't look up until it sounded as if this car had become entrenched in a muddy shell-hole. The noise of the revving engine as the driver tried to get it out like a sword passing through his pain-racked body.

'You're making things worse doing that,' he yelled.

'Then get up off your arse and do something to help,' came the vulgar reply, though the voice sounded distinctly feminine.

He got up reluctantly and slouched across. When he stood still he was swaying with tiredness. An orderly in Medical Corps uniform opened the door at the back of the ambulance, jumped down and made straight for the driver.

'What the hell do you think you're doing? There are two very sick men in here, one with serious head injuries.'

'I didn't make the bloody hole.'

The girl switched off the engine and got down. She was of medium height and dressed in khaki. Her hair was tucked up inside a military tin helmet, and William was not sure whether the marks on her face were freckles or mud.

432

The orderly got him to help lift out the stretchers bearing the two wounded men and they laid them on the side of the road, then William went behind the ambulance and heaved his shoulder against it.

'You're not trying,' the girl accused, also using brute strength, and so close beside him he could see that she had green eyes.

'Get in and start the engine again,' he ordered.

Several more battle-weary soldiers came to give assistance, but even with their combined strength it took several more minutes before the vehicle was once more on comparatively level ground. The men went back to laying rails. Only William stayed with the girl.

Damage had been done to the engine. It coughed and spluttered, then ceased altogether.

'Let me try,' said William. But when he urged her to move over so that he could take the wheel she was angry and obstinate.

'I've been driving and mending one of these things for the last three years. I know a damned sight more about it than you do.' She got down again and lifted the bonnet.

'Linnie, if we don't get goin' fast it'll be too late,' called the orderly, who was holding a bowl of water to one of the wounded men's lips. The other was moaning in agony.

The girl called Linnie struggled with spanners, her head under the bonnet of the ambulance. She was swearing like a man, and although she wore an American uniform her accent sounded British. William made another attempt to help, having seen what was wrong, but she kicked his shin, forcing him to stand aside. As he watched he felt an ache growing inside him which was totally separate from bodily exhaustion. This girl was at breaking point. She was trying to work in a frenzy and accomplishing nothing. The dampness he had seen on her cheeks and thought was sweat became an unstoppable stream of tears.

He risked further assault from her heavy footwear and moved closer, taking the tools from her feverish hands. This time she put up no resistance.

'You've had enough,' he said gently. 'No one expects you to carry on until you drop.'

'Yes, they do. No one cares as long as the ambulance gets through.'

'Well, if you go on like this you'll be in it instead of driving it.'

'I've got to get these men to the hospital.'

She started sobbing and he knew instinctively it was the first time she had given way. A great feeling of pity welled up in him and he cursed the war more vociferously than at any other time. Women ought not to be subjected to this. It was far more than their weaker constitution was meant to stand, and if he could have demanded her withdrawal from the front line right then he would have done so. His anger at her plight was so strong it diminished his own exhaustion.

Without any embarrassment he drew her into his arms and cradled her there for several minutes while the sobbing wracked her body.

It was the first time he had held a woman since he had left the States and the feel of her was disturbing, even through the coarse uniform. Her tin hat fell off and rolled between their feet. Her head came to rest against his chest. He found himself murmuring words of comfort against her ear, and a silent bond seemed to be forged even though she was a complete stranger. With rough hands he stroked her hair. It was dark with grease and badly in need of a wash, yet as it fell over her shoulders it was more beautiful than anything he had touched in over a year.

'Linnie, for God's sake get that vehicle moving,' yelled the orderly, from the side of the road.

'I can't do it,' the girl wept. She jerked out of William's embrace and clasped her hands against her temples. 'You'll have to drive the bloody thing yourself.'

One of the engineers picked up some tools and started working on the ambulance's engine. Another joined him. The moans of the soldier with blood-soaked head bandages turned to screams. The girl let forth at William with new bitterness.

'Aren't you ashamed to have been sitting down? This is the Paris to Nancy trunk route. It'll save hours getting ambulance trains to the Channel ports, and time can save lives.'

He was impressed with her knowledge. 'This part of the line's been German controlled almost since the war started. The track might not take ambulance trains yet.'

'You don't know what you're talking about, mister.'

'And you do, I suppose?'

'I should. I own a company that's been building them.'

William stared at her in amazement, his red-rimmed eyes stinging as they widened, and a rash reply came without thought. 'Half a company.'

'What did you say?'

'I said you only own half a company, Galina.' It was her turn to stare. 'You *are* Galina Devlin, aren't you?'

'I don't know you. How do *you* know me?'

'I'm your cousin, William Berman. My father owns the other half of Court Carriages and he's willed it to me, so mind what you're claiming as your own.'

'William! Oh, my God!' Tears sprang afresh to her eyes and she trembled visibly. 'I never used to swear. Uncle Max would be horrified.'

'I won't tell him,' he promised.

After several awkward moments he reached out and drew her close again, holding her as if they were lovers reunited. He could feel her heart beating against his own, strong as a traction engine, and when he reluctantly let her go he brought her calloused palms to his lips and kissed them tenderly. It was the most extraordinary meeting. Then she drew away.

'I've had a grudge against you for years,' she said. 'I swore you'd never get your hands on my company. Why is it I'm ridiculously pleased to see you?'

436

'We're family, and the war changes everything,' said William. 'Tell me where I can find you. I must see you again soon.'

'I'll write. Give me your field address.'

The stretcher cases were back in the ambulance and the orderly caught sight of his driver being overfamiliar with an Army Captain she'd only just met. 'What the bloody hell's going on?' he demanded furiously. 'I'm going to report you, Devlin.'

Galina lifted her arms in the air as if in praise of the Powers above, and she turned a complete circle. Her face no longer registered defeat, but shone with unexpected joy.

'I've found my Cousin William,' she cried, so that everyone could hear. 'Isn't it amazing!'

The men gathered round, hungry for every scrap of good news, and they were noisy in their appreciation. Their respect and affection for their commanding officer was much in evidence.

'I'm due a few days' leave soon, William,' Galina said. 'I plan to spend it in Paris.'

'You haven't had a break since we came out here, sir,' said one of the engineers. 'You deserve a spell of furlough if ever anyone did.'

William hesitated, then smiled as he looked at his cousin. 'I'll be there.'

The orderly knew the urgency to get moving and went back to the ambulance, stepping on the footplate preparatory to climbing in behind the wheel. Galina raced over.

'Get down from there, you bastard,' she cried,

437

but this time without animosity. 'No one does my job for me.'

She pushed him away and slipped into the driving seat, filled with renewed energy.

'Goodbye, William,' she called, waving as she started off along the shell-cratered road. 'See you in Paris.'

TWENTY-ONE

At the beginning of November 1918, Ellie found herself on a train to Southampton, something she had vowed she would not be doing. Not all her memories of the time she had spent in the town were unpleasant, but a phobia about the dockside lingered, and if she'd had to arrive at Southampton from America in her Red Cross capacity she dreaded to think what sort of state she would have been in.

Her destination in the town was also a place she had never wanted to see again, but her orders to go there had been issued by the top authority at Richmond Hospital. The hospital was now fully functional and her own work there as an administrator had grown less demanding.

'It's important that one of our senior staff inspect the ambulance train, Mrs Berman,' she had been told. 'Court Carriage Works have done a wonderful job, I hear, but before it's shipped to France we need to be sure it contains all the

438

necessary medical equipment. It's the first one they've built for us Americans.'

After Max's visit to the hospital she'd heard nothing from him. It was ridiculous to have felt disappointed. She had made her views so crystal clear he had obviously accepted them as final, which was what she had intended ... at the time. Since then she'd reflected on what she had done, and in the empty hours between every sunset and sunrise she'd come to realise the cost of her unyielding pride. Max was still the only man she had ever loved, yet fear of being hurt again made her continue to reject him. She wished he hadn't given up so quickly. It made the mockery she had suspected of his loving declarations. What she had needed and hoped for was persistence capable of breaking down her contrariness, but he had failed her in that, the same as in everything else.

She had written a very formal letter to tell him of the Red Cross's wish that she should carry out an inspection of the mobile ambulance facilities. By return of post all she had received was an equally formal acknowledgement.

She was going to arrive quite late. There'd been no car or driver available to take her so it had meant travelling by train, and as there were no timetables she'd not been able to check on the journey beforehand. It had been necessary to change trains twice before she was on the right one to Southampton, and it had been badly delayed so she wouldn't get there until late afternoon, which was particularly annoying as she might now have to stay somewhere overnight.

Sitting in the crowded train she had time to study her fellow travellers, mostly servicemen with kitbags and young women making the harrowing journey to spend every precious last second with their menfolk leaving for the front. Demonstrations of affection which would have been frowned on before the war were now commonplace, and Ellie's heart melted to see tears in the eyes of a young wife as she rested her head on her soldier husband's shoulder.

Life was such a fragile thing. This had been brought home to her with great clarity since the hospital had been filled to capacity with the wounded and dying. It was a terrible tragedy to see the state of young men who had gone to war full of vitality, now with limbs missing, brain damage and gas poisoning. For Ellie, the trauma of witnessing their injuries was magnified by the fear that one day she might look down at a stretcher and see William.

How wicked, therefore, to waste the only things of real value in life—to let pride stand in the way of love. She wondered what these young women would say if they knew how she persistently refused to forgive her husband for a youthful wrongdoing he had admitted was the biggest mistake of his life.

The coming meeting with Max filled her with the same apprehension as before. She wondered how he felt, knowing she was on her way.

She had never seen West Station so crowded. Carts and wagons were piled high with the luggage of troops in transit, and mostly khaki uniforms coloured the scene in a drab yet brave monotone. Ellie elbowed her way through, her Red Cross cape held round her to keep out the cold sea air on that autumn day. The buildings of Court Carriages loomed ahead of her as soon as she came out into the forecourt, and seeing them for the first time in twenty years brought a lump to her throat. She remembered Oliver and Grandfather Cromer. Memories of Julian came crowding back. She would take the opportunity to visit him and Millicent while she was in Southampton, though she felt a certain reluctance.

She was glad of the walk. The fresh air helped to clear her head. There was a new branch line leading from the station which hadn't been there before, and she guessed it must be the mile-long link-span which connected with the train ferry now operating between Southampton and Dieppe four times a week carrying wounded. Apart from that, not much had changed that she could see, and as she walked into the main office at Court Carriages it seemed like only yesterday that she had left. One big difference here, however, was the replacement of Mr Carew with a female clerk.

'Oh dear, we thought you weren't coming after all, and Mr Berman's out,' the girl said, flustered.

'Out?' Ellie's arched brows rose even higher. At her most imperious she could make junior nurses quake, and now she had the same effect on the clerk. 'He knew I would be here. Why couldn't he have waited?'

'We expected you this morning. And something important cropped up.'

Ellie was livid. It sounded as if she had been deliberately snubbed and, unreasonably, all her magnanimous thoughts on the journey down dissolved in a mist of fresh disillusion. Yet she *was* late. Max had had every right to give up on her.

'If you'd like to wait...'

'No, I would not like to wait. I shall carry out the inspection I was sent to do, and be on the next train back to Richmond.' She brushed the girl aside impatiently when she offered to escort her. Truth to tell, she was near to tears. 'I don't need anyone to show me the way.'

'Mrs Berman, you can't go on your own.'

'If my husband returns from his urgent appointment in the next hour tell him he'll find me in the Red Cross train.'

'Mrs Berman, I'm not to let anyone go through to the Works unescorted.' The clerk earned Ellie's respect for her efficiency. 'I'll arrange for someone to go with you.'

Ten minutes later she stalked through the yard in the company of an elderly gentleman in a black suit called Mr Thorne, who had a job to keep up with her. Her heels clipped the cobbles, her attaché case was gripped firmly in her right hand, and she made straight for the vast bodyshop where she was used to seeing upwards of twenty car bodies in various stages of construction. The men working there now were all over conscription age, and were mostly carrying out repairs. Some of the jobs, such as painting, were being done by women.

The poor man tripping along in her wake tried to make conversation but she was in no mood for it.

'Did you have a good journey, Mrs Berman? Was the train unbearably crowded? How long is it since you've been here?'

'Twenty years, Mr Thorne, and little has changed apart from the war work. I expected to see signs of modernisation.'

If only Max had waited. She could hardly think of anything else.

A few interested eyes turned to Ellie as she walked between the lines of bogies and made for the ambulance coaches which stood isolated at the far end, conspicuous by their newly-painted white roofs and red crosses. Now work had finished on the American train no one was near it. There were wooden steps up to the doors of the sixteen bogie vehicles, the elevation being too great for admittance from ground level, and Ellie stood aside at last for Mr Thorne to precede her up the first of them. Then she lifted her grey skirt slightly to negotiate the steps. The door was locked.

'Oh dear, oh dear.' The old man was fumbling through his pockets and getting very agitated. 'I seem to have come without the keys. Will you excuse me while I go back for them?'

There was nothing else she could do. She tapped her fingers on the wooden balustrade impatiently, then tried to see through the window. This was a pharmacy car containing an operating table, treatment room and office for the doctors. In service it would have to be coupled between the ward cars.

Exasperated at the delay, she spent the time looking at the once-familiar scene around her, and beyond the body shop she saw there was a new building. It was well-lit within, though she couldn't see the purpose of it, and curiosity got the better of her. She went back down the steps and left the shop by a rear door which had once opened out onto another yard, but now led through to a dark passage between the two buildings.

It was quite a long passage with a couple of doors leading off and a large set of double doors at the end with glass top-panels illuminated by the internal electric lights. The windows were the right height for her to look through and she saw a huge machine shop with rows of long benches at which sat a hundred or more women of all ages, elbow to elbow, mob-caps on their heads, engaged in assembling shell-fuses. Overseeing them were men in cloth caps, probably invalided out of the Army and glad to be involved in very essential war work.

Ellie watched undetected for several minutes, fascinated by the speed with which the women worked, but when someone who looked like a security guard appeared she realised how bad it would look if she was caught spying. She darted back down the passage to one of the heavy side doors which was ajar, and slipped inside to let him pass.

The room was obviously a storeroom, and

much bigger than she would have expected. There was very little light, but she could make out boxes of parts for fuses stacked on shelves from floor to ceiling, with little space to walk between them. The smell of dust and cardboard made her want to cough; luckily she didn't.

She was waiting to make sure the coast was clear when she became aware of another presence in the storeroom. Furtive movements made her shrink back between two of the shelves, and her heartbeats quickened as a shadowy figure crossed her path. She realised she was trapped; to be discovered here would be even worse than by the double doors in the passage, which at least was a fairly public place.

He knew she was there. Oh, dear Holy Virgin, what was she to do? The man was extremely quiet as he moved stealthily to the door to cut off her escape, and she daren't leave her hiding place. She held her breath, expecting to be seized at any minute and hauled out to face charges, but when she peered out fearfully she had the surprise of her life.

The other occupant of the storeroom stood for a few seconds in the dimness looking up and down the passage. He turned briefly to face her direction, as if checking something, and Ellie's stomach muscles suddenly contracted. It was her uncle, Julian Cromer!

She'd understood from both William and Max that Julian no longer had anything to do with Court Carriages, but times were difficult. She had only to think of the quavering voice of Mr

445

Thorne to understand how the shortage of male staff was affecting the company, so no doubt it had been necessary to ask Julian back. Surely it had been short-sighted to let him go in the first place.

He'd seen her, she was sure of it, and she almost called out his name, but stopped herself. She wanted to speak to Julian, but first she needed to extricate herself from the suspicious circumstances her curiosity had created. It wouldn't do for him to find her in an obviously sensitive part of the works, where she had no business to be. She must be able to greet him openly.

His eyes glittered in the half-light, and his searching glance passed over her. With a sigh of relief she realised he hadn't noticed her hiding place after all. He took an anxious look outside and then left, closing the door behind him.

Ellie allowed a few seconds to elapse, then tried the door. It wouldn't open. Julian had turned the key in the lock.

With sickening alarm she had to face the fact that she was locked in, and nobody knew she was there.

William was looking for a dark-haired girl. He'd thought he wouldn't have the slightest difficulty recognising her, especially as she would be wearing American Army uniform, but as he stood at the station entrance searching the faces milling past he began to think he couldn't trust his memory. When he tried to picture her, he found it almost impossible, because what he

446

remembered was intangible. After that briefest of meetings he'd been left with a feeling of completeness, though he hadn't been aware before of an inner void, and of course allowances had to be made for extraordinary circumstances playing havoc with his emotions. Even so, he knew it had been one of the most important days in his life. Inner recognition had been what mattered, not facial details.

Galina had been continually in his thoughts since that meeting on the road near St Mihiel, keeping him sane in conditions so appalling he wondered each night if he would live to see the next sunrise. He had lost two of his best men the week before, when a booby-trapped bridge was destroyed. The offensive was gaining momentum, the enemy being driven back towards Belgium, but for the advance party of engineers with the job of opening up roads and railways destroyed by the Huns in retreat, there was always the danger of setting off primed explosive devices, no matter how careful the preliminary inspection.

The communication Galina had sent was brief. *'Paris, October 12th, 3.30 pm, Gare de Lyon, main entrance. Make it if you can, Galina.'* The telegram was in his hand, though the contents were engraved on his mind. He looked at his watch and saw the minute hand had crept on another five minutes, making it almost four o'clock. He didn't know what he would do if she didn't turn up after all. It had been difficult enough to get forty-eight hours' furlough. He didn't think he would ever be able to return to

447

the front if he didn't see her.

He'd had no proper sleep for weeks. His face was gaunt, his eyes haunted, and he shivered with cold and disappointment. A chill wind was whistling through the station and he was glad of his long khaki overcoat. An Austrian knot in black braid on each cuff indicated his Captain's rank, and he was obliged to acknowledge many a salute while fearing the distractions might make him miss the one person he was desperate to see.

Five more minutes had slipped by when the voice he longed to hear came from behind him.

'Hello, soldier.'

He turned. He stared. He faltered over her name. 'Galina?'

The girl smiling up at him was the most ravishing redhead he had ever seen, and if it hadn't been for the green eyes and dusting of freckles he would have sworn she was a complete stranger. Not only was her hair a different colour now that the grease was washed out of it, her clothes were different too. She wasn't wearing uniform.

'Were you here to meet anyone else?' she asked, laughing. 'Sorry I'm late. I got here a few hours earlier and managed to do some shopping. I felt I'd die if I had to wear khaki any longer.'

'You look lovely,' he said. The words were inadequate. She looked wonderfully Parisienne in a golden-brown tunic dress reaching well above her ankles, a brown velvet coat and a

448

small green and gold plaid hat with a single feather at the back. Her laced boots were black patent leather with gaberdine tops, and the high heels gave her added grace. 'Wherever did you manage to buy such finery?'

'There are still places if you have the money.' She slipped a gloved hand through his arm. 'Come on, I'm starving. Let's have some real food, shall we?'

They started to walk, but had gone only a short distance when William stopped and turned her towards him.

'Galina, we've both been over here too long. It affects the mind. Meeting you was like a miracle.'

'I know.'

'But let's be realistic. If we'd met in Southampton at Court Carriages I would have barely been polite. I've never liked you since you kicked me when I was a kid.'

'And I hated you. Spoilt brat ... Mama's pet! I've always been determined you wouldn't get your hands on any of *my* company.'

'Which you acquired fraudulently. Your father embezzled my mother's money to get it. One day I'll find a way to get you out.'

'Never.' She stamped her foot, and he was glad of the protection of his knee-length leather boots in case she aimed a pointed toe at his shins.

There was a glint in her eyes, but it wasn't malicious. The shine in his own was humorous, and full of admiration. She was so exquisite.

'Okay, so that's settled ... we hate each other,'

he said. 'Now let's forget it and enjoy the next couple of days.'

'Suits me,' said Galina. 'I didn't bring up the past in the first place.'

After an adequate meal in a bistro they wandered the streets of Paris, her gloved hand tucked through the crook of his arm. Signs of the German bombardment had left scars in places, but the beauty of the city remained intact and it glowed in the dwindling light of the cool autumn evening. Wall posters advertised *Le Casino de Paris. Les Dernières Nouveautés d'Angleterre et d'Amerique dans* LA GRAND REVUE. They bought tickets and laughed at the antics of Boucot, sang along with Rose-Amy, and tapped their feet to the music of the Sherbo-American-Band. For William there was the thrill of seeing forty-eight beautiful dancing girls, but when Galina teased him he said that none could equal the way she looked that night.

After leaving the Casino they walked some more, Galina chattering all the while about inconsequential things while William listened and marvelled at the warmth of her low voice. Not a single swearword escaped her. She was different entirely from the female Army driver he had held in his arms and comforted only a few weeks ago, and his affection grew.

'Why are you with the Americans?' he asked. 'Why don't you drive for the British Army?'

'Because I am American,' she said. 'Have you forgotten I was born in Chicago?'

'So you're still a US citizen?'

'Uncle Max never suggested I become

450

anything else. I ... we've got umpteen more cousins over there. Do you ever see them?'

'No. After Grandmother Berman died, my father's brother and family moved out to the country and we lost touch.'

'We were never good enough for you. I wonder your mother didn't change her name back to Harvey.'

He was rattled. 'My mother isn't a snob. If she had been, she wouldn't have married my father.'

Galina squeezed his arm and smiled disarmingly. 'Let's not fall out.' It was getting very late, and the moon which had cast a bright path across the river earlier had become obscured by cloud, making the streets dark. 'I saw the hotel where I want to stay,' she said. 'It's a big place not far from the Madeleine.'

'*I* shall choose where we stay,' said William.

Their wandering had brought them to the Hotel de France in a street called rue de l'Arbre Sec; it was a small establishment with fancy wine bottles in the windows either side of the door and thick lace curtains at the windows above. It looked clean and cosy, and very anonymous. The woman who booked them in was plump and homely, her dark hair drawn into a plain knot at the back of her head.

'*Deux chambres?*' she asked, raising her eyebrows in Gallic surprise when William asked for separate rooms.

'I think this must be a *"maison d'assignation"*,' giggled Galina. But she was already enchanted with it. The stairs were narrow, the bedrooms quaint and typically French with their heavy carved furniture, dark patterned wallpaper and lace bedspreads. The pillows were long bolsters. 'I love it. I can't remember when I last smelt lavender.'

'Sleep well then,' William said. It seemed appropriate to kiss her lightly on both cheeks before retiring to the room next door.

It was the first night he'd been in a proper bed for many months and he ought to have slept soundly. He closed his eyes, savouring the luxury of sheets and blankets and certain that within minutes sleep would claim him, but his mind was over-active. He kept reliving the events of the day, and he was very conscious of the girl in the next bedroom. Shame at the way his body reacted to thoughts of her made him deliberately try to keep her from his mind, but the more he tried the worse it became. Galina was his cousin, yet he wanted her so desperately he couldn't lie still. Finally he slept, only to dream of her.

At breakfast next morning Galina looked as if she had spent an equally wakeful night. Her eyes were less bright and she was very quiet.

'I guess I've gotten used to sleeping on the ground,' William said. 'I found the bed a mite strange.' The red check tablecloth dazzled his eyes, and the coffee served in bowls without handles taxed his patience when he was so thirsty.

'The pillow hurt my neck,' said Galina. 'I had to throw it out.'

They ate French bread in silence, but every

time they looked up their eyes met, and when both reached for the jam at the same time their fingers touched. She drew hers back as if they had been in contact with a flame.

Presently he gave up all pretence. 'I couldn't sleep because I was thinking of you,' he admitted.

'And I just lay there waiting for morning to come.' She, too, was candid. 'I wanted to be with you again.'

He felt better knowing this madness was shared. He'd been afraid she would laugh and call him a fool.

'We've got a whole day to ourselves,' he said. 'Let's not waste a minute of it.'

He booked the rooms for a second night before they went out into the garlic-smelling street. Restrictions governed what they could do in war-time Paris, but it didn't matter. They were content just to be in each other's company, and as they walked hand in hand between the lime trees in the Luxembourg Gardens they scarcely noticed the presence of French tanks and troops. The air was fresh, the sky a clear blue, and there was no sound of gunfire to dampen their spirits. They had so much to talk about, yet in moments of silence it seemed much more was said. William had never met a girl with whom he was so immediately at ease.

Later, in Les Halles, he bought flowers for Galina, an armful of red roses too big for her to carry. She gave all but one away, some to a girl with a screaming baby, more to an old woman in black with the sorrows of the world in her eyes.

'I wish everyone could be as happy as I am today,' Galina cried. 'I wish the day would never end.'

'We'll have it to remember.' They had been laughing, but thoughts of returning to the front line sobered them temporarily. William carried her hand to his heart and held it there. 'Promise me you'll take care. I've never had anyone to worry about before. If anything happened to you I'd be devastated.'

'Nothing's going to happen to me,' she said. 'Or to you either. We'll both be around to fight over Court Carriages when the war is over.'

They ate at a café in Les Halles where an old man was playing a harp and thick brocade curtains with tassels down the edges were drawn at dusk to black out the light. A candle flickered in a glass on the table. And as it burnt down they were increasingly aware that their time together was getting shorter. William caressed Galina's cheek with his fingertips. Her skin was soft in spite of the amount of time she spent outdoors, and it had the pale clarity which went with red hair, a creaminess he could almost taste.

She quivered at his touch. He saw the pulse beating rapidly in her throat, and she drew his hand away from her cheek and up to her lips. Time seemed to stand still. Presently he kissed her. She leaned towards him in anticipation, and when their lips met the gentle touch sent a shock through every part of his body.

'Galina, I think I'm in love with you.'

The words were drawn from him involuntarily. He expected her to tell him not to be absurd, but instead she cupped his face between her hands and repeated the kiss he had instigated.

'I love you too.'

'What would you say if I asked you to marry me?'

The question took her by surprise, in spite of their declarations. 'Marriage? No, William, that's not possible.'

'Give me a good reason why not. And don't say it's because we're first cousins because the law doesn't forbid it.'

'There's more to it than that,' she said. 'I'm half Irish Catholic and half Russian Jew.'

'And I'm half Russian Jew and half American Catholic. Does it matter?'

'I've been brought up Jewish.'

'And I'm Catholic.' He smiled into her eyes. 'But only in name. I've no great attachment to the church of Our Lady even though the family are devout.' He paused. 'Do you believe in God?'

She said: 'Yes, implicitly, in spite of all the atrocities and bloodshed I've seen.'

'So do I. So let's trust in Him to guide us without caring too much about the route we take,' said William.

But Galina was not persuaded. She sat back in her chair and gave him a teasing smile. 'I think you're only asking me so that you can be sure of having Court Carriages.'

He laughed. 'Perhaps I am.' Then he became

serious again. 'Galina, I wouldn't care if the whole Works went up in smoke. I want to take you back to America after the war ... as my wife.'

'It's too sudden. We must give ourselves time. Emotions are strained and unnatural during a war. No one can count on even seeing the next day. If we still feel the same way when all this is over, then perhaps I'll think about it. I can't make decisions now.'

He knew she was right, and he accepted it. But he also knew that he would feel exactly the same tomorrow and in twenty or more years' time. From the moment of meeting there had been something special between them, a bond which bridged the years since childhood. He remembered the saying that hatred is akin to love. She had made a great impact on him as a small boy and he had never forgotten her, though he had allowed the memory of their juvenile antipathy to linger on as intense dislike, when all the time it had been love waiting to be awakened.

'I'll write to you whenever I have the opportunity,' he said. 'Every night if I can.'

'I'll do the same,' she promised.

'And I'll be thinking of you every minute.' He held her hands again and pressed them between his own. 'I'll leave instructions for you to be told if anything happens to me, though I know we'll both come through.'

'I know it, too. But I'll do the same ... just in case.'

'I love you, my darling,' he told her again,

and she responded by kissing him full on the mouth with lips which quivered deliciously.

When they got back to the Hotel de France the concierge at the desk was shaking her head at a young French soldier and his girl obviously wanting a room for the night. Galina took her key and offered it to the soldier.

'You can have my room,' she said, in perfect French. 'We shall only be needing the one.'

Max had been expecting Ellie to arrive in the morning. He had planned to take her out for a special lunch, but when it was way past noon and she hadn't turned up he had no appetite for eating alone. His disappointment at the delay made him restless.

He was longing to see her—no good denying it. Since their unsatisfactory meeting in Richmond he had been waiting for an opportunity to see her again in surroundings more conducive to a reconciliation, but he knew arrangements had to be handled carefully. Ellie was more prickly than a porcupine and her willpower as strong as iron. It would have been no good writing with yet more abject apologies and demands for her to reconsider. Appealing to her had no effect whatever.

The only way to get results, Max decided, was to approach the matter underhandingly. So he had written to the American Red Cross on the completion of their ambulance train with a request for a senior administrator to approve the equipment before it was shipped out, though it had already been checked according to British

457

regulations. It had been a risk. They could have sent a man, but knowing the character of Ellie's job had made him fairly certain she would be the one detailed to undertake the task, and he had been right.

Had there been a chance to take her in his arms that afternoon at the hospital he was fairly sure she would have succumbed. She was ready for love. It had been evident in her posture, in the way she had leaned towards him without being aware of it, and in the way she had moistened her lips. Today his plan had been to woo her with the best food and wine available, and to charm her out of the remnants of opposition he knew she clung to through obstinacy. But three o'clock came and she still hadn't arrived. And after that a most unexpected telephone call changed everything.

The call came from Millicent Cromer. 'Mr Berman, I must see you urgently. Now, today.'

Over the years he'd had very little to do with Julian's wife. Her snobbery aggravated him, and when she had found he was not interested in being helped up the social ladder she had abandoned all pretence of friendship. They were just not compatible, and she had certainly never made a personal call to him before.

'Can't you tell me the problem now?' Max asked.

'No,' she said. Her economy with words should have alerted him. She usually indulged in flowery language.

'Well, I can't leave the Works today on any

account. If Julian's ill, call the doctor.'

'If you value your life and the safety of the company, you'll come straight away.'

With that the telephone went dead, and Max was left holding the receiver in stunned silence. He had no idea what was behind the call, but the reason must be extremely urgent for Millicent to have made it. It couldn't be ignored.

He had to give priority to Millicent's problem, no matter what Ellie might think when she came. It was most unlikely the melodramatic announcement had been a hoax or a ploy to get him away from the Works for some reason. Millicent was not the type to practise such deception, so the extraordinary warning had to be taken seriously. He would go straight away, find out what the trouble was, and with any luck, be able to leave again almost immediately with little time wasted.

He drove recklessly to Fortune Cottage, and had hardly switched off the engine of his motor car before Millicent was at the front door. Her short figure had filled out from the onset of middle-age and she was now very plump. But her pink and white complexion was still good and her face almost unlined. The new style of dress with less restriction suited her.

'Please come in,' she said, hastily ushering Max inside as if afraid there might be someone watching. 'I'm sorry to have sounded so mysterious on the telephone, but I couldn't say more in case there was anyone listening

459

in, and I wanted you here at once while Julian is out of the house.'

'Where is he?'

'I don't know.' She showed him into the drawing room. 'I'm very worried, Mr Berman. You see, I'll come straight to the point. My husband has had visits recently from a man I don't trust.'

'Who?'

'He says his name is Walter Goddard.'

It appeared the man had arrived one day while Millicent was out visiting, so she hadn't seen him initially, but Julian had been in an excited state on her return. He'd told her a long, involved story about Mr Goddard having heard news of their daughter Charlotte through friends of friends which he had hastened to bring, and Millicent had been so overjoyed to hear that her daughter was safe, she hadn't thought to question the source of the information too deeply. It hadn't even occurred to her that there might be something suspicious about news coming from inside Germany. The man had returned two days later with a brief letter from Charlotte, in her unmistakable handwriting, in which she hadn't said anything much except that she was safe and well. Lack of detail wasn't surprising, though, in view of censorship. When she'd asked Julian later why Mr Goddard hadn't brought it on his first visit he had been very vague, but that wasn't surprising either since he was vague about a lot of things lately.

'What does the man look like?' Max asked.

'He's young and appears to be very fit, fit

enough to be serving his country.'

'So is Francis, I believe.' He had no patience with conscientious objectors, and made it known.

Millicent's lips tightened, but she let the remark pass. 'Last night Mr Goddard came again, wearing a Royal Flying Corps uniform. Oh, he's very charming. He brought me a box of chocolates such as I haven't seen since before the war, and Julian a case of brandy. A whole case! Of course Julian insisted he sat down to dinner with us.' She paused. Then: 'I don't know why, but I asked him if he had trained at Farnborough, and he said he had. So I said he must have met Squadron-Commander Willard Preston there, and he replied that they'd spent many jolly evenings together in the mess. Now, it didn't occur to me until we had finished eating that Willard Preston, who was a frequent visitor here in the days when I did a lot of entertaining, is in the Royal Naval Air Service. He wouldn't have been at Farnborough.'

Max's opinion of Millicent went up by leaps and bounds.

'Have you discussed this with your husband?'

'No—for a very important reason. The man was lingering, I could tell. I had the feeling he was waiting for me to leave so that he could talk to Julian privately, so I yawned a few times and asked if he would excuse me if I retired to bed, something I would *never* say to a guest normally, you understand.'

'Of course.'

'I then committed the sin of eavesdropping.'

461

Millicent was very serious. 'There is a service lift for food trays from the dining room to the kitchen below stairs, no longer used as we haven't got the servants. I made sure the upper hatch doors were very slightly ajar, then went down to the kitchen and opened the lower ones. I heard Mr Goddard open the case of brandy and I feared they were embarking on a heavy drinking session, but Julian was asking questions about a job to be done tomorrow ... that's today.'

'A job? Did he say what?'

'No—only that the money wouldn't be paid until afterwards. For now Julian would have to make do with what had been given him.'

Max was becoming very intrigued. 'Secret work for the Flying Corps? Brandy being the reward.'

'No,' she said again. 'I've given it much thought, but the possible truth didn't occur to me until a little while ago.'

'Go on,' he urged.

'Well, it sounded as if Mr Goddard had given Julian a clock as a present. He was telling him how to set it. But I couldn't think why—'

She didn't have to say any more. Max got up, his face draining of colour. 'Court Carriages! Oh, my God!'

'Quite,' said Millicent. 'You know Julian has been very bitter about the company since you took over complete control. He had just gone out when I telephoned you, and he had some sort of box with him.' She hurried after Max when he dashed towards the door. 'Mr Berman,

462

I might just be imagining things. Perhaps I'm just a stupid, interfering woman.'

Impulsively he leaned forward and kissed her forehead, a liberty he would never have taken half an hour ago. 'Mrs Cromer, you are very brave, and very intelligent.'

He didn't wait for Millicent to show him out. He was already climbing into his car when she came puffing up to it.

'The main purpose in telling you is to save my husband from trouble. You must find Julian if he's at the Works and stop him from doing anything terrible!'

'Don't worry, I will.'

His speed on the return journey tested the engine's capability to the limit. He had never driven so fast.

Even allowing for the urgency of her telephone call he hadn't expected to hear anything like this from Millicent Cromer. It smelt of sabotage. There was strict security throughout Court Carriages, particularly since the War Office had extended the Works to include a munitions department. Shell-cases had been made there since 1915. Now there was the machine shop assembling fuses. Security guards would challenge any stranger seen on the premises. *But Julian Cromer was not a stranger.*

Max entered the yard with a screeching of brakes and steam coming from the bonnet of the engine. It was five o'clock and workers leaving after an early shift stopped at the gate to stare at him with curiosity. He was out of the car

463

and in the main reception office within seconds, desperate to know whether Julian Cromer had come visiting.

'Mr Cromer? No, he hasn't been here, sir,' the clerk said. 'But—'

The young woman had no chance to finish. Max began issuing dramatic orders which required such urgent attention everything else was forced from her mind.

'I want the whole of the Works evacuated. Everyone must leave immediately.'

'What? Beg your pardon, sir—you mean evacuated!'

'NOW! Find Mr Wilkinson at once and see that the managers of every shop and office are told and comply without question.' He went through to his own office, talking as he went. 'Get me the police and the Security Services on the telephone, Miss Cobham. And I want to speak to Army Headquarters in the town.'

'But Mr Berman, I can't do everything at once.' Miss Cobham followed him, plainly bewildered and flustered by his frenetic instructions. 'What shall I do first? Are we in danger?'

'Heaven preserve me from women! Get Mr Wilkinson and tell him to start the evacuation. Some of the secretaries'll help you with the telephones. I want everyone out of these buildings as quickly as possible ... everyone! Do you understand?'

'Yes, sir.'

A few minutes later, bells began sounding. It

took half an hour to get the vast number of people employed at Court Carriages assembled outside in the street, and then moved to a safe distance. There was confusion and a certain amount of panic, no one knowing the reason for the emergency as police arrived, and Army personnel on motor-cycles drove into the front yard.

'Mr Berman! Mr Berman!' Miss Cobham called to Max, hurrying back into the yard after him when the list of employees was complete and everyone had been accounted for. 'There wasn't time to tell you your wife got here soon after you went out this afternoon.'

He swung round. 'Where is she now, then?'

'I don't know, sir.' The girl was very upset. 'I sent Mr Thorne over with her when she insisted on seeing the ambulance train without waiting, but Mr Thorne came back for the key, and when he went to find her again she wasn't there.'

'Do you mean she left?'

'No, sir. I didn't see her leave, sir, and I was in the office all the time. She would have had to come out that way. No one's seen her at all.'

Max's head was throbbing. Ellie couldn't still be inside any of the buildings. Someone would have seen her and told her to leave with the staff. So where had she gone?

A few minutes later the first terrible explosion shook the machine shop, blowing out windows and shattering glass in every building round a wide area.

465

TWENTY-TWO

The day came for Julian to carry out the instructions of his blackmailer before he had time to think properly of the consequences. In order to save Charlotte, and to improve his almost non-existent bank balance, he had agreed to do an appalling thing which would damage the war effort, probably destroy the company begun by Millicent's father, and put countless people out of work. He would be obliterating all his own life's work, though in recent years he had been systematically robbed of credit for what he had done. He hadn't dared to think in depth of any of these things.

He felt a certain exhilaration as he set out for Court Carriages with the case containing the means to kill people. Killing wasn't his intention. He was to plant the device and prime it go off at midnight, but as he no longer had his own keys, and had not been given any, he needed to be there while it was still daylight.

This was an opportunity to take his revenge. It was going to make certain Court Carriages no longer existed, and Oliver Devlin's pushy daughter would be deprived forever of her ill-gotten inheritance. He saw it as a means of putting to an end Max Berman's powerful and successful bid for full ownership of another man's company. There would be nothing left.

He avoided the main office. The yard entrances were guarded by men invalided out of the services but still able to perform useful civil duties, which presented a problem as Julian was not known to any of them, but he was undeterred. He knew the premises so well it was relatively simple to slip through a small side-gate at the back of the timberyard. From then on he was free to wander where he liked as most men recognised him and presumed he was there by invitation or arrangement.

'Nice to see you, Mr Cromer,' one man said, doffing his cap.

'Welcome back, Mr Cromer, sir,' said another.

The acknowledgements warmed his heart, but didn't weaken his resolution. The one person he didn't want to meet was Max, but he doubted if he would be around the part of the Works for which he was heading.

Following instructions, he made for the body shop, no longer trying to be inconspicuous. He'd asked Walter how he knew so much about Court Carriages but had been silenced by the reply that the less he knew the better. He had the first slight misgiving when he saw the new ambulance train and realised he was probably about to deprive wounded troops of transport back home, but as it was for the American forces the feelings of guilt was less. He had no cause to love the Americans.

The passage between the body shop and the new munitions section was helpfully dark and he didn't need to go as far as the double doors at the end. His mission was to plant the small bomb in a components storeroom to the rear of the machine shop, where a single explosion would be guaranteed to set off a succession of others.

As luck would have it there was no one around to see him unlock the storeroom with a key that Walter had provided, and go inside. The job would only take a few minutes so he left the door slightly ajar to get away quickly. He knew exactly what to do. Walter had gone over it with him several times until it was absolutely clear and there could be no mistake. He looked and saw the exact shelf against the wall separating the store from the machine shop where boxes were marked with a red star to indicate they contained combustible material, and opened the case to set the device inside the way he had been shown. His fingers were clumsy and trembling, and he had to blink away a film from his eyes as he felt in his top pocket and realised with consternation that he had forgotten to bring his magnifying spectacles. Luckily he could see enough without them.

There, the thing was set. No going back now on the agreement. He was about to close the lid of the case when he began to feel dizzy and strangely light-headed, as if he were someone else entirely seeing the scene from another sphere. It was frightening. A flask of brandy was in his hip pocket. He took a gulp from it and felt a little better, his nerves steadying again. But the feeling of unreality persisted, and he decided it was the claustrophobic atmosphere.

The sooner he was back home the better.

Wait! Someone was watching him. The hair at the back of his neck seemed to lift like a dog's before a fight, and his blood turned to ice even though he suddenly sweated profusely. He mustn't be found with the case on him. He closed the lid without a sound and stowed it between the boxes on a lower shelf, covering it with the piece of cloth he'd been told would be there for the purpose.

He looked round fearfully, trying to locate where the vague sound had come from to disturb him. It must have been his imagination overworking: there was no one there. Nevertheless he stepped almost silently and with extreme caution towards the door, and glanced quickly up and down the passage. Then for some reason he felt compelled to take a last look back in the storeroom before leaving, and it was then he knew his mind was playing dangerous tricks. In the shadows he saw a figure, completely motionless and unreal. It could only be in his mind because the figure looked like Ellie, and he knew for certain she was thousands of miles away. The spectre made no sound, but eyes like the ones he had carried in his memory for more than twenty years seemed to stare back at him, condemning him for the terrible thing he had just done.

He must be ill. He wasn't drunk. Fear of discovery was now secondary to the worry over his mental state, and he stepped out into the passage without caring, thankful to be turning the key on his weird fantasies.

Alarm bells started to ring before he was even through the body shop, and shouts for the Works to be evacuated were carried from mouth to mouth. Julian froze. No one could have known about the bomb. No one could have suspected his motive for being there, unless there was an inside agent working for Walter who had turned counter-spy and reported his activities. He felt like a fly caught in a bottle, not knowing which way to turn.

The decision was made for him when panic-stricken employees started carrying him along on the tide of their anxiety to be out of the building. He was pushed towards the far doorway opening onto the yard, which was too narrow to let the swell of people through other than a few at a time, and they crushed together like water building up against a dam. Julian had no choice but to go with them. He could feel the fear of these people, mostly women, and was infected by it.

Suddenly, and with terrifying clarity, he knew he had set the timing mechanism wrong on the device he had planted. Without his spectacles the numbers had been blurred and he'd had to go by the upright position on the dial to ensure it would go off at midnight. But in his haste he hadn't checked. Seeing it now in his mind's eye he knew he had primed it for six o'clock instead, having had to open the case the opposite way round in the confined space, with the lid towards him. Fear made his stomach lurch almost uncontrollably.

'What the hell's the delay,' he called from

behind. 'Get a move on. There may not be much time.'

He pushed with the rest, but his voice only added to the pandemonium. A large railway clock on the wall above the door through which he was being pressed showed the time to be ten minutes to six now. He was almost the last to reach the yard, and he started to run so as to put as much distance as possible between himself and the explosion he knew would happen within minutes. Most of the employees had congregated in the road outside the main entrance, herded together for their names to be checked. He couldn't go out that way.

He went round the side of the reception office, intending to make for a gate which would lead him into Western Esplanade, but through an open window he heard a quavering voice he recognised as belonging to Mr Thorne. It made him stop abruptly.

'Are you *sure* no one saw Mrs Berman leave? There was no sign of her...'

Ellie. Astonishingly, the figure he'd thought was only in his imagination had been Ellie for real. For some extraordinary reason she'd been hiding in the storeroom and—my God, he'd locked her in!

Julian's head was swimming, his heart pounding. All the passionate feelings he'd had for his niece flooded his mind, blocking out all else, and his eyes were wild as he looked back. He must return through the body shop and into the store before it was too late. The key was already in his hand as he set off, ignoring a staccato command to halt.

Max was chasing him. Max was yelling at him to stop as he gained on him.

'You bloody traitor, Julian. You'll hang for this if what Millicent told me is true.' The younger and fitter man caught up with him just inside the now empty body shop, and he nearly wrenched his arm out of its socket as he swung him round. He had him by the throat. 'Damn you! I've ordered your arrest.'

Julian could only gasp and choke on the words he had to get out. 'Ellie's ... in the ... storeroom...'

Max had been shaking him like a terrier with a rat, but he stopped dead, letting him go. 'You're mad.'

'She's there, I tell you! It's where the bomb is. For God's sake, if we don't get there now it'll be too late.'

Without another word Max set off again, this time streaking ahead as he ran between the construction lines of vehicles and machinery to the rear door, but by the time he reached the passage Julian was close behind. The storeroom door was open and Max rushed inside, yelling his wife's name.

'Ellie! Ellie, where are you?'

It was then the place was torn apart by a massive explosion which buried them both under bricks and glass and packing cases as the machine shop and everything in its vicinity was destroyed.

When she realised she was locked in, Ellie banged on the door until her knuckles were sore, but no one heard her. No doubt the noise would be mistaken for hammering in the body shop, which at times could be deafening. She shouted herself hoarse, but no one came. Where were the security guards? Admittedly the walls were thick and the door heavy, but surely someone must walk along the passage and hear her soon.

What an absolute fool she'd been, not to have revealed her presence to Julian. A reprimand for being nosy would have been infinitely preferable to imprisonment in this vast, airless storeroom which was beginning to make her feel she couldn't breathe.

It was strange that Julian had been in the store at all. She'd been shocked by his appearance in that brief glimpse. He'd looked gaunt and old, his eyes almost glazed, but probably the dim light had just made him seem like that. His movements had been furtive, though, as if he didn't want to be caught there any more than she did. If it had been anyone but him she would have been slightly suspicious.

She must find another way out. Utterly frustrated and angry with herself, she started to walk through the maze of metal shelves and packing cases. She ought not to have moved from the spot where Mr Thorne had left her. The man would wonder where on earth she had gone, but he wouldn't think to look for her in a components store. She looked at her watch. It was nearly six o'clock. The women she'd seen assembling fuses would be going home, and new supplies wouldn't be wanted until morning, which meant no one would be coming to the storeroom again tonight. Ellie's skin became goose-pimpled. She was trapped here, and already it was beginning to get dark. The thought of spending the night in such surroundings filled her with terror. When it was completely dark she wouldn't dare to move for fear of dislodging something.

At the far end there were narrow windows, but they were securely locked and only looked out on a narrow yard and a brick wall. No one would be going past to see her. She turned to her right and dodged between packing cases stacked on top of each other like building blocks, and ended up at the same door she had been assaulting. There wasn't another one.

She sat on a box to consider her position. It was then the alarm bells started sounding with harsh insistence, almost deafening her, and she was on her feet again, desperate to know the reason for them. She could hear voices shouting. It sounded as if the building was being evacuated. For a moment Ellie was paralysed with fear: then she started kicking the door until her toes felt broken and her legs were trembling too much to hold her.

Something very serious was happening for alarms to ring. Something life-threatening, if the building was being cleared. She was petrified. There must be a fire.

Ever since the blast in Max's apartment in Pullman, Ellie had been frightened of fire, but that fear had increased to an obsession after Grandfather Cromer had died in the inferno at the Iroquois Theater. She began to shake from head to foot. No one knew she was here, and she wouldn't stand a chance if fire swept through as far as the store. She didn't know precisely what the boxes contained, but she imagined they were combustible. Gulping, dry-eyed sobs of terror escaped her.

When the door was suddenly unlocked and two men appeared in the doorway her relief was so great she pushed past them to escape like someone demented. But she had only gone a few yards when one of them caught her in a grip of steel and forced her to stop.

'Not so fast!' he bellowed. He was in the uniform of a security guard and carried a gun. 'What were you doing in there? Where do you think you're going?'

'Fire! I've got to get out,' she cried, in terrible distress.

'How do you know there's a fire? Have *you* started one?'

'No, of course I haven't!'

His mate took her other arm and they hauled her along, through the double doors into the machine shop, between the deserted work-benches and out at the far end by a new entrance connecting the munitions department with the Western Esplanade. Groups of police and Army servicemen were gathering outside.

'Let me go. I can walk on my own.' She struggled and protested, furious at their treatment of her, but she couldn't get away.

'Will you take your hands off me!'

Her hat was somewhere in the storeroom where she had taken it off in the stifling heat. The pins were falling from her hair and she looked too dishevelled to be anyone of importance. An officer stepped down from an Army vehicle and came towards them arrogantly, his eyes flicking over the captive woman with contempt.

'What's this? What's she done?'

'Suspected arson, sir. Found her lurking in a storeroom by the machine shop. Could be high treason.'

'Who is she?'

'I can speak for myself,' shouted Ellie. 'High treason, indeed! What are you talking about? I'm Mrs Berman of the American Red Cross, and I demand to see my husband.'

'Papers.'

'I beg your pardon?'

'Have you got papers to prove who you are?'

The time was six o'clock. As a distant church clock chimed the hour, an appalling, ear-splitting explosion rocked the earth under their feet, and Ellie, along with everyone else, was knocked to the ground by the blast. Her head hit a stone and she lost consciousness.

After a few eerie seconds of silence, men began picking themselves up. What remained of Court Carriages' machine shop and body shop was settling into a heap of twisted metal and bricks, and a cloud of dust was rising into the atmosphere.

476

It was almost dark, and Ellie Berman stayed unconscious for several more minutes. The woman they had found in such suspicious circumstances and dragged from the building with scarcely a minute to spare, lay on the ground where she had been thrown, her eyes closed and her grey cape with the Red Cross emblem on the shoulder spread across her. The officer who had demanded evidence of her identity ordered one of his men to get her in the lorry, but as she revived she tried to fight off all efforts to force her.

'Don't touch me.' It was difficult to speak. Her throat felt tight and painful, and her eyes wouldn't focus properly.

Bruised and dazed she managed to sit up, and she was sickened to the core as with blurred vision she witnessed the death throes of the company she had once helped to prosper. Treason. Did they really think she was capable of destroying something belonging to her family, Max's company to which he had given twenty years of his life? And after all she had done to help the war effort it was ludicrous to suspect her of sabotaging it.

Was it treason? She felt ill as she remembered Julian's strange behaviour, but even if she tried to incriminate him she doubted her word would be believed.

'You've no right to do this to me,' she wept, as cruel hands dug beneath her armpits to lift her.

'Get her in there,' the officer commanded, losing patience.

'If you'll telephone Richmond Hospital they'll tell you why I'm here.'

'Tie her up if necessary.' Her plea was completely ignored.

No sense in resisting further if she didn't want to be hurt any more than she was already. There was a lump on her temple which throbbed, and she couldn't seem to see properly, but no one cared. She was bundled in the lorry, and no help was offered when she stumbled on the iron step.

They were about to drive off when a girl in a black office skirt and white blouse came running to the Army Lieutenant, her face white, her hands shaking.

'Sir, I'm sent to tell you Mr Berman's been killed. He went in the Works to find his wife. Oh sir, all this is my fault because I didn't tell him she was here. I didn't know where she'd gone.'

The officer slammed his hand against the side of the vehicle to delay its departure. He opened the door at the back which had just been fastened and a guard positioned in case the prisoner tried to escape.

'Do you know this woman?' he asked the clerk.

Ellie was crouching on the floor, her head in her hands, but she looked up with relief at hearing a slightly familiar voice. *Please* tell them who I am,' she begged.

The girl put her hand to her mouth. 'Oh, mercy! It's her. It's Mrs Berman.'

'Thank you, Miss...'

'Cobham, sir. Miss Cobham. Was it her who done it? And to think Mr Berman died trying to save her...'

The door was slammed shut again.

Ellie didn't make another sound. Her breathing was laboured, her shoulders hunched, and her arms were crossed so tightly against her breast it seemed she was crushing her heart.

'Oh no,' she murmured. 'Oh, no...'

The soldier sitting next to her showed no sympathy. She fell against the cold, hard side of the lorry, her spirit broken, and the present dissolved away.

Above the noise of the engine and the rattling wheels she heard herself in the past when she had accused Max of not really loving her. Words, she had said. Just words which meant nothing, and she'd insisted she wouldn't believe him until he proved he loved her. And now he had done it.

He had made the ultimate sacrifice by giving his life for her.

She wanted to die herself.

TWENTY-THREE

From the moment William fell in love with Galina the war took on a new significance. He no longer had to think only of his own survival. Galina was constantly on his mind, and he worried about her far more than he did about himself.

She was true to her word and wrote to him every day, even if it was only a single line to say that she loved him, and the letters got through several at a time. He tried to write to her as regularly, but the offensive continued and life behind the lines was brutally hard, so there were few chances to put pen to paper. He tried to make up for quantity by putting his heart into every missive he sent.

'My darling Galina,' he wrote. 'I grudge every hour, every minute I am not with you. I long to hold you in my arms again, and pray we will win this war before many more weeks have passed. I lie on my groundsheet at night and remember the wonderful feel of your body close to mine. Memories of your hair sliding through my fingers tease me until I can't sleep, even though I am too weary to remove my boots.

'Loving you has made me hate what is happening to the world. With you I see a bright new beginning where everything is golden, and I ache for the suffering of innocent people who will never again know love. My dear girl, you have given a whole new meaning to my life and I can't wait for the day when we'll be together always.

'Say that you'll marry me. I shan't give you any peace until you promise to be my wife. Who cares if our children will be Russian-Irish-Jewish-Catholics? Nothing and nobody will stop me from making an honest woman of you.

'I'll love you forever, William.'

The American First Army had now joined forces with the Second French Army of Verdun, and under the genius of General Pétain, the Hun was swept back in orderly assault. A combined Franco-American effort gained the high hills on the west side of the Argonne, and in the forest along the Aire River the United States troops won a substantial victory by driving the enemy clear of the railway line at Marcq.

The campaign was complicated by the desperate stratagems of the retreating Germans. When the fighting eased there were still ambushes to fear and traps to avoid. At one place in the advance they came to a stagnant pool of poisonous gas which made men terribly ill. At other times there were trip- and pressure-mines and the ever-present danger of one false step leading to Eternity. And always and everywhere, there were the dead. In other wars there had been time to bury the dead. In this one the numbers killed were so colossal, the weapons so destructive, that often there was nothing left of a man's body to bury. William had seen mass burial-grounds blown open again by shells, even corpses stacked together to help form barricades, and the smell of death hung about him continually.

'We've been fighting our way through fields of wire and barricades,' he wrote to Galina. *'I look upon it as an obstacle course through which I have to struggle before we can be together.'*

'Take care, my dearest William,' Galina wrote back. *'I love every single part of you, and I know them all. You are the most precious being in my whole life and I'll not settle for anything less than*

the complete you.

'I can't tell you where I am, but I've been moved to a sector quite a way to the north of you where casualties are high. Even so, I still look for you along every road in the hope we might one day meet again like we did the first time.

'My darling, I'll not give you an answer to the marriage proposal until the war is over. Who knows how differently we might look at things when the circumstances are changed.

'The change will not be in me. I shall always love you. But I have to give you the chance to change your mind. You are always in my heart, Galina.'

The Argonne terrain suited the Americans, and they pushed forward through high wooded country, poor roads, rain and bad visibility, initiative on the part of patrols and platoon commanders bringing them safely through tunnels and wolf-pits and entanglements, and dodging the ever-present machine-gun posts.

At the end of October, the French and American armies linked around Châtillon in an enveloping movement, and conquered the Argonne Forest with its outside railway system and two valley tracks. The enemy was crippled, left without power or communication facilities, and the Americans pursued them in their retreat along the Meuse.

It was while working on the captured light railway that William's luck began to run out. The fractured lines had to be pieced together, bolted and ballasted and re-laid, to link up with a main railway point further down in order to feed thousands more tons of shells and ammunition to the advancing troops. Most of the once-wooded hills overlooking the valley had been cleared of trees during the trench warfare, and the vast American tented encampment had moved on. But higher up the valley there was enough vegetation for isolated German batteries to escape detection, and it was one of these which opened fire on the engineers while they worked in the open, vulnerable targets for the besieged enemy.

William had come through the fighting unscathed, believing in his own immunity to such an extent that he took risks without considering the danger. The mortar shell, which killed and wounded several of his men, buried him in a fallen dug-out near the line. After a few minutes he recovered enough from the shock to realise his left arm was useless, agonisingly painful, and badly broken, but apart from that he seemed to be intact. He began to shout to his trapped comrades, encouraging all who could to start digging their way out of the débris, and he set an example by using his good arm to shift clods of earth and timber until he was free.

'Keep down,' he yelled, lying on his stomach as another shell landed several hundred yards away, smashing the newly-repaired line. 'Dawkins, organise the men behind that promontory and return fire. Watts, get as many of the wounded as you can to a safer position. Hilton, the engine's intact. Get it going. We've got to get the wounded back to the rail-head.'

Blood was seeping through his khaki jacket sleeve.

'We'll be sitting targets in the trucks, sir,' said Hilton, his second-in-command. 'We'd never make it. The Hun'll just pick us off from up there.'

'I said get the engine going! By the time you've done that it should be safe.'

Another shell exploded close by. 'That arm looks bad, sir.'

'It'll be seen to later. I've a job to do.'

A stench of blood and explosives hung in the air as William moved back with Dawkins and put two grenades in his right-hand pocket.

'Keep Lieutenant Hilton covered as best you can,' he ordered. 'I'm going up the hill.'

'But, sir...'

'The bastards've got to be put out of action.'

He judged by the short-range mortar fire that the enemy position was hidden in a clump of trees not far above the working party and he climbed up stealthily, the pain in his arm so excruciating he hoped he would make it. A twig cracked beneath his foot and he stopped, but there was no sign he'd been detected, and after a moment he moved on up, crouching in places where there were only bushes for cover. There was nothing to guide him, other than instinct. At any minute he could stumble across the battery and that would be the end of him. He couldn't defend himself with his arm the way it was.

A low-velocity shell whined past quite close to his right, pin-pointing his objective. Another few yards and he could hear guttural voices. Yes, he could see the battery through the branches. There were only two soldiers operating the muzzle-loading gun behind a barricade of rocks, and they were too engrossed to suspect retaliation. He went on climbing a step at a time, pausing, listening, watching, holding his breath until he was past the enemy bunker and ideally positioned above it. Using his uninjured right arm he threw the first grenade, seeing it explode just wide of the mark and alerting the soldiers. But the second was right on target. It killed both men instantaneously, and destroyed the gun. Only then did William pass out.

He was vaguely aware of being taken down the line to the field hospital. Loss of blood had weakened him considerably, and it was several days before he was fully conscious again. Shell splinters had been removed from his arm and the shattered bone set as well as possible, though it would never be completely straight or the arm capable of heavy use.

Nurses ministered to him, their white caps fluttering before his eyes like butterflies, their hands gentle yet competent. Soft voices murmured above him, but he couldn't hear properly what was being said. Fear of gangrene in the wound seemed to be the concern of the doctors and the dressings were changed often, causing fresh, unbearable pain which necessitated another dose of morphine. But gradually he began to recover, and one morning he was told he could have a visitor. It was his Commanding Officer, a man by the name of Colonel MacDonald.

'Glad you're on the mend, Berman,' the Colonel said. 'Bad luck copping it just before the end.'

William was propped up on pillows, his left arm strapped close to his chest. 'You mean the war's over, sir?'

'Good as. I hear the Germans are on the point of admitting defeat.'

'Great news.' But surely it didn't merit a special visit from his superior.

'Great indeed. And it wouldn't have been possible without men like you. Every one of our troops are heroes, but some show greater heroism than others. I'm here to tell you, Captain Berman, that the French are awarding you the Croix de Guerre for what you did in the Argonne Valley.'

William sat up. 'I'm no hero,' he protested. 'It was the only logical thing to do.'

'By putting the enemy battery out of action you saved the lives of a whole lot of men. Wounded, too. To me that deserves the highest gallantry award. I salute you, Captain.'

After the Colonel had left William drifted into a dazed sleep, and he awoke feeling certain it had all been a dream. But people came to congratulate him, including Lieutenant Hilton and some of the men who had got out of the valley alive, thanks to his brave trek alone up the hillside.

He wanted to share this moment with Galina. As he lay there dwelling on what had happened he felt an overwhelming desire to see her. Hilton had brought in the latest batch of letters from her and he started to read them with joy, noting that each one became more passionate.

The last letter had been written four days ago, and it made his heart sing.

'It's too long since I heard from you, William,' she wrote. *'I'm worrying about you incessantly. I know it's difficult to get mail through, but we've always managed it and I've been expecting some to arrive. My darling, if anything should happen to you I think I'd want to die. Isn't that melodramatic!'* And then he read what he wanted to hear more than anything else. *'Darling, I know I said I wouldn't make any decisions until after the war, but I've got the strangest feeling I must give you an answer to your proposal now. Call it premonition or whatever you will, but something tells me all isn't well, and I want you to know I'll marry you at the earliest opportunity. And that means taking you on, no matter what. Am I being morbid?*

'Please get in touch, dearest William. Tell me you're safe and unharmed. I'm worried sick. I'll love you till eternity and beyond. Galina.'

He smiled as he put the letter back in the envelope. Her intuition had proved right, but things could have been a lot worse. Thankfully his wounds were healing and he was gaining strength every day to hold her close by his good arm. He couldn't wait for it to happen.

The letter was in his hand that evening when the lights were low and the time was right to talk to his favourite nurse.

'I'm getting married, Sister,' he said.

'I thought you looked a lot happier.' She

stood beside his bed, a plain woman with a Brooklyn accent and the smile of an angel. 'I've some more good news for you, Captain Berman. You're being sent to England on the next ambulance train.'

He was pleased. He didn't want to stay a minute longer than necessary now peace looked certain, but he desperately wanted to see Galina first.

'Is there any chance of seeing my fiancée?' he asked. 'She doesn't know I'm in here. She's an ambulance driver.'

'I'll get word to her if it's at all possible,' the Sister promised.

'Her name's Galina Devlin.'

The woman's face changed, as if a mask suddenly covered it, and she turned away abruptly. William sat forward, his heartbeats quickening uneasily.

'What's the matter?' He touched her sleeve. 'Tell me.'

When she turned back there were tears shining on her cheeks, glistening in the dim light. Her hand covered his.

'Three days ago Galina Devlin's motor-van hit a mine on a road north of Verdun,' she said, her voice calm but her hands trembling with sympathy. 'She was bringing us more wounded. They were all blown to bits.'

William felt as if his own life ended there. He sank back against the pillows.

He didn't talk to anyone for several days, by which time he was on his way to a Channel port and a boat bound for England. He didn't care

488

where he was sent. Without Galina everywhere was a desert.

For many hours after the destruction of Court Carriages, Ellie was still in shock and took no interest in anyone or anything. She couldn't seem to focus her eyes so she closed them against the bare ugliness of the police cell, and as her ears still echoed painfully from the explosion she didn't hear the arguments and accusations going on around her. She sat on a hard bench as if she were blind and deaf, responding automatically to commands without really knowing what she was doing.

She didn't know how long she had been there when someone came to say they were sorry.

'It was a terrible misunderstanding, Mrs Berman. We ought never... You shouldn't have... If only someone had known you were there... Please accept our... I've been in touch with the American Red Cross.'

Everything sounded disjointed, and it really didn't matter. She didn't answer.

Someone helped her out to a car and she was driven a short distance through the town. It was pitch dark. Soon she was in a house and another person was getting her into bed. During the night she felt her wrists to see if they were handcuffed or tied, but there was nothing restricting them or stopping her from relaxing on the soft feather mattress.

Half-asleep, half-awake, her mind wandered through the past, taking her back to the days in Pullman with Max, and she thought the pain in her body had been caused by the women kicking her during the strike. She called out for Max, but of course he wasn't there. He was never there when she needed him. He would never be there again.

Max was dead. He had given his life for her.

She wept over the wasted years of their separation which could have been spent so differently if only they'd been able to make allowances for each other. She'd thought the overpowering love she had lavished on him in the early days could survive everything. How she had deceived herself. The kind of love she'd believed in would have been strong enough to withstand far worse things than desertion, and would have accepted Max's weakness as part of him. A true and lasting love would have grasped at the chance of reconciliation and worked at overcoming the faults in herself which had been a cause of the break-up. She'd told William she had loved too much, but it wasn't that at all. *She hadn't loved enough.*

She'd failed Max. She had been too full of her own importance to try and see things from his point of view. They'd both been too proud. He, too arrogant to be beholden to anyone else; she, too proud and stubborn to accept he hadn't adored her like everyone else, or been willing to always put her needs first. She had been intolerant.

Now they would never be able to start again. He had died before she could tell him how sorry she was for not trusting him.

It wasn't until daylight that she realised she was at Fortune Cottage. Not that she had ever been in one of the bedrooms before, but fully awake and with her vision restored she saw a familiar painting on the wall of Francis and Charlotte when young, and a photograph of Millicent and Julian resplendent in evening dress. There was a soothing smell of jasmine on the pillow, and she lay still, recalling what had happened and why she was there.

Millicent came in later, carrying a tray of tea and some light breakfast. She looked drawn and tired.

'You shouldn't be waiting on me, Millicent,' Ellie said, sitting up in bed. 'How very kind of you to have brought me here.'

'It was the least I could do. You had the most terrible shock. I've been sitting with you most of the night.'

'There was no need...'

'I didn't want to be on my own.' She shuddered. With slightly unsteady hands, Ellie's aunt by marriage put the tray on the bed and sat on the chair she had used to keep the night-time vigil. She was neatly dressed in a black gown which disguised the extra weight she had put on in middle age, and now she smoothed it over her knees with studied care while she sought for words to speak of what was on her mind. 'Ellie, I want to talk to you about Julian before you hear things officially which will brand him a traitor to his country.'

'I don't understand.'

'You're here because of what I told the police

last night when I heard you were being held responsible for the bomb. I didn't even know you were in this country.'

'The police came here?'

'To tell me Julian had died in the blast.'

Ellie closed her eyes in anguish. 'Julian, too.'

'I told them it was he who planted the bomb.'

'To save me from being blamed?'

'It was the truth. I can only say it's a mercy he's dead. He planted it, you see, to save Charlotte's life in Germany. He was being blackmailed.' Millicent swallowed hard and looked down at her hands. 'Julian wasn't a bad man, but he was weak, and lately he'd come to rely too much on brandy, like his father before him. What I want you to know, Ellie, is that I loved him, and would never have stopped loving him in spite of what he's done. I shall defend him with every breath in me.'

It was so awful Ellie could hardly take it in. Her immediate thought was that Julian had killed Max, and for that she could never be so magnanimous as Millicent. Whatever his motive, whatever excuse his wife made for him, there could be no such loyalty from his niece. In a way the revelation was not surprising when she remembered seeing Julian's furtive exit from the storeroom, but she would never have suspected him of treason. Never. Or of murder, for that was what it amounted to.

She ached unbearably as she stared, dry-eyed, at her aunt, whose loyalty to her husband put

Ellie to shame. It was impossible not to admire her. She had always dismissed Millicent as frivolous and extravagant, a snob of the highest order with whom she'd had nothing in common. In the past there'd been no clue as to the strength of character behind the luxury-looking exterior.

'I don't know what to say, Millicent, except that we must somehow console each other since we have both suffered a terrible loss. I'm very grateful for what you've done for me.'

Millicent bent over to kiss her forehead where the swelling of last night was turning to a black bruise. 'I wanted to be able to tell you myself, my dear. You would have heard the truth from another source, but I begged to be allowed to speak to you first.'

'I'm glad you did.'

'And I'm so very sorry about Max. I know you never forgave him, but he was a good man for all that. He loved his niece and brought her up like a daughter. I think he wanted a wife and family, but we all knew no one could take your place.'

Ellie swung her legs out of bed so that she could draw Millicent into her embrace, the sensitive words having touched her so deeply there was nothing to say in reply. She ached to give way to her misery, but Millicent's fortitude had a strengthening effect. In some ways it was worse for her aunt. There'd been no break in her marriage to Julian. They had been with each other all their married life, and her grief must be devastating.

Ellie's grief was compounded by guilt that she and Max had spent hardly any time together at all.

The two women held each other silently for several minutes, sharing their suffering. Then Ellie got out of bed.

'I'm going to get dressed, Millicent,' she said, forcing herself to sound stronger than she felt. 'There's going to be a lot of things to do, and we'll both feel better if we tackle them together. First, I must use your telephone, if I may, to let the hospital at Richmond know what's happened.'

A little later in the morning there was yet another ring at the front doorbell. An incessant string of callers had been told by the only remaining maidservant to please go away, but this time Millicent looked round the door of the drawing room where Ellie was desperately trying to compose a letter, yet unable to think of anything but Max.

'You have a visitor, Ellie,' Millicent said, the first smile of the day touching her lips.

'You know I won't see anyone.'

'But this is someone very special.'

With that Millicent opened the door fully, and Ellie saw a very tall young man in military uniform standing there, his left arm in a sling tight to his chest.

'William!' she breathed. After a second's heart-stopping delay she ran to him, halting only just in time before throwing herself against him. He was wounded. 'Oh, my darling, how wonderful! When did you get back? How did your arm get broken? How did you know I was here?'

'Mother, forget the questions. Just let me hold you with my good arm,' he said. The strength in it more than compensated as he drew her against him and kissed her.

She began to weep at last. 'Oh William, your father's been killed and I don't know what to do.'

'I know, Mama.' He stroked her hair soothingly. 'If only I'd been here yesterday.'

William had sailed on a train ferry from Dieppe to Southampton. With his shattered arm he was among the mobile wounded so he was able to sit in the officers' mess where there were wooden armchairs and a round covered table with a vase of flowers in the middle. The train itself was on a track through the centre of the ferry, and the lorries parked on either side of it made it impossible to see much. Not that William wanted to see. He had taken little interest in anything since learning of Galina's death, and England wasn't home.

'Hope there are no Boche U-boats in the Channel,' said the 1st Lieutenant next to William. 'I can cope with being shot at but I'd hate to drown.'

'It would be last-minute desperation if we were attacked,' William said.

'Yeah, the Boche are running scared of us Yanks,' said a very young 2nd Lieutenant. 'They've heard about our mighty men and machines.'

'They've been defeated by our Allies.' William hated the smugness and boasting of some of his comrades. 'We came in too late to take that much credit.'

'What'll you do when it's over, Captain?' the first man asked.

'Get back to the States as soon as I can.'

'You're an Engineer. I hear they're drafting them on to Russia to fight the Bolsheviks.'

'I won't be with them. I face a few operations.'

He'd heard some Americans were being sent to help cool the Bolshevik revolution, but the state of his arm ensured his exemption, and he was glad. He didn't want to go to Russia. In one of his more sensible conversations with Galina in Paris she had said that perhaps the Bolsheviks had a just cause. He had learnt for the first time that his name was in fact Bermanovitch, and she had told him gruesome tales of the persecution of their Russian grandparents by the henchmen of Tsarist nobility because they had been Jews. Who knew which side was right, if either of them were.

He had only known Galina such a short time, had only met her twice, yet his feelings for her had been stronger than for any other girl he'd previously encountered. Even making allowances for the emotional circumstances of their meeting he was left in no doubt that they could have married and been happy. Successful marriages didn't always follow a long courtship, and he had loved her from the moment his arms had gone round her to give comfort. He wondered what would happen to her share of Court Carriages. She'd been a very rich young woman and doubtless they would have feuded over the company. He didn't want to see it, but he would have to.

He was bound for the American hospital at Richmond, and couldn't wait to get there. The most recent letter to reach him from his mother had been to tell him she herself was at Richmond. It was wonderful news and he longed to see her. His father might have already been informed about Galina. He would visit him just as soon as he was allowed a pass to travel.

The ferry had only just docked when word of the sabotage to Court Carriages got around. A bomb, they said. Very little left, but few casualties as the place had just been evacuated.

'My God!' William was on his feet, suddenly galvanised into action, which puzzled his companions. He began tussling with his jacket, trying to get his right arm in the sleeve but failing in his haste.

'Why so bothered, man?' asked the 2nd Lieutenant. 'Where do you think you're going, for God's sake?'

'Court Carriages belongs to my father.'

He left the men in the officers' mess frustrated not to learn more, and sought someone in charge who would give him permission to leave the train. A short time later he was standing in the Western Esplanade, staring at the ruins of Galina's inheritance and his father's hard-earned business.

He couldn't believe the devastation. The air

was still filled with dust and the smell of crumbling bricks and mortar. In France he had seen the same scene hundreds of times and accepted it as the inevitable result of war, but here in England it was somehow obscene. He felt so angry and revolted by what he saw it screwed his stomach up. The traitor who had perpetrated it should be hounded mercilessly until he was caught and hanged. The damn awful waste, the wickedness!

'My poor darling Galina,' he said to himself. 'There is now nothing left for us to fight over.'

Soldiers and civilians were working together on the rubble, cranes lifting metal girders, men shifting débris with their bare hands. Others watched as if unable to believe it had happened. A column of masonry fell as he watched, crumbling slowly and sending up a fresh cloud of brickdust.

'Bloody awful affair,' said an old man leaning on a stick near to William. 'Not safe in our own country these days.'

'No one was killed, though,' William said.

'Two was. One was the owner, name of Berman. They say he went in at the last minute to rescue his wife, but she was already out. He were a hero if ever there was one. The tale goes the wife was suspected of treason, but that were daft and now she's been took to Mr Cromer's home. I remembers her. She was here when I worked for the company back in—'

William didn't wait to hear any more. The

anger inside him was nothing to the agony which had now overtaken it.

The telephone call came less than an hour after William's arrival. Ellie had just been hearing about his extraordinary meeting with Galina Devlin and had hardly had time to absorb the fact that she'd been killed in France, when Millicent was told there was an urgent call. She came back into the room a few minutes later, her expression inscrutable.

'What is it, Millicent?' It seemed to be further trouble and Ellie's question was fearful.

Her aunt came and took her hand. 'There's someone alive in the ruins of Court Carriages,' she said. 'That was Mr Wilkinson. He owes his life to Max, and he wanted us to know straight away.'

Ellie could hardly breathe. She clasped William's hand so hard her knuckles were white. 'Who? Who's alive?'

'They don't know yet.' Millicent was trembling so much her teeth began to chatter. 'I ought to hope it's Julian, but I can't, for his sake. What good would it do for him to survive this, only to be hanged for treason.'

'Come and sit down, Aunt Millicent,' said William, extricating himself from his mother and helping the older woman to a chair.

A prickling sensation coursed down Ellie's spine, and there was a singing in her head.

'We've got to get down there,' she said, her spirits beginning to soar. 'Straight away. We mustn't waste time.'

'Take care, Mother,' William warned. 'Don't build your hopes up too high. It might not be Father.'

'I know. But oh, William, you don't know how hard I'm praying it's him. I'm sorry, William.'

'It's all right, I understand. And I can't come with you.' Tears filled Millicent's eyes. 'If Julian *is* alive he'll find out I betrayed him and he'll never forgive me.' She got up again and went to the window. 'There are sightseers outside, would you believe? Take Julian's car, William. It's in the garage at the side of the house.'

'I can't drive with only one arm. We'll have to get a cab.'

'There's no time, I can drive,' said Ellie.

But William was inexplicably upset at the idea. 'No, Mother. I won't let you.'

'Don't be absurd. You can tell me what to do if the car's very different to ones I've handled before.'

'I said no. Women shouldn't drive cars—it's too dangerous.'

Then she understood. 'You're thinking of Galina,' she said gently. 'She was killed driving a lorry—but it's not going to happen to me. This is England.'

'I couldn't bear to lose anyone else I love.'

'You loved Galina?' Ellie's surprise showed in her tone and her raised eyebrows.

'We would have married as soon as the war's over.'

'Oh, William. Oh, my darling ... I'm so sorry.' She hugged her son fiercely, sympathy for him bringing fresh anguish to darken the day. Then she took a deep breath and stood tall. 'We'll talk about it later. Right now, whether you like it or not, we're taking Julian's car to town.'

She had never driven a vehicle in England but that didn't deter her. Of course William wouldn't let her go alone. He got in beside her, no doubt thinking she was being manipulative again, but she couldn't help it. She would tackle anything to get to Court Carriages in time to be there when that survivor was brought out alive. The car was a 'Prince Henry' Vauxhall which Julian had bought just before the war. It had been his pride and joy, and he had always made sure the silver fluted bonnet and red bodywork shone like mirror glass. For the last three years there had been no chauffeur, but he had taken pleasure in driving it himself.

The hood was up, and Ellie sounded the horn to clear people away from the gate as she drove out into Lance's Hill.

'The left-hand side of the road, Mother,' shouted William, when she would have set off on the right.

She soon got used to the controls, and it wasn't too bad having the steering wheel at the wrong side, once she adjusted to driving on the left. A few more shouts from her son saved them from any mishap, and she was quite proud of the way she handled the large car. It felt as if she were flying towards Max.

Her hopes went on growing. It had to be him. If there was any fairness in the world, surely it couldn't be Julian who was spared after what he had done.

The busy roads into town meant they were held up at several places and her impatience was voiced aloud. 'Why didn't they let us through before they closed the gates?' she exclaimed, when they had to wait at a level crossing. 'The train's miles away yet.'

'Calm down, Mama,' said William. 'A few minutes is neither here nor there. You're doing very well—I'm amazed at your driving ability.'

'Your Uncle Drew taught me.' Her foot touched the accelerator pedal and they were on their way again before the gates were fully opened. 'He said I was not too old to be fully emancipated.'

When they reached Western Esplanade, crowds of morbid sightseers were being held back by the police, but enough débris had been cleared for traffic to use the road if involved in the rescue work.

An Army sergeant flagged them down and came over to the large Vauxhall.

'I must ask what your business is,' he said, after first saluting William. 'No vehicles are allowed past this point unless authorised.'

'I'm Mrs Berman,' said Ellie. 'I understand there's someone being brought out alive and I must be here in case it's my husband.'

'You can't drive any further, madam.'

'Then I'll walk.'

'I'm Mrs Berman's son,' William told the soldier. 'I'll go with her.'

They were permitted to leave the car by the

military lorries, and set off on foot, picking their way over glass and rubble to get to a place opposite to where the main work was going on. Ellie could see it had once been the body shop, but they were ordered to stay by the road and not go anywhere near the operations.

Nothing seemed to be going on. A team of men was standing by an excavated area where twisted metal and wood suggested the remains of the ambulance train had been reached, but they were standing with their arms folded.

'Why aren't they doing anything?' Ellie asked William, her tone edgy and fretful.

'I guess they're afraid to move anything else in case the whole lot falls in.'

'Oh no, it can't. It mustn't.' She pressed her hand to her mouth.

'He might be very badly injured.'

'I'll devote the rest of my life to nursing him if I have to,' Ellie said. 'I've been so selfish, William. I can never make it up to him.'

They had been waiting fifteen minutes when a cheer went up, and William had to grasp his mother's arm to prevent her from rushing forward into the danger zone to see what was happening.

A man came off the site. 'They're bringing a stretcher out,' he told them. 'I think it's Mr Cromer they've rescued.'

Ellie's heart plummeted. She was shaken and afraid, but her courage didn't desert her. After a moment in which she almost crushed William's good hand she prepared to go and look at the man on the stretcher. There was no life. A sheet was covering the body completely, and silence fell on the crowd as a policeman lifted the covering off for a second to disclose that it was indeed Julian Cromer.

Heartbroken, Ellie buried her face against William's chest while people continued to mill round. She didn't see men at the excavation site helping someone else to the surface.

'It was a miracle if ever I saw one,' one of the stretcher-bearers was saying, before they moved off with Julian's body. 'Packing cases had fallen in such a way there was space like a tomb in the rubble with metal shelves holding it up. Fallen crossways, like. Another few minutes and it would've caved in.'

Ellie couldn't look any more. 'Take me back to Millicent's, William,' she whispered. Her shattered hopes added to her previous grief and it seemed as if her own life was draining away.

Suddenly she felt William's body tense. 'Mother, look!'

The urgency in his voice revived her and she lifted her head. She rubbed her eyes and stared, then began to shake uncontrollably, for there across the rubble, covered in dust but walking unaided, was Max.

She left William's side and stumbled across the débris, tearing her skirt when she tripped, but picking herself up again and staggering forward to meet her husband. Tears of joy rained down her cheeks and she was murmuring his name with every breath. When she reached him he held out his arms.

504

'It's all right, Ellie,' he said. 'It's all right, I'm here.'

His clothes were torn and he was bruised, but he was all in one piece. She touched him tenderly, her fingers caressing his face.

'I knew you wouldn't leave me again,' she sobbed. 'You know how much I need you.'

'I know how much I love you.'

'I love you too. I've never stopped loving you. I never will.'

One of the medical team took hold of Max's arm. 'Come along, sir, we must get you to hospital.'

'I'm going with him,' Ellie cried. She took his other arm. 'William's here too, Max.'

So many people came rushing forward to greet him the police had to clear a path. At the end of it William stood waiting, his hat tucked under his arm in respect, and he began walking towards his parents with a smile so warm it seemed to brighten the leaden sky.

EPILOGUE

Early in the spring of 1919, Ellie Berman stood on the deck of the liner *Mauretania* as it made its way down Southampton Water en route for New York, and she watched the town of Southampton fading into the distance with mixed feelings, knowing that she would probably never see it again. Many major events in her life had taken place there, most she would prefer not to remember, but the last months had been so happy.

When they passed Netley Hospital on the port side where for a long time yet the war wounded would continue to be cared for, she gave thanks that William's injury had been no worse. While at Richmond, he'd had two operations on his arm which had almost straightened it, and there was hope that he would be able to use it normally in time. The wound taking longer to heal was the loss of Galina. It was a good thing he had been sent back to the States in February. Ellie in no way minimised her son's feelings for his cousin, but she took heart from the brevity of their relationship and hoped it wouldn't be too long before there was another girl to fill his thoughts.

Of course Max had shared William's grief. As Ellie hadn't seen Galina since she was a small child, she'd felt shut out when her menfolk talked about her, but she gave comfort whenever it was needed, and she understood.

Max himself had suffered no lasting physical effect from his entombment beneath the rubble of Court Carriages. He had been discharged from hospital after a few days, and Ellie had had to return to Richmond, leaving him to start sorting out enormous problems to do with the company. He had decided not to rebuild. The business had gone, and with Eastleigh likely to become the most important post-war carriage-building works in the south of England it seemed pointless to once more set up in opposition. He had lost all enthusiasm for it. Instead he made plans for the future with the compensation he seemed set to get.

'We'll design furniture together, Ellie,' he said. 'I was starting to make a success of it before. With you to help me we'll take the interior design world by storm.'

It was an exciting thought, but she didn't mind what they did as long as they were together.

Max came along the deck and leaned against the rail with her. The eastern end of the Isle of Wight was in view, and once clear of that there was open sea before them as far as the Atlantic coast of America. He put his arm round her waist and drew her close.

'I've arranged for breakfast to be brought to the cabin each morning, Mrs Berman,' he said. They were travelling first-class. 'Every minute alone with you is precious.'

She planted a kiss on his cheek, and the

gesture prompted a meeting of their lips which lingered on as they were the only couple outside braving a cold north-easterly wind.

'Max, do you remember the train crash at Quincy when we first met?'

'Of course I do.'

'You saved my life then.'

'So you always tell me.'

'You did. And then you tried to do it again in Southampton. When they said you were dead I thought things had come full circle and it was the end of everything.'

Max held her so tightly she felt as if they were part of each other. 'No, my darling. It was a second beginning.'

The crossing was uneventful. There were no rough passages, and in the cabin booked by Max and Elena Berman there was love. They wished the voyage could last forever, but in no time at all, it seemed, they were seeing Brooklyn Bridge to the starboard, the Statue of Liberty, and the awe-inspiring buildings of Manhattan. They were home at last.

The war had changed things in New York. There were not the men available to see to arrangements at the dockside when a liner berthed, and after the baggage had been unloaded it was left to every passenger to look after his or her own luggage, transfer-agents being in short supply. In all the noise and bustle it was difficult to get anyone to handle anything, but Max was determined to get assistance.

'We can't manage all this on our own,' he

said. 'Stay with it, Ellie. I'll go and find someone.'

She sat down on one of the boxes and watched his tall figure disappear amidst the throng in the disembarkation lounge, but she wasn't afraid.

This Large Print Book for the Partially sighted, who cannot read normal print, is published under the auspices of

THE ULVERSCROFT FOUNDATION